RISE OF THE
ORDER
THE SORCERER'S REBIRTH

BROCK E.
DESKINS

He mentally prodded Klaraxis, the demon lord trapped within the black stone set in the pommel of his sword, and drew upon his abyssal power. Darkness, deeper than a full eclipse, enveloped the duelers. Bojan yelped when Daebian's obscured blade slipped past his guard and scored his flesh.

The eldritch glow surrounding the Ordinator's shield and sword increased until they glowed like miniature suns and obliterated the darkness. Daebian had anticipated such a response. While the brilliant light dazzled their eyes and destroyed the black miasma, it also created deep shadows across the ground. Daebian leapt into one and vanished only to emerge from another behind his enemy. Daebian buried his blade in the man's vulnerable back and drew his soul from his body to feed Klaraxis. While nowhere near as powerful as the god-forged soul sword he once possessed, his new blade was sufficient for keeping his pet demon satisfied.

Daebian cast his gaze across the small battlefield and did not like what he saw. While his people had emerged from their homes and businesses in droves to defend what was theirs, they lacked the training, arms, and armor of these professional soldiers. Even had the legionnaires not possessed weapons and shields bolstered by strange magic, the fight would have been a costly one. With them, they were almost certainly doomed to defeat.

Ellyssa hurled lightning and fire at the invaders, but little if any harmed those protected by the ward enveloping them. Arrows and crossbow bolts sent streaking into their ranks bounced off their shields as well. Ellyssa used her magic to pry large stones from beneath the sand and soil and hurled them with as much force as she could muster.

The soldiers' wards flared beneath the impact and caused the front rank to stagger. Finally seeing some effect, she continued her barrage with renewed vigor. A quarrel slipped through a crack in the shields and felled a man. More islanders rushed at the centuria from behind and clubbed and hacked at the rear elements.

CHAPTER I

The abyss. It was never dark and yet there was no light. It was neither hot nor cold. It was a place of death and misery, but no odor fouled the air. It was a land where tormented souls wandered until consumed by demons, and yet it was bereft of spirit. No wonder some people called it hell. Azerick simply called it home.

He stood in the middle of Sharrellan's garden, the one thing of beauty in this gods' forsaken abyss. Forsaken by all but one god. Crystals sprang from the ground like shoots of grass between plants and flowers seen nowhere else in any world he could imagine. The colors were so vibrant it was a joyous assault on the eyes.

It could be that the dreary landscape of the abyss made them appear bright, but he doubted it. Azerick had no idea how long he had been here. Longer than the last time for certain. Time was as meaningless and incomprehensible as everything else around him.

A soft, rich, seductive voice broke Azerick's solitude. "You know, I spent a millennium crafting this garden, making sure every crystal and flower caught the light so as to be the most vibrant and spectacular creation known even to the gods. And yet your very presence makes it the gloomiest spot in all the abyss."

Azerick looked over his shoulder at the goddess as she slid her around his stomach from behind. Her jet-black hair contrasted starkly with her alabaster skin. Her full lips, lavender to match her eyes, both of which changed colors to fit her whims, pulled up into a smile.

"After all these years, why must you still be so dreary? I thought you had accepted your place in the universe."

Azerick looked away from her as he spoke. "Accepting something does not mean welcoming it."

Sharrellan's lips drooped into a frown and turned deep blue. "I hope you are referring to the place and not the company. I grant you far more leave than anyone else in my realm, but not even I know how far my tolerance goes. It would be best not to find out."

Azerick, lord of the fifth circle of the abyss, found his smile and turned into her embrace. Riling the moody goddess was one of the few pleasures he found in this hellish place. He conjured a simple globe of light and enjoyed the rainbow of colors the crystals cast across the ground and on the nearby colonnades.

The iridescent reflections wavered and bent to his will and became bright silhouettes of Miranda, Raijaun, Daebian, and Ellyssa. Within seconds, he had recreated his entire school in light—before the Scions had destroyed it.

"I see you are going to be in another one of your moods," Sharrellan said. "You know, there are thousands of mortals who would literally trade their souls to be my consort."

"And I would gladly change places with any of them. Even if it were an old cripple on his death bed. To see my wife, to touch her one last time with mortal hands, would be the greatest of gifts."

"Ugh, you may as well be mortal. You certainly share their predilection for not appreciating what you have. I will leave you to sulk. Attend me when you are done with your little pity party."

"It's a good thing you're immortal. You might be waiting quite some time."

The goddess let out a growl and shattered the crystals into sand with a flick of her finger before turning and storming away. Azerick chuckled, amused to have gotten under her skin once again. It was not as though he hated being with her, he had accepted his role long ago, but the memory of his mortality, of his ability to experience true pleasure, was too fresh in his mind to bury the pain it caused. It was an old wound, but it still bled. Probably because he would not stop picking at it.

Azerick gathered up the glittering sand with magical hands and sculpted it into his characters. Wolf and Ghost ran from the kitchen, chased by Agnes for stealing a ham. Having escaped the angry cook, the food thieves found Sandy in the woods and all three ate their pilfered meal.

He sent Grick and Ellyssa, a much younger Ellyssa, down into the tower sublevels to kill rats. A smile tugged at the corner of his mouth even as a tear rolled down his cheek. He wondered what had become of his adopted daughter.

Azerick understood her need to get away, to try to leave the pain behind. But her choice to go with Daebian worried him. His son had his own demons, but unlike his father, he did not fight them. He welcomed them. Ellyssa had battled hers long ago, but he feared his son's influence could bring them back. Azerick knew better than anyone that demons did not stay dead. Not the real kind nor the metaphorical ones.

He released his hold on the magic and let the sand fall back to the ground. Despite his assertions, Azerick had too much time on his hands to spend it sulking. Besides, he had actual responsibilities. Demons could not be left to their own devices for long before they got bored and caused trouble. Not a day went by, as far as he was able to discern time, that some group or another did not decide to declare war, on each other or with him.

His minions despised him. The demons of the other circles openly threatened him and made repeated petitions to Sharrellan to either destroy him or allow them to launch a full-scale attack in an effort to unseat him as the master of the fifth circle. In their black eyes, he was a mortal soul and usurper that Sharrellan had elevated above them all, including greater demons that had waited centuries to become her favorite.

Azerick did not care. Every few years, a demon lord, either alone or as part of a larger assault, would challenge him, and each time he destroyed them with various levels of difficulty. None matched his power in the abyss, except the goddess herself, and nothing short of a full-scale planar war could unseat him from his throne. And with the goddess' support, not even that. It was another reason to stay in her good graces.

He knew Sharrellan was merely annoyed and would not seek to punish him despite her warnings, but Azerick decided he had done enough sulking for one day. He would bid her farewell before returning to his demonic kingdom. His absence only increased the conspiracies against him, so he preferred not to stay gone for too long.

Azerick stood and turned to leave the garden but paused when the hairs on his arms and the back of his neck stood up. It was the only warning he got before the world exploded. He was barely conscious of the fact that his feet no longer touched the ground and that he was flying backward at a phenomenal speed.

It took several seconds before he returned to ground, his body bouncing and rolling dozens of times before sliding to a halt, leaving behind a trail not unlike that of a meteor strike. Azerick climbed to his feet the moment he came to a stop, summoned his staff to hand, and shifted into his natural demonic form, ready to do battle despite struggling not to fall down.

The staff looked incongruous in his enormous, onyx hand, but there was nothing absurd about the power it possessed. He had been denied its reassuring presence during his first tenure as demon prince and was properly grateful to have it this time. It was what elevated him far above even the most powerful of demon lords.

Shaking the stars from his eyes and forcing clarity back into his mind, Azerick took in the destruction around him. The garden, and much of Sharrellan's godly palace, lay in ruin. He beat his bat-like wings and lifted into the air for a better view of what had happened. The sight from on high did nothing to improve the scene, and in fact, he now saw the totality of the devastation.

Whatever had struck had created a perfect circle of annihilation several hundred feet across, destroying not just the heart of the palace, but appeared to punch straight through Sharrellan's celestial plane. Azerick reached out with his arcane senses, trying to detect the goddess' presence but found none. Sharrellan, goddess of death, was gone.

CHAPTER 2

Daebian opened his eyes as the sun streamed through the glassless window. He yawned, stretched, and kissed the woman next to him until she opened her eyes. Ellyssa smiled even as she turned her head aside.

"Morning breath!" she squealed.

The two had not become lovers until several years after leaving the shattered kingdom of Valeria following the cataclysmic war with the Scions and their horde. Daebian provided the quickest way out, to escape and leave behind her former life, shattered every bit as much as the land itself, and to start anew.

Over the years, she and Daebian had grown closer. No longer feeling as though he were in his father's shadow, Daebian's sharp edges softened just enough to become tolerable company, more than tolerable for those with sufficient strength of character. They were more than lovers now. While having never formally cemented their relationship with a ceremony, the two had been together for some twenty years and partners for the majority of that time.

"I am a dragon!" Daebian crowed. "I will lay waste to your village with my fiery breath!"

Ellyssa pushed his face away with her palm. "The only thing you're laying waste to is my eyebrows!"

"That's a good thing. They're only about three hairs away from meeting in the middle."

"Liar!"

"I overheard people call you magess unibrow."

Ellyssa hurled away the thin sheet covering her and raced across the room to the mirror hanging on the wall. "You are such a liar."

Daebian rolled out of bed and put his arms around her from behind. "I know, and I'm sorry. I got you a gift I thought you would like."

Ellyssa looked down at his closed fist resting against her bare stomach. "What is it?"

Daebian uncurled his fingers and revealed his surprise.

Ellyssa scowled, snatched the tweezers from his hand, and hurled them at his back as he fled the room. "You ass!"

"Ow!" Daebian cried when the tweezer points pierced his skin at the base of his neck. "I think you drew blood."

"Not nearly enough. Shouldn't you be at breakfast before tormenting the populace?"

"What? My people love me."

"Love is a strong word."

"So is execution. Given a choice between the two, I think they've made the right decision."

Ellyssa rolled her eyes. "Just go eat. I imagine they are waiting for you."

Daebian frowned. "I'm sure they are. I find that annoying."

"You find everything annoying."

"Not you."

"Then I need to try harder."

"You do. You're slipping in your old age."

Allyssa's hairbrush followed a trajectory similar to that of the tweezers. "Who are you calling old?"

Daebian ducked the projectile and laughed. "You, Grandma. What are you, forty now?"

Mock fury contorted Ellyssa's face. She gestured at the bed. The blankets and sheets flew off of it and wrapped around Daebian's legs and arms. He tried to run, but that only caused him to fall over and strike the floor with a heavy thud. Ellyssa leapt on his writhing form and pinned him down. A mischievous smile splayed across her face as sparks arced between her fingers.

Daebian cried out as she ran her hand down his chest. "Ow, ow, ow! OK, I'm sorry!"

"Do you still think I'm a grandma?"

"Maybe a sexy grandma."

More sparks crackled across his skin. "OK, you're not a grandma!"

"I'm young and beautiful."

"Absolutely."

"And I don't have a unibrow."

"And you don't have a unibrow." Daebian grinned. "Or a mole on your back with a three-inch hair growing out of it."

"What?"

Ellyssa pushed off of his chest and sought the mirror once more. She turned and craned her head around to glimpse her back.

"I don't see a mole!"

Daebian threw the bedsheet over her head, smacked her on the backside, and ran out of the bedroom laughing before Ellyssa could retaliate. He snatched up his clothes and sword on the way out and made it to the end of the hall before something wrapped around his ankles and sent him sprawling headlong.

Daebian rolled onto his back, looked at his feet, and found the bedsheet wrapped around his legs. With warbling laughter, he pulled his sword from the scabbard and sliced through the linens. He scrambled to his feet as a vase and several knickknacks levitated off a small bureau.

"Hey, no throwing!" Daebian cried as he took shelter behind the open front door.

The hallway decorations went flying as if hurled from a ballista and shattered against the door he closed behind him. He cracked it open, reached through, and grabbed the clothes he had dropped. Once dressed, he turned away from the house, still chuckling, and found a stableboy with his horse waiting for him.

Daebian lifted himself into the saddle and looked down at the boy. "Word of advice. Never marry a wizard."

The boy squinted up at him. "Couldn't you just not make them mad, sir?"

The island governor looked out toward the beach and frowned. "I don't know. I don't think I've ever tried that."

"Might not get so many things thrown at you."

"You may be right, but what's the fun in that?" Daebian replied with a wink.

The boy tittered. "Have a good breakfast, sir. Say hi to Willoughby."

Daebian scowled, wheeled his horse around, and nudged it into a trot.

A fishmonger was setting up his table. He stopped and waved as Daebian rode past. "Morning, Gov'ner. Having a bite of breakfast at Willoughby's? Hard to believe it's Friday already."

Daebian narrowed his eyes as he continued on toward the tavern. A man sitting on a barrel and repairing a net looked up from his mending.

"Ahoy, Gov'ner. Going for a swim in the lagoon after your breakfast at Willoughby's?"

Daebian kept his eyes set straight ahead. His jaw muscled clenched as he gnashed his teeth. He urged his mount to a canter, eager to get off the streets and away from his people.

A man pushing a cart full of fruit and coconuts smiled and waved. "Gonna take the *Dark Shard* out around the island after your swim?"

Daebian spurred his horse into a gallop with a frustrated, strangled cry. It's hooves pounded against the hard-packed streets and created a spray of sand when he reined it in before the tavern. He tossed the reins over the hitching bar without bothering to tie them and stormed inside.

Willoughby, the tall, portly proprietor beamed at the governor's entrance. He disappeared into the kitchen and reemerged seconds later with a plate of eggs, sausage, potatoes, and buttered toast. He set the laden plate down before the island ruler.

"Right on time, Gov'ner. I hurried the butcher yesterday to have the sausage fresh for you today."

Daebian stared at the tendrils of steam coming off the timely, well-prepared meal as if it were offal. He stood up so abruptly that his chair toppled over backward in his haste to leave.

Willoughby called after the upset governor. "Is something the matter with it? I can make you something else, sir."

Daebian shouted over his shoulder as he stalked toward the exit. "No, it's exactly what I wanted, how I wanted it, and when I wanted it, and that's the problem!"

He slammed the door on his way out, leapt into the saddle, and raced back to his manor. Daebian blew through the house like a spring tempest and found Ellyssa reading in the study.

"Pack whatever you can't bear to part with. We're leaving."

Ellyssa looked up from her book. "Leaving? Whatever for? This has been our home for ten years."

"Which is several years too long! We've become complacent and—" Daebian held his hand over his stomach and made a sickly face, "—predictable."

"What are you going on about?"

He waved his hand around the room. "Everyone on this island knows what I'm going to do and when I'm going to do it. They smile and wave and ask me about my breakfast or my swim or taking my ship around the island. It's sickening. I'm sickening."

Ellyssa smiled, stood, and wrapped her arms around him. "You are a good leader, and the people love you. It's their way of showing they appreciate you."

Daebian scowled. "I should set fire to the whole damn island and show them just how much I appreciate them. I bet they won't predict that!"

"You're being ridiculous, and you will not set fire to the island or anything else."

"I still refuse to stay here one more minute. I have become what I despise most—my father. He had his tower, and now I have this stupid island. He had Rusty and his wizardly sycophants, and I have these pirates and fishermen, all bowing and scraping and 'morning Gov'ner,' 'nice day, Gov'ner.' 'Going for a swim, Gov'ner? It's Friday after all.'" Daebian stepped away from his wife and shook his finger in her face. "No, it's moving day!"

"Where are we going to go?"

"We'll go west, like we've been doing. We'll find a new land and new people for me to rule, and this time they will be properly respectful, and I won't be so damned predictable."

"These people do respect you."

"But it's respect without the underlying hint of fear. Without it, it's meaningless."

Ellyssa let out an exasperated sigh. "You're being ridiculous."

"I'm being unpredictable." He turned toward the open door and shouted. "Bradley!"

A man dressed in a crisp steward's uniform appeared. "Yes, sir?"

"Get a few men together and have them move mine and my wife's belongings onto the *Dark Shard*."

"Very good, sir. And how long should I expect you to be gone?"

"Forever. We aren't coming back."

"But…you are the governor."

Daebian stepped up to the man, removed the seal of office from around his neck, and held it out. "Now you're the governor. Congratulations."

"Daebian," Ellyssa started to say, but a bell rang in the town, its klaxon cutting her off. She cocked her head and narrowed her eyes. "That's the warning bell."

"Impossible," Daebian replied. "No one has been stupid enough to attack my island in years."

"So it's your island again? I thought Bradley was the governor now?"

Daebian pursed his lips. "It appears I may have acted hastily. Bradley, do you mind if I resume my duties until I have dealt with whatever this is?"

"It would be my pleasure, sir."

Daebian slipped the seal of office back around his neck and let it dangle on the outside of his shirt. "Wife, are you prepared to greet our uninvited guests?"

Ellyssa slid a wand into the belt around her waist and adjusted the magical rings and bracelets she wore. "I am. Let's go see what all the fuss is about."

The pair left the house and walked toward the town square. The island was not large, only about twenty square miles, and the town housed just a couple thousand residents with maybe two hundred more on outlying farms and plantations. There was a sense of urgency in the citizens' furtive movements as they ran toward their homes and away from whatever was causing the commotion.

Daebian looked up at the sky when a large shadow raced across the ground as if cast by an enormous bird or small dragon. Shielding his eyes with his hand, he saw a man astride a strange vehicle with short, fixed wings circling over the town.

"Well, you don't see that every day," he remarked.

"Nor them," Ellyssa said as she pointed toward the town square.

A squad of soldiers stood in orderly ranks. Gleaming helmets, greaves, breastplates, and bracers atop bare skin or leathers comprised their armor. The metal appeared to be bronze with silver inlaid designs. Ellyssa knew at a glance the sigils were more than mere ornamentation. She could sense that the pieces were imbued with strong magic.

The soldiers wielded short spears and bucklers, both made of the same materials and design as their armor. Most of the soldiers were dark-skinned, ranging from deep tan to almost black with dark, straight hair sticking out from under their helmets, but the variety in some of the men's features hinted of a mash of nationalities.

As the couple approached, another vehicle looking like a wagon but hovering about a foot off the ground appeared and disgorged its load of another twenty soldiers. It was made of the same metal as the people's armor, and the silver runes set into its surface glowed with power. Ellyssa marked the driver, an older man shackled to the device, as a mage. His chains radiated magic, and a shudder ran up her spine.

"I'm certain no one predicted this," she said in an attempt to relieve her mounting anxiety.

A tall, muscular man with skin the color of dark walnut beneath his silver armor stepped to the fore. He bore no weapons other than a dagger sheathed at his hip and small, silver, rune-scribed bucklers strapped to each forearm. He traveled his eyes across the group of townsfolk gathered before him and settled his gaze on Daebian and Ellyssa.

"I am Ordinator Bojan Archelaus. Are you the leader of these people?" he asked, his voice deep and his words clipped.

Daebian glanced over his shoulder and found that scores of his people had gathered behind him, many gripping weapons in their hands or touching the hilts of the blades strapped on their hips. "I am Daebian Giles, governor of this island and its people. What brings you and your soldiers to my island, Ordinator Archelaus?"

The soldier's eyelids narrowed to slits as he locked eyes with Daebian. "Your eyes…"

"Captivating, I know," Daebian replied with a smirk.

"Are you demon spawn? A warlock?"

"I have no idea what a warlock is. As far as being demon spawn," Daebian shrugged, "I'm told I get them from my father. Unless you want to discuss my other extraordinary physical endowments, I ask again, what do you want here?"

"I come bearing the gift of the Order and the peace, security, and prosperity that comes with it. All you need do is swear fealty to the Order and recognize Emperor Leontius Attar and Empress Noela Attar as your divine rulers, and your lives will continue much as before. As to your peculiar features, the inquisitors will determine your status."

"I see. So because of my eyes, I get handed over to some uptight men with hot pokers and other contraptions of sadistic entertainment. And what manner of festivities do my people get to enjoy under your peaceful and prosperous rule?"

"One in five able-bodied men are afforded the glory of joining the legion to help purge the world of the foul beasts plaguing it these last twenty years. Any who possess magical talent are conscripted into the legion and hold special positions within its ranks."

Daebian glanced at the older man who appeared to be chained to the floating troop wagon. "I see the *special position* you afford them. It looks more like slavery."

Ellyssa shook her head, her face a mask of suppressed fury. "It is far worse than slavery. It is worse than death."

The Ordinator flicked his fingers over his shoulder and waved the shackled man over. The man withdrew a rod attached to his shackles from the machine and strode to the Ordinator's side. He held his head high, and his eyes did not portray the look of subservience or reflect the broken spirit of a downtrodden man.

"Arcanus Filipov, are you a slave?" Ordinator Archelaus asked.

The man set his jaw and gazed over Daebian and Ellyssa's head. "It is my pride and duty to serve the Order as the Order serves me, my family, and my people."

"Why are you shackled, Arcanus?"

"For my protection and the protection of my people and so I may best serve the Order."

"Are you compensated for your duties?"

"An Arcanus under conscription is paid and housed as an optio. Arcanus who have completed their conscription but continues to serve in the legion is compensated as an ordinator, or even a primus depending on their years of service and accomplishments."

"Thank you, Arcanus. Return to your station."

The mage turned but leaned in to whisper to the Ordinator. "Beware the woman. She is a wizard of substantial ability if my assessment is accurate."

Ordinator Archelaus nodded and set his eyes on Ellyssa. "Arcanus Doncho Filipov was free to leave the legion seven years ago, but he stayed to serve his family and his empire. He, as does every man and woman who fights this scourge the old gods set upon our world, knows his sacrifice ensures the safety and prosperity of his family. Does that sound like a slave to you?"

"Then why is he shackled like an animal?" Ellyssa demanded.

"Only the godly Emperor and Empress and their children are trusted with unrestricted access to arcane power. Magic is too dangerous and tempting to be left unfettered in the hands of lesser beings."

Daebian said, "As great as all that sounds, I'm afraid we must decline your generous offer. My people are not fond of rules and stricture, and your Order looks as though rules abound. But you and your men are welcome to rest here and enjoy whatever services my people offer—as long as you can pay of course."

The dark-skinned man's eyes hardened. "You mistake my meaning. There is only the Order and enemies of the Order. You do not want to be my enemy, Governor. Kneel to the empire, and, as long as you are not a warlock or other abomination, you will retain your position."

"And my wife?"

"She is a wizard, yes? The law requires her to be forever shackled and conscripted into the legion for a term of ten years."

"Like hell!" Ellyssa seethed as she began to draw power.

"You heard the Lady. It's time for you to leave."

"You will yield, or we will break you. There is only the Order. You can join the Order or die. Those are your two options."

Daebian gripped the sword sheathed at his side. "I know nothing about your Order, but I am quite familiar with death. You can go play tin soldiers somewhere else or join the line of people who can kiss my taut, supple ass. Those are your two options."

Ordinator Bojan matched Daebian's grim look. "After I carve your black eyes from your skull, I will put your woman in chains and conscript your people. There is only the Order."

"You think that because you have never met true chaos. Allow me to introduce you."

Daebian's sword leapt from its scabbard and whistled toward the small gap between the Ordinator's helmet and pauldron. The blow should have been as decisive as it was swift, but Bojan's arm came up, and a violet ring of energy the size of a round shield surrounded the silver buckler strapped to his left forearm.

Amethyst sparks flew as enchanted steel struck arcane shield, the jolt knocking Daebian back on his heels. Purplish-blue energy leapt from the Ordinator's right bracer, this one in the shape of a longsword. Bojan held the shimmering apparition aloft in salute.

"There is the Order and death. You have given me your decision, and I accept it."

Bojan's shimmering blade arced toward Daebian's head. Daebian ducked beneath the swing and lunged, his blade once again deflected by the soldier's shield. The governor retreated as Bojan reversed his stroke, a feat that would be almost impossible to achieve with a steel sword.

Ellyssa gathered arcane power from the ether and prepared to come to her husband's aid, but the soldiers lowered their spears and marched forward, each step punctuated by a short, wordless shout. She turned her attention to the oncoming men and unleashed lightning into their ranks.

The bolt struck near the center of the forward line, dropping two men, but before she could rake her lightning across the front echelon, the soldiers raised shields similar to that of their commander and closed the small gap left by the fallen men with expert precision. Ellyssa followed up her attack with half a dozen arcane orbs and a fireball, but the soldiers' shields expanded until they formed a potent ward that covered them in a dome of energy and limned their spears.

The sailors and islanders hurled stones, bottles, and knives, but the missiles were no more effective than Ellyssa's magic had been. The wizardess mimed clawing at the ground and spread her hands wide. A crack opened near her feet and created a gash in the street that streaked toward the ranks of soldiers, widening as it drew nearer as if to swallow them whole. However, like water around a boulder, the rent raced around the arcane shields' border, doing little more than to buckle the cobblestones beneath the invader's feet.

"Daebian!" Ellyssa called out.

Daebian spared her a quick glance that almost cost him his head. "I'm a little busy, dear!"

Ellyssa's eyes flashed between her husband and the soldiers, unsure who was in the greatest danger. Daebian was the most skilled swordsman she had ever seen, but the ordinator had him on the defensive.

Daebian ducked beneath the ordinator's swing and backpedaled. He darted in to take advantage of a small opening, but the soldier interposed his shield between him and Daebian's blade. Bojan's riposte forced him back once again, fueling Daebian's ire by thwarting every one of his attacks. The man's skill with shield and sword was remarkable, but Daebian's talents were not limited to just martial ability.

He mentally prodded Klaraxis, the demon lord trapped within the black stone set in the pommel of his sword, and drew upon his abyssal power. Darkness, deeper than a full eclipse, enveloped the duelers. Bojan yelped when Daebian's obscured blade slipped past his guard and scored his flesh.

The eldritch glow surrounding the Ordinator's shield and sword increased until they glowed like miniature suns and obliterated the darkness. Daebian had anticipated such a response. While the brilliant light dazzled their eyes and destroyed the black miasma, it also created deep shadows across the ground. Daebian leapt into one and vanished only to emerge from another behind his enemy. Daebian buried his blade in the man's vulnerable back and drew his soul from his body to feed Klaraxis. While nowhere near as powerful as the god-forged soul sword he once possessed, his new blade was sufficient for keeping his pet demon satisfied.

Daebian cast his gaze across the small battlefield and did not like what he saw. While his people had emerged from their homes and businesses in droves to defend what was theirs, they lacked the training, arms, and armor of these professional soldiers. Even had the legionnaires not possessed weapons and shields bolstered by strange magic, the fight would have been a costly one. With them, they were almost certainly doomed to defeat.

Ellyssa hurled lightning and fire at the invaders, but little if any harmed those protected by the ward enveloping them. Arrows and crossbow bolts sent streaking into their ranks bounced off their shields as well. Ellyssa used her magic to pry large stones from beneath the sand and soil and hurled them with as much force as she could muster.

The soldiers' wards flared beneath the impact and caused the front rank to stagger. Finally seeing some effect, she continued her barrage with renewed vigor. A quarrel slipped through a crack in the shields and felled a man. More islanders rushed at the centuria from behind and clubbed and hacked at the rear elements.

Several javelins flew out of the enemy ranks toward Ellyssa, but none came near to hitting her and stuck up out of the ground like tent poles waiting for canvas. She reached for more energy to fling another boulder into the mass of soldiers, but the moment she touched the Source, she felt her wards drop, and bolts of lightning leapt from what she had thought were poorly cast javelins, each one striking her in the chest and back.

Ellyssa cried out before slumping to the ground, stunned and struggling to hold onto consciousness. She braced herself for another agonizing strike as she reached for the Source, but it felt weak and far away. Electricity arced across the javelins' length to give a warning of what was to come if she continued to draw power. The mage glared at the javelins creating a rough circle around her and saw the runes adorning their lengths.

She tried to crawl out of the punishing ring, but the soldiers rushed forward, pushing through the defenders with grunts and shouted orders from their leaders and descended upon her. Ellyssa looked up at the men surrounding her, spears held aloft and ready to plunge into her body should she resist. Dazed, her body and magic struck numb, she knew she could do little more than spit at them in defiance. So she did.

"Hold!" an officer, shouted, an order meant as much for the remaining defenders as to his own men.

The ranks parted so Daebian could see his wife, subdued and at their mercy.

"Yield, warlock, or we will put you, your woman, and all who continue to resist to the blade," the officer commanded.

Daebian studied the battlefield with a professional eye and knew his people were defeated. Were it not for Ellyssa, he would escape and wreak his vengeance upon them in the night, slaughtering them one by one in their sleep or standing at their guard posts. But unable to get to his wife, he could not risk them punishing her for his actions.

He slammed his sword home in its sheath, unbuckled it from around his waist, and cast it into the sand at his feet. It was not just being beaten that galled him, but for the weakness he showed in letting his sentiments for Ellyssa stop him from winning at any cost. There was a time when victory was all that mattered, and no cost or betrayal too great to achieve it. Clearly, that time had passed.

The officer, Optio Grigor Flavius, looked at Arcanus Filipov and jerked his head toward Ellyssa. "Arcanus, shackle this wizard. You men, secure the warlock."

"What in the abyss is a warlock?" Daebian shouted as several soldiers grabbed him by the arms and clamped manacles around his wrists and ankles.

The old mage, Doncho, strode forward with a pair of manacles identical to the ones he wore. Ellyssa's eyes went wide and her face drained of color as old horrors leapt into her mind. She struggled against the hands holding her in place, her feet churning in the sand beneath her. A scream tore from her lips as Doncho knelt before her.

"Leave her alone, you bastards!" Daebian yelled, earning him a spear butt to his stomach.

The Arcanus' eyes filled with sadness and sympathy. "You have been shackled before? By whom?"

Ellyssa gasped and fought to swallow her fear. "By people who also sought to use me, to kill for them, and to torture me if I refused. I would rather die than be subjected to that ever again!"

The older man shook his head. "These are not devices for torture or to rob you of your free will. They merely restrict your access to magic for the safety of you and those around you. You have my word. Should you ultimately refuse to serve the Order, you will simply be restricted to quarters until the end of this dreadful war. You will not be harmed or punished. That is not the way of the Order. We are here to save humanity, not destroy it."

"You invaded my home. Murdered my friends. What good is your word?"

"You were warned not to resist. Had you complied, all of this would have been avoided."

Ellyssa looked to the black-skinned officer and back to the wizard. "You aren't from their land. Did your people comply when the Order came for them?"

Doncho cast his eyes to the ground. "Not immediately, and many people died because of it. Could I go back in time, I would urge them to obey, even if we could have defied them. Their cause is just and necessary. Only the Order can save us. There is only the Order."

"Spoken like a true zealot," Ellyssa spat.

"No, just a man who has seen enough evil to understand the truth. Please, you must wear these. I will be personally responsible for you, and I promise I will not harm you or let you come to harm as long as you pose no threat to me or the Order."

Ellyssa glared at the man, sent emotional fire into his kind eyes, and held out her hands. She shuddered and fought the urge to vomit as the cold metal clamped around her wrists.

"Arcanus," Optio Flavius called out. "This man claims to know nothing of warlocks, yet he reeks of their foul magic."

Doncho gave Ellyssa one last smile and nodded before climbing stiffly to his feet and standing before Daebian. "His eyes are certainly interesting, and the aura of magic surrounding him is similar to that of a warlock, but it is not the same. Certainly not the same as that used by the betrayers."

"What do you recommend we do with him?"

Doncho spared Ellyssa a look over his shoulder. "The woman is a very capable mage. If this man is not in league with the betrayers, it might be best to return him to Syrna. He defeated an ordinator and would make a strong soldier. Keeping him alive should also make the woman more compliant."

Optio Flavius nodded. "I concur with your assessment." He turned and issued orders to his men. "This island is small and its people appear to be mostly pirates and vagabonds. We will conscript three out of five. Secure a number of them and load them on a ship for reeducation. I will send word to the cohort to come and take the rest."

CHAPTER 3

Azerick returned to the arch that would take him back to his citadel, or anywhere else in the abyss, only to find the gateway destroyed. The white marble doorway lay shattered amidst the debris of Sharrellan's once opulent plaza.

Bits of silvery arcanum runes that once adorned the arch shone amongst the wreckage. Azerick focused on his staff and created a bond between its arcanum components and the runes. Broken stones lifted from the ground and assembled themselves before the demon lord until they reformed the gateway.

The structure held despite the network of fissures marring its form, and the runes complied to Azerick's silent command and flared to life. He walked through the arch and stepped into his throne room.

Azerick stood in his vast hall, wary. Something was not right. He sent his senses down the citadel's vast, labyrinthine corridors. The black fortress, like his staff, was an extension of himself, linked by blood and soul. Before he could react to the intruders, every door leading into the throne room burst open or shattered, and scores of demons poured in like water through open floodgates.

Azerick glared at the demons and sneered his contempt and ire. He knew the attackers played a role in what had happened to the dark goddess. They caused his pain. Pain fueled his rage. Rage demanded vengeance. Vengeance required blood.

The lord of the fifth circle raised a ward just as the demon horde swarmed over him, tearing at the invisible barrier with their claws and gnashing teeth. Azerick brought the butt of his staff cracking against the stone floor, dropping the ward at the same time. Powerful energy erupted around him and flung demons, and pieces of demons, away in every direction like chaff in a tornado.

Azerick swept his staff before him in an arc, sending an arcane blade streaking across the room and scything down everything in its path. Succubi and other flying demons dove from the high ceiling. The demonic sorcerer spared them little more than a glance.

The black walls wept blood, but the ichor did not trickle down its ebony surface. It lanced out and solidified into spears, stabbing into the plummeting traitors and reeling them back up into the vaulted shadows.

Throughout the citadel, bloody tendrils sprang from the walls, floors, and ceilings, piercing demonic flesh, and consuming their souls, their life energy feeding the fortress and its master. Azerick slashed at the air with his staff and opened a gate to the tallest of the citadel's towers. What he saw left him awestruck.

Demons swarmed outside of his fortress as far as he could see. Flying demons darkened the skies like flocks of starlings during migration. He knew there were more fiends assaulting his home than resided within the entire fifth circle. The attack was far more coordinated any previous attempts at usurpation. It appeared other circles had joined in a unified cause. Perhaps all of them.

As powerful as he was, Azerick knew he could not defeat such a horde. It was only a matter of time before the throng breached the walls and tore him apart, but he would not go quietly. There would be hell to pay for this effrontery, and with Sharrellan gone, hell belonged to him.

Drawing power from the citadel's deep reserves, Azerick sent stones soring into the strange mauve sky, the missiles moving at such velocity they blasted through any demon unfortunate enough to be in their path. The rocks streaked back to ground as fiery meteors, sundering the land around them and obliterating scores of monsters with every strike.

"Skulk!" Azerick shouted above the continuous, thundering impacts of meteors.

A loud pop and puff of sulfur produced the small demog, who cowered against one of the tower's crenellations next to Azerick's feet.

"Master! The ungrateful scum have rebelled," Skulk cried. "Skulk wanted to warn the master, but the others would not let him."

"What have they done with Sharrellan?"

"Skulk does not know. The traitors, they whispered in shadows where Skulk could not hear. They knew Skulk was loyal to the master and the glorious goddess. Skulk will rejoice in their cries when the goddess returns and punishes them!"

Azerick chewed his lip and frowned. "Sharrellan may never return unless I can rescue her. Someone has to know what happened, someone who will tell me."

Skulk scratched his bald head hard enough to score the bright pink flesh. "Krade, Krade knows everything in the abyss!"

"Krade…" Azerick said, his voice thick with disgust at the mention of the devil's name. "Keep your head down. I don't know how long the citadel can keep them out."

"Skulk be fine. Demons only want to kill you."

"Lucky you," Azerick replied with a grunt.

He tore another hole through the fabric of reality and fell the moment he crossed through. Still in his demonic form, he snapped his enormous, bat-like wings open and glided over the reddish landscape miles from the siege. Even this far out, demons streamed across the ground toward his citadel, which meant those tasked with guarding the portals between the five circles of the abyss let them through or were defeated. Since neither he nor Sharrellan had received a warning, Azerick assumed it was the former.

Even in a realm where conspiracy and betrayal was the norm of everyday business, this level of treachery was unheard of. Assuming the goddess was still alive, Azerick could not imagine the retribution she would impose on her denizens when he returned her to her seat of power. What he could envision made him smile.

Azerick rolled in flight, putting his back toward the ground, and stabbed out with his staff. The arcanum orb adorning its top stretched out into a spike and pierced the succubus' heart before she could land her surprise attack.

A dozen more flying demons, a mash of succubi, incubi, and grackin, dove at Azerick's larger form like swallows harrying a crow.

Fireballs and lightning leapt from their hands, and small but deadly blades slashed at the demon lord's wings and body as they flitted past.

Azerick landed with an explosion of rock and sand to create a moment of respite from the demons trying to mob him from both the air and the ground. He lashed out with magic, talons, and staff at any creature appearing within the dust cloud, rending and scorching flesh. Demonic cries of pain and fury resounded across the abyssal plane, many cutting off and silenced forever.

The ground shook, and a hulking silhouette appeared in the haze. Azerick recognized the mountainous behemoth's form a moment before it coalesced into a wall of shaggy, ruddy fur and malice. Behemoths were supposed to be guarding the gateways between the five circles, its appearance this far from its home giving evidence to the level of betrayal rife throughout the abyss.

A massive paw tipped with claws as long as swords enveloped Azerick's torso. The enormous demon lifted him off his feet and smashed him against the ground, raising another thick pall of dust. Air blasted from Azerick's lungs under the impact, and his ribs sounded with an ominous cracking.

Azerick felt himself floating upward once again in preparation of a second dashing. He stabbed the tip of his staff into the creature's forearm and send a powerful jolt of electricity into the shaggy limb. The behemoth released its hold on him with a bellow so loud it made the stones tremble.

The demon lord dropped twenty feet before landing in a painful crouch, his fall only slightly slowed by his broken wings. He formed his arcanum spear tip into a blade as thin as a razor and the length of a two-handed sword. Azerick watched the enormous hand reaching for him.

He swiped at the creature's paw and severed the appendage just behind the wrist. The behemoth pulled back its gore-spewing limb with another bellow of pain. Azerick reeled back and hurled his staff, empowering it with sorcerous energy. The weapon hummed with power as it streaked between the small gulf separating foes and blasted through the behemoth's chest and out of its back.

The monstrosity stared at him a moment with an uncomprehending gaze before pitching forward and falling onto its hideous face. A cry of outrage issued from the remaining demons as they charged forth once more. Azerick sent demonic power into the behemoth's corpse, tore its entrails from its body, and sent them into the onrushing horde.

The blood and offal writhed like tentacles as they plunged into dozens of demons. He siphoned their life energy from their bodies, using it to heal his wounds, and left desiccated corpses in his wake. Hundreds of demons converged on him, but he had already wasted too much time. Opening another gate, he fled the battlefield.

Azerick shrouded himself in concealing magic hoping to continue his journey unnoticed, or at least ignored. He flew over mile after mile of mauve desert, his pace broken up with a series of portals he wrenched open to span several leagues in an instant.

Fatigue began to wear on him by the time he reached the entrance to Krade's Valley of Lies, but he was far from exhausted. Regardless of how his denizens felt about him, he was the master of this world, and its resources were his for the taking.

The narrow valley spread out before him, its features familiar and haunting. While named The Valley of Lies, and Krade being the master of lies, those deceptions and deceits were tools to uncover truths, all of them painful.

The valley responded to his presence the moment he entered. Krade's magic invaded his mind, seeking his greatest failures, doubts, and guilt.

"You let them take me," Andrea, his boyhood friend said as she appeared from the shadows of the cliff looming over him to his left.

Bran stepped up beside her. "You let me go after her alone, and we both became prisoners. You said you were our friend."

"What sort of friend abandons his family when they need it most?" Andrea asked.

Azerick forced himself to keep his eyes locked ahead, refusing to acknowledge their accusations.

"It's what he does. He calls me his daughter, but he let slavers take me away, torture me, and turn me into a weapon as I fell into madness."

Try as he might, Azerick could not ignore the girl's words. He turned his head and gazed upon Ellyssa's haunted visage. It was a younger Ellyssa, but she aged before his eyes.

"You left me again when I needed you most. Do you know what happened to me after the war? Do you know if I'm even alive? Do you care?"

"Of course I care," Azerick whispered as he hastened his steps.

Miranda appeared wearing a widow's black gown. "He cares only for himself. He left me to raise a child on my own, a child tainted with his demonic seed. Is it no wonder he became a monster?"

"Nonsense. Father loves his monstrous progeny," Daebian replied as he materialized a few paces away from his mother. "He welcomed that freak brother of mine with open arms while spurning me, driving me to prove to him I was as worthy to be called his son every bit as much as Raijaun, despite my lack of magic."

"At least you were a product of a loving union," Raijaun replied. "I was a construct, a tool used to help him further his own aims. Using my power is agonizing, but he pushed me, used me with no thought of what it was doing to me."

"Enough, Krade!" Azerick shouted, his booming voice echoing off the canyon walls.

"Enough he says," Allister's gruff voice replied. "When has anything ever been enough? Certainly not enough death. How many people died for your glory, for you to become a hero only to be reviled and cast out by those you sought to save?"

Aggie, Jon Locke and his extended family, the children that perished in the ravager attack at the Academy, his mother and father, Jansen, and everyone Azerick had ever watched die filled the valley.

"Were we enough?" they droned as Azerick shoved past them. "Who else must die for your glory?"

With a roar of defiance, Azerick ducked his head, held his arms crossed before his face, and bulled through the crowd of ghosts. Not until he felt alone once more did he slow to a walk and lower his arms. Azerick looked behind him, but his eyes beheld only a barren valley. He lowered his head and continued through the vale, which in reality was little more than a wide gorge, its very name a lie. In the distance, he spied something in the middle of the chasm, too uniform to be a mere outcrop of stone.

He raced ahead, the site spurring him on as the shape came into view. Sharrellan stood upon a large round dais with her hands chained above her head to a white marble pillar jutting up from its center like an enormous sundial. Azerick tried to climb the steps, but an invisible force with the tangibility of a brick wall stopped him.

"I knew you would find me," Sharrellan said as Azerick took a step back and studied the feature upon which she stood.

"What happened?" Azerick asked.

"That vile Krade conspired with the other demon lords to chain me so they could destroy you. It was a foolish plan, and they will all pay dearly for it, I promise you."

"How was this even possible?"

The goddess looked askance. "They took me by surprise with a spell of impressive power. It required the combined magic of the four lords and many of their ilk to effect it, and I imagine a great number of sacrifices. Once transported to this damned place and chained to the pillar, I was helpless. The magic has cut me off from my power."

Azerick ran his hand across the barrier. "This is an exceptionally powerful ward."

"They put a great amount of thought and effort into its construction, but I believe you can destroy it with the joint use of your sorcerous and demonic power."

Azerick nodded his agreement. "I don't know if I can do it without hurting you."

"Don't worry about me. The power that keeps me locked away protects me. I will be fine. Just destroy the damned thing."

The goddess' consort raised his staff and unleashed a ray of black and silver energy. The barrier flared with blue fire as it tried to resist its own destruction. Sweat beaded on Azerick's brow as he poured more power into his attack. His staff heated in his hand until its touch would have charred his flesh had he been mortal.

The ward shattered under his assault, exploding outward in an azure fireball. The force of it hurled Azerick to the ground and scorched his exposed skin. He climbed to his feet and mounted the few steps to the pillar. Forming the arcanum sphere atop his staff into an axe head, Azerick severed the chains holding his mistress prisoner.

Sharrellan dropped her arms around Azerick's neck. "I knew you would come for me. I will make Krade and the rest of these vermin pay for their impudence!"

"Are you sure you're well? Do you need a minute to recover?"

The goddess traced Azerick's jaw line and pulled him close. "I suppose I could use a few minutes to...recover."

Before he could reply, Sharrellan pressed her lips to his and quested the inside of his mouth with her tongue. It was fortunate that Azerick had no real need to breathe in this realm else he might have suffered hypoxia before she released him.

"Come, my love, let us return to what remains of my palace so I can plan my revenge," Sharrellan said as she pushed Azerick away.

"Of course," Azerick replied. "I need to do one thing first."

"What's that?"

"This." Azerick thrust his spear-tipped staff through Sharrellan's body and pinned her to the pillar.

The goddess pursed her lips as she glared at the weapon impaling her through the chest. "Is that any way to treat a lady?"

"Enough of your games, Krade! Where is she?"

Sharrellan's body morphed into something more devilish and far less feminine. "What did I do wrong?"

"Sharrellan would never call me her love," Azerick replied with a smirk.

"Well shit. Admit it, I was doing well until then."

Azerick sent a jolt of electricity through his staff and into Krade's body. "Tell me where she is!"

"Ow, fine! You don't have to be so brutal. Violence isn't really my thing. I mean, inflicting it sure. Not so much a fan of receiving it."

"You're going to receive a great deal of it if you don't tell me what I want to know."

Krade slumped his shoulders in defeat. "OK, fine, I admit it. You're a decent kisser."

The devil cried out as Azerick sent an agonizing wave of pain through his body. "All right! Firstly, you should know I had nothing to do with what happened."

"Nothing?"

Krade shrugged. "Next to nothing. I took no active part in her imprisonment."

"Then she's alive?"

"Gods yes! Could you imagine what would happen to this place without the goddess of death? The insane would be running the asylum."

Azerick narrowed his eyes at the devil. "How inactive was your part?"

"Extremely. Practically non-existent."

"Explain it to me."

Krade bobbed his head from side to side. "Well, I may have made an offhand remark that someone repeated to someone else who told another. Then those demons got together and turned my innocent, hypothetical comment into an actual plan they then executed with a surprising measure of success."

Azerick shook his head. "And they don't plan on killing her?"

"Of course not. I would never permit it. I am far too loyal a subject to allow any harm to come to my queen."

"But you're fine with imprisoning her for eternity?"

"What? No. Just until you're dead and we feast on your soul. Then Sharrellan's captors will make a truce with her and set her free."

"You can't believe Sharrellan will forgive those responsible for killing me, destroying her home, and locking her away."

Krade belted out a laugh. "Absolutely not! That's what makes this whole thing so deliciously hilarious! She'll slaughter them like diseased cattle and torture the ones she lets live for the next century."

"What do you get out of this?"

Krade shrugged. "With you and the lords dead, or at least no longer rivals, I'll be her favorite again."

"Where is she, and how do I free her?"

"The lords have her trapped between planes. The best way to reach her is tearing through the veil where they took her. The spell did a lot of damage, and it will be weakest there. I should warn you, they expect you to come for her. It's probably a suicide mission."

Azerick tore his staff free from Krade's torso. "I've gotten good at being the one who walks away from suicide missions."

Krade prodded the hole in his chest with a long, slender finger. "It will take days for this to heal."

"It's going to take even longer to get the taste of your tongue out of my mouth," Azerick replied with a grunt as he descended the dais steps.

"Perhaps, but try as you might, you'll never get it out of your mind."

Azerick gestured over his shoulder, and stone spikes shot out of the pillar and pierced Krade's body in several places, each one curving outward to secure him in place.

"Oh, now that's just rude. And incredibly painful," Krade whined.

CHAPTER 4

Two soldiers of the Order escorted Ellyssa from the small, locked room in which they detained her for the last day and a half. The deck under her feet rolled over the waves. She had spent years at sea with Daebian, and it posed no difficulty to her walking.

The Order had taken her, Daebian, and thirty men from the island aboard one of their ships. They were returning to Syrna for indoctrination and training of their newest "recruits." The armada comprising the prima cohort would conscript the others into their ranks and reeducate them en route to Valeria once they reached the island.

Ellyssa tried to keep her eyes off the shackles binding not just her hands but her magic. While they felt different from the ones she had been forced to wear before, she could not keep her heart from racing and her breathing steady. Ellyssa was on the precipice of panic, peering over the edge with terrified eyes, but she refused to give in to her fear.

The lead soldier opened a door and gestured her inside. Arcanus Doncho Filipov sat at a small table bolted to the floor and was reading Ellyssa's spell book. The chamber was only a little larger than the one in which they held her but better furnished, and she was certain his door was never locked.

"Please have a seat," Doncho said as she entered. He nodded to the guards. "You may leave us."

Ellyssa looked over her shoulder at the sound of the door closing before returning her gaze to the mage. "What do you want with me?"

"In this moment? Just to talk. There are some very impressive spells in your grimoire. Can you cast them all?"

"Take these chains off and I'll show you."

"I don't think that would be a wise idea. If you are capable of controlling such forces, it is a good thing we caught you unprepared."

Ellyssa's face darkened. "You have no idea, and you would be a fool to think I'm the biggest threat."

"The potential danger your man poses is what we must discuss. I think it would be best to learn as much about you and Daebian as I can before reaching Syrna."

"Why?"

Doncho pressed his lips into a thin line and drummed his fingers upon the tabletop. "Your husband, he is your husband, yes?"

"It's as good a word as any."

"Then we shall use it. Your husband, Daebian, presents a problem for us."

"How so?"

Doncho leaned back in his chair and took a deep breath. "A proper explanation requires a history lesson. If you will indulge me a lecture, I shall tell it to you."

Ellyssa shrugged and rattled the chain connecting her manacles. "You have a captive audience."

"So I do. Syrna has always had a contentious relationship with Castracene, their neighbors to the north and east. The dark-skinned people are almost all from Syrna. While a smaller nation than Castracene, the Syrnese are a magically adept people, mostly sorcerous. The average citizen has a minor talent in the arts, but the empire have more than their share of adepts and masters. It is why Castracene was never able defeat Syrna although it was not for lack of trying. Some twenty years ago, transdimensional rifts opened across the land, disgorging horrifying creatures that appeared to desire nothing but to slaughter everyone in their path."

"It was the return of the elder gods, called Scions," Ellyssa said. "They came to our land as well, and not just their foul creations. We had to battle the gods themselves."

Doncho pursed his lips. "That is a remarkable addition to history if true."

"It is true."

"It doesn't matter. Truth has no bearing on where you are going. As I was saying, when the creatures invaded, Syrna and Castracene formed an alliance to battle a common foe. With Castracene's large army and Syrna's sorcerers, they pushed back the tide of death and closed many of the rifts."

Doncho's visage darkened. "Once victory appeared at hand, Castracene turned on Syrna in a vile act of betrayal. Syrna lost many powerful sorcerers while battling the abominations. Sensing weakness, the Castracene committed an unforgivable act of betrayal. Several Syrnese towns and cities fell to Castracene swords and a new, dark magic. How they came to possess it, no one is certain, but their sorcerer scholars believed it was tied to demonic power, or perhaps the spawn. They called these wielders of the black arts warlocks. Just as it appeared Syrna would fall, the royal family performed a miracle. They became gods. The emperor and empress and their chosen few slaughtered the Castracene using power never seen in this world. They hued down entire armies with fire and lightning, driving them out of Syrna."

The old mage became animated as he regaled his guest with his tale. "Rallying behind their new gods, Syrna continued to drive the Castracene out of their own homeland and into the northern badlands. Far from Syrna's border, where the Castracene could no longer pose a threat, the empress and emperor raised a great wall of ice and stone and bound it with magic to make sure they could never again pose a threat to Syrna."

"How did they become gods?" Ellyssa asked, interrupting the old mage.

"The gods had abandoned the world to its fate. They allowed the creatures to invade and did nothing to stop Castracene's treachery despite the prayers of millions. The rulers declared the gods to be dead and took their places. How, I cannot say, but to lay eyes upon the emperor and empress removes all doubt."

"The gods did not abandon us. They were fighting the Scions alongside my people. Serron, god of the sea, died fighting them. Died for us!"

"Fact or fiction is irrelevant at this point. We must deal with the matters at hand regardless of how we got here or why we chose the path that led to our encounter. Now we get to the problem of your husband."

Ellyssa levied a fierce glare on the elder mage. "Because he is different."

"Because his abilities and countenance resembles that of the warlocks. He defeated an ordinator in single combat, something I had thought impossible of a mortal man."

"To be fair, I'm not sure he is mortal," Ellyssa replied with a smirk.

Doncho bobbed his head. "It is this, and his coming into being, that I want you to share with me. If I can prove he is not a warlock, perhaps I can spare him from execution."

"You would kill him for defending himself and his people?" Ellyssa demanded.

"Warlocks are a pestilence we must eradicate wherever we find them." He held up a hand to forestall the woman's pending rebuke. "I believe neither of you know anything about the warlocks. I need you to help me convince the higher powers. What do you know of his…creation."

Ellyssa took several deep breaths and fought the urge to lunge across the table and strangle the man with her bare hands. "I know everything about him. I've known him since birth, and I knew his father and mother years before that."

Doncho leaned back in his chair and smiled. "Enlighten me. I have told you our story. Now tell me yours."

"On one condition."

"Which is?"

"You allow me to be with my husband."

The mage's mouth turned down into a frown. "I cannot allow him to stay in your room. It is not secure enough."

"Then let me go to him."

"You would prefer the brig to your room?"

"I would rather live in a sty with Daebian than a palace without him."

"As you wish. Your tale, please."

Ellyssa placed her palms flat on the tabletop and leaned back. "Daebian's father, Azerick, adopted me when I was young. He is a powerful sorcerer, and he taught me how to wield magic."

"He did a fine job."

Ellyssa smirked. "Your people caught me unprepared. It won't happen again. A group of wizards captured him once and sacrificed his body to a demon named Klaraxis, the lord of the fifth circle of the abyss, so he could return to our world and wreak havoc. Only Azerick was stronger. He suppressed the demon's will and took control of his power. That was the first time he returned from the abyss. His wife became pregnant with Daebian. While both his parents were human, some of the demon's essence affected the baby, and that is how Daebian came into being."

Doncho nodded and stroked his chin. "I see."

"No, you don't. Azerick was later struck down, and returned to the abyss once again, his soul too entwined with that of the demon's. This time he took over Klaraxis' body. The Scions' prison was failing, and if they got free, they and their scourge would destroy the world as we know it. He escaped the abyss a second time. He came for me the last time someone put me in chains. Azerick led an army and crushed a powerful city full of wizards and sorcerers. He returned from the abyss to battle, and defeat, the old gods."

"Your master sounds formidable. Let us pray he does not come back a third time."

Ellyssa threw back her head and laughed. "Azerick is not the one you should fear. Even if he did somehow return, he is good and merciful. Daebian is not. Had you not captured and threatened me, you and your men would still be on that island, fighting and dying while your corpses provided fertilizer for the palm trees. I have managed over the years to get a good grip on his leash. I've even gotten him housebroken. It will end badly for you if I let him loose."

"You are not making it easy for me to save him."

Ellyssa leaned forward and bore her eyes into his. "I'm not trying to save him from you. I'm trying to save you from him. Let us go. Go fight your crusade somewhere else. We won't stop you. My people have suffered enough and have no desire for war with anyone."

The mage shook his head. "There is only the Order and enemies of the Order."

Ellyssa stood. "Then we have nothing more to discuss. Take me to Daebian as you promised."

"Legionnaire," the arcanus called out.

The door opened, and two soldiers crowded into the room.

"Take the woman to the brig and confine her with her man. And double their guard," he ordered.

Doncho drummed his fingers on the table as he processed the woman's words. The Order had faced formidable foes before, but all fell to their might. However, if even half of what she had said was true, it would be foolish to discount the threat. There was certainty in her words that gave the old mage pause. He knew there were heroes and villains in this world, their power bolstered by fate. For the first time since accepting the Order, he had to wonder which side fate had chosen.

A chill crawled up his spine and made him shudder. He told himself it was just the cold draft coming off the sea and finding its way into his cabin.

CHAPTER 5

A zerick drew a talon across the palm of his hand and made a ring around him with the black blood. His blood linked him to his citadel, and opening a portal back to it was a simple matter. The landscape blurred in his vision for an instant before resolving into his throne room.

The once-human demon lord looked around the chamber, wary of attack, but none came. It appeared as though the horde had not yet penetrated the interior. He teleported to the top of a tower and studied the chaotic scene below. Demons still laid siege to his citadel; their numbers even greater than before.

The mass of flying demons were so thick they almost blotted out the sky. Winged creatures hurled fire and even their own bodies at the parapets only for the bastion's formidable wards to rebuff them, often with significant violence. Ambulating monsters covered half the height of the walls as they climbed over each other in an attempt to breach the top.

Azerick thrust his staff into the black stones atop the tower. Bloody spears erupted from the lower walls and impaled hundreds of invaders. A burst of energy sent thousands more flying, their charred bodies trailing streamers of smoke. Confident that the citadel's defenses were strong enough hold a while longer, Azerick returned to his throne room.

He strode to the portal to Sharrellan's abode with great urgency. His defenses would not hold forever, and he knew he was unable to defeat the combined fury of all five abyssal circles. He had to rescue the goddess. Only she could save him from a slow, torturous death preceding oblivion.

Destruction surrounded him once again. Nothing had changed during his short excursion. Azerick peered into the rubble with more than his eyes and reconstructed in his mind what had happened. The five demon lords had a portal leading from their realms to that of their goddess. Powerful energy, far greater than Azerick was capable of producing even by using the power of his citadel and staff, had torn through the other four gateways and ripped a hole through the veil between planes.

It was this confluence of power that had destroyed Sharrellan's home and stolen her away. Azerick knew it was possible to imprison a god, but how the demons had managed it he could not fathom. But he meant to find out.

Azerick found the weakness at the point of confluence where the demon's had torn through the veil. He stabbed his staff into the ground and sundered the veil, tearing open the weakened fabric of reality and threw himself into the void.

Azerick materialized more than fell into the demiplane. He stood upon grey sand in an otherwise featureless plane and took in everything at a glance. Demons encased in womb-like cocoons dotted the landscape out to the horizon.

Hundreds of thousands, if not millions, of seemingly lifeless lesser beings surrounded a small plain. Umbilical cords crawled across the ground from the cocoons and connected to the bottom of a transparent sphere the size of a tiny room. Inside the transparent prison stood Sharrellan, a cold, petulant look on her pristine face.

Her red lips curled up into a smile at the sight of her paramour, but it vanished just as quickly. The assault came without warning. Black rays of abyssal power slammed into Azerick within seconds of his arrival.

His instincts allowed him to raise a hasty ward, but enough of the combined attack got through to send him tumbling across the ground. He ignored the pain shooting through every inch of his demonic body, rolled to his feet, and slashed his staff in a semi-circle.

Power scythed through the air and struck three of the four demon lords, but they were better prepared than he had been. Their wards flared, and they took a step or two backward, but Azerick's swift reprisal was far from a telling blow.

The demon Azerick had missed in his counterattack lunged forward with black energy shooting from his hand. Inael, the devilish master of the fourth circle, wielded a black saber alongside his powerful magic.

Azerick shielded himself from the magical attack and blocked the sword with his staff. He lifted a powerful leg and kicked Inael in the chest. He sent a black and silver ray lancing from his staff and struck the demon on the downward apex of his flight. Inael collided with an invisible barrier fifty yards away.

Azerick embraced his demonic rage, spun on the other three lords with a bestial snarl, and met their charge head on. Magic crashed into wards with deafening cracks like lightning. He raised a field of crystal spears from the ground between him and his foes. Amoodan, the lord of the first circle, collided with the diamond-hard shards. Those that did not shatter under his bulk stabbed into his ghastly, dire-bear-like body. He roared in pain and outrage, but Azerick knew his wounds were far from mortal.

Zanehis, a thirty-foot long serpent demon with four arms, swept his enormous halberd with its six-foot blade out before him and hewed a path through the spires. Tapuriel's form was similar to Azerick's but female. She spread her large wings, vaulted over the spikes, and landed in a cloud of dust as she swept her three-headed flail before her.

Azerick leapt back to avoid the strike, but the weapon's chains stretched out like vipers, their attached spiked orbs glowing red with malevolent intent. The three heads struck him in the chest with explosive effect and blasted him backward several times his own substantial height.

Zanehis had hacked his way through the crystal spikes and was on Azerick before he was able recover. The serpent demon's halberd came down, aiming to cleave Azerick's head and chest in twain. Azerick raised a pillar of stone beneath Zanehis' feet and catapulted him straight up into the air. His staff humming with power, Azerick clubbed Zanehis just before he struck the ground, sending him crashing onto the crystal spires.

Inael had pulled himself off the spikes and struck Azerick with an eldritch blast. His ward flared as the impact drove him back. Tapuriel's flail lashed out and clouted him another blow. His ward failed under the twin assault, and he found himself on his back once again.

Azerick opened a portal beneath his prone form and gated to the far side of Sharrellan's prison. He knew he could not defeat all four demon lords, at least not on a battlefield of their choosing. He unleashed his abyssal and arcane power through his staff and struck the goddess' cage with all his might. The sphere's walls flared in response and keened like a banshee's wail, but they did not yield to his assault.

Two more black beams impacted his torso. Their combined attacks tore through his newly erected ward and sundered his ebony flesh. Azerick struck the invisible barrier between him and the cocooned demons beyond and left a bloody smear like a swatted fly on a window.

Conceding defeat, Azerick channeled power into the blood pooling around his body and returned to his citadel. He lay on the cold stone floor a moment, using the bastion's stored energy to heal his gruesome wounds.

Unwilling and unable to spare more time to his personal misery, Azerick crawled to his feet and flopped onto his throne. He needed help, but there was no one in the abyss who was going to offer it, and he had no time to search for them if there was. His citadel's power was waning, and it would not be much longer before the invaders breached its walls.

Azerick's claws gouged the skulls adorning his throne as he thought. If he was unable to find help within the abyss, perhaps he could get it from without. He cut his hand, filled the upturned skull at the end of his throne's armrest with blood, and channeled magic into the inky liquid as he focused on those with whom he sought to commune.

"Solarian. Ellanee."

It was a terrible breach of protocol, but Azerick was an exception. He had been instrumental in saving the gods' lives and defeating the Scions. All but Serron, god of the sea, who had perished in the battle.

Azerick opened his eyes and found himself in a verdant clearing. Two radiant beings sat upon marble seats adorned with clinging ivy next to a pond with water so clear it was impossible to accurately gauge its depth.

"Hello, Azerick," Ellanee said. "It has been a long time, as mortals would consider it."

He knew he was not physically here. A denizen of the abyss was not allowed leave the hellish plane much less enter the celestial realm of the gods of light and nature. He was only a projection, but the sight, feel, and smell of nature surrounding him felt real, and it filled him with longing for the life he once had.

Azerick shook off his nostalgia. "I've come—"

Solarian raised a hand. "We know why you are here, and the answer is no."

"No? How can you just say no? Sharrellan is trapped, and her realm is in chaos!"

Ellanee replied, "The abyss is a place of chaos. It is that way by her design. Our realms are sacrosanct, and we may no more interfere in hers than we would allow her to do to ours."

"She is a prisoner, cut off from her power."

"But in no real danger of harm," Solarian said. "The demons' desire is quite clear. Sharrellan created this problem and eventuality when she enlisted you as her hand and awarded you the highest position under her."

Azerick's face flushed at the double meaning Solarian intended to convey with his words. "So I should just let the demons destroy me so that everything can return to normal?"

"You do not have to *let* anyone do anything," the god of light returned. "That is the nature of free will. You may do whatever you can to free Sharrellan. It is the same free will that bars us from interfering."

"But I cannot free her on my own. I need help!"

"We believe you are correct in that regard," Ellanee replied.

"I have no one else to turn to."

Ellanee smiled. "Don't you? Goodbye, Azerick. We wish you success."

Azerick found himself back on his throne and crushed the skull beneath his hand. Ellanee had hinted that there was someone who could aid him, but there was no one in the abyss who looked upon him favorably, and none were able enter it without the express consent of the goddess.

A smile crept onto Azerick's face. Except one.

CHAPTER 6

The soldiers led Ellyssa down the steps and into the bowels of the ship. The air was dank, stale, and smelled of sweat, grease, tar, and the odor of fetid water seeping through the deck from the bilge. As far as ships went, the vessel was immaculate, but no level of cleanliness and order could prevent those kinds of smells.

The brig was a series of iron cages bolted to the ship's frame. Up to half a dozen men crowded each of the cells, except for Daebian, who stood chained to the wall in a cage of his own. It appeared the soldiers were taking no chances with him.

One of the three Order soldiers guarding the prisoners opened Daebian's cell to admit Ellyssa. "Looks like you're getting a conjugal visit, warlock. Hope you enjoy an audience."

Daebian's chin rested against his chest, but he looked up and smiled at the man's words. "Do you know what time it is?"

"Why?"

"I like to chronical certain events in my life. It is likely that you people hold the record for the longest time remaining alive after having offended me. Enjoy what little remains of your lives."

"Big talk for a little man in a cage," the soldier returned.

"You're on a ship surrounded by miles of water. We're all in a cage, and when I get loose, there will be nowhere to run."

"We are the Order!" the man spat. "All fall before our righteous might, just as you and your witch did."

"I think I'll kill you first."

"You squawk like a chicken being taken to the headsman. I wonder if you'll flop around after he takes your head?"

Daebian said nothing more as Ellyssa's escort gave her a light push into the cell. Ellyssa rushed over to Daebian. Because of her shackles, she had to raise her arms over his head and drape them over his shoulders.

"Are you all right?" she asked in a hurried voice.

"Other than my bruised ego, I'm fine."

Ellyssa whispered into Daebian's ear. "We have to escape. I think they want to execute you for being a warlock."

"Yeah, I'm still not sure what that is, but that's the impression I got."

"I spoke to their wizard. He said he wanted to help, but I don't think he can. I can't touch the Source with these manacles on, so we must figure out another way to free you."

Daebian's mouth turned up into a grin. "I already have a plan to get us both out. I've just been waiting to see you before doing anything."

"What is it?"

"I still have Klaraxis' stone."

"What? How?" Ellyssa asked with a small gasp.

"I hid it where no one would find it."

Ellyssa pushed him away at arms' length. "You don't mean…? Oh, gods."

"Yeah. Clearly, I can't reach it with my hands chained to the wall, so…"

"Oh, gods!" she exclaimed again.

"Relax. I think I can get it out. I just need you to pick it up."

"You'll need to relax far more than I," Ellyssa said with a chortle.

Daebian scowled at her as he wiggled and hopped up and down to dislodge the soul stone. "Uh oh."

"What?"

"It's stuck."

"Maybe you need to push harder and relax more."

Daebian cocked his head and scowled. "No, I mean in my trousers."

Ellyssa tugged at his lacings. "I told you not to wear such tight trousers."

"Hey, if you had an ass like mine, you'd want to highlight it too."

"I have a fabulous posterior!"

"Sure, for a woman your age…"

"Are you seriously going on about that again?" Ellyssa snapped.

"Hey, what are you two doing in there?" a soldier demanded as he looked up from the card game he was playing with two others.

"We're comparing asses," Daebian replied as he tried to turn his back toward the men. "Your honest opinion, gender and sexual preferences aside, which of us has the better butt? Based on tone and shape."

The soldiers turned their attention back to the game with muted grumbles.

Daebian nodded toward his feet. "It's next to my foot. Pick it up and give it to me."

"I'll give it to you. Right back up your shapely ass," she muttered as she retrieved the stone.

Daebian snapped his head forward and gave Ellyssa a quick peck on the lips as she pressed the soul stone into his hand. "You know I think you're beautiful when you're angry."

"Get these shackles off me and you'll see the most gorgeous woman on the planet."

"I already do."

Ellyssa blushed. "Aw! Now show these fools what happens to people who threaten us. Try not to kill Doncho. He seems a decent man. The crew is unlikely to be a threat either. I can deal with them. It's only the soldiers we need to worry about."

"Anything for you, my love."

That was the most unpleasant experience of my life. And mind you, I've lived in the abyss for a thousand years, Klaraxis said in Daebian's mind.

I think you'll find it was worth it after the feast I'm about to give you.

Daebian wielded the demon's dark power, and the chains tethering him to the wall disintegrated like ash. He turned his attention to the two lanterns burning near the opposite ends of the brig and extinguished the flames within.

"What in the abyss?" a soldier cried out amidst a chorus of surprised shouts. "Get those lanterns lit!"

Sparks flew as one soldier struck flint and steel and lit a short length of rope permeated with oil.

"I told you I'd kill you first," Daebian whispered in the man's ear.

A shadow blade, not unlike the conjured weapon wielded by the ordinator only black, sprouted from his hand and plunged through the man's back without the slightest resistance. The soldier dropped the burning cord to the deck as his assassin dragged him from the feeble circle of light.

Daebian was a wraith within the darkness, moving with no more noise than a draft, his victims feeling nothing more than a chill run up their spine before joining the ranks of the dead. He picked up the burning cord and lit the lanterns. Light splayed over the gruesome scene of five corpses, the terror of their deaths etched forever on their faces.

He did not bother to find the keys to the cells, instead, he destroyed the locks as he had his chains. His men hastened from their cages and retrieved the fallen soldiers' weapons.

Ellyssa rushed over to Daebian and held her shackles up. "Can you get them off?"

Daebian took the chain in his free hand. "I'll try. These aren't exactly ordinary chains."

He closed his eyes and focused Klaraxis' abyssal power into the enchanted metal. The chains grew warm then hot beneath his touch. His eyes snapped open at the sound of Ellyssa stifling a cry of pain.

She shook her head. "Keep going!"

Daebian bent his considerable will to the task. The metal blackened and cracked beneath his hand. He could smell the odor of burning flesh, but still Ellyssa refused to vocalize the agony he was sure she must be suffering. The magic buttressing the shackles surrendered to Daebian's toxic power and crumbled.

Ellyssa let out a gasp and took several deep breaths. Daebian took her hands and gazed at the blistered flesh around her wrists.

"I'll be fine," she said. "I'm better than fine. I'm free. Doncho has my spell book. Your sword is probably in their leader's cabin."

Daebian shrugged. "The sword is little more than a trinket without the stone in it, but it was a nice one, and I want to get it back."

He looked to his men waiting for orders. "I'll go first. You men stay concealed until you hear an alarm. Don't waste your time with the sailors unless they are a problem. We have to eliminate these soldiers quickly. We've seen what they can do once organized. I plan to create as much chaos in the Order as I can, and we all know I'm good at that."

His men chuckled and shuffled toward the ladder leading to the sleeping berths above. Daebian did not bother climbing the steps. He had memorized the deck layouts and noted every shadow when brought to his cell. He stepped into a patch of darkness and emerged on the deck.

Daebian preferred the weight of solid steel in his hand as he set about his grisly work, wielding an Order soldier's dagger. With silent steps, he glided between sleeping men, an awakened nightmare extinguishing their lives as they dreamt. Daebian took no pleasure in the task. He never fancied himself an assassin, but these people had invaded his home, taken him and his men captive, and shackled the woman he loved more than anyone else in this world, binding not just her hands, but her spirit. The anguish on her face when the arcanus had stripped away her power was an icy stake through his heart, and they would pay for their abuse.

More than half of the dozen soldiers lay dead at Daebian's hand by the time the first of his crew slinked up the stairs. Hands clamped over the mouths of sleeping soldiers, and fists gripping knives and spears pumped with deadly efficiency.

Only a few soldiers woke to issue a muffled cry, but he stilled them before they could get sufficient air to create more than a coarse gasp. Daebian's sailors worked with the same silent ruthlessness as he did. This was their one chance at survival, and there was no room for conscience or mercy.

"Same plan," Daebian said when they extinguished the last Order life on the berth deck. "I'll go topside and take down as many soldiers as I can. Once someone sounds an alarm, I'll take out their captain or whatever he calls himself."

"Optio Flavius," Ellyssa supplied.

Daebian nodded. "That's the one. He probably has my sword, and I want it back. That's when you men charge onto the deck."

Daebian pictured what he saw of the upper deck in his mind and melded into the nearest shadow. He emerged behind several barrels filled with fresh water and surveyed his surroundings. Most of the men on deck were sailors working to keep the ship steady and on course. He did not expect them to pose much of a problem.

But there were half a score of legionnaires standing watch in small groups, their spears and breastplates gleaming in the moonlight. A door, a head shorter than an average man's height, led into a room beneath the forecastle. This was likely where the Order officer resided. The ship captain's cabin would be beneath the stern castle.

Daebian could not trust his shadow blade to deliver an instant death, so he relied on his pilfered dagger to do his dirty work. He lurked in the shadows, stalking his prey until one peeled away from the group. Sliding out of the nearest patch of darkness, Daebian wrapped a forearm around his target's neck and plunged his blade into the base of the soldier's skull. His shadow-limned blade froze the unfortunate man's voice in his throat as his killer dragged him to the deck.

He executed four soldiers before a small group found the first body and raised the alarm. Daebian's men burst forth from the berthing deck and charged into the nearest knot of soldiers, ignoring any sailor that got in their way unless they posed an obstacle.

Cries of alarm sounded across the deck, but the noise of battle drowned them out. The remaining Order soldiers tried to form ranks, but Daebian's crew fought to keep them separated. Unable to form a cohesive unit, the soldiers' shields failed to offer adequate protection from the assaults coming from all sides.

Daebian blinded a group of Order soldiers with conjured darkness but kept his attention fixed on the officer's doorway. The door flew open with a bang, and Optio Grigor Flavius stood within its aperture. Surveying the battle, he knew in an instant his men were losing.

Grigor's spear and shield hummed with eldritch energy. Daebian's eyes cut through the darkness and scanned the cabin's interior through the open door. His senses, combined with those of his enslaved demon lord, detected his sword's magical signature within.

Daebian traveled through the shadow ways and emerged within reach of his blade. He took up the weapon and set Klaraxis' stone within the prongs at the base of its hilt. The metal came alive and clutched the onyx jewel with its arcanum claws.

Grigor sensed Daebian's presence and spun around, interposing his shield between him and his attacker's charge. Daebian sprinted the three steps across the room and thrust his blade with all of his physical and dark, spiritual might. The blade punched through the shield and the officer's breastplate with a brilliant flash and the crack of thunder. The light in the officer's eyes died along with that of his shield and weapon.

Ellyssa almost collided with Doncho when he pulled open the door of his cabin to respond to the hue and cry on the deck. The old mage's eyes widened in surprise at the sight of the woman, enlarging even farther when she brought her hands up and he saw that she was no longer shackled.

A giant, invisible fist crashed into his body and sent him hurling headlong into the far wall. Timbers creaked in protest under the impact. Doncho fought to fill his lungs and crawl to his feet, but another force hefted him into the air and pinned him against the bulkhead.

"Your ship, and lives, are ours," Ellyssa said between clenched teeth.

"H-how did you break free?" Doncho asked, his words weak as he struggled to pull in enough air to speak.

"I told you; someone chained me before. I warned you it would not turn out well for you, just as it had not for them."

The old man's eyes narrowed in defiance. "What will you do with me now?"

"You will tell the rest of the crew to stand down."

"And then?"

"Then we will set you adrift in longboats." Ellyssa stepped forward and locked eyes with the magus, their noses just inches apart. "We do not enslave our enemies. We're better than that."

Doncho wilted under her glare and shook his head. "You do not understand."

"I understand plenty. What you and your people need to understand is that we will not surrender ourselves into the bonds of servitude. Tell your emperor and empress that. If you come for us, we will destroy you."

The wizard smiled, his courage returning. "They will come for you, and you cannot stop them. You do not understand what you face."

Ellyssa gestured with her hand, and Doncho fell to the deck. "They aren't here tonight. On your feet. If I sense you reaching for the Source, I will crush every bone in your body and throw you to the fish."

Doncho climbed to his feet, straightened his robe, and walked out of the room with as much dignity as he could muster. When he and his captor arrived on the main deck, the fighting was almost over. A few soldiers and the bulk of the crew crowded the sterncastle and fought to hold off Daebian's men on the stairs. The battle had broken into little more than insults and taunts.

Daebian appeared at Ellyssa's side. "Nice of you to join us. Ready to put an end to this?"

Ellyssa nodded. "I am. What about you, Arcanus? Will you order these men to surrender, or shall we see it to its bitter end?"

"I, and the Order, have no desire for unnecessary bloodshed," Doncho snapped. "I will order them to surrender as long as I have your word that no harm will come to them."

"You have it."

Doncho shuffled to the base of the sterncastle and took a deep breath. "Ground your weapons, men! The night is lost, but we shall live to fight another day."

The Order soldiers and crew looked to one another with muttered curses before dropping their weapons to the deck. Daebian's men charged up the stairs and prodded them down the steps to the main deck.

"How are our casualties?" Ellyssa asked.

"We lost a few men, and several more are unfit for duty for at least a few days, but we have enough to crew the ship," Daebian replied.

"Good. Let us see these men to the longboats and turn us about."

"It would be best to toss them overboard, or at least the mage. It might give us a head start on anyone who might pursue us."

Ellyssa shook her head. "No, Daebian. Even had I not given my word. That is not what we are. This Order of theirs justifies their actions through their sense of moral superiority, and I won't prove them right."

Daebian grinned and flashed her a wink. "It's a good thing you're a wonderful wife, because you make a terrible pirate." He turned to his men and shouted. "Drop the longboats and swab my deck clean of these Order pricks!"

His crew replied with a loud huzzah and lowered the boats into the water.

Ellyssa called to Doncho once he was in the small watercraft. "Remember my words, Arcanus, and relay it to your empress."

The old wizard looked up, his face bearing a look of calm resolve. "And you remember mine, magess."

Ellyssa looked to Daebian. "Let's go home."

CHAPTER 7

A cacophonic boom heralded the citadel's breached defenses. The howls and cries of demons echoed down the vast labyrinth of corridors as they fought each other for the glory of being the first to spill Azerick's blood.

Furious cries grew louder as the demon horde approached the throne room. The floor and walls shook under their combined steps and vocal reverberations. The colossal doors blew apart in a spray of fire, wood, and metal. Demons swarmed into the enormous hall only to smash into an invisible barrier just before the throne upon which Azerick sat.

"You have forgotten who is the master of this realm," Azerick's voice boomed over the demons' furious wailing. "It is time I remind you."

The demon prince cut his palm with a razor-sharp talon, crossed to the back of the chamber, and slapped a bloody handprint onto the wall before disappearing through a portal. Eldritch light limned the citadel's every brick like luminous mortar. A keening arose so loud that it drowned out the demons' cries. Their instinct for survival washed away their fury as they tried to claw their way out of the great hall, but there was nowhere in which to flee.

Succubi and other demons capable of magic tried to gate out, but the black fortress refused to allow anyone to escape. The bastion exploded with such force that a shock wave shattered stone and killed every creature within several miles. A great tsunami of wind and dust traveled several times farther than that before dying away and leaving behind a titanic circle of death and destruction.

Azerick did not lament the annihilation of his abyssal home. He knew there was no coming back, regardless of his plan's outcome. He hesitated just a moment before tearing open the veil between planes once again and throwing himself into battle.

The demon lord exploded onto the demi-plane containing Sharrellan's prison. Azerick struck like a meteor, sending a blast of fire and stone in every direction. He leveled his staff and lashed out with arcane and demonic power, destroying scores of the cocooned demons whose life force kept the goddess imprisoned.

But his efforts was like swatting at a swarm of mosquitos. For every one he squashed, there were thousands to take its place, and these pests had mighty defenders. Tapuriel struck Azerick with a powerful black ray as she beat her wings and lifted into the air. The impact struck him a glancing blow but still landed with enough force to spin him around and send him stumbling to the ground.

The monstrous, bear-like Amoodan sank his claws into the ground and hurled himself at the usurper demon lord. Azerick struggled to his feet just in time to meet the creature's charge. Both demon princes went tumbling in a flurry of claws and snapping teeth. Azerick got his feet beneath Amoodan's great bulk and heaved him skyward with the help of a blast of magic.

Azerick had no time to wallow in pain and forced himself to his feet. He raised a powerful ward just in time to deflect a magically hurled spear of stone cast by the devilish Inael. Zanehis slithered forward with the speed of a galloping horse, his enormous halberd a blur in his hands.

The master of the fifth circle raised a wall of rock fifty feet high and ten feet thick between himself and the charging serpent. Zanehis struck the barrier hard enough to shake it. With a magical push from Azerick, the wall exploded outward, blasting him a hundred yards back and pelting Inael with a hailstorm of rock.

Azerick deflected another lancing bolt from Tapuriel's hands and conjured a powerful maelstrom. The demon fought to control her flight, but winds battered and whipped her about like a kite in a hurricane, forcing her back to the ground.

Amoodan bore down on Azerick once again before he could take advantage of Tapuriel's disorientation. Azerick leveled his staff and prepared to unleash its fury upon the charging demon, but Amoodan opened his fang-filled maw and roared so loud Azerick thought his bones would shatter. Scarabs erupted from the demon bear's mouth in a swarm so thick Azerick could see nothing but a black, biting cloud.

The Scarabs rode the sonic wave through Azerick's ward and chewed on his flesh, their sharp mandibles ripping out thumb-sized pieces of tissue with every bite. Azerick immolated himself in fire so hot it melted the stone beneath his feet and turned the swarm into ash.

He conjured whirling blades of energy that expanded in an enormous cyclone with him standing in its eye. The vortex expanded around him, and the luminous knives of pure energy clashed and sparked off the demons' wards. Azerick fought desperately as his foes unraveled his conjuration. His spinning blades burst into moats of light and died like embers carried on the wind.

Azerick grabbed at more power to unleash against his enemies, but they were not going to allow him to continue his offensive. Inael and Tapuriel let loose a barrage of demonic power, driving Azerick back and forcing him to focus every ounce of his will into defending against them.

Zanehis rushed forward and tried to cleave Azerick in half with his enormous halberd, but Azerick deflected the blow with his staff. Before he could counter, the serpent demon's tail whipped around and caught him in the chest, sending him sprawling.

Azerick struggled to his knees when Amoodan crashed into him at full speed. The bearish monstrosity wrapped Azerick up in his powerful arms, his claws sinking deep into his flesh as they both rolled across the ground in a deadly embrace. Amoodan's massive maw opened wide, unleashing a pall of fetid breath. He got his arm up before the demon sank his fangs into his throat.

Azerick cried out as his tough flesh yielded to Amoodan's bite. He could feel and hear the fangs grinding against bone. The other three demons hurried forth and loomed over the two combatants locked together on the ground.

"Did you think you could defeat us, arrogant imposter?" Zanehis jeered as he raised his halberd like a headsman's axe.

Blood trickled out of the corner of Azerick's mouth as he looked up and grinned. "No. I'm just the distraction."

The four demon lords snapped their heads toward Sharrellan's prison and cried out at the sight of Azerick's son, Raijaun, standing just a short distance from the goddess. Raijaun raised his hands and unleashed a torrent of demonic, arcane, and guardian magic at the shimmering sphere.

A sharp keening filled the air and raised to a deafening level as the orb's walls reverberated under his assault. Raijaun's agonized cry was lost in the sound of the prison's imminent destruction as the three conflicting forms of magic sought to tear him apart.

The demon lords raced toward Raijaun, but the sphere shattered before they could cross half the distance to their target. Time stopped for everyone within the eye of Sharrellan's furious storm. Outside its now peaceful center, white fire burst outward toward the horizon and beyond, immolating the cocoons and the lesser demons trapped within.

Azerick and Raijaun was able to move again as Sharrellan descended invisible steps and sashayed toward her frozen captors. The goddess bore a wide smile that contained not a hint of kindness or even amusement. It was the grin of a predator just before it devoured its prey.

"It appears I have been far too beneficent to you lot," Sharrellan said as she glided between her chosen, occasionally reaching out to stroke one with a delicate finger.

Unable to move, the demon lords' terrified eyes tracked their goddess and rolled back in their sockets in silent agony every time she touched them.

"I think a few centuries of starvation and deprivation will help cull your numbers," she continued. "I will allow no more souls into the abyss for your consumption for, oh, I don't know, 300 years. How does that sound? Perhaps the few who please me will earn my boon once more and be properly grateful and respectful from here on out."

Sharrellan sauntered over to where Raijaun kneeled and fought to catch his breath after the toll using his magic had taken on him.

"My dear Raijaun, my beloved's greatest creation. How can I repay you for coming to my aid once again?"

Raijaun stayed kneeling and ducked his head. "Goddess, I came at my father's behest. I only beg that you grant him his wish."

Sharrellan spun around and stalked toward Azerick, who was just now climbing to his feet. "No! I cannot do that."

"Can't or won't?" Azerick asked, his voice tight and defiant.

"Take your pick. I am a god, and one is the same as the other."

"They are not the same. You brought this upon yourself. You placed me above the others despite knowing full well how they would react. My existence will only continue the discord. It is only a matter of time before something like this happens again. They will eventually kill me even if they have to destroy you to do it. They will find a way if it takes a thousand years."

A fierce scowl crossed the goddess' face. "It will be far longer than that before they forget the lesson I will teach them for crossing me."

Azerick shook his head. "They will not care. The abyss is suffrage. Pain and fear is the norm, and they will pay any price to see me destroyed."

"I cannot do it."

"You are a god. You can do as you please."

Sharrellan ground her teeth together, her fury hanging over them like a dark cloud. "You will give up your immortality, your power."

"I have never cared about power for power's sake. I only sought it to protect myself and the people I care for. It is time to send me back."

Sharrellan sighed and her delicate shoulders slumped. "What you ask is beyond my power. I will have to petition the others, and I cannot guarantee their compliance. There are rules that govern even the gods, and you are asking us to break them."

Azerick grinned. "What are rules for if not to break them?"

Sharrellan's lip curled up in a smirk. "You really do belong here with me, you know that?"

"You're probably right."

"Of course I'm right. I'm a god." She turned to Raijaun. "On your feet. We'll need your help, handsome."

Before Azerick or his son could respond, they found themselves back in the same beautiful clearing where Azerick had petitioned the gods of light and nature and been denied.

Solarian looked up from the tome he was reading next to the pond. "Sharrellan, you are back. That did not take long."

"No thanks to you lot," the goddess snapped.

"I like to think we played a part," Ellanee said.

"A small part. You would have been just as pleased if I stayed in that damnable prison for a thousand years."

Solarian shrugged his wide shoulders. "We all need a break from time to time."

"We also must recognize and reward our most faithful followers when they deserve it. It is time—"

"No," Solarian said with finality before Sharrellan could even finish making her request.

"No?" Sharrellan practically shrieked. "You listen to me, you glowing pompous prick!"

"Charming as ever," Ellanee drawled.

Sharrellan stalked toward the goddess of nature until she was nose to nose with her. "Do you remember the last time you refused me? That century of death and darkness will seem charming compared to what I will do if you open your gob to shut me down without so much as considering my petition."

"It is forbidden," Solarian said. "The All Mother—"

"The All Mother can kiss my perfect ass!"

Their celestial kingdom rumbled beneath their feet.

"One should not forget whence one came," Ellanee quipped.

Sharrellan snapped her gaze back to the goddess. "One should also recognize the sacrifices made in their name and do what is right and just."

"When have you ever given a damn about what is right and just?" Solarian asked.

Sharrellan turned toward the god of light with a smile on her lips. "When have you not?"

Solarian sighed. "Azerick, do you know what this means for you? We cannot simply return you to the mortal world. We will have to remake you in your mortal form where you will suffer the pain and frailties of any other man."

Azerick nodded. "I understand and accept that."

"Very well. Lie on the ground next to the pool."

Azerick did as they ordered. The three gods and Raijaun hovered over him as he gazed into the brilliant blue sky. Solarian took out a golden dagger and drew it across his palm. Silver blood trickled from the cut and dribbled onto Azerick's chest.

"I bestow unto you my blood so you may be reborn of light, honor, and goodness," Solarian intoned.

Ellanee took the blade and cut herself. "I bestow upon you my blood so you me be reborn a mortal man, a creature of nature and purity."

Words filled Raijaun's head the moment he grasped the knife. "I bestow upon you my blood to bridge the gap between this world and your own."

Sharrellan took the knife from Raijaun and touched its edge to her delicate flesh. "I bestow my blood upon you so you will know free will and not be a boring, stuffy sot."

"Sharrellan," Solarian rumbled.

"Oh, shut up. You know the words are bullshit."

"By the light, nature, and darkness, you are reborn," the gods chanted in unison.

The ground beneath Azerick churned, and he sank into it as if it were water. The feeling of drowning washed over him, and earth filled his mouth as he screamed.

CHAPTER 8

Doncho hovered over A bowl of water with the glittering sand of powdered quartz covering the bottom of the basin. The quartz sand glimmered as the arcanus dribbled magic into the small scrying pool. The wizened face of Primus Arcanus Pavel Veselin projected off the sand and filled the bowl's surface.

"What is it, Arcanus?" Pavel asked, his clipped words reminding the summoner that his time was important.

"Primus Arcanus, I am Doncho Filipov of the 5th Legion, 2nd Expeditionary Prima Cohort. Several days ago, Primus Lycus Ploutarch dispatched the 6th Centuria, formerly under the command of Ordinator Bojan Archelaus, to investigate a small island some fifteen-hundred leagues off Murwell's eastern shore."

The Primus Arcanus scratched the white beard covering his chin. "That is well beyond our farthest eastern front."

Doncho nodded. "Yes, Primus Arcanus. With Murwell almost pacified, Primus Ploutarch petitioned the emperor to allow him to take his legion farther east. He was certain another continent lay in that direction."

"And was he correct?"

"I believe so. We encountered a community on the island we were surveying. A man not native to the region governed the island. This governor also had a ship's compliment of non-native peoples under his command. When he refused to yield to the Order, my centuria set about pacifying the population."

"I assume you were successful," Pavel asked.

Doncho took a deep breath as he contemplated his next words. "Partly. The governor was a…unique individual with power similar to that of a warlock."

Pavel's face darkened as his mouth turned down into a scowl. "A warlock so far east? This does not bode well."

"I do not believe he was a warlock as we understand them. He was certainly not Castracene. He managed to slay Ordinator Archelaus in single combat."

A woman's aged but flawless face replaced that of the Primus Arcanus. "Tell me of this man and what has become of him."

Years of servitude caused Doncho to drop to his knees. His sudden, wild movement caused him to strike the table with his shoulder. Water sloshed from the scrying bowl onto the table.

"Empress! I was not aware you were with us," Doncho exclaimed as he fought to control his thudding heart.

"I am always where I am needed. Tell me of these people you encountered. Were you able to capture them alive? And off your knees, Arcanus. I prefer to see with whom I am speaking."

Doncho climbed back into the chair next to the table. "We did, Empress. The man was an exceptional fighter, and his wife a formidable wizard. We were of course able to pacify the island and took our quota of their men for conscription. Unfortunately, they managed to escape and captured the vessel tasked with returning them to Syrna for questioning and reeducation. They killed most of the soldiers aboard and set me and the rest of the crew adrift in longboats. It was fortunate that I was able to contact an arcanus in the cohort and our main force retrieved us."

The empress looked pensive a moment before responding. "An interesting if troubling account. Instruct Primus Ploutarch to follow the vessel and discover the whereabouts of these people's mainland. We are in need of new forces, and this may prove an excellent opportunity to acquire them."

"Yes, Empress." Doncho hesitated before speaking his next words. "Empress, the wizard I mentioned. She claimed her master fought alongside the gods to defeat more ancient gods that had been imprisoned millennia ago. The monstrosities we battled then and continue to fight today are but their minions, and that the true war occurred in their land."

Empress Noela Attar's image scowled at the arcanus, making him wilt under her steely gaze. "A fanciful tale and nothing more. The gods abandoned us, and We are their successors."

"Of course, Empress. But…she claims they defeated these old gods. If anything in her story is true, then we could face a formidable enemy."

"I understand your meaning, Arcanus. You are part of an expeditionary force. Discover the location of this new continent and perform reconnaissance. I will order three legions to follow you."

Doncho rocked back in his chair. "Three legions? That is a significant force, Empress."

"As you said, these people could be formidable, and that makes them valuable."

"Yes, Empress."

"And Arcanus," Empress Noela said before breaking the magical connection. "You will not speak a word of any gods, old or ancient, to anyone."

Doncho bobbed his head. "Yes, Empress."

The empress vanished, and Doncho stared at his own reflection within the glittering bowl of water. He took several deep breaths to steady his nerves before searching out Primus Ploutarch.

He found the cohort commander on the main deck standing next to the ship's captain.

"Primus, I communed with the Primus Arcanus and received orders from the Empress."

Primus Ploutarch's thick, dark eyebrows lifted. "The Empress? What is her command?"

"She desires that we follow the escapees to discover their homeland. Once we locate their home, we are to scout the area, gather information, and await the three full legions she has dispatched to pacify the population."

The primus' face clouded with suppressed anger. He had been Primus of an expeditionary prima cohort for more than seven years and ached for promotion and command of his own legion. He had set out on this expeditionary mission to bring glory to his name, and now that he was on the brink of success, the empress' orders would see his work and sacrifice given to another. Likely to Imperator Aquila Martinus. The two had attended the officer academy together, but Aquila came from a better family and thus promoted ahead of him. A fact for which the Imperator enjoyed reminding him every chance he got.

"Arcanus, have your brethren conjure a wind to speed our pursuit. We will intercept the vessel and learn the whereabouts of their continent firsthand through interrogation."

"Primus, the Empress' orders were to follow them and conduct reconnaissance only," Doncho reminded the primus.

Lycus turned his glower onto the arcanus. "The Empress ordered us to discover the location of this new land. These people were well-established on that island but were not native. They probably left their homeland long ago, and we cannot be certain they are returning to it. They may well lead us on a chase across the face of the world until they sail off its edge."

"The world is a sphere, Primus," Doncho hesitantly corrected his leader.

"Carry out your orders," Lycus commanded in a tense voice that left no room for argument.

"Yes, Primus."

Daebian stuck his head through the doorway to the captain's berth. "Learn anything about their weapons?"

Ellyssa set the magnifying glass on the table and turned around in her chair. "Not much. They are rune-empowered, but I don't recognize the language or sigils, nor how to activate them. Doncho said the Syrnese were sorcerous, and I assume that they are able to use their inherent affinity with the Source to power them."

"Much as my father did with the mage novices and his constructs."

Ellyssa nodded. "Very much so. I tried to channel power into them myself but nothing happened. I believe they might be tied to the wielder, but I cannot determine how. How are things topside?"

"Smooth sailing so far. No sign of pursuit."

Ellyssa chewed her lip and furrowed her brow. "That's odd. I could have sworn we were being scryed."

A shout rang out from high in the rigging. "Sails aft!"

"It appears I spoke too soon," Daebian said with a shrug.

The pair strode out onto the deck and mounted the sterncastle. Shielding their eyes from the sun's glare with a hand, the two gazed out over the rolling waves and saw the Order's red sails poking above the horizon like bloody teeth.

"Can we outrun them?" Daebian asked.

Ellyssa watched the sails grow taller until she could make out the ships that flew them. "No. They're using magic to hasten their speed. I could do the same, but I'm by myself. They have more arcanus in their flotilla than just Doncho. They can maintain a wind far longer than I."

Daebian grimaced and gripped the hilt of his sword. "How do you suggest we face them? We don't have the element of surprise, and we're outnumbered. I'd rather not see a repeat of what happened on the island."

The wizardess leveled her baleful eyes onto the approaching ships. "They caught me unawares before. The Order only met Ellyssa Jansen the mage. It's time I acquaint them with the witch of North Haven."

A wind surrounded Ellyssa and whipped her clothes and hair about. She lifted off the deck and plummeted into the warm, tropical waters. A swell rose off the stern and raced toward the pursuing vessels, growing higher and higher as the gust became a hurricane-force gale.

Water spray flew off the roiling whitecaps and lifted into the sky to fall back down as torrential rain. Daebian's stolen ship sailed on, leaving the tempest wall behind them. The storm that was Ellyssa grew ever more powerful as she bore down upon the Order flotilla.

She looked upon them from the crest of her towering wave and saw soldiers band together and raise their shields. While their erected wards might help protect them from her wrath, it did little for the ships beneath their feet.

Her wall of water crashed against the lead vessel. Ellyssa felt a magical force slam into her like a shield trying to deflect her attack. Her aqueous body parted around the powerful wards before she slammed into the deck. While blunted, her assault still wreaked havoc on the masts and rigging and those unfortunate enough to be caught in the open.

Ellyssa's storm tore into the other ships. She was a force of nature with her fury focused on the Order troops and vessels. More defensive magic lashed out at her, but she was everywhere. Lightning cracked and sundered masts, and wind shredded sails like they were paper. When another force tried to push her away, she aimed her wave below a ship's hull instead of trying to bury it in a watery avalanche.

She disappeared beneath the vessel and rose up, causing the ship to list violently. It continued to roll across her back until reaching its tipping point. Her fury drowned out the cries of the men as their ship foundered and the sea claimed what was hers.

Ellyssa swam beneath another ship and lifted it high upon her swell. Magic pummeled her back and forced her to retreat. The vessel streaked down from her wave's summit and clipped another ship at its base. Wood crashed and sundered, and men cried out as they rolled across decks or over rails.

The arcanus found the core of her conjured being and began pulling her storm apart with invisible hands. Exhausted, Ellyssa gave up her assault and retreated. She rose from the sea on a column of water and lay on the deck near Daebian's feet.

Daebian dropped to his knees and cradled his wife in his arms. "Are you all right? What happened?"

Ellyssa looked up into his face and gave him a weak smile. "I'm fine. Just tired and bruised. I gave them a thrashing they won't soon forget. It should be at least a couple of days before they can resume their pursuit."

"What do we do now?"

"We have to go home. There's no other choice."

"And lead them to our shores?"

Ellyssa pressed her lips together and shook her head. "It's a large continent. They'll find it eventually. At least we can warn them what's coming."

Daebian sighed. "You're right. At least this time it's you and I coming to save Eidolan and not my father," he said with a grin.

CHAPTER 9

Azerick felt the cool air caress his hand's exposed flesh when it burst through the ground and into the light. He bolted upright and clawed the damp earth from his face and gasped in air. Air. Real air, chill and sweet carrying the scents of evergreen trees, flowers, and...something else.

The sorcerer found the strength to force open his eyelids and stared up into the greying muzzle of a large black wolf. Habit forced him to reach for his demonic power, but it was gone. He sought the Source and felt its familiar warmth trickle into his fingertips. Before Azerick could shape the magic into a spell, the wolf dragged its hot, moist tongue across his face.

"Ew, he kissed him!" a girl's voice cried out amongst a chorus of giggles around him.

Azerick grabbed at his jumbled thoughts and tried to put together the wispy pieces. "Ghost?"

A strong, chiseled face pressed next to that of Ghost's and beamed at him with a grin that tried to touch the pointed ears just poking through his thick, black hair. "Took you long enough to get back," Wolf quipped.

Azerick could not contain his smile and did not try to hold it back. "Sorry. I guess I got distracted. Can you help me stand? I'm having a hard time getting my muscles to work."

Wolf reached down and hefted Azerick to his feet with little effort. Dirt ran off Azerick's body like snow from a shaken branch. He summoned his staff and used it to bear his weight.

Azerick looked around at several children ranging from toddlers to preteen. "Who are these children, and why are they naked?"

Wolf crouched, turned around in a circle, and charged at the kids with a roar. "Because they're little savages!"

The kids shrieked and raced away. A few dropped to all fours, fur sprouting from their bodies so fast it looked as if they had crossed through a dark shadow and come out the other side a wolf.

Wolf turned back to Azerick with laughter in his eyes. "A better question is why are *you* naked? And how are you so young?"

Azerick looked down at himself and blushed. "That's a bit of a story."

"Don't worry about it. We're rather uninhibited around here, as you can see. Modesty's more of a human thing."

"Speaking of which, what's with the wolf kids?"

"That's also quite a story. Short version; they're lupin. So is Ghost, and his mother is Den Mother of their lupin pack."

Azerick shook his head and regretted it as the world began to spin. "What's a lupin?"

Wolf pointed in the direction in which the children had run. "Naked little savages that can turn into wolves."

Ghost stood on his hind legs and morphed into a man. "Technically, we're wolves that can turn into naked savages."

"Yeah. I'm having a hard time with my thoughts and body just now, so I'll try to process that later. I don't suppose anyone has a spare set of trousers?"

Ghost shrugged. "I'd give you a pair of mine, but I don't own any."

Wolf laughed and took Azerick by the arm. "I'm sure we can find something in the village."

The half-elf guided Azerick through the forest. Ghost returned to his natural form and loped ahead of them. Azerick saw they traveled on a narrow game trail barely distinguishable to his human eyes. He figured it probably looked like a cobblestone street to Wolf and his people.

He was concerned that with so little apparent traffic on the trail that the village might be some distance away. Azerick doubted he had the strength to walk very far. He was already winded and stumbling over every root, rock, and pinecone on the path. Which is why it came as a surprise when they pushed past some low-hanging boughs and stepped into the edge of the mostly treehouse village.

Other than a smith's workshop, a small stable, and a large gathering hall, the other structures were built high off the ground in the trees. Unlike proper elven homes, which they grew and shaped from the trees themselves, these were built much as any structure in a human town.

Catwalks connected the homes, and counterweighted lifts and ramps provided access to them from the ground. The adults he saw were at least clothed, which made him feel a little more comfortable but also keenly aware of his own nudity. His lack of attire did not seem to faze anyone. Their querying looks at his arrival held no more interest to them than the appearance of any stranger, clothed or not.

"This is quite a place," Azerick said as he gazed up into the treetops.

"It is! While I enjoyed my wild, solitary life, this has really turned into a blessing."

"How did this come about?"

"The war displaced a lot of people, and not just humans. Ghost's pack came to help us fight off the ravagers and other spawn and stayed afterward. Word started going around, mostly from Luna's people, and other lupin and half-elves looking for a home and community began showing up. It wasn't long after the war we built this."

Azerick tried to take a rough count of the people he saw, minus the lupins. "How many people live here?"

"About a dozen half-elf families plus Luna's pack."

Azerick was thankful when Wolf guided him onto a lift instead of the ramps encircling the enormous trees.

The lift bumped against the landing in front of the treehouse door, and Wolf guided him inside. Several children, at least half a dozen in number, stood in the large living room, peered out from behind the few pieces of furniture adorning the chamber, or around doorways.

"Go get dressed, you wildlings!" Wolf snapped in a playful tone. "Lynx, we have a guest in desperate need of clothing."

Children scurried about and disappeared with a chorus of giggles. A half-elf woman with long, soft brown hair and large, green eyes walked into the room with a stack of folded clothes and passed them to Azerick.

"This is my mate Lynx," Wolf said. "Lynx, this is Azerick."

The woman's eyes lit up and she gasped. "The Azerick you've told me about?" She wrapped the human in a tight hug. "I'm so happy you made it back! Wolf said you would someday."

Azerick's entire body burned from within as a deep blush reddened his face and presumably much of the rest of him. "Uh, yeah…If I could just put these on…"

Lynx released him and backed away. "Of course! So sorry. We're a little more informal than humans are accustomed to."

"No problem," Azerick replied as he tugged on a pair of trousers and pulled a shirt over his head. "Considering where I've been all these years, nothing should surprise me, but this recent ordeal has me shaken."

Wolf gestured to a chair. "Sit and tell us what happened."

Azerick sat, grateful to get off his feet.

"Azerick, would you like something to eat?" Lynx asked.

He had not given food much thought in decades, but his stomach rumbled so hard at the mention he was certain the chair vibrated beneath him.

Lynx laughed. "I'll take that as a yes. Wolf can tell me everything later."

Azerick looked over his shoulder until Lynx disappeared into what he assumed was the kitchen. "She calls you Wolf too?"

"Oh yeah. Few half-elves use their given names. I barely remember what mine is. Hers is Lana-something hard to pronounce. We both prefer Lynx."

"It's a great name. Were all those kids yours?"

Wolf's typical grin spread across his face. "Them and then some! When you're free from the trappings of so-called civilization you have a lot of free time. And when you have a mate as beautiful as mine, well…"

Azerick shared his friend's smile. "She seems wonderful. I'm happy for you."

"I'm happy you're back. So what happened?"

Azerick let out a long sigh and sank into the chair. "The demons never accepted me. Hated my favored position with Sharrellan. In an unheard-of act of solidarity, they trapped the goddess and came after me en masse."

"So, you escaped or what?"

"No. I managed to free her and demanded that she send me back. It took the gods and Raijaun to do it, but here I am."

Wolf's thin eyebrows rose. "You saw Raijaun?"

"I did. I couldn't have freed Sharrellan without him."

Wolf ran his eyes up and down Azerick's form. "What's with the fresh look? You look like the day we first met."

"I'm not sure. I think they remade my body. Maybe they thought reconstructing me in my prime was a favor or something. I don't know. Gods aren't real forthcoming with answers."

Wolf pursed his lips. "So you're not really you? They just stuffed you into a new body like a pig in a blanket?"

"Pretty much," Azerick replied with a chuckle. "I'm an old sausage in fresh bread."

His stomach growled again at the mention of food.

"Lynx, hurry up before Azerick's stomach eats him from the inside!" Wolf called out.

Lynx bustled into the room a moment later bearing a tray of reheated stew and a small loaf of bread. "You poor thing. When's the last time you ate?" she asked as she set the tray on his lap.

"I suppose this is technically the first thing I've eaten in my entire life," he replied before dunking the end of the bread into the stew and stuffing it into his mouth.

Wolf did not interrupt Azerick with chatter while he ate. In a rare show of patience, he let him finish his meal without speaking. Satiated, Azerick leaned back and closed his eyes. Wolf thought he had fallen asleep until he spoke.

"How far are we from the school?"

Wolf shifted in his seat. "Not far. Maybe ten miles. Azerick, you should know…A lot has changed since you left. Those gods and their creatures, they destroyed the new tower and most of the buildings. Miranda has done a great job of rebuilding the school, but it's not the same."

Azerick took a deep breath and let it out. "Then she's still here."

"Yeah but…people move on. She waited a long time, but…"

"It's all right. I told her not to wait for me. I wanted her to find happiness. Did she?"

Wolf shrugged. "It's been difficult. It was hard on her, but I think she's happy."

Azerick nodded. "Good. That's all I ever wanted. I should go see her tomorrow."

"Sure. That's a great idea. She'd love to see you—to know you made it out."

"If you don't mind, I'm going to take a little nap."

Wolf stood and laid a hand on Azerick's arm. "Come sleep in my bed."

"No, I'm fine here. I don't want to put you out."

"Are you kidding? I've never gotten used to the thing. I'm more comfortable on the ground sleeping next to Ghost. You know that. And now I get to sleep next Lynx. She's not quite as warm, but she smells a lot better."

Lynx shouted from the other room, "You better hope he's available, or it's going to be a damn cold night for you!"

Azerick grinned and let Wolf show him to the bedroom. "Looks like I got you in trouble."

"Are you kidding? Trouble is my middle name. Don't go taking credit for my accomplishments. I'll wake you in the morning."

Azerick nodded drunkenly and flopped onto the bed. "Thanks, Wolf. Not too early though, huh?"

"Sure, buddy."

"Did he die?"

"He looks dead."

"Poke him."

"I'm not going to poke him, you poke him!"

"Give me a stick. I'll poke him."

The babble of children's voices intruded into Azerick's dreamless sleep. He forced his eyes open and turned toward the nearest voice. Talking turned to screeches and giggles accompanied by the pounding of bare feet as Wolf's kids fled the room.

"I told *one* of you to go see if he was awake!" Lynx's face appeared around the edge of the doorframe. "Sorry. They are very much their father's children."

Azerick sat up and yawned. "That's fine. They bring back a lot of memories."

"Good ones?"

"Mostly. At least everyone is wearing clothes this time. How late is it?"

"A little before noon. How did you sleep?"

Azerick swung his legs over the bed, stood, and stretched. "Like a dead man, hence my critics. I feel better today. Stronger."

Lynx smiled. "I imagine living in the abyss for twenty years and being resurrected takes its toll on a body."

"It certainly does. Where's Wolf?"

"He's packing a few things in case you wanted to leave soon. You're welcome to stay as long as you want though," Lynx amended.

"No, he knows me too well. I need to get home."

"I have lunch prepared."

Azerick returned to the same chair he had sat in the previous day. Wolf arrived just as he was finishing his meal.

"Hey, you're up," he said as he set a laden pack near the door. "I hope my terrible children didn't disturb you." Wolf mock glared at the faces watching them through a bedroom doorway. "Lynx says I don't beat them enough."

High-pitched shrieks filled the air as his kids raced through the living room and out of the front door. Some sprinted down the ramp while others threw themselves off the platform and slid down the ropes used to raise and lower the lifts.

"I think they're great," Azerick said.

"Right? I never got beat a day in my life and look how well I turned out."

"As I recall, that's only because the cooks couldn't catch you."

Wolf blew off his comment with the wave of a hand. "Some people don't appreciate the importance of a proper lesson."

"The lesson being?"

"That the haves need to share with the have nots. Especially in pie-related matters. Besides, I was just a kid."

Lynx rolled her eyes. "You stole two pies from their kitchen last week. What kind of person hikes ten miles each way just to steal a pie?"

Wolf pursed his lips and refused to meet her gaze. "Pilfered pie has a special flavor that can't be duplicated. It has the spice of..."

"Larceny?" Lynx said.

Wolf jabbed a finger at his mate. "That's the one! Sweet yet tangy larceny. You can't put that in a bottle."

"I'd like to put you in a bottle," Lynx muttered as she took Azerick's empty plate to the kitchen.

Wolf stuck his tongue out at his wife before turning to his guest. "I figured you'd want to get home, so I packed a few things. Are you up for traveling?"

"I am. I feel stronger this morning."

"We have a few horses in the village. You can ride one of them so it doesn't take us an entire day to get there."

Azerick nodded, glad for the help. While he felt better than yesterday, a ten-mile hike through the mountains would have tested his limits.

"I'm ready to go when you are," Azerick said.

Wolf grabbed the pack he had set down. "Woman, we're leaving!"

Lynx rushed from the kitchen and hugged Azerick as if he were an old friend. "I hope you find the peace you deserve."

"If history is any indication..." Azerick replied, leaving his ambiguous response hanging in the air.

He followed Wolf down the winding ramp to the small stable he had seen on his way into the village. A young half-elf woman Azerick's apparent age handed him the reins of a saddled mare. Wolf secured his pack behind the saddle and helped Azerick mount.

"She's the only horse in the village that will take a saddle, as we ride bareback. She's also the least likely to do something crazy," Wolf said as Azerick settled himself.

"That's good to hear. I never was much of an equestrian."

Azerick looked around as Wolf guided them out of the village. Ghost appeared in wolf form and loped next to them.

"I'm sorry for not staying longer," Azerick said as the forest swallowed them. "I would have loved to have seen more of your village and people. The lupin sound fascinating."

Wolf flicked his eyes toward Ghost. "Yeah, the novelty wears off pretty quick. They're not much in the way of conversationalists."

Ghost growled in response and picked up his pace to leave the two bipeds behind. Wolf laughed as Ghost trotted away with the fur between his shoulders bristling.

"It's nice to see you two are still the same," Azerick remarked.

"Not a chance. Ghost is my best friend in the world. Always will be. No offense. You're a close second, but he's my brother."

"Has Sandy come around over the years?"

Wolf's smile vanished. "She stopped by about twelve years ago. Nothing before or after then. She didn't say much about where she was or what she was doing. I got the feeling she was with other dragons and might have taken a companion."

"Was she happy?"

Wolf shrugged. "More or less. You leaving took a toll on everyone, more so on her. At least as much as Ellyssa and Miranda."

"You know I didn't have a choice, right?"

"Yeah, I know. We all know. Still didn't make it any easier. But hey, we've coped in our own way."

Azerick stayed quiet most of the way while Wolf chattered on about everything that popped into his head. His anxiety increased the closer they got to his former home until it felt as if he had swallowed an active beehive when they emerged from the woods and looked upon the enclave located just a few miles from North Haven.

"The tower is gone, but it looks like they rebuilt the wall," Azerick said as he studied the unfamiliar buildings.

"Yeah. I saw the giant glass castle fly over and blast everything to pieces. The wall's important. We don't get a lot of spawn this far north and west, but they're out there. Ghost's people are good at dealing with them when they do show up. It's just part of our way of life now."

"Is it worse elsewhere?"

Wolf's head bobbed up and down. "Oh yeah. The interior of Valeria, especially closer to where you fought those old gods, is rife with the creatures. King Miles and Duke Thomas are constantly sending out patrols to destroy the infestations. Duchess Paulina of Argoth too. Because the war took such a toll on the population, particularly soldiers, they haven't been able to send much help to the smaller towns when there's trouble. That has made them less than popular outside their cities and immediate surroundings."

"What do the people who don't get help from their leaders do? Those ravagers and other creatures are terrifying."

"The ones who can afford it hire mercenaries. There's also been a resurgence of adventuring groups who enjoy the fame and thrill of killing monsters. The king and dukes pay a hefty bounty for killing spawn. For the others, they move or die," Wolf said with a shrug of his shoulders.

"Sounds terrible."

"As I said, it's our way of life now. We should walk the rest of the way in if you're up to it. The horse will find her way back on her own."

Azerick swung from the saddle and tested his legs. "Other than the usual saddle soreness, I'm fine."

"I imagine this is going to be a very personal reunion, so I'll leave you to it. Ghost and I will be out foraging if you need us."

Azerick reached out and clasped Wolf's forearm. "Thanks, Wolf. It's great seeing you again."

"It's good to have you back."

Azerick turned toward the small town, took a deep breath, and began walking. There was no cry of alarm as he approached the wall, but eyes tracked his every movement. He thought he recognized some of the faces staring back at him, but it was hard to tell. Twenty years did a lot to change a person, and most of whom that were here when he left had been children.

"You have business here, friend?" a young man guarding the open gate asked.

Azerick tried to place his face but failed. "I'm visiting friends—family."

"I don't recognize you. Have you been here before?"

"Yes. A long time ago."

"Then you know the Lady doesn't tolerate poor behavior. Behave yourself and be welcome."

Azerick ducked his head as he passed through the gates. "Thanks."

He headed for the manor built where his new tower had once stood. He recognized a school and temple, but neither were the same buildings he had left behind. Everything around had been rebuilt from the rubble of what had once been his home.

A beautiful, stately woman strode through the manor's front door. Grey streaked her flowing, auburn hair, but her brilliant green eyes and face hid more than a decade of her sixty years of life.

Miranda stood before the open door; her hands clenched into fists before her face as Azerick approached. "Is it really you?"

Azerick stopped a few paces away and smiled. "It's really me."

Miranda rushed Azerick with a sob and threw her arms around him. "You made it back!"

Azerick fought to choke back his tears. "Sorry it took so long."

Miranda ran her hands through his hair and across his smooth face. "You look just like you did when we first met, only cleaner."

"Yeah, I'm fresh from the mold. The clay probably isn't even all the way dry."

"Clay?"

"Metaphorical clay," Azerick replied with a grin.

"Then you're really you?"

"I'm really me. Really, really me."

"No demon?"

Azerick shook his head and beamed. "No demon."

Miranda sobbed anew as she squeezed Azerick so hard he thought she was trying to snap him in half. She regained her composure and gazed into his eyes. "A lot has changed while you've been gone."

Azerick looked around. "I can tell."

"I don't mean just the buildings."

Azerick's face grew somber as he looked over her shoulder at the man exiting the house. "I know."

Miranda looked back and released Azerick from her embrace. The man was sixty if he was a day, but he still carried himself with a strong, proud bearing. He was a few inches taller than Azerick was with broader shoulders even today. His once dark hair had surrendered to the gray with only a few holdouts still fighting the battle. A groomed, grey beard covered his square jaw, and he wore a smile that was open and friendly. He was the kind of man people immediately liked, so of course Azerick hated him right away.

"Is it true?" he asked Miranda as he stood by her side and wrapped an arm around her waist. "Is it really him?"

Miranda swallowed and nodded. "It is. I have no doubt."

The man smiled and extended his hand. "Tim Kubrick. Miranda's husband, Lord of North Haven, and former captain of the Duchess' guard. I led her army in the Gods War."

Azerick returned a smile that lacked an ounce of sincerity and tried, and failed, to crush the man's hand in his grip. "Nice to meet you, *Tim*. I'm Azerick Giles. Also Miranda's husband, Lord of the Realm, Defender of the Crown, Lord of the Fifth Circle of the Abyss, and consort to the dark goddess Sharrellan. I fought against the old gods and helped save the world from perpetual darkness."

"It is not a contest, Azerick!" Miranda said, knowing what her former husband was doing.

Azerick locked eyes with the older man and chuckled. "Good thing for *Tim*. Am I right, *Tim*?"

"Azerick Giles!" Miranda snapped. "I understand you have been through a great deal, and all this comes as something of a shock, but that is no excuse for being so rude!"

Tim laid a hand on her shoulder. "Azerick is clearly having a hard time adjusting to what must be difficult changes. I'll go see to preparing a guest room."

Azerick spun on his heel and stormed away. "This was a huge mistake. I'm sorry."

"Azerick!"

Azerick ignored her cry and strode through the town without thought or direction. He chose a random building, punched the wall, and cradled his injured hand with a curse.

"Did it help?" Miranda asked as she caught up with him.

"It helped remind me of the suckier aspects of being a mortal human."

"I'm glad it hurt. You deserve it. I don't recall you being such a colossal ass."

Azerick rolled his eyes and smirked. "Yeah, well, they say memory is the first thing to go. That and the breasts."

Miranda reeled back and punched him in the chest.

"Ow, you hit hard for an old woman!"

"What is wrong with you?" she shrieked.

A gleeful smile spread across Azerick's face as he took her by the shoulders. "I'm jealous!"

Miranda narrowed her eyes and scowled back at him. "People are not normally so enthusiastic to admit such a thing."

"Jealousy," Azerick affirmed, "a real human emotion! You don't understand what it's like to have been stripped of your humanity for so long and then suddenly find it once again. It's akin to having been born blind and crippled and waking up to functional legs and eyes. It's…indescribable."

Miranda sighed and laid a hand on his cheek. "I can't imagine the horrors you've suffered in your life. This must be hard for you, but you must accept that life went on without you, that things changed. I thought you wanted me to go on with my life?"

"I did, and I'm glad you found *Tim* if he makes you happy."

"He does, and you need to accept that he's my husband now and has been for a long time. Longer than you were," she finished with a whisper.

"I know, and I'm sorry—for everything. Maybe I'm not ready for all this just yet. I can find a place to stay in town or in the city. Please, apologize to *Tim* for me."

"Don't be ridiculous. This is your home too, and you'll stay here until you figure out what you're going to do. And if you want to apologize to Tim, you can start by not saying his name like that."

Azerick averted his eyes. "Like how?"

"*Tim*, as if you stepped in something foul," she replied with a shake of her shoulders.

"I'll try, but it's a stupid name."

"How is it a stupid name? What's so great about your name?"

Azerick held up his hand and counted off on his fingers. "It's unique, it has more than one syllable, and it isn't *Tim*. Tim sounds like the name of the town idiot who likes to expose himself in public."

Miranda responded by punching him in the chest again. "Say it right!"

"*Tim*."

"Try again."

"T-*im*."

"Once more."

Azerick scowled. "Maybe I should give him a nickname."

"He has a nickname, but you'd like it even less."

"Why?"

"Because I only use it in the bedroom."

Azerick gasped and clutched his chest. "You are an evil woman!" He took a breath and set his jaw. "Tim."

Miranda patted his cheek. "Very good. You can join us for dinner in an hour."

"Sure. Just for the record, I think your breasts look amazing."

Miranda chuckled and tugged at the corset beneath her dress. "Trust me, there's more cloth and lines holding these things up than are in a ship's rigging. Why don't you take a walk around and get your bearings?"

"I will," Azerick called out at her back as she walked away. "Don't step in any Tim on your way back."

"Ass!" Miranda shouted over her shoulder.

"What? I said it right!"

He turned with a huff and found Wolf sitting on a barrel next to Ghost. Wolf held a pie in his lap with a handful lifted partway to his mouth.

"Larceny pie?" Wolf offered with a grin.

CHAPTER 10

Primus Lycus Ploutarch studied the distant city through a powerful spyglass mounted to the rail of his ship. Runes cast feint light as their magical properties turned night into day. The escapees with their absconded vessel had bypassed what was a major port city and had continued to sail north.

He knew he would not catch them before they made landfall, so he had decided to investigate the port city. If he could not present the empress with prisoners, perhaps he could give her something better, something to cement his name in the annals of military history.

Capturing this city would be an enormous achievement. Possibly enough to put him at the top of the short, selective list of considerations for promotion to imperator. The city would provide the perfect staging area for their approaching army, and he would hang their pennants from the towers welcoming them.

"Craft approaching," a lookout said in a hushed call.

Lycus aimed the spyglass lower over the water and twisted the long barrel to decrease its magnification. He spotted the small vessel a hundred yards from the ship.

"It's ours. Stand down and prepare to bring them aboard," he ordered.

Several minutes later, a junior officer named Varius Timaeus, bedecked in dark clothes resembling the local style, stood before him and saluted. "Sir, we have finished scouting the city."

"Report."

"It is a mid-sized city with a light population. The number of derelict buildings, homes, and districts give evidence it was once a major port with a thriving trade, but it seems to have been in decline for many years. I estimate the total population to be around thirty thousand at most."

The primus nodded as his brain calculated his odds and formulated plans of attack. "Military capabilities?"

"There is a significant local constabulary and militia totaling perhaps a thousand men. Best we could discover in a short time, there are an additional five-hundred trained soldiers."

"Any word of spawn activity?"

"Yes, sir. These people fought the creatures in a major battle back during the time of the initial incursion, and they still plague the land to this day, but most of the trouble is concentrated in the continent's interior."

Lycus smiled to himself at the report. Spawn-plagued are far easier to pacify as the people understand the benefits of joining the Order instead of fighting them. They provided security, prosperity, and a rich culture that raises them above their crude, barbaric ways.

"There is one other thing to note, sir," Optio Varius said. "The city is home to some sort of arcanus academy."

Lycus' eyes snapped back to the young officer. "An academy? How many arcanus?"

Varius beckoned over his shoulder. "Arcanus Nikandros was able to infiltrate their grounds undetected and can better inform you, sir."

Chains jingled at the arcanus' approach. "Sir, Arcanus Grozdan Nikandros."

"At ease, Arcanus. Tell me of this academy."

"Like the city, it was once much more populated. There are three primary sections. One for military officer training, scholarly studies, and then the arcanus halls. The martial grounds has a large stable but is at most filled to half capacity. The same with the study halls and quarters, the arcanus dormitories being less than a third occupied given the lights in windows and outside movements I saw."

"How many spellcasters? What kind?"

"Maybe a score of full wizards, likely instructors, and perhaps a hundred and fifty students of varying abilities, sir. Of the auras I was able to detect, none were sorcerous or those of warlocks."

"What are the odds of us establishing a nullification field large enough to ensnare them without raising an alarm?"

"I think good, sir. The students and masters are housed in one wing. I am confident we can pacify the vast majority of them with four arcanus and two centuria of legionnaires. We'll have to neutralize the light guard they post at night, but that shouldn't pose too great a challenge."

"Excellent work, Arcanus. Optio Timaeus."

The young officer snapped to attention. "Sir!"

"Any further intelligence to report?"

"Yes, Primus. I have procured a local map and one covering the kingdom. I marked the locations of several barracks, armories, and Watch houses on the city map. There is another large nation to the east and south called Sumara that we will also need to pacify."

"Outstanding work, Optio. Your reconnaissance may well be the key to our successful pacification."

Varius brought his fist to his chest. "I live to serve the Order."

Azerick returned to the manor, entering through a side door to avoid any confrontations, and sought his room. He tried to duck out of sight at the sound of footsteps descending the stairs.

"M-master Azerick, is that you?" a soft, nervous voice asked.

Azerick froze, his shoulder's bunched with tension, and turned. A small, hunched old man stood with one hand gripping the banister and the other linked through the arm of a stately woman of similar age.

"It's me. Simon? Teresa?"

The aged accountant pushed his owlish spectacles up and smiled. "H-how wonderful to see you again! You are so young!"

"Yes, the gods did a fair job of putting me back the way they found me. It's nice to see you both."

"Simon always said you would return one day," Teresa, his school's former headmaster, said. "I'll be honest, I did not expect to see it in our lifetime."

"I'm glad to disappoint," Azerick replied with a grin.

"There is nothing disappointing about it," Teresa replied, her stern visage not cracking for an instant.

"Give me time."

"M-master Azerick, I can bring you the ledgers at your earliest convenience. Perhaps after dinner?" Simon shuffled his feet. "I'm afraid the accounts are significantly depressed since your last accounting."

"They aren't my accounts anymore, Simon."

"Oh, ah, yes. Quite right. Forgive me. Old age and all that."

"It's fine. If you could point me to the guest room, I would be much obliged."

"Second floor, east wing, last door on your left," Teresa supplied. "Will you be joining us for dinner?"

"I'm afraid not. I'm weary from my travel and need to rest. Please apologize to my hosts."

Azerick moved past the elderly couple and found his room. He lay on the bed and closed his eyes. His ride from Wolf's village had left him too exhausted to attend dinner, or so he told himself.

He enjoyed another night of dreamless sleep, a luxury considering that his last couple of decades were a sleepless, waking nightmare. Demons did not sleep. They did not rest. Every minute of their existence was focused on achieving their own desires and destroying those of everyone else.

Azerick's desire had been to exist as lord of the fifth circle as best he could without having to fight his minions at every turn. The demons' wants ran contrary to this, and so there existed a constant battle of will and power between two entities that neither rested nor yielded to the other.

Oblivion was the closest thing to pleasure Azerick thought possible for him—until now. Even though Miranda had moved on, found a new love and remarried, he was happy to see her with his own eyes. Eyes not clouded by inner darkness and suppressed fury.

Faint light seeped through the bedroom window, heralding the morning. It was something so simple and yet it filled him with joy. A real sun announcing a new day for his new life.

He found fresh clothes on a chair near the door and donned them before going downstairs. A servant ushered him to the dining room where he found Miranda and Tim seated for breakfast. He sat on Tim's left, across from Miranda. Azerick smiled at the servant who set a plate of food in front of him.

Hunger, at least stomach hunger, was another sensation Azerick had forgotten, and he dove into his food with great enthusiasm. He paused between mouthfuls to talk to Miranda.

"I notice Rusty and Colleen are not here."

Miranda gave him a slight shake of her head. "No, they moved back to Southport after the war. They haven't come back to visit, but Colleen sends letters often. Their twins are grown, and both have Rusty's penchant for magic. They have another daughter, but she shows no sign of the gift."

"And your mother is well? I can't help but notice you are not living in the castle."

"She still rules and is as sharp and beautiful as ever. I swear the woman is a secret sorceress herself. We almost look like sisters these days."

Azerick took a breath and steeled himself for the answer he knew was forthcoming. "Ewen and Zeb?"

Miranda looked at her plate. "Both passed years ago. Balor is in charge of the shipping company now, and Derran captains one of the ships."

"Balor is a good man. I can't imagine Derran as a captain. He was just a kid when I left," Azerick replied, shaking his head in disbelief.

"The company rightly belongs to you, Azerick. I will have Simon draw up the papers to return it to you."

Tim snapped his head up. "Miranda..."

"We talked about this, Tim. Azerick created it. It belongs to him."

"We cannot move our goods by land because of those blasted highwaymen," Tim refuted. "Those ships are the only thing keeping us and this city solvent."

"What's this about highwaymen?" Azerick asked.

Tim turned toward Azerick, a disgusted look upon his face. "A gang of rogues that have set up a base of operations somewhere between North Haven and Southport."

"Can the cities not spare soldiers to deal with them?"

"It's a large band. Scores, maybe more than a hundred men. They're well-armed and organized. I've heard they have even begun targeting caravans headed east to Brightridge and Brelland."

Miranda looked at Azerick, her eyes filled with remorse. "They have several mages amongst them. Some I fear were former students here."

"My students became criminals?"

Miranda nodded. "A few. Others left the Academy. It's been hard for everyone after the war, and many of our students..."

"Were street children accustomed to surviving in such hardships," Azerick finished.

"They reverted to their former ways."

Azerick scrubbed his face with his hands in frustration. "It's just as the Academy feared. They warned me of the dangers of putting such power in the hands of people like them. I thought I knew better, that they would change, that I could change them."

Miranda reached across the table and laid a hand on Azerick's. "You did, for all of them, but the war changed some of them back."

"Which is why we have to have those ships," Tim said.

"We will manage without them," Miranda said with finality.

Azerick raised a hand to forestall further argument. "Miranda, I appreciate the gesture, but I relinquished my claim to the company long ago. I am nothing if not industrious. I'll be fine."

"Are you sure?" Miranda asked. "It was your dream to take after your father."

"It was the dream of another man. That man is dead. I am starting over, and I cannot do that if I cling to the past."

Tim looked at Azerick with a nod and grunt of appreciation. "Thank you, Azerick. That's very generous of you."

"On the topic of clinging to the past; _Ti—_" Azerick cleared his throat. "Tim, I want to apologize for my behavior yesterday. It was unseemly and unwarranted."

Tim flicked the knife he was using to slather a biscuit with butter. "Think nothing of it. I can't imagine what you've gone through. That you held onto even a shred of your sanity is an amazing testament to your character and fortitude. I've seen men's minds and discipline break in battles that would seem like a walk in the park compared to what you have witnessed and suffered."

"Thank you for understanding. I promise to avoid being…" Azerick's mind fought for the proper word.

"An ass, I believe is Miranda's preferred word," Tim said with a look to his wife.

Miranda nodded. "An ass, that's the one."

Azerick smiled, accepting the rebuke as his penance. "An ass. Thank you."

"Anytime," Miranda replied.

"Speaking of asses, have you heard from Daebian these past years?" Azerick asked.

Miranda scowled, her face losing its former traces of humor. "He is your son, and no, I have not. Not much. Ellyssa has sent a few letters over the years, either by way of ships sailing to Southport or through magical transcribing with mages at the Academy and couriered to us here. The last I heard they had settled on an island far to the southwest, well beyond Lazuul. Daebian was setting himself up as governor. But that was years ago."

"They're still together then?"

"They are. From what I could garner from Ellyssa's letters, she has had a calming effect on Daebian. I believe she has steered him away from blatant piracy and dulled his rougher edges."

Azerick nodded as some of the tension he had not realized he held loosened its hold on his chest. "That's good to hear. Given the darker periods in Ellyssa's life, I was worried the influence on each other might have gone the other way."

"But no concern for your son?"

"Of course I worried for him, but Daebian chose his path long ago, and any trouble he found would be of his own making."

"Really? Like yours was?" Miranda snapped. "Daebian's faults are entirely his own, but you are a victim of circumstance?"

"I never claimed to be a victim of anything," Azerick responded in a tense, measured tone. "But our experiences are very different. I grew up on the streets of Southport after someone murdered my family. Sharrellan pressed me into her service when I was just a boy. I knew little to nothing but loss, pain, and betrayal. Daebian grew up in a nice home with a loving mother and wanted for nothing."

"Nothing but a father who loved him for him even for his flaws. And when you returned, what did you do? You spent every minute with Raijaun."

"I had a war to fight and world to save! I could not have connected with Daebian even if he wanted me to, which he made clear he did not."

"You didn't try."

Azerick opened his mouth to argue, but he closed it when he heard the door open and two people stepped into the dining room.

"By the gods, Father, how many times must you be banished to deepest pits of hell before you find the common damn courtesy to stay there?" Daebian asked with a scowl on his face. "Honestly, at this point you're just being rude."

"Azerick!" Ellyssa cried and rushed across the room.

Azerick stood, knocking the chair over in his haste, and engulfed Ellyssa in his arms.

"I knew you'd come back," she sobbed. "I just knew it!" Ellyssa gazed into Azerick's eyes. "It's really you."

"It's really me," Azerick said with a smile.

"How?"

"Work of the gods, clearly," Daebian said. "Only they can make an entirely new body from a single old asshole."

"Daebian!" Miranda snapped as Tim choked on his biscuit.

"Don't Daebian me, Mother. I heard you two. How is my ugly brother? Still a virgin I imagine?"

Azerick sighed and faced his son. "Hello, Daebian. It's good to see you are well."

"The feeling is not mutual."

Ellyssa spun on her ersatz husband. "Daebian, stop it! We have more important things to do than bicker."

Daebian expressed his disagreement by curling his lips almost in a knot and looking away but remained silent.

"What's wrong?" Miranda asked. "I assume your timely visit is not mere coincidence."

Daebian scoffed, "Coincidence? When the crap hits the fan, it's usually father turning the crank."

Ellyssa spun on her husband. "Daebian, this has nothing to do with Azerick."

"Doesn't it? Tell me, father, how is it you have miraculously returned from the abyss once more at the same time we face yet another world-shattering event?"

Azerick returned his son's petulant look with a stern gaze. "The demons led a revolt against Sharrellan and took her captive. With Raijaun's help, I freed her. In exchange, I demanded that she return me here."

"I see. So, they had the power to return you to the living all this time, but saving their lives and dominion from the old gods wasn't enough. You had to perform yet another act of heroics."

"It wasn't like that," Azerick insisted.

"Of course not. It's just coincidence that this Order denounced the gods and replaced them with their emperor and empress and are now converting the entire world. If you could pause your cranking just a moment, perhaps you can tell me what happens when gods no longer have anyone following them?"

Azerick opened his mouth and snapped it shut.

"Yeah, I thought not. You are so stupidly oblivious."

"Daebian, that's not fair," Miranda said.

"The truth rarely is."

Azerick took a deep breath to still his inner rage. He should have known better. Sharrellan had given in to his demands far too easily. The gods were not being just or merciful. They needed to use him once again.

"What is this Order, and what do they want?" Azerick asked.

"They're an army, or a nation, or a religion—take your pick," Ellyssa replied. "They came to our island and took one out of every three men and anyone capable of wielding magic as conscripts into their army."

Azerick looked at his son. "They took you?"

"We weren't ready for them, and even if we had been... They were formidable, and we only faced a single detachment," Daebian said.

"Their soldiers were equipped with shields that could project a barrier that was all but invulnerable to my magic," Ellyssa added. "They hurled spears that weakened my ability to touch the Source and struck me when I tried. Azerick, they shackled me. They shackle everyone capable of wielding magic and use them like the Mushadan had."

"What do they want?" Azerick asked.

"To conquer everyone and enlist them in their crusade against the Scions' spawn," Ellyssa said.

Miranda asked, "Can we not treaty with them? If all they want is to destroy the spawn why not work together? If we could prove that we are not a threat to them, surely they will see that avoiding war is better for everyone."

Daebian shook his head. "They are fanatical. They feel the gods abandoned them when the spawn appeared and now despise them. I think their leaders control the mages' access to the Source through the shackles, and they brainwash them into accepting them as their gods."

Ellyssa looked at the floor. "And we may have led them straight here after we escaped with one of their ships."

Azerick wrapped an arm around her shoulder and drew her close. "It sounds as though their arrival was inevitable, but at least now we know they're coming and can prepare. Do you know where they are now?"

Ellyssa shook her head. "I sped our escape as best I could, but I don't think they're more than a few days behind us. I tried to scry them out, but their mages blocked my attempts."

"But you're sure they followed?"

"I'm sure I felt them scrying us on a few occasions. I'm not well-versed in divination."

Azerick bit his lower lip. "Neither am I, but perhaps together we could glean something of their whereabouts, if you're willing to try."

Ellyssa blew out a breath and nodded.

Azerick found a clean, silver serving dish on the table and fill it with water. "Seek them out. I'll join you once you think you've found them."

Ellyssa braced her hands against the table and stared into the water as she held Doncho's image in her mind. Trying to scry the old mage carried the greatest risk of discovery, but his was the only face amongst the Order she knew.

"I think I've found them."

Azerick laid a hand atop hers and slipped into the invisible stream of magic. He felt a barrier separating them from their target. Azerick pushed hard, and the arcane wall crumbled beneath his assault.

For an instant, he looked upon the shocked face of an older wizard as he fought to resist the intruders' prying eyes. Azerick had no interest in the mage and lifted into the sky. Four ships of foreign design bobbed on the sea. Soldiers in piecemeal armor and plumed helmets crowded the decks.

Azerick flew higher and recognized the city and shoreline in the distance. A powerful wave of magic crashed into him and sent him reeling. The water in the silver dish exploded in a spray, pelting everyone around the table.

Daebian wiped a hand across his eyes and flicked the droplets to the floor. "Well, I'm glad you didn't use tomato soup."

"What did you see?" Miranda asked.

Azerick shook his head to clear his disrupted thoughts. "Four ships laden with soldiers anchored not far off Southport's shore."

"What were they doing?"

"I can't say. We were repelled by at least four mages before I could discern much beyond their location."

"Can you warn Southport?" Miranda asked. "Through someone at the Academy, perhaps?"

Azerick motioned with his hands, and much of the water floated back into the dish. He focused his magic upon the vessel once more. "I don't think so. If I was stronger maybe, and better versed in the craft, I might break through, but they're aware of me now and appear to be making an active effort to block me."

"If they don't want anyone contacting the Academy..." Daebian said.

"They're preparing to mount an assault on the city," Azerick finished, coming to the same conclusion.

"What should we do?" Miranda asked.

Azerick replied, "You need to warn your mother and prepare defenses and arm everyone you can. If they take Southport, they will use the city as a staging point for further conquest. I'll ride to Southport and speak to the headmaster in person."

"Daebian and I will go with you," Ellyssa said.

Azerick shook his head. "No, you two should stay here and help defend the city. Whatever students are still here will need your leadership."

Ellyssa sighed and clenched her jaw. "You must at least take Daebian. He's seen these people firsthand, and you'll need as much credibility with the Academy as you can get. You aren't exactly popular there."

Azerick thought back to the time of the spawns' initial incursions. The Academy had rebuffed his warnings and suffered for it. He could have aided them, but he had let them die to drive home the importance of preparing for what was coming. It was the greatest source of his nightmares.

"I'm not leaving you here," Daebian said.

Ellyssa spun on him. "Yes, you are. I'll be fine, and Azerick will need your help more than we will."

"Fine," Daebian huffed. "We can take the ship I stole."

"No," Azerick said. "Their mages are certainly watching the seas for approaching vessels, and we would be at a severe disadvantage. We'll ride south and should be able to enter the city undetected."

"That will take several days more travel. The city might be under siege, if it hasn't fallen by then," Daebian rebutted.

"If these people are as adept at warfare, especially against magic wielders, as you say, that will be the case no matter which form of transportation we take. I can gate us a great distance, so we'll take no longer getting there on horseback than by ship. Possibly faster."

"Oh, joy, several days of horseback travel with my father," Daebian drawled. "I can't wait."

CHAPTER II

Optio Varius Timaeus led his centuria across one of the Martial Academy's drill fields in the dead of night. The gates leading into the school from the city were less guarded than its outer perimeter, indicating that the inhabitants were more concerned with attack from without than within. However, the city watch made the exterior approach the better option. Primus Ploutarch would deal with them.

His legionnaires had draped netting with strips of dark cloth over their heads and shoulders to blend in with the ground and to prevent any errant rays of moonlight from glinting off their armor. His centuria contained six arcanus who used their magic to further conceal and muffle their approach.

They reached the wall without raising an alarm. The centuria cast off their camouflage and pressed themselves against the tall stonework. A pair of arcanus breached the barrier by creating magical gates that allowed the soldiers to pass through the wall as if walking through a tunnel.

Camouflaged scouts neutralized an Academy guard with a muffled cry above and the sound of a body striking the causeway. They stalked the top of the wall, unseen and unheard thanks to their concealing, magical armor.

Four teams split off from the main contingent, each one taking an arcanus with them and several nullification standards. The standards looked like military guidons, but arcane sigils adorned their length instead flying unit flags. The advance teams placed the standards around the primary Magus Academy building, which housed most of the students and faculty.

Headmaster Maureen Florent woke with a gasp and bolted upright in her bed. She felt the loss of the Source as if something had cut off her airway. She reached for the magical energy, but she would have had more luck finding a fresh spring in the middle of the sun-parched desert.

The archmage focused on the magical artifacts adorning her fingers, wrists, and neck and found them functional. She grabbed the staff leaning against her bedpost and found it too still held power. At least she was not defenseless, and she knew without a doubt that her school was under attack once again. Maureen stormed from her chambers and found two of her instructors racing down the hall toward her.

"Headmaster, the Source!" Magus Megan Pugh called out in a panicked voice.

"I know. Sound the alarm. We must get to the students."

Magus Mason King, one of the Academy council members looked at the headmaster, his eyes wide with fright. "How? We cannot use our magic!"

"The old-fashioned way, you damned fool!" Maureen snapped. "Beat upon the doors and bring everyone you can to the central auditorium. From there, we will find out what is happening. Send someone to the Martial Academy, the castle, and the Watch. If we are under attack, we'll need them all."

The two mages ran back the way they had come, shouting, as the Headmaster pounded upon the doors in this wing. After the slaughter of hundreds of students and staff during a massive ravager incursion, scores of them her own magus students, she refused to be more than a few steps away from them.

It was easier now. There were barely five-hundred people enrolled in the entire Academy, the vast majority of them being martial students. She counted only ninety-seven magus students, more than half of them adults or nearly so.

Children of their society's upper-echelon filled most of the Academy's ranks, but the Gods' War had ripped Valeria apart. The war had leveled not just homes and businesses, but the very foundations of their civilization. The cunning, strong, and ambitious rose once more to what counted as prosperity, but they were few. Most of them had wealth and power before the war and were lucky enough to survive it and return to something akin to their former stations.

The rest fought just to survive and could not devote the time or resources needed for an education, particularly the kind that required total devotion and significant cost. Soldiers were easier to train and much cheaper to enlist. Seventy percent of the Academy's population were martial students. Even the Scholar's Academy was all but vacant. How do you convince people that education was the key to rebuilding what they had lost when they could scarcely find enough food to keep from starving?

Most of the students in the first dorm room were awake, blinking the sleep out of their eyes with looks of fright and confusion.

"Headmaster, what's going on?" a teenaged girl in a night robe asked.

"I'm not sure yet, but we need to get to the auditorium," Maureen replied. "Out of bed, quickly."

"I can't reach the Source," a boy cried as he shuffled behind the headmaster.

Maureen's expression was grim as she locked her eyes down the hall. "I know. None of us can."

She tried to block out her students' worried mutterings as she led them through the long corridors. She pounded on doors and called out to the students inside their dorms. The headmaster turned right at the next junction, but the crack of lightning, shouts, and the sound of clanking armor stopped her in her tracks.

Maureen turned around and chose another hall. "This way, children!"

"What's happening?" a young voice cried.

Their detour added precious time to their escape, but they made it to the auditorium. Maureen beckoned to the two other instructors she saw inside the chamber.

"What's our situation? Have you seen any others?" the headmaster asked as she tallied the number of students huddled together.

Magus Armand Trent said, "I caught sight of Magus Lewis leading a group of students here, but soldiers cut her off. She had a wand, but..." he looked around the auditorium. "It does not appear she or her students made it."

Maureen's face clouded and her brows drew together. "What soldiers? Who is attacking us?"

Armand shook his head. "I don't know. I only glimpsed them. Their armor was unfamiliar, and many of them had dark skin."

"Sumarans?"

Many people feared that the Sumarans, who had fared far better than they had in the Second Gods War, would seize upon their weakness and invade, but their alliance had held so far.

"No, darker even than that. I'm quite certain they are foreign."

One of the auditorium doors burst open, and Magus Megan Pugh rushed in behind a stream of students, unleashing fireballs down the passageway with a wand as she rushed inside the room.

"Bar the doors! They are upon us!" the magus shouted.

Doors slammed shut, sturdy crossbars dropped into place, and arcane runes carved into the doorways and across supporting arches glowed brightly enough to provide dim blue light throughout the enormous chamber. The auditorium was built as a panic room large enough to hold every student from all three branches of the Academy. Maureen shuddered as she looked around and saw far too many empty seats.

Something heavy crashed into two of the doors leading into the auditorium. The thick wood banded in steel shook but held. Silence reigned for several minutes until a firm but polite knocking sounded from the other side.

"Hello in there. My name is Optio Varius Timaeus of the Order. My soldiers have this room surrounded and have secured the entire building. Please surrender, and I promise none of you shall come to harm so long as you do not resist."

The archmage strode to the door. "I am Archmage Maureen Florent, Headmaster of the Academy. Your people will not breach this room before our soldiers drive you out."

"My arcanus are siphoning the power from your wards, and no one is coming to your rescue. Your young soldiers are engaging my troops, but they will not be successful. As for your city's defense forces, they are too busy fighting the bulk of our cohort. The castle and your wards will fall within the hour. Help me prevent unnecessary death by surrendering and encouraging your soldiers and leaders to stand down."

"You attack us without provocation! How could I possibly trust your word?"

Varius' voice dropped as he adopted an earnest tone. "Headmaster, I know it is difficult to accept the words of a stranger, but know my people value an oath above our lives. To break an oath is to forfeit one's life. By my word, in the name of Emperor Leontius Attar and Empress Noela Attar, the Twin Beacons of Syrna, I will allow no harm to come to you or anyone who submits to the Order."

Maureen looked to her fellow mages.

Megan laid a hand on the runes glowing around the doorframe. "The wards are failing."

"Headmaster, please," Varius said. "Your students are dying despite my best efforts to prevent bloodshed. You must tell them to stand down."

"What of my other students and their instructors, the ones from the magus hall?" the headmaster asked through the door.

"We have detained them, nothing more. You have my word of honor. Surrender and order your soldiers to lay down their arms."

Maureen squeezed her staff until her knuckles turned white and her fingers ached. She settled her eyes onto her frightened students before turning them to her cadre. Each of them gave her a curt but resigned nod.

The headmaster turned back toward the door. "All right. I am lowering the wards and unbarring the door. We surrender."

Maureen leaned her staff against the wall, deactivated the wards protecting the chamber, and stood back before the door as two of her fellows withdrew the thick bolts securing it closed. The headmaster braced herself as the two mages opened the doors.

A young man with dark skin and wearing silver armor adorned with arcanum runes stood in the doorway. He held a short spear at the ready in one hand and a buckler that emitted a larger, arcane shield in the other.

Varius lowered both when he saw that the archmage and her fellow wizards showed no sign of attacking. He gestured to the score of soldiers forming ranks behind him. They streamed past him in two columns, splitting to both sides of the doorway, and encircled the students and instructors.

Several soldiers broke ranks and advanced on the mages and oldest students with shackles. Varius strode forward and presented Maureen with a pair.

"What is this?" the headmaster asked, flinching away from the device as she tried to interpret the sigils carved into the metal.

"They are for your protection and mine," the young officer replied. "They will not cause you any harm."

Maureen sneered at the man as he clamped the manacles around her thin wrists. "You attack innocent people and children in the night without cause and claim to cause no harm. The harm you have caused is already extraordinary."

"I assure you, Lady, our cause is righteous, and you and your people will one day thank us for our arrival."

"The dead can't thank anyone, and I doubt the families of those you have murdered this night will either. To the abyss with you, your people, and your *righteous* cause."

Varius had the decency to look chagrined as he led the headmaster from the auditorium. She could hear shouts and the clash of weapons down the hall. Order soldiers parted to allow the archmage and her captor to pass through the clogged doorway leading into a courtyard.

At least three-score Order soldiers stood in ranks just beyond the door, securing the entrance against three or four times as many of her Martial Academy students and faculty. Several bodies littered the space between the two groups, all of which belonged to her people.

It was far from a slaughter. Maureen and most every adult of middle years and older had seen true carnage during the Gods War, but such knowledge did little to dull the pain of witnessing yet more blood spilled upon Academy grounds.

A flight of arrows streaked across the courtyard only to strike the Order shields. Ripples like raindrops on a pond ran across the arcane shields created by the Order soldiers, the missiles clattering to the ground.

Maureen looked over the crested helmets and saw the Martial Academy's chancellor, retired General Barret McGill, prepared to lead his young men on another fruitless charge that would result in nothing but more needless death.

There was no mistaking the tall headmaster in her archmage robes as she pushed through the Order's ranks and stood between the two warring factions.

"Hold!" the senior mage called out. "The battle is over."

The aging veteran held out his arms as he took several steps toward Maureen and the enemy line. "Headmaster, what are you saying? Our casualties are light."

"And theirs are nonexistent. The Mage's Academy has fallen with nary a spell unleashed. We are defeated, Barret."

The general's thick, white mustache quivered with anger. "We're still standing, and the Watch and city forces will be here in minutes!"

Varius stepped forward. "Our main force should have your castle walls secured and infiltrated the castle itself. If your leaders have not already capitulated, it will not be much longer before they do. Your men fought well, sir, but all fall before the Order."

"To the abyss and back with your damn Order!" Barret seethed.

"There is nothing for us to gain by continuing this fight, Barret," Maureen said. She looked past him to the frightened but determined young men behind him. "Lay down your arms. All of you."

The soldiers looked to their commander. Barret glared fury at both the headmaster and the invaders but threw down his sword and shield. Steel rang on stone as his troops followed suit with muttered curses.

Varius strode up to the general. "You made the wise decision, sir. My men will escort your people to the auditorium until the situation in the city has been resolved."

Barret set his fierce gaze on the young man. "You may have won this fight, but Valerians will never yield. We have defeated armies of monsters, dragons, and even gods. We will beat you as well."

Varius smiled as he wagged his head. "Four continents, a dozen nations, scores of societies; all spoke the same words. All fell. There is only the Order."

CHAPTER 12

Order soldiers poured through magical breaches in the walls surrounding Southport's castle. The moment the advance cohort was through, the arcanus closed their magical gates and erected nullifiers, cutting off those inside the walls from the Source. Their approach had not gone undetected. Despite their arcanus' best efforts to conceal them, it was impossible to veil almost a thousand soldiers as they double-time marched through the city.

While Watch patrols were heavy given the city's population, coordinating a viable defense was slow due to the efforts of a few legionnaire platoons and arcanus providing misdirection through false attacks. By the time the city organized its militia and soldier garrisons, the bulk of Primus Lycus Ploutarch's expeditionary cohort was inside the bailey walls and storming the castle itself.

Lycus led the infiltration centuria himself while the rest of the cohort secured the walls and inner courtyards. The castle grounds were expansive, but the defenders fell to the Order's superior training, tactics, and armament. The battlements were theirs within minutes.

Someone inside had the presence of mind to secure the castle doors, and with the nullifiers in place breaching them by arcane means was no longer possible. Lycus strode up to the formidable barrier with a confident swagger and hued into the door with his eldritch blade. The blazing arcane weapon cleaved through the wood and stout iron hinges with just two strokes.

The doors fell to the ground with a crash. Crossbow bolts streaked through the opening before the slabs of wood and iron struck the ground. The quarrels bounced off the legionnaires' shields or sailed overhead. The Order soldiers charged through the breach with cadenced steps, shields held before them, their weapons poised to strike.

Lycus led the charge. His sword made of pure energy cut through armor, shields, weapons, and bodies alike. This was a blitz. There was no time to ask for quarter. The invaders stormed through the castle, cutting down anyone who raised a weapon in defense. Within minutes, Lycus and his infiltration centuria reached a hall packed with soldiers standing guard over a set of doors behind them. Before the primus could order them to surrender, Duke Terrance's house guard charged the invaders with fierce battle cries.

Lycus' shimmering blade cut a swath through the brave fighters as his centuria pressed in behind him, their spears thrusting between shields to strike down those soldiers that flanked their leader. Having cut a bloody path through the guard, Lycus stood before the barred doors. He stabbed his energy blade between them and cut through the crossbar holding them closed.

With a strike from his booted foot, the doors crashed open to reveal an older man in nightclothes with a hastily thrown on breastplate covering his torso. He stood before his wife brandishing a sword that looked far more ornamental than it did a true weapon. An effect highlighted by the fact that the duke held it with an unfamiliar grip.

Two guards in full plate armor rushed Lycus from each side of the doorway. The Primus reacted with expert reflexes. His glowing weapon cut through the first guard's sword, shearing it off just inches beyond the hilt. He spun around and deflected the second man's attack out wide. Lycus pumped his legs as he bashed the soldier in the chest repeatedly with his shimmering shield, driving him backwards, staving in the breastplate, and knocking him to the ground.

Lycus turned toward the duke who stood rooted in place. "Enough! Order your men to stand down and surrender your city."

Duke Terrance looked to his two guards, both of whom would defend their liege to the death, and at the bloody hallway packed with enemy soldiers. He dropped his ornate sword to the ground and took a backward step toward his wife with his arms outstretched.

"I yield and throw myself at your mercy," Terrance said with as much courage as he could muster.

"Surrender your city and swear fealty to the Order."

"Who are you? What Order?"

"The Order is the righteous sword and shield of the divine emperor and empress of Syrna and all the world," Lycus declared.

Terrance looked around once more at the soldiers, the dead and wounded, and spared his wife a glance before shaking his head. "No. I surrender myself and will command those within these halls to lay down their weapons, but I will not hand my city to an unknown invader even upon pain of death."

The primus' sword and shield vanished with a thought. He took the recalcitrant duke by the arm and pulled him from the room. All but a handful of legionnaires formed ranks and marched behind their commander. Terrance ordered any of his people he saw to surrender. He knew the battle, at least for the castle, had been lost.

Lycus led him onto the battlements. Southport's soldiers pressed against the walls and gates, some bashing at them with makeshift rams. Arrows and quarrels arced overhead and struck Order shields with ripples of energy.

The Primus found one of his optios. "Clear the gates!"

The optio shouted commands to his centuria and formed ranks. Those guarding the gates threw them wide, and the centuria clashed with the city soldiers. Order shields flared with light whenever struck while their spears passed through the arcane barriers without resistance. The Order's enchanted weapons had no problem punching through the soldiers' armor, be it steel or leather.

The city's militia fell back before the charge, leaving bodies and dropped weapons to litter the ground. Not until the centuria had cleared a square a hundred feet on each side did they retreat through the gates. The city militia flooded in to fill the hole, but not until after the gates slammed shut.

"That was but a hundred men," Lycus said as the duke watched in horror at how easily the foreigners had cut through his soldiers. "I have close to a thousand at my disposal. We do not hide behind these walls for our safety. We hold here to spare the lives of your people. Be warned, I am not a patient man."

Terrance looked out over his city toward the Academy which was strangely dark.

Lycus followed his gaze. "We have already brought your wizards to heel. They will not come to your rescue. No one will. Surrender, and most of your people will go on living just as they have been, only better. Mine is but an expeditionary force. The main host brings with it engineers to improve your roads, bridges, and defenses. Our legionnaires will scour this land clean of the vile spawn that has plagued the world these last two decades. That is our righteous cause, and we will not allow man, beast, or nation to stand in our way."

Terrance was not a military man, but even he recognized a lost battle. "What will happen to me and my family?"

"We will conscript any children you have into service to fulfill a role that best suits the Order. Do you have children?"

Even after all this time, losing his son Travis caused him grief. "No. Some nieces and nephews on my wife's side."

"We will send some of them back to Syrna for indoctrination and to guarantee your continued compliance. You, as long as you faithfully serve our divine lords, will hold a role similar to what you enjoy now. You will have overseers for a few years to ensure you remain true, but you will be harmost to this city."

"Harmost?"

"Governor, I believe is your term. There is no royalty but the emperor and empress and their children."

Terrance cast his eyes to the street. "Gods preserve us."

Lycus leveled his gaze onto the defeated duke. "There are no gods but the emperor and empress either. It is they who will preserve us and purge the land of spawn and infidels."

Rusty woke to the sound of klaxons shattering the stillness of the night. He leapt from his bed and hopped around the room as he tried to pull on a pair of trousers.

"What's going on?" Colleen asked as she sat up in bed.

Rusty shuffled to the window and looked out over the courtyard. "I don't know. There are people running down the street."

"Ravager attack?" Colleen asked in a trembling voice.

"This near the city center? I can't imagine so."

"Where are you going?"

Rusty paused in the doorway as he shrugged on a coat. "To see what's going on."

Colleen's voice rose to a higher pitch. "You're leaving me here?"

"I didn't think you'd want to come with me."

"I don't! But I don't want you to leave me here by myself," Colleen shouted as she chased after her husband.

The pair almost collided with Rusty's mother and father in the hallway as they rushed for the stairs. Their two live-in servants stood in the downstairs living room gripping the fronts of their robes and looking both confused and worried.

"What's happening, son?" George huffed as he tried to keep up with Rusty.

"I don't know yet, Father. If you would all just stay put a moment, I'll go find out."

Rusty left his family huddling in the open doorway and jogged across the courtyard to the street. He spotted another group of city militia charging up the road and called out through the iron gate.

"You there. What's happening?"

"The castle is under attack!" a man exclaimed.

"By whom?"

"Don't know. Some soldiers I hear. Foreigners."

"Sumaran?"

The man shook his head. "Even more foreign."

"Where did they come from?"

"Ships I think," he replied before running off to catch up with his group.

Rusty hurried back to the house. "Soldiers have attacked the castle."

His family exchanged worried glances. Colleen moved in close and pressed her hands against Rusty's chest as she looked past him toward the street. "Who's attacking us?"

Rusty hugged his wife and kissed the top of her head. "I don't know yet. I need to get to the Academy."

Colleen recoiled with a gasp. "Dear gods, the children."

Rusty nodded. "They'll need all the help they can get."

"You're not a warrior mage, son," George said.

"No, but I'm no stranger to fighting, and Vera isn't a mage or a warrior. I must make sure they're safe. Secure the gates behind me, lock the doors, and shutter the windows. I am sure this will be over soon, once we marshal the Academy mages."

Rusty jogged down the street against the flow of militia and ordinary citizens running toward the castle. Despite his improved longevity, due to his being a mage, he was still a middle-aged man who had lived a sedentary life after the war, and his bones and muscles reminded him of the fact. He drew in power from the Source and used it to fuel his flagging strength, giving them the energy they needed to propel him down the road.

After the war, Rusty had replaced his father as the city's Minister of Finance. It was a challenging post. It took years to restore the city's banks and commerce, and they were still in recovery today. Southport, like most every city in the kingdom, had been ravaged during the war. The fell spawn and dragons had laid waste to much of the structures, ships, and dockyards.

Rusty looked over the rooftops toward the Academy towers, but he saw only the dark, clouded night sky and a few faint windows glowing with lamplight. A sense of dread ran through his body. The Academy was always well lit, its towers standing like beacons visible for miles. His fear urged him to greater speeds. He was unsure what the darkness portended, but he knew it could not bode well.

He reached the gates and felt relief when he saw that they were still intact, and that soldiers stood guard. Rusty grabbed the gate's iron bars and tried to see beyond them and into the gloomy courtyard.

"Hello!" Rusty called out to the shadowy silhouettes. "The city is under attack. We need to rally the mages."

Several soldiers strode toward the gate. The first thing Rusty noticed were the crested helmets, the sight of which caused his unease to resurge. Southport's military did not have crested helms. Three foreign soldiers approached the gate. They had skin darker than any Rusty had ever seen.

"This area is closed until further notice," one man said through the gate.

Rusty swallowed the lump in his throat and licked his lips. "My children are in there. Can you bring them to me?"

"Who are you?"

"My name is Franklin Cossington. I am the finance minister," Rusty replied.

"No one goes in or out until the city is pacified. Return to your home and stay off the streets, or we will arrest you."

Rusty's eyes flicked to the enormous scholars building. "My youngest daughter is sick. I have medicine she needs. Surely you would allow me to bring it to her?"

The soldier opened his mouth to respond then closed it as a woman wearing no armor and bearing no weapons stepped to his side and said something into his ear. It took Rusty only a second to realize the woman was a wizard, and not one he recognized. It was evident by her clothes she did not belong to the Academy, and likely not even to Valeria.

The soldiers opened the gate and advanced. "Sir, you need to come with us," the speaker of the squad said as he removed a pair of manacles from his belt.

Rusty had returned to Southport and taken the job of finance minister because he had no desire for combat. He was weary of war and the destruction it wrought, and so created a life for himself and his family that avoided conflict greater than a council debate on appropriations and spending.

While the number of criminals and fell spawn attacks had decreased over the past decade, it was still a dangerous time, and Rusty was prepared to defend himself should it arise. He lashed out with a quick spell, striking the squad with a wave of force. Two went sailing backward and rolled across the flagstone courtyard with a raucous clanging of metal. The mage brought up a ward that blunted the sudden attack enough so it only knocked her back a few steps. Soldiers brought up small shields that erupted with halos of azure light, blocking the spell's effect.

The foreign mage retaliated with a similar cone of force. Rusty erected a ward, but the blow still staggered him, and he tripped backward onto the street. He gained his feet with speed borne of fear and hurled a fireball into the advancing group of soldiers. The fiery orb burst into an explosive inferno and lit up several blocks with orange light.

Darkness flooded back in an instant after the fireball struck his own ward, the only thing that had kept him from scorching himself. Through dazzling motes of light, Rusty saw the iron gates warped from the extreme heat, but it had no effect on the soldiers. He knew if he could not harm his foes with magic, he would lose this battle. Who then would save his children?

Rusty mimicked one of Azerick's favorite spells, raising a wall of stone spikes in front of the soldiers to slow them. He turned and ran, figuring it wiser to retreat and regroup, as it was clear he could not defeat these people on his own. A soldier behind him blew a long, trumpeting note on a looping brass horn.

The hairs on the back of Rusty's neck stood up just before an invisible fist collided with his back and sent him tumbling once again. Javelins arced toward him, their points sinking into or between the cobblestones. Rusty got back to his feet and tried to raise another ward, but electricity shot from the javelins and arced into his body the instant he reached out for the Source.

His eyes wide with panic, he now understood the javelins' purpose and that the soldiers did not miss him because of terrible aim. He tried to run out of the ring of spears, but a braided cord with weighted ends wrapped around his ankles and he went sprawling a third time. Stars flashed before his eyes as his head bounced off stone and a warm trickle of blood flowed down his face from a gash in his forehead.

Rusty struggled to get up, desperate to escape. Rough hands turned him over onto his back. He glanced at the manacles clamped around his wrists and tried to curse his captors, but his complaints and curses came out as nothing more than a pathetic moan.

His excuse of wanting to rally the Academy forces had been only partially true. Mostly, he was worried for his children, especially Vera. The twins, Trisha and Elias, were both capable wizards. But Vera was ungifted and was a student at the Scholars Academy. Younger than her siblings by some twenty years, he still saw her as his little girl, which she was. Although nineteen, she was small and studious with a weak constitution.

A sickly child, Vera needed regular doses of medicine to clear her lungs. The prospect of her being in danger terrified Rusty. Fear from what was happening could trigger her breathing difficulties, and if she did not have her medicine, it could kill her. If he did not save her, who would?

CHAPTER 13

Azerick and Daebian woke early in the morning. They had said their goodbyes the night before and stole out of the manor before most of the house was awake. Azerick smiled at the short man with wild, straw-colored hair standing in front of the stables with two horses saddled and ready to go. A woman of sturdy build, with blond ponytails hanging past her shoulders towered a full head over him. Her broad smile matched the one Peck wore.

"I'm glad to see you're still here, Peck," Azerick said.

Peck shrugged. "It's where my horses are, so there's nowhere else for me to be." He looked up at the woman next to him. "This is my wife Nicolette, or Niko for short."

Daebian's lip curled up in a smirk. "Oh, she's your wife. I thought you had decided to go with us and had brought out three horses."

Peck balled up a fist and made to step forward, but Niko laid a hand on his shoulder. "Ignore him. Tiny men need to say terrible things to cover for their own inadequacies."

"Well, you know all about tiny men," Daebian replied.

"Peck is more of a man than you in every way that counts."

Daebian rolled his eyes. "I'm sure not in every way."

Niko tilted her head and narrowed her eyes. "*Every* way."

Daebian's mouth curled down, and he leaned back as he studied Peck. "Well...good for you, Peck."

"Even better for Niko," Peck replied with a grin.

"Still, I killed a god. Good luck on that."

Niko scoffed. "And who killed your sense of decency?"

Daebian jerked a thumb toward Azerick. "Blame it on poor parenting. You know what they say about apples not falling far from the tree."

"Azerick was like a father to us, to a lot of us, and we turned out well," Peck replied. "If you want to find the fault for your own shittiness, you only have to look in a mirror."

"If you looked in a mirror occasionally your hair wouldn't look like a chicken's nest."

"I'd say you look like a horse's ass, but that's an insult to horses."

Daebian took a step toward Peck. "Don't presume to speak on behalf of horses when you have one right here that can speak for herself."

Azerick thumped his staff into Daebian's chest. "Enough! There are more important things to do than pick fights!" He nodded at Peck and Niko. "I'm very sorry for my son's behavior."

"Don't apologize for me!"

Azerick snapped his head around and glared at his son. "Someone has to, and far too often!"

Daebian scowled at his father. "If you want to apologize for someone, apologize for yourself."

"I've made most of my apologies to everyone who deserves them, including you. If you're too angry or hard-headed to accept it, then the problem is yours. If you can't be civil, then at least be quiet."

Daebian stared at Azerick a moment before flashing him a wink and turning to Peck. "Which horse is mine?"

"The mare," Peck replied. "And I expect you to treat her decent."

Daebian lifted himself into the saddle and grinned. "Don't worry, I've outgrown abusing dumb animals…except for Father." He nudged the horse into a canter, leaving them alone.

Azerick shook his head and sighed. "I'm sorry again. I don't know what to do with him."

"I don't think there's anything you can do," Peck said.

"You could always try beating him," said Niko.

"Believe me, nothing would make me happier," Azerick replied with a chuckle.

"Just be careful out there on the road," Peck said.

"I'd heard there were creatures and bandits around causing problems, but I can handle them."

"There are other monsters than just creatures and bandits," Peck said, his voice somber. "Some of them are much more dangerous and very close."

Azerick looked to where Daebian waited by the road leading away from the small town. "Yes, there certainly are."

Vera leaned back in her chair and yawned. She held her thick, round spectacles in one hand and tried to rub the gritty sleep out of her eyes with the other. She often found herself in the library long after hours. Not only did she enjoy her research, she preferred being alone. Even the quiet of normal library hours was more interaction than she cared for.

Noise in the hall pulled her out of her thoughts. Vera looked up at the clock and saw it was after midnight. Curfew had long passed, and she decided it would be best to return to her dorm. She slipped her civil engineering book into a small backpack and slung it over her shoulder.

Voices, footsteps, and raucous sounds greeted her in the hallway. The halls should be deserted at this hour, and she wondered what could cause such a commotion. Vera left the library and followed the source of the unusual noise. She rounded a corner and saw the backs of four men in unusual armor. Two of them had skin darker than any Sumaran she had ever seen.

"Um, excuse me," Vera called out to the squad.

The soldiers stopped in their tracks, spun around, and leveled weapons at the young woman. They snapped their spears up when they concluded that she posed no threat.

"Who are you? What are you doing in the halls?" one of the men asked.

"My name is Vera. I was in the library and am returning to my dorm. Who are you?"

"We are the Order. Students and faculty are required to be in their rooms. You need to return to your dorm."

"Uh, yeah. I just said that's where I was going."

"You need to return to your room," the soldier repeated.

"Wait, now I'm confused. Are you saying I should return to my room? Because I thought I was supposed to go to my room, but you keep telling me to go to my room."

"Return to your room!"

"So I *should* go to my room. Sorry, I want to make sure I understand you."

The three soldiers standing with the speaker of their squad grinned, but their leader was not as amused. "Where is your room?"

Vera pointed at the door next to them. "It's the one you are blocking."

The speaker opened the door and made room for her to pass.

Vera stopped near the open door and turned toward the one on the other side of the hall. "Oh wait, it's that one."

The soldier shut the door, crossed the hall, and opened the other door.

"I am so sorry. It was the first one. The sight of so many strange, dangerous men must have me frazzled."

The leader's cohorts snorted laughter as he slammed the door shut hard enough to rattle the hinges, threw open the other door, and shoved the girl inside. "Stay in your room!"

"You mean this room with the locked door and armed guards? How would I do elsewise?" Vera asked through the door. She looked at the eleven other girls in the dorm and asked, "What is going on?"

Kaelyn, the self-appointed dorm leader, said, "Are you serious? Foreigners have invaded the city and taken over the entire Academy! Maybe if you closed your stupid books once in a while you'd see what in the abyss is happening around you."

"And maybe if you opened a book half as often as you open your legs you wouldn't be failing most of your classes and spending so much money at the chemist's trying to contain whatever zoological experiment you have going on down there."

"I do not have...anything going on down there!"

Vera walked past Kaelyn as she headed to her bunk at the back of the room. "Please, it's like an incubated petri dish with pubic hair."

Kaelyn seethed. She knew she would lose a war of words with the bookworm, but it did not stop her from trying. "Tell me Vera, how exciting was it for you when that soldier shoved you, being the first time a man has ever touched you?"

Vera looked up from where she was packing clothes and essentials into a bag. "Given that we are at the mercy of men who are likely to rape, kill, or sell us into slavery, it's nice to know you have the presence of mind to still be a total bitch. So courageous."

"You're a bitch!" Kaelyn said over the garble of frightened voices Vera's comment had elicited.

"A truly brilliant retort," Vera said with a sigh.

Kaelyn watched her packing. "What are you doing?"

"Uh, leaving."

"You can't leave, stupid."

"Of course I can. I'm certainly not staying here with them."

"There are soldiers standing right outside the door. They won't let you leave."

"That's not the only door, and I don't plan on asking permission," Vera said.

"There's another way out?" a girl asked.

"Is what Vera said true? Are they going to hurt us or sell us?" another cried.

Kaelyn raised her voice. "Vera doesn't know what she's talking about. She's just a scared little girl. The soldiers promised that they wouldn't hurt us and that everything would soon be back to normal."

Vera slipped her backpack on and gripped the handle of the alchemy set her father had given her as a young girl with both hands. She had always been jealous of her older siblings' ability to use magic, and alchemy was the closest thing she could come to being like them. Alchemy had become one of her favorite hobbies and her second greatest pursuit next to engineering.

"I'm leaving, if anyone wants to go with me."

"The only way anyone gets hurt is if we break the rules. No one is going anywhere, including you, Vera. You could get us in trouble."

"If you want to stay, fine. I'll be better on my own without dragging dead weight along with me, but I'm not sticking around on the promises of an invading army."

Kaelyn stalked across the room and glared at the smaller girl. "I said you're not leaving. If you try, I'll tell the guards so you're the only one who gets in trouble."

Vera glared up at the girl before laying her alchemy set on the bed and shrugging off her pack. "Fine, you win."

Kaelyn strode away with a triumphant smile on her face. Vera flipped the catches on the small trunk and pulled out vials filled with powders and liquids. She set a small glass jar half-filled with purple powder on the floor in the center of the room and poured the liquid contents of a vial into it.

"What is that?" Kaelyn asked.

"It's a flameless candle. Lilac scented I think."

Kaelyn smirked at her. "I hope it's strong enough to cover the smell of loser."

Vera donned a leather mask with glass lenses and a metal canister attached to it.

"Nice mask. You should wear it all the time. It's an improvement over your face. Maybe someone will ask you to the dance now."

Vera flashed her a thumb's up and smiled behind her mask as the girls began yawning and rubbing their eyes. Some had the wherewithal to lie down before the sleeping gas knocked them out. Those who did not, like Kaelyn, fell to the floor and lay in a heap.

Vera shouldered her pack once more, closed the lid on her alchemy set, and slipped behind the tapestry near her bed where the secret door lay. She cast a final glance back to the unconscious girls.

"Later, bitches," she said, her voice muffled by the mask.

Vera removed the gas mask as soon as she closed the door behind her. The three Academy buildings contained many secret passages. It was an inefficient use of space and building materials, and she had often wondered why any engineer wasted their time with such designs. The foreign soldiers' arrival had answered her question for her.

While she had not agreed with the construction, it did not prevent her from appreciating it even before the invasion. It was a good way to sneak out of the dorm when the other girls became intolerable, which was almost every day. Unfortunately, they did not all connect. That would have been an architectural impossibility given the many wings, rooms, and intersections.

The secret passage she was using ended just a short distance ahead where a large portrait concealed the door into the hall. Its proximity to the library was why she chose to share the same dorm with Kaelyn all these years. She opened the door and listened from behind the painting before pushing it aside and stepping through.

The library's bookshelves hid more than one passageway, and she hurried down the hall as quickly as she could. Lugging the alchemy set slowed her, but there was no way she would leave it behind. It was the greatest weapon in her arsenal, other than her wits, both of which were quite formidable. She reached the library's big door and tugged it open.

"Hey, you, halt!" someone shouted just as she closed the door.

A pair of Order legionnaires burst into the library with the clanging of armor a moment later. They searched the numerous aisles of bookcases but failed to find anyone.

"Are you sure you saw something?" one asked.

"I thought I did. Maybe I imagined it."

"Your mind is probably inventing things because we're stuck on this boring babysitting detail while the rest of the cohort is having all the fun."

"Probably."

Vera listened to the men from behind the bookcase concealing the hidden passageway until she was sure they had moved on. This was not a passage she normally used, and it had no source of light. She set the alchemy chest on the floor, opened it, and selected two vials and a small jar. She mixed the chemicals together in the jar, screwed the lid on tight, and shook it.

The liquid inside glowed a bright green, illuminating several yards of the passageway. Vera tied a length of cord around the glowing jar and hung it from her neck. This kept her hands free, and she could drop the light inside her coat to conceal it. It would be hard enough sneaking past the soldiers without glowing like a ghostly apparition.

This corridor led to a hallway that took her to the kitchen. She tucked the glowing jar inside her shirt and emerged from behind a tapestry. This was the riskiest stretch of her journey as it left her exposed. She trudged down the hallway lugging her trunk. Voices from around the corner alerted her to the presence of soldiers.

Vera peered around the edge of an intersection and spotted a cluster of men. None were looking her direction, so she darted down the passageway in the opposite direction, praying that none turned around. She had been so eager to get out of eyesight of the squad behind her she failed to look before rounding the corner and ran straight into another trio of legionnaires.

Both parties stared a moment before one of the men said, "You should be in your room."

Vera rolled her eyes. "That seems to be a common theme with you people. You are obsessed with sending girls to their rooms."

"Why is your face glowing?" one asked as they walked toward the girl.

"Oh, that? Because of this."

Vera reached inside her coat, pulled out a glass vial, and hurled it at the lead soldier. It shattered against his breastplate and unleashed the most god-awful stench ever devised. The three men stopped in their tracks and wretched. Even from where she stood, the odor made Vera gag as she ran the other direction.

The soldiers' noisy expulsions alerted their brethren, who came running toward the source of the disturbance. They cursed as they waded into the noxious fumes. The stricken group shoved them forward and waved them toward the fleeing girl.

Vera heard the heavy footsteps behind her, and they were drawing closer. She reached the kitchen, threw open the door to the cellar, and pulled out her glowing jar before descending the steps. Twice she almost tumbled headlong down the stairs thanks to her cumbersome burden.

She found a two-wheeled sack truck amongst the clutter, set her trunk on the foot, and pulled it behind her as she searched for the secret door she knew existed somewhere along the east wall. Which way was east? Vera needed time to find the entrance to the sewer, so she grabbed a board that was once part of a shelving unit, ran back up the stairs, and wedged it between the door handle and the top step. She had just gotten it into place when the handle rattled and someone pushed hard against the door.

"I think she's down here!" a soldier shouted.

The door shook but held as someone kicked it. "Find something heavy to use as a ram."

Vera raced down the last few steps and slung sacks of foodstuffs, old, discarded kitchen equipment, and other pieces of debris away from the wall. She ran her hands along the rough stone in search of the hidden door.

The door above splintered under the heavy pounding. She found the hidden entrance behind some barrels. The opening was small, but she was able to get the sack truck bearing her alchemy set through by laying it flat on its back and pushing it ahead of her.

She closed the door behind her and wedged it shut with a piece of wood. The small landing upon which she stood had stairs leading farther down before ending inside the sewers running beneath the city. Vera had spent so much time studying their layout she could traverse them as easily as the streets above.

She squealed and performed an impromptu dance when a rat ran across her foot. Gods how she hated rats. Vera had no problem working with the creatures in a laboratory setting, but vermin in the wild was an entirely different thing. She unslung her backpack and rifled through it until she found what she was looking for.

It was a metal device that looked a bit like a hand crossbow with a canister of special oil protruding from beneath the body. Vera pumped the plunger sticking out of the back, pressurizing the flammable contents inside the canister. She lit a small flame from the fumes escaping from the nozzle using a striker from the alchemy set. A squeeze of the trigger opened a valve and shot a gout of flame several feet, immolating any rat that sought to challenge her.

Vera pulled the sack truck behind her and directing her flamer ahead as she navigated the walkway running beside the slow-moving, fetid water. Vera had not walked more than two hundred yards when she found her way blocked by thick, iron bars. The impediment was not unexpected. There were barriers throughout the sewers, particularly the sections that led to important areas like the Academy, castle, and wealthy districts.

She retrieved a glass bottle from her haversack and poured the thick liquid onto three of the bars. The metal hissed and let off an acrid smoke. Vera was careful to stand away from the toxic vapors while the acid burned through the metal.

With a few careful kicks, the bars fell away, and she continued her trek. She began seeing people as she neared the lower quarter, likely those familiar with using the subterranean passageways when they felt the need to avoid the Watch. Vera kept a wary eye on them as those accustomed to sewer travel were usually of the unsavory variety.

While every set of eyes noted her approach, no one accosted her. She saw entire families huddled around metal barrels and makeshift braziers, casting orange light from their fires and warding off the dank chill that seeped through clothes and deep into flesh.

Vera surmised they were fleeing the invaders. While the thought of their homes being pillaged filled her with unease, she was glad the refugees had something to keep them distracted. She doubted that she would have had such an easy time going through the sewers had they not.

There were three entrances to her destination, but the first two had people lingering about, and she did not want anyone else to discover it. She neared the third entrance leading into the sewers and felt a glimmer of hope. No light of a burn barrel shone at the dark dead end. She slipped her glow jar into her shirt and turned down the flame on her flamer to its lowest setting so that the light it created only illuminated a small area around it.

It took her a minute or two to find the loose stone in the wall. She pulled it out as far as it would go and turned it. A section of the wall opened just a crack. Vera set the stone back in its socket, pushed the door open wide enough for her to pass, and went inside. Phosphorescent lichen covered the walls, but its bluish glow was insufficient to illuminate the passageway.

A few steel crossbow bolts lay on the floor. Vera found the small holes bored through the stone and knew these were remnants of sprung traps. Since there were no bodies, she figured that time and the elements, or possibly rats, had sprung them. That did not mean that some might not still be active, so she proceeded with caution.

The passageway opened into an intersection. The four halls contained several rooms filled with ancient furnishings, rugs, and desiccated foodstuffs. As she had expected, no one had been here for a long time. Thirty-five years to be precise. Her father had told her stories about Azerick's old lair.

While it did not show on any of the city schematics she had studied, it was easy for her to figure out where it was. All she had to do was study what was shown and what was not but should be. The place stank of musty, decaying furnishings and needed a great deal of cleaning, but at least she knew she was safe.

CHAPTER 14

The last three days of riding had been an unflagging barrage of Daebian's verbal sniping broken up by long periods of awkward silence. Awkward for Azerick anyway. Daebian appeared as comfortable with the silence as he was the constant criticism.

Having reached the end of his patience, Azerick asked, "What is it I have done that makes you detest me so?"

Daebian stared ahead a moment as he thought. "At this point, I'm not sure I recall."

"Then why must you continue your disparaging remarks?"

Daebian shrugged. "Because I enjoy it."

"That is an unacceptable answer."

"Why?"

"Because I'm your father, and it's just plain lazy."

Daebian sputtered. "You're hardly my father."

"You refer to me as your father."

"I say it ironically."

"My blood runs through your veins."

"Blood is immaterial. It is about emotional and intellectual connections," Daebian countered.

Azerick nodded as he swayed with the horse's gait. "Ah, I see. So how is it you became so comfortable with incest?"

Daebian whipped his head toward Azerick. "What in the abyss are you talking about?"

"I consider Ellyssa my daughter, and I am certain she sees me as her father. You know, in an emotional and intellectual connection."

"She is not your daughter by blood. It is not incest."

Azerick grinned at his son. "I thought blood didn't matter?"

"It does for this!" Daebian turned almost sideways in his saddle. "You want to know why I hate you?" He lowered the dark glasses he wore to hide his black eyes and peered over the gold rims. "Because you gave me these. You are the reason I aged at a freakish rate, leaving behind what should have been a normal childhood in a handful of years. You gave me the ability to see the world around me as it truly is, in all its ugliness, without the filters normality creates to protect innocent minds as they grow. And when you finally returned and had the chance to help me, to guide me through the ugliness, you gave all your precious time and attention to Raijaun, because he was useful to you, and I was not."

"I see. Because I placed the needs of the many above those of the one, you feel it is proper to torment me?"

"Pretty much. The shit you gave me in the beginnings of my life entitles me to give you shit for the rest of your life."

Azerick nodded his head. "You may have a point. There is one thing I should have given you but did not that might have helped, and perhaps if I gave it to you now, it still can."

Daebian cocked his head. "And what would that be?"

"A proper ass whooping."

Daebian laughed. "You cannot be serious. Maybe when I was a child, and you possessed Klaraxis' body and wielded his power. But now? Not a chance. Not man to man. You are a pathetic imitation of what you once were."

"You think so?"

Daebian lowered his dark glasses. "I know so. I see everything, remember?"

Azerick flicked a finger, and an invisible force knocked Daebian from his saddle. "Did you see that?"

Daebian twisted in midair and landed with a measure of grace. He rolled to his feet and drew his sword.

"You want to test me, old man? Come and fight me like a man, without your tricks!"

Azerick swung from the saddle and slid his staff out of its holder. "Fine, but the same goes for you."

"I don't need magic to defeat you."

Azerick spun his staff around in his hands. "You think so, do you?"

"I know so. You are weak. Without your magic, you are nothing," Daebian replied as he circled his father.

"I was fighting for my life long before I knew anything about sorcery."

"I know the stories. I am not some thief or pathetic slaver."

"No, you're not. You're a spoiled little boy who has become a spoiled little man with daddy issues."

Daebian waded in, his face contorted in fury, his sword slashing and thrusting in a fierce attack routine. Azerick's staff whirled as his son forced him into a retreat. Enchanted sword and magical staff collided with showers of sparks as one resisted the force of the other. Azerick focused his attention on defense, unable to launch an attack even if he wanted to. Daebian's assault was too ferocious, his skill with the blade too great to overcome.

Sweat poured down both men's faces as the duel continued. Daebian's attack was reaching the ten-minute mark, and it showed little sign of abating. Neither of them spoke. Both focused entirely on the fight and unable to spare a thought or breath on pointless taunting.

Daebian's fury only mounted as he could not bring an end to the battle. He had fought some of the greatest swordsmen plying the seas and inhabiting taverns in a dozen foreign cities. None had challenged him as much as Azerick was doing at this moment, and the man was not even a fighter. Daebian determined he must be cheating. Somehow using his magic to increase his strength and speed in a way he could not detect.

Daebian began to feel the effects of fatigue and steered the fight toward the shadows created by the trees lining the road. Once the shade enveloped them both, he disappeared into the shadow ways and sprang out at Azerick's back. The move was almost instantaneous and gave him an open shot at his father's unprotected rear.

A shimmering portal opened between Daebian and Azerick. Unable to halt his lunge, Daebian leapt through and found himself where he had been but with his back facing his foe. He whirled around, slashing blindly with his sword. The arcanum ball at the end of Azerick's staff struck him in the midriff with the force of a mule kick and sent him flying headlong.

Daebian lay sprawled on his back, his hands over his stomach as he fought to regain his breath.

"You cheated," he said in a wheezing breath.

Azerick grinned at him. "You cheated first."

He reached down to help his son up, but Daebian swiped at his hand with his sword. Azerick left him on the ground and mounted his horse. Daebian recovered his breath and his feet and followed suit a minute later. The pair rode in silence for the better part of an hour before Daebian got over his petulance.

"Just so you know, I held back. I could have beaten you had we not chosen to limit ourselves," Daebian said.

Azerick chuckled under his breath. "You think so, huh?"

"Hey, I killed a god. I can damn sure defeat you if I really wanted to."

"You stabbed him in the back with a sword crafted by Sharrellan and designed to kill gods."

"Still…You did fight better than I expected."

"Almost three decades in the abyss, you learn a few things."

Daebian kept his eyes locked on the road ahead. "What was it like in the abyss?"

Azerick took a deep breath and stared into the distance. "You're surrounded by misery and suffering. As lord of the fifth circle, I felt it all. I felt the anguish of every tortured soul in that place. The denizens of that realm felt I was a usurper, that I did not deserve the title. Each day was a battle for survival. Not only did every demon on my plane want to devour my soul, I had the other rulers out for me as well."

"So not much different from what you left behind?" Daebian asked with a grin.

Azerick chuckled. "No, I guess it wasn't."

"Did you ever wonder what became of us after you left?"

"Every minute of every day. I knew life would be difficult for everyone, and I hated that I could not be there to help."

"Even me?"

Azerick looked over at his son and sighed. "Yes. Perhaps even more than anyone else. I understand your anger more than you believe. I know the darkness that lurks around the edges of that anger, waiting to pull you in and never let you go."

"How did you avoid it?"

"My compassion for others I suppose; placing more value on the lives of those I cared about than my own. Many times, I came close, teetered on the edge. Somehow, I always stepped back at the last moment. What about you? What kept you from taking that plunge into darkness?"

"What makes you so sure I haven't?"

"You're not the only one who can see more than what is in front of their eyes."

Daebian sighed and shook his head. "Mother, Ellyssa. Mostly Ellyssa. She never looked at me like a freak. Mother tried her best, but she could not hide it from me. It was there. But so was her love. I guess I did not want to disappoint either of them even if it meant being boring and predictable. I also could not stand the thought of proving you right."

"Right in what way?"

"Being hopeless, succumbing to the dark desires because I was too weak to resist them."

Azerick nodded. "It was one of my greatest fears, but you are probably the strongest man I know, Daebian, and I knew you could overcome the curse I passed onto you if that was your desire."

Daebian shifted in his saddle. "Can we find a different topic of conversation? Any more sharing of feelings and I am likely to start lactating."

Azerick pursed his lips as he thought. "We could badmouth Tim."

"Seriously! What was Mother thinking? The guy is as exciting as a plain cheese sandwich on stale bread, and it is missing the cheese."

"I guess she wanted someone safe and stable after what I put her through."

"Yeah, I get it, but she went entirely in the other direction. I mean, *Tim*? Sure, you have a stupid name too, but at least it is original and more than a single syllable."

Azerick threw up his hands. "That's what I said! I guess it's short for Timothy or something, but still."

"It's not! I had Ellyssa ask in one of her letters. It's just *Tim*. I guess even his parents knew he was going to be so dull that there was no point in wasting the effort or ink in coming up with a proper name."

"Awful."

"Horrible."

Father and son rode on with an unvoiced, tenuous truce between them. Azerick knew it was likely a temporary cessation of hostilities. Daebian had an acerbic personality by nature, and one would have better luck teaching a cat to bark than expect him to change. They were two days ride from Southport when a chill crawled up Azerick's spine.

"Something is watching us," Azerick said, turning his head to search both sides of the road.

"They've been pacing us for the last fifteen minutes just beyond the tree line."

Azerick tried to see past the dense foliage and deep shadows of early evening. "You can see them?"

"I told you; I see everything."

"Why didn't you say something?"

Daebian shrugged. "It did not seem urgent, and I wanted to see how far your weaknesses go. I have added poor eyesight to the list."

Azerick blew a frustrated breath out through his nose and shook his head. "Human?"

"Not even close."

"How many?"

"At least a dozen."

"Why haven't they attacked?"

Daebian jerked his chin toward the road ahead of them. "I imagine they're waiting until we get near the other group prepared to ambush us at the bend."

Azerick looked at the curve in the road less than a hundred yards ahead. "How many are there?"

"About the same number, more or less."

"Damn it! If we ride into the ambush, we're almost certain to lose the horses."

"We'll probably lose them regardless."

"Do you mind fighting dismounted?" Azerick asked.

"I prefer it. I do not mind having a rolling ship under my feet, but horses are unpredictable creatures."

Azerick stopped his mount and swung from the saddle. "Get down. I have an idea."

Daebian dropped to the road and held his horse by the reins. Both animals stamped their feet in agitation. They could sense the predators lurking just beyond their sight. Azerick slashed the air in front of him with his staff and tore open a portal. He slapped both horses on the rumps, urging them through the gate. The two animals obliged with only a moment's hesitation, figuring whatever danger the portal represented, it had to be less than whatever was stalking them.

Daebian looked at Azerick when the portal snapped shut. "Why didn't we go through with them?"

Azerick grinned at his son. "Because I wanted to see how far your weaknesses go."

Daebian glared at his father as he drew his sword and woke Klaraxis from his slumber inside the soul gem. "You'll find no weaknesses in me, old man."

Azerick laughed as he armored himself in several wards and prepared to meet the enemy. Realizing that their ambush had failed, the spawn exploded from the tree line with savage, bestial snarls, and howls. Red-skinned ravagers gripping short, curved blades in each hand ran on bare feet and knuckles. Daebian took several steps back in the face of their numbers and sheer ferocity.

Azerick made an up-thrusting clawing motion with his free hand and raised a field of stone spikes in the ravagers' path, impaling the ones in the lead. Those farther back and able to react, leapt high into the air and sailed over the deadly barrier. The ravagers' bound carried them twenty yards, and they dropped just before and right on top their prey.

Azerick reinforced his ward and added an electrical effect to it a moment before two of the creatures landed atop him. Bright sparks crackled around him as the two ravagers rebounded off the shield, patches of their red hides blackened and smoking. The sorcerer whipped his staff in an arc, striking several more creatures with an invisible wave of force while they were in mid-leap. The airborne ravagers reversed direction and went crashing back into the brush.

Daebian reversed his retreat and ran beneath the creatures that tried to pounce on him like a cat on a mouse. His advance put him within striking distance of the next closest creatures. His sword sang as it cut through the air before meeting flesh. Black blood flew from the blade as he performed a dance of death, ducking, dodging, and leaping out of the monsters' reach.

The second group of spawn abandoned their ambush and charged down the road. Azerick raised a massive wall of fire backed by another field of spikes, creating a deadly surprise for any creature foolish or brave enough to run or jump through the flames. Cries of pain cut through the air as several made the attempt.

Azerick had no time to witness the success of his trap as more ravagers converged on his position. He sent arcane bolts streaming into their midst, some with enough power to blast a hole clean through them. His eye caught a flicker of movement, and he spun just in time to deflect an obsidian knife aimed for his vulnerable back. The onyx blade opened a wide but shallow gash in his side. Azerick kicked the blue-skinned, goblin-looking creature in the chest. He recognized the spawn from the Gods War and knew how it had ignored his wards.

Runes carved into its body flared. Without a second thought, Azerick lifted the ripper with a magical hand and hurled it into a knot of ravagers skirting the wall of fire. It exploded with violent force, as its suicidal runes were meant to do, killing two of its brethren and maiming several more.

Daebian intercepted a ravager's slashing knife, removing the creature's arm at the elbow. He ducked low, spun in a circle, and lopped the leg off just below the knee of another. He squared off against three more of the creatures as they circled him. They had learned to be wary of his lethal blade.

The ground shook, and Daebian glanced toward his father thinking he had caused it with one of his spells. The look on Azerick's face indicated that it was not. The ravagers trying to surround him began backing away. Anything that made the murderous creatures hesitate gave him good reason for concern. Tall saplings folded over as whatever was coming bulled through the forest's edge.

Daebian's eyes went wide, and he scrambled backward. Had the ravagers not been trying to get clear, he would have retreated right into them. The creature was the size of a horse but bipedal and bore a vague resemblance to a bear with no forelegs and a thick tail that stuck out behind it as it ran. Its head and muzzle were wide, only slightly more so than its thick neck. When the devourer opened its enormous mouth and unleashed a bone-rattling roar, Daebian could swear he could see the creature's stomach at the end of the huge cavern.

Daebian's feet did not stop churning until his back fetched up against a tree. The devourer ducked its head, mouth wide to display rows of needle-like teeth the length of a man's finger. He caught a whiff of the creature's foul breath before he fell back into the tree's shadow. There was no way he was going to stand and fight such a monstrosity. Daebian decided the best tactic would be striking from the shadow ways, cutting pieces out of its shaggy hide and darting away before it could stomp him into a paste or swallow him whole.

From within the impenetrable darkness, he picked an exit point that put him at the creature's back, but a sixth sense sent a tingle up his spine. He was not alone. Daebian caught movement out of the corner of his eye as a black shape leapt from the darkness, its elongated fingers and nails like daggers protruding from its hands. He jumped away and felt a warm trickle of blood flow down his side. The shadow stalker melted back into the darkness where not even Daebian's unnatural sight could find it.

Azerick saw the devourer bearing down on his son and unleashed a stream of arcane missiles into its side. Other than scorching patches of bristly fur from its hide, the attack did little to harm it and nothing to deter its charge. Daebian disappeared into the shadows, leaving the devourer to crash headlong into the stout tree. The tree shuddered and dropped a shower of autumn leaves like giant orange and brown snowflakes. The devourer shook its enormous head before laying a baleful gaze with its beady black eyes onto the sorcerer.

With its original quarry having escaped, the monstrosity focused it ire upon the other human. It bellowed as its clawed feet churned the earth beneath it. Despite its size, the devourer was swift and agile. Azerick unleashed a continuous bolt of electricity but only grazed his target as it juked to the side without breaking stride.

The lightning bolt seared a stripe along its side, further infuriating the creature. Azerick opened a gate and escaped through, emerging at its exit point a hundred yards up the road. The devourer tore through the air where Azerick had been standing. Its claws sank into the road, tearing loose what few cobblestones remained on the neglected, dilapidated path. The creature tossed its head around in search of its prey and trumpeted an ear-piercing shriek when it found him.

Azerick summoned a shower of enormous ice spires that crashed into the ground with enough force to leave an aftermath of frozen potholes. The devourer danced left and right, avoiding most of the glacial shards. Those that struck home shattered against its broad back, bruising but not stopping it. Azerick was growing frustrated with his spells' lack of effect, and now a group of ravagers were trying to flank him. It was time to end this.

The sorcerer opened another portal in front of the rampaging devourer, swallowing the creature whole. Seeing the behemoth disappear into the gate, the ravagers advanced. Azerick let them approach to within a few yards before leveling his staff in their direction.

"Stop!" he shouted, his voiced laced with magic.

The ravagers stopped, hefted their blades, and hissed their hatred of the human. Azerick flicked his eyes upward and pointed at the sky. The ravagers looked up and caught sight of the plummeting devourer an instant before it crushed them. Blood, bone, and entrails erupted outward like a stone thrown into a bucket of water. The offal struck and parted around Azerick's ward, leaving a red and black ring of gore in the middle of the roadway. Azerick looked around and saw a few ravagers melting back into the forest, but there was no sign of Daebian.

The creature was swift, silent, and all but invisible. It was a situation Daebian was not accustomed to being in, and he found it disconcerting. The shadow spawn struck the moment he tried to leave the shadow ways, keeping him on the field of battle of its choosing. Only his quick reflexes, heightened by the power he drew from Klaraxis' soul stone, allowed him to keep the creature at bay and from inflicting more than superficial wounds.

Bleeding from several cuts, Daebian faked left before dashing to the right in an attempt to return to the prime material plane. He doubted the spawn could take Azerick down, but he hated not being part of the battle. It was less about concern for his father and more a point of pride.

The shadow spawn was not fooled by Daebian's feint and lunged. Daebian expected the attack, ducked, and spun, his sword slashing in a wide arc. The spawn leapt back into the deep shadows, hissing in pain when the human's blade found flesh. Daebian took another cut on the back of his shoulder, but this time he had given as good as he got.

I could really use some light, Daebian said, sending his thoughts to Klaraxis.

I am a creature of darkness as are you. There is no light within me to bring forth.

Maybe you could find another way to be useful. If you have not noticed, I'm having a bit of trouble.

Useful beyond improving your pathetic mortal abilities and being your greatest source of power? Klaraxis responded, insulted by Daebian's comment.

Yes, because those are not doing me much good at the moment.

You're still alive. I would argue they are doing a great deal.

Daebian was losing what little patience he had. *This really is not the time to argue. I need to see this thing so I can kill it.*

You rely too much on your vision.

I cannot hear the damn thing either! It does not make any noise.

Because you aren't listening. If it cries out, it breathes. If it bleeds, it has a heartbeat.

Daebian grudgingly admitted to himself that Klaraxis was right. He had always relied upon his preternatural vision. He closed his useless eyes, held his breath, and even slowed his heartbeat until it all but stopped. Without the sound of his own labored breaths and the oceanic sound of blood rushing through his ears, the silence was profound.

He turned his head, focusing his senses outward. To his right, just a few strides away, he could detect the dull thrum of a heartbeat and of lungs filling and evacuating air. A drop of blood spattered onto the ground like a roof with a slow leak. He stood stock still, letting the creature sidle toward his back.

Daebian could not hear the shadow spawn's movement, but he felt the air being displaced on the back of his neck and heard the heartbeat move closer. He ducked, spun, and thrust his sword out the instant the creature lunged in for the kill. Daebian's sword pierced its black heart as the spawn's blade nearly parted the hair on his head.

The shadow spawn released a final, shuddering breath and died at his feet. Daebian spared a second to spit on the creature before leaping out of a shadow several paces from where his father stood wrapping a bandage around a minor wound that was already clotting.

CHAPTER 15

Daebian looked at the pile of gore in the middle of the road. "What in the abyss happened here?"

"Spawn soup. Just add one part devourer, three parts ravager, and pulp thoroughly," Azerick replied with a grin.

"Subtle."

"What happened to you," Azerick asked, looking at Daebian's wounds.

"I got trapped in the shadow ways by a creature even more at home in that lightless realm than I am."

"Ah, shadow spawn. I'd read about them in the codex, but I don't recall seeing any in the war. There are similar creatures in the abyss."

"This will be an issue for me if it continues."

"I'm sure you'll figure it out. After all, you killed a god."

Daebian curled his lip and glared. "Your concern is touching."

Azerick shrugged. "I never was the nurturing type. Let me help you bind those wounds."

Daebian took off his shirt and let Azerick apply a poultice and bandages he kept in a pouch on his belt.

"Do you want me to kiss them for you too?" Azerick asked as he wrapped a strip of cloth around Daebian's upper left arm.

Daebian jerked his arm away and finished the job himself. "Mother's right. You are an ass."

Azerick pointed his finger at himself then Daebian. "Tree, apple. Remember?"

"Whatever. Can you open one of your portals to our horses, assuming they haven't been eaten or run on to Southport without us?"

Azerick slashed at the air with his staff and opened a gate. They stepped through the shimmering portal out onto the road a mile from their battle with the spawn. The pair looked around and found the horses standing with several people a hundred yards farther up the road.

Azerick raised his free hand as they approached. "Hello. Thanks for minding our horses. We had some trouble up the road."

The man holding onto Daebian's mount smiled. "We thought you might have. As to the horses, well, that's where we might find ourselves in a disagreement. These are our horses, but since we're such amenable folks, we'll sell them back to you and allow you passage on our road, assuming you've enough coin to purchase both, or either."

Three men carried weapons and looked like your typical roughnecks. The one woman in the group was a mage of moderate talent if Azerick's assessment of her aura was accurate. She could be masking it, as he did, but it was more likely that she lacked the skill or inclination to do so.

"There are five more nearby," Daebian said out of the corner of his mouth. "Two on the left side of the road and three on the right. Both groups have a wizard amongst them."

"Strength?"

"Not impressive, as far as I can tell. One is probably decent. I will kill him first."

"Let's try diplomacy first." Azerick's smile grew wider. "Ah, you're the highwaymen I've been told about. I was hoping to run into you."

"You'd be the first," the man replied. "Most folks do their best to avoid us. They more often than not fail and hand over their coin, just as you're going to do."

"I'm not most people, so I won't be doing that."

The man narrowed his eyes and studied the two men. "You from the Academy?"

"Not for a long time."

"Well, I got five men and three wizards that says you will."

Azerick's hand tightened around his staff. "Anyone who draws a weapon or readies a spell will have the rest of their lives measured not in years but in seconds. I suggest you and your people consider well their next course of action, because their lives depend on it."

The man, Joah, shifted his stance. He was not accustomed to being challenged, particularly with such confidence. "Who are you?"

Azerick raised his voice so that everyone could hear him. "Azerick Giles."

The highwaymen exchanged looks with Joah who said, "Azerick Giles would be near fifty, or sixty even, if he was still alive, which he ain't."

Azerick shook his head. "You've got it wrong. I was never dead, just gone. If you know even a fragment of my history, you should know looks can be deceiving, especially in my case."

A man of about thirty stepped from the trees onto the road and approached to within a dozen steps of Azerick and Daebian. He studied Azerick's face. "Master Azerick?"

Azerick tried to place the man's face, but he would have been ten years old at most the last time he had seen him, and failed. "It's me. You are?"

"Abner. Abner Porter."

Azerick nodded. "You were a student in my school. A novice, but skilled enough to control a construct during the war. I'm glad to see you've survived, but I'm more than a little disappointed at the life you've chosen."

Abner dropped his gaze to his feet. "It's been difficult, sir."

"Abner, you saying it's really him?" Joah asked.

"I think so. He's younger than I remember, but he was in the body of a demon then, so he could look like anyone he wanted I imagine."

"What do you want, *Azerick*?" Joah asked, not convinced of the man's identity.

"I need to speak with your leader."

"That ain't gonna happen. Marley doesn't take visitors."

"He'll make an exception."

Joah set his jaw. "And if I refuse to take you?"

"Then we go find him ourselves, but I won't be so diplomatic."

Joah turned his head, his gaze flicking between his people, those visible and the ones concealed nearby. "I still have three wizards to your one."

"I'm not a wizard, I'm a sorcerer, and they aren't enough."

Azerick stopped suppressing his aura and let its radiance shine to its fullest. Invisible to most people except Daebian and mages putting forth the effort to look for it, he shined like a miniature sun. It forced Daebian, even with his dark glasses, to look away. The bandit wizards gasped, whatever confidence and resolve they had shattered beneath its glare.

Shevon, the woman standing next to Joah, said in a tight voice, "Do as he says, or we are done in this life."

Shaken by Shevon's insistence, Joah licked his lips and nodded. "All right, but if you ain't who you say you are, you won't leave alive, sorcerer or no."

Joah whistled, and the other members of the bandit group emerged from hiding. They took up positions behind Azerick and Daebian while the others led the way. The three men carried heavy crossbows and wore longswords at their side. They did not return their horses, so Azerick and Daebian walked along with the rest of them.

Abner sidled up to Azerick but kept a fair distance between them. "Master Azerick, can I speak with you?"

"It's just Azerick. I'm no one's master."

Abner bobbed his head. "I was just wondering, what happened to you after the war? Some said you left with the gods and that you replaced Serron. Others said you gave yourself to Sharrellan and ruled the abyss by her side."

Azerick chuckled and shook his head. "I suppose the latter is more accurate than the former, but both are wrong. Because I inhabited a demon lord's body and wielded his power, I had to return to the abyss."

My gods-be-damned body! Klaraxis railed from inside his prison.

"So you weren't wed to the dark goddess?" Abner asked.

"That's...complicated."

"He was her joy toy until she tired of him and tossed him back to us," Daebian said.

If he's done with my body, then the goddess should return me to it!

Quiet, demon, Daebian commanded. *She gave you to me, and here is where you'll stay.*

Of course, Klaraxis cooed. *Where else would I want to be but by my son's side?*

A droning hum filled the air and drew nearer.

"Everyone off the road!" Joah ordered.

Azerick and Daebian followed the bandits as they dove into the forest. A moment later, a man astride a strange device flew overhead and disappeared in the distance.

"What in the abyss was that?" Azerick asked.

Joah said, "We don't know yet. That's the fourth one we've seen in the last couple of days. Don't know who they are or what they want, but it's best we avoid them."

"The flying machine is called a skimmer, or a glider. Definitely Glider," Daebian answered. "The skimmer hovers only a couple of feet off the ground and is the size of a wagon. They are vehicles used by the Order. If they are flying around, I do not think we will find good news in Southport."

"Do you know how they work?" Azerick asked.

Daebian shrugged. "Rune magic powered by mages from what I gathered, but many of their soldiers can also use them. The ones with arcane ability, anyway. Some of their weapons and shields work on a similar principle."

"I see what you mean by them being a formidable people. Soldiers with that kind of equipment would be a strong force," Azerick said. "How many did you say were chasing you?"

"The arcanus, what they call their mages, I spoke to, said their unit numbered near a thousand."

"How many of these arcanus?"

"He did not say, but I got the impression they do not rely heavily on magic for their battles. From what I have seen of their fighting ability, they do not need to. They are adept at countering mages, probably even sorcerers," Daebian said, giving Azerick a pointed look.

"Come, we need to stay off the road," Joah said, leading them deeper under the forest canopy. "It isn't much farther."

The group came to a stone archway inscribed with runes, similar to the ones Azerick had created to evacuate the cities during the war only smaller and simpler. Shevon lifted a pendant attached to a gold chain around her neck and pressed it into a matching relief. The archway's interior shimmered into a portal.

Abner saw Azerick looking at the arch. "We designed it after the ones you made. It can't take us as far, but it works just as well."

Joah led them through, tugging the horses after him as they resisted the thought of having to use a magical gateway once again. They exited in an area so similar to the one they just left that if it were not for the disorienting effects of gate travel, Azerick would not have known they had gone anywhere.

Daebian leaned his head toward Azerick and said, "There are several armed men and two more mages watching us from behind blinds."

"I can see the mages' auras through the foliage, but that's it. They're well-camouflaged."

"They certainly do not want visitors. I put it at even odds we have to fight our way out, whether they believe in the legendary Azerick Giles or not."

"I hope it doesn't come to that. I knew some of these people."

Daebian gave him a sidelong glance and grunted. "Hm."

"Hm what?"

Daebian shrugged. "I find it interesting that you place so much more value on a life because you are familiar with it. I thought with your vaunted moral superiority you would be above such a thing."

"It's natural to care more about people you know."

"Not for me, and if a person is truly good it should not for them either. The inherent value of a person's life extends beyond another person's familiarity with them, even someone who counts gods amongst their social circles. I have done a lot of traveling in my life, and I know the world is a bigger place than what is in my immediate reach."

He pointed at Joah's back with his chin. "Same with the people in it. Just because you do not know someone or value them does not mean that someone else does not. Every man might be a husband, father, or son to somebody. Does the value they place on that person not matter as much as yours? Why not, because you have a statue of yourself in every damn city?"

"I never said that, and I never asked for anyone to raise a statue of me anywhere," Azerick snapped.

"But there they are, and here you are with the men and women you might soon have to destroy."

"What is your point, Daebian?"

"My point is that it should not matter if you know them or not, but whether they need to die. They all share the same inherent value until their actions decree otherwise."

"You pose an interesting philosophical quandary, but you're hardly one to preach morality."

"Trust me, I am not preaching. They are all equally worthless to me. I would stamp the lives out of every one of them with no more thought or remorse than swatting a fly."

Joah stopped and spun around. "I can hear you! We can all damn well hear you, so I'd appreciate it if you didn't talk so freely about killing us."

Daebian twitched his shoulders. "I wanted you to know the likely consequences of your actions should you make a poor decision. If you did not want people discussing your imminent demise, you should have chosen a profession that did not draw the attentions of those willing and able to bring it about."

Joah looked as if to issue a retort, but words failed him, and he turned back around and stomped away. The others gave the two more space, moving away from them as if they carried a terrible disease.

"Sensitive bunch for highwaymen," Daebian said.

The forest opened into a grove containing several cabins surrounding what appeared to be a large hunting lodge. Sod covered the roofs of every building from which sprouted grass and even shrubs. Since the flying vehicles' appearance was a recent event, Azerick assumed it was to aid in hiding from mages trying to scry their location or seeking them out through other remote viewing spells.

Men and women sat or stood guard under trees and porches. A few children scurried around but stayed within sight of their parents. The group headed straight for the hunting lodge where several men stood beneath a sod-covered porch.

A large man blocked the steps. "What is this, Joah?"

"These two insisted on seeing Marley," Joah replied.

The man glanced at Azerick and Daebian before settling his confused look back on Joah. "Marley doesn't see visitors. You aren't supposed to bring people to the village. You know that."

"Yeah. This is a special circumstance, Kord."

"Who are they?"

Joah looked at his two guests and took a deep breath. "Best they tell Marley themselves. It's…complicated."

Kord stared at the two strangers a moment before deciding. "All right, but however this turns out, it's on your head. No weapons," he said to Azerick and Daebian.

Azerick shrugged, nodded to Daebian, and leaned his staff against the porch railing. Daebian unbuckled his belt and set his sword in the corner where the stairs met the raised porch.

"Nobody touch it," Daebian said as he wrapped the ends of his belt around the sword hilt.

Satisfied, Kord opened the door and entered first with three other men. Daebian and Azerick followed Joah up the stairs with the rest of his group trailing behind them.

Everyone turned around as a man's anguished and horrified screams filled the air. One of the guards failed to heed Daebian's order and touched the gem set in his sword's hilt. The man's hand was a blackened claw, and decay continued to climb up his arm as they watched.

Kord burst from the lodge, saw what transpired, and bulled through the group of people. Thinking fast, he drew his sword and hacked the afflicted man's arm off just above the elbow. Others leapt to the fore to staunch his bleeding. Kord turned and glared at Daebian.

Daebian shrugged his shoulders. "I warned everyone not to touch it."

Kord's teeth sounded like stone blocks sliding together. He held whatever threats he desired to make and stormed back into the lodge. It wasn't as if the newcomer was likely to be alive much longer. Marley did not take kindly to visitors.

The first floor of the lodge was an open meeting and dining hall. A stone fireplace sat at one side and had a fire blazing within its pit. Several people sat at tables nearest the fire. All eyes turned toward them as they entered. Several ravager and other monstrous heads adorned the walls.

"I see we have guests," Marley said. "Welcome to Freehold." He locked eyes with Joah, who wilted under his stare. "Why do we have guests? New recruits?"

Marley was a middle-aged man in his forties with long, wavy black hair and a short but full beard. He had the look of a man accustomed to power.

Azerick did not wait for introductions. "No, we are not here to join your band of criminals. We're here to convince you to put an end to your predations."

Several people in the room joined Marley's laughter. "Is that right? You wouldn't be the first. Who are you to make such a request of me?"

Azerick had no problem picking out the mages amongst the people in the hall. He stared each of them in the eyes before saying, "Azerick Giles."

The room filled with hushed muttering.

Daebian took a step forward. "And I'm Daebian Giles."

Marley looked him up and down. "His name I know. Never heard of you."

Daebian's face reddened. "Daebian Giles! I'm the only one in the Gods War to have actually killed a god," he sputtered. "Not even one of our gods managed kill one of the old gods!"

"Still never heard of you."

"Now I remember why I left this dung heap of a kingdom."

Marley returned his attention to Azerick. "Even assuming you are who you say, why should I accede to your request?"

"Make no mistake, it is an ultimatum, not a request."

Marley flashed a confident smile. "I have six wizards and a dozen hardened fighters just in this room."

"Like I told your man on the road, it isn't enough."

"No? There are nearly two hundred people in my little town, more than half of which are ready and capable of defending their home. Those fighting men and women are bolstered by more than a score of competent wizards."

Azerick shook his head, his face impassive. "Still not enough."

"How do I know you are who you say? Last I heard, the gods sent you back to the abyss."

"It's not the first time that place has spit me back out." Azerick looked around the room, picking out the faces of those able to wield magic. "One of your mages knows me for who I am. I'm sure others here remember me. Ask them what your chances are should you refuse me."

Azerick summoned his staff to hand and struck the floor with its butt to punctuate his demand. Those in the room gripped their weapons in tight fists or readied spells to defend themselves. Marley looked to his wizards, half of whom gave him a nod and wore looks of concern.

Marley's confident smile returned. "All right, I accept your claim, but I reject your demands."

Azerick met the man's smile with a steely gaze. "Are you sure? It would be imprudent for the last decision you make in this life to be a foolish one."

Marley continued to smile and wagged a finger. "I don't think so. You see, I know your history. Who doesn't these days? The hero of Valeria, right here in my home! You think we're just a band of highwaymen, picking on poor merchants and travelers on the roadway?"

He pointed an arm toward the door. "We provide a service to the people and to those same travelers. The only reason they have a chance of surviving their journey is because me and my people hunt those abominations that prey on them. Do we demand payment? Of course! There are families here just trying to survive; wives, children."

He leaned forward in his chair and pierced Azerick with his gaze. "You don't like what we do? Too bad! We do what we must to survive. The king can't help us. The city won't help us despite the fact we are the reason those creatures aren't climbing the walls in the middle of the night and slaughtering them in their sleep. Do they thank us? No, they label us as criminals. They sent soldiers and their precious Academy wizards to destroy us, but we're still here."

Marley swung his finger back to Azerick's face. "You see, that's the problem with heroes. Your conscience won't allow you to do what you have to do to stop us. Sure, people speak your name with the same reverence as the gods', and maybe you are everything the stories say you are and can snuff us out like that," he said with the snap of his fingers. "But there's no way you do it without killing everyone, those women and children who have committed no crime."

Marley looked triumphant when the sorcerer's face fell. He had seen the bluff and called him on it.

Azerick took a deep breath. "How many of you were at the Academy when the ravagers attacked it in the night and slaughtered so many of you?"

Several hands flicked up.

"I am responsible for that dreadful night. While it haunts me to this day, I would do it again, because I have always done, and will always do, what is necessary to protect the people. I sacrificed those children, because it was the only way I could get the Academy to act, otherwise we were doomed. Tell me if you think me unwilling to do what must be done."

Marley looked to his people and saw his support vanish. They would not fight this man. He shrank under Azerick's glare and hung his head.

"What do you demand of us?"

Azerick relaxed his posture. "I understand what you've done here, what you're trying to build. It's not that different from what I did in North Haven a long time ago. But you're building your home on a foundation of extortion, and it will inevitably collapse." He glanced at the heads on the walls. "You and your people hunt these things?"

Marley followed his gaze. "Damn right, and we've gotten good at it too. Joah and his team were on their way to check out a sighting when they must have run into you."

"It's a good thing we found them first. It was a large pack. More than a score in two separate groups. They were laying an ambush."

Marley furrowed his brow. "An ambush? Never seen them strategize before. That's a bigger host than we normally see too, at least in the last ten years."

"It's possible they were being directed."

"Directed? By who?"

"My guess is the Scions. It's possible they know of my return."

"You mean the old gods? I thought they were destroyed in the war."

Azerick shook his head. "No, merely defeated and imprisoned once more."

"Except for the one I killed," Daebian quipped. "Fed it to my demon."

Marley inspected Daebian with newfound respect. "He's serious about that?"

"Yeah, but it's best to let it go or it will go to his head," Azerick replied.

"Needs to be going to everyone's head," Daebian muttered.

"How do I support my people?" Marley asked.

"Just as you have been. Collect your tolls, but properly and with fairness. I'll speak with the people who control the purse strings in Southport and North Haven and get them to funnel resources to you and your village. It's the least they can do."

Marley scoffed. "You think you can get them to do anything?"

"I can be very convincing."

Marley nodded. "Yes, so I've seen. All right, Lord Giles. I'll tell my people the new rules."

"I'm no one's lord anymore."

Marley responded with another nod, glad to be rid of the honorific that stuck in his throat. "Not to be rude, but now that our business finished, I expect you'll want to be on your way."

Azerick smiled at the man's obvious dismissal. "We have urgent business in Southport."

"I think you might find an invading army has disrupted most business in the city."

"What have you heard?"

"Not much. We have people in Southport and other cities who inform us of things of importance. Some of them fled Southport when the invaders came. The castle was under siege and the Academy was silent. Now we see flying machines overhead at least a few times a day. Reconnaissance is my guess."

"Then the city has fallen," Azerick said in a hollow voice.

"Most likely."

"Then our business is now more urgent than ever."

"I'll have Joah show you out."

"We can make our own way."

"Yes, I'm sure you can," Marley replied, his voice deadpan.

Azerick and Daebian left the lodge. Daebian found his sword untouched where he had left it. With Southport potentially occupied, Azerick decided it was best to leave their horses in Freehold. He opened a portal that deposited them back on the road. Marley's news troubled him. If the city and the Academy had both fallen so quickly, the Order was a far more formidable enemy than he had thought. An unusual feeling came over him, one he rarely experienced; doubt.

CHAPTER 16

Vera spent the entire night and most of the morning hard at work with the alchemy set. She was not a mage like her siblings or even a fighter. Her weapons were her mind, courage, and her determination, and she needed to employ them all if she would have any effect on the situation that had unfolded last night.

Most people in her position would have been overwhelmed by the chaos of finding their school and city under siege, but Vera was not most people. She knew life, no matter how many obstacles it might hurl in her path, was nothing more than a series of single events. All she needed to do was to resolve the challenge before her and move on to the next one until she reached her goal.

Last night, while terrifying, had been no different. She needed to get out of the school so she could find out about her family and defeat the invaders. First, she had to get past the soldiers to reach her room so she could procure her things. Then she had to get out of the Academy, find a place to hide, and craft things that would help her defend herself. Now, she was ready to seek her family, get information about the invading army, and figure out a way to drive them off.

While a seemingly monumental task, once broken into its constituent elements, it became manageable. The last step would be a significant challenge, but she did not have to worry about it until she had completed the ones before it.

Fatigue brought on from lack of sleep and the heavy demands she had been placing on her mind was the current task at hand. That one was easy to resolve. She spiked a large cup of coffee with a special brew she had learned to concoct years ago to allow her to spend most of the night studying. It was how she had crammed some twenty years of experience and research into ten years of academic pursuit.

Now that she was alert, if a bit jittery, she needed to find out what had happened to her family. Vera left her secret lair while it was still light out. Darkness would help her move through the city unseen, but she knew those who controlled the city probably established a curfew. From what she had seen from the soldiers in the Academy, it was likely that the common people within the city were not all under arrest. There was no sense in risking being caught out at night and getting arrested if she could simply walk down the street to her home.

Vera stored several small vials of various concoctions inside her coat. The larger ones she carried in a small haversack slung over her shoulder. She chose an exit that deposited her in what records stated had once been a warehouse but was now nothing more than a stone foundation littered with debris. Pieces of rotted wood, bits of stone, and dirt slid off the trapdoor when she opened it.

She blinked against the sudden light and peered through the narrow opening before throwing it wide and climbing out. Vera kicked the debris back onto the hatch to keep it hidden. This area was dilapidated and mostly abandoned before the war and was worse off now than it had been. Or maybe better. She could not be sure.

There were several collapsed buildings but also shacks built from their remains along with newer materials desperate people had collected to create shelter. The bedraggled citizens stood in doorways or peered through glassless windows, but only a few ventured outside. Vera paid them no more attention than they gave her as she headed toward the castle. Her home was located near the castle's inner curtain wall, so it would be a long walk.

She could have used the sewer system to take her closer, but there were elements, both human and otherwise, Vera wanted to avoid. She also needed to get an idea of what was happening throughout the city first-hand. The streets were ominously quiet and all but deserted. Most of the shops were closed, and people stayed in their homes. She spied several foreign soldiers stationed at key intersections or patrolling the streets, but none did more than give her a cursory glance. Vera looked up at the sound of a low droning coming from overhead. A strange metal machine looking vaguely like an enormous bird with short wings and a soldier seated in a saddle on its back flew overhead.

Well, that's interesting, Vera thought to herself.

She received another surprise when a horseless wagon floating two feet off the ground and carrying a squad of Order soldiers glided by. When she reached the merchant district, she saw that a few enterprising people had set up their stands as if it were business as usual, taking advantage of the new customers within the city. Vera had not made it far into the quarter when a squad of soldiers stopped her.

"You there, girl, come over here," a soldier ordered.

Vera cast her gaze around the market. There were few locals out, and those that had decided that the business they needed to conduct outweighed whatever risks leaving their homes posed, looked away and cast their eyes to the ground. Vera knew the expression. It was the look of a defeated people.

She kept her eyes on the cobblestones ahead of her as she walked toward the soldiers. Vera hunched her shoulders and bent her knees, further shrinking her tiny, five-foot frame.

"Yes, sir?" she asked in a quiet voice.

"Do you have your papers?"

"Papers? What papers?"

"All citizens must take the oath of allegiance before being allowed on the streets," the soldier said. "Where are you going?"

"I was going home, sir. I was staying at a friend's house when you attacked the city. I didn't know about having to get papers."

"The Order does not attack cities, it liberates them."

"Yes, sir, my apologies. It was so very frightening. I just want to go home to my family."

"Where do you live?"

"In the upper ward. My father is, or was, the minister of finance."

Vera knew using her father's position was risky. She knew through history books that a conquered city often retained some of the senior governmental positions, as long as they swore fealty, to use their influence and knowledge to create an easier transition for the conquering army. There were also instances of entire purges of heads of state and their families to remove any chance of rebellion.

The soldier's stance relaxed, and Vera knew she had chosen correctly. "Go straight home and then find a registrar. There's one just outside the castle gates. Go nowhere else but those two places until you get your papers."

"Yes, sir, I will. Right away."

Vera hurried toward her home. She noted every guard station and patrol she saw so she could plot them on a map later. She slowed her pace whenever she spotted a patrol so as not to draw attention. Vera reached her home and found the gates locked, so she pulled the cord that rang a bell inside the house.

Her mother flung the gate open a moment later and ran out to wrap Vera in her arms. "Oh, thank the gods you're all right! I've been worried sick."

Vera craned her head to look past her mother and saw her grandparents and two armed men standing in the courtyard. "Where's Father?"

Colleen ushered her daughter into the courtyard and locked the gate. "He went looking for you and your brother and sister when these soldiers attacked the city. You haven't seen any of them?"

"No. I escaped the Academy last night. The soldiers ordered everyone to their rooms. I assume Trisha and Elias are still there if they haven't come home. Maybe Father is with them."

Colleen clutched her fist to her chest. "I fear you are right."

"I'm sure they'll be fine. I didn't hear any fighting at the Academy. From what I understand once they take this oath of fealty they'll be let go."

"No, not the wizards."

"What do you mean?"

"The Order has issued proclamations. One of them is that anyone with magical talent is taken to their homeland for indoctrination training. After that, they're conscripted into their army along with one out of five men of fighting age."

Vera bit her bottom lip. "I don't see Father going along with that."

"Neither do I, and if they have him..."

"I must get them out."

Colleen gasped. "You can't! You're not—"

"What, a powerful wizard like Father and his favorite children?"

"Vera, you know that's not what I mean."

"Isn't it, Mother? I got out of the Academy on my own, and I can get back in. I'm not as helpless as everyone around here thinks."

"No one thinks you are helpless, but you aren't as strong as they are. That's not an insult or meant to be demeaning. It's just a fact."

Vera narrowed her eyes. "Then it's a good thing there's no problem in this world that can be solved by strength that can't be worked out with intelligence and determination."

"Vera, I never said—"

"I know what you said and I know what you meant, Mother." Vera turned around and bobbed her head as if looking for something. "Apparently I need to go get some papers in order to walk around the city."

Colleen spun Vera around by the shoulder. "You can't break the oath. These people are fanatical when it comes to oaths. It's a death sentence. There are already people hanging in the streets near the castle."

"Did you swear the oath? Do you have your precious papers?" Vera asked in a challenging voice.

Colleen stiffened her back. "We all did. We had no choice."

"Really? All? Do you think Father did as well?"

"If it meant protecting his family, you're damn right he did."

"I guess we'll find out when I rescue him and my siblings."

"Vera, please!"

Vera ignored her mother's pleading, threw open the gate, and stormed away. She had always been a willful child, particularly when it came to her mother. Not being magically gifted like her siblings, Colleen had tried to mold her into something like herself, a Lady who attended parties, wore gowns, and mingled with polite society. By the time Vera was five, it was clear she would have none of it.

It was her father who read with her and pushed her to learn everything she could when he was not busy tutoring Trisha and Elias with their magical studies. He had told her she could be anything she wanted and gave her everything she needed to become whatever she desired. As much as Vera loved attending school at the Academy, she missed reading with her father, and she would not let these people take him away.

Her stressful encounter with her mother had caused her breathing condition to flare up, but she refused to let her mother see it. Vera waited until she was outside the gate before digging through her satchel and retrieving her spray bottle. She squeezed the rubber bulb and inhaled the mist, which cleared up her lungs in just a few seconds.

Despite her frequent use of the Academy's secret passageways, Vera had no desire and little skill to go skulking around the city, so she headed toward the castle and find this registrar. She would take their stupid oath, get her papers, and figure out a way to free her father.

Her courage waned when she saw the first bodies hanging from hastily erected gallows. Each one had a sign dangling from their neck declaring their crime. At least half were oath breakers.

By the time she reached the long line stretching out from the registrar's table, she saw almost a dozen gruesome hangings, and her courage fled. Her mother had been right. These people were serious about their oaths. Vera turned around and walked away, deciding that it was better to risk getting caught without papers than breaking the Order's oath of allegiance.

Vera had almost made it back to the merchant district when she rounded the corner and collided with an Order soldier. His hand snaked out and grabbed her upper arm as he readied his spear. He relaxed when he saw it was just a girl and not an insurgent. While the city was largely pacified with little in the way of battle, the corpses hanging in the squares was a testament that not everyone welcomed the Order's beneficent presence.

"Watch where you're going, girl," the soldier snapped.

"Yes, sir. Sorry." Vera pushed her glasses higher on her nose. "I don't see that well."

"Have you taken your oath and gotten your papers?"

By the gods, these people had a limited vocabulary. Go to your room. Where's your papers? She thought to herself.

"No, I was just on my way to do that."

The soldier tugged on her arm. "I'll take you to the nearest registrar."

Vera tried to pull away, but the man did not ease his grip. "I can find it. No need to bother yourself with me."

"It's no trouble. My station is near the registrar in this district."

It was a problem for her though. Fed up with being manhandled, Vera reached into her coat, selected a vial, flipped the cap off with her thumb, and pressed the saturated sponge lodged in the opening to the hand clamped around her arm.

The soldier jerked has hand away and rubbed at the wet spot. "What was that?"

"That was a paralytic toxin extracted from sea snake venom. You should lose control of your muscles right about—" The soldier crumpled to the ground and lay perfectly still, his eyes wide with fear. "—now."

Vera replaced the cap on the vial and put it back in her coat. She looked around for the quickest way off the street. The few people out on the streets stared at her and the fallen soldier in shock and silent applause. A cry broke the silence as a squad of soldiers pushed through the crowd that seemed intent on getting in their way without looking as if it were intentional.

Vera sprinted down a side street with the soldiers pounding after her. She ducked into every narrow passage she came across, but whenever she thought she had shaken her pursuers, another group appeared and forced her to run once more. Her airway began seizing up again and forced her to stop for another dose of medicine.

One of the strange flying machines appeared and hovered over her. The man astride it shouted and pointed. Vera took off, but the glider kept pace and reported her location to the soldiers on the ground. She burst out of the alley almost into the waiting arms of a patrol. She ran the other direction with the soldiers close on her heels. Vera was never much of an athlete, and they were closing fast.

She ran down another narrow passage and erupted out onto a side street. The glider hummed overhead, and she continued running, darting into a narrow fissure between two buildings. A wagon loaded with bundles of straw blocked her path. Dropping to her hands and knees, Vera crawled beneath it and out onto the street. She reached into her coat, pulled out two glass vials, and hurled them against the cobblestones beneath the wagon.

The bottles shattered with a whoosh of combustion when the two chemicals mixed. The soldiers on the far side slid to a stop as the wagon and its contents burned. Vera snapped her head around when more men ran at her from down the street, shouting for her to stop.

Vera snorted as she thought, *Like I'm going to do that.*

She took off at a dead run, but her breathing was getting worse, and she was becoming weaker and slower by the second. The chase was winding down, and not in such a way that was likely to see her escape.

Vera loped into another alley, sprinting its length before barging out onto another secondary path. The pursuing squad was close on her heels, and she had only a second to choose her next route. She ran toward another narrow gap between buildings when the sound of a wagon's creaking wheels behind her made her look back. The heavy cart rolled forward, blocking the alley she had just vacated and the men chasing her.

The soldiers cursed and shouted as the men maneuvering the wagon struggled to hitch it to a recalcitrant horse. Not questioning her good fortune, Vera turned away but stopped when a pair of men beckoned her from the narrow egress.

"Come on, girl, unless you'd rather try your luck with the soldiers," the taller of the pair said.

Figuring she had more in common with these men than the invaders, Vera hustled across the street. The men pulled her farther into the alley before one wrapped his arms around her and the other dropped a sack over her head.

"Let me go you rancid dung heap!" she shouted as she kicked her feet and struggled to get away.

One of her captors grunted in pain when one of her flailing feet caught him in the shin. "Stop your struggling or we'll give you to the soldiers!"

"What are you doing with me?"

"Taking you away from this place. Someone wants to talk to you."

"I can walk, and I don't need a sack over my head to talk!"

The man holding her set her feet back on the ground but maintained his hold on her arms. "It's how he prefers to make introductions. Now be quiet and play nice so we can get you someplace safe—and *secret*."

Vera concluded these men might be part of a fledgling resistance group, which explained the sack. She did as the man told her and ceased her struggling. If they proved to be a danger, she had things in her pack and jacket that might convince them to let her go. The men guided her through several buildings, never taking more than a few steps outside. Twice her ears picked up the sound of one of the flying machines, and they rushed inside and waited for it to pass before moving again.

They guided her through buildings and across streets for another fifteen minutes before descending a set of creaking steps. Someone pulled the hood off Vera's head and freed her arms. She righted her glasses and looked around. In addition to her escorts, two men stood next to the stairs, and two much older men sat behind a large desk.

The old man seated off to the side was nondescript other than being perfectly bald. He looked to have once been a large man, but age had shrunken him down. The man sitting in the desk's center appeared to be the same age, close to seventy was Vera's guess, but that was where any similarity ended. He was shorter and dressed in fine clothes and sported several pieces of expensive jewelry.

He traveled his eyes up and down Vera's form and looked unimpressed. "My name is Andrill. And who might you be?"

"What do you want with me?"

Andrill looked over at Braxis sitting in the chair an arm's length away. "Youth these days, no appreciation of pleasantries."

Braxis twitched his shoulders and grunted, failing to open his disinterested eyes more than halfway.

Andrill returned his sharp gaze to Vera. "What is your name, girl?"

"Vera. Why bring me here?"

"I heard you had done a fine job of stirring up our new masters. I instructed my men to bring you to our secret lair should it appear they would capture you. I believe the term you are searching for is thank you."

"You expect me to thank you for putting a sack over my head and kidnapping me?"

"I like to consider it more of a rescue than a kidnapping. As for the sack, well, this is a *secret* lair. I can't have just anyone knowing its location, particularly considering the new regime. Many of the people decorating the gallows were my men. I could appreciate their remarkable talent in conquering, pacifying, and enforcing their laws upon the populace if it weren't so bad for my business."

"Secret lair?" Vera looked around the chamber. "You mean the hidden basement beneath the Sow's Ear buttery room?"

Andrill's eyes narrowed to slits, and he pursed his lips. "What makes you think that is where you're at?"

"I counted my steps and noted my bearing whenever we made a turn. I have an excellent sense of direction. My father often joked that I was part homing pigeon. I'm also familiar with the city's layout and technical drawings of many of the buildings in it. It was simply a matter of tracking my direction and distance traveled, even when they doubled back several times to throw me off. Also, you got the information about my flight almost immediately, which means you must have been close by. Couple that with the tavern's smell, and it wasn't that difficult to figure out."

Andrill smiled, but it was not a friendly gesture. "Clever girl, but your cleverness poses a problem for us both. Yours being the greater one."

"How's that?"

"I can't allow you to leave with the information you now possess. Moving about the city is difficult at the moment, as you well know."

Vera felt her chest tighten, and she drew in deep, wheezing breaths. "I need my medicine," she said, and gestured to her rucksack.

Andrill shrugged. She set the pack on the floor and retrieved a flask wrapped in thin rope to prevent it from rattling around and breaking, followed by a small vial from her coat pocket. She flipped the wire latch off the cork sealing the flask and removed the stopper from the vial.

Vera tilted the vial and held it over the flask's mouth. "I think you'll want to change your mind about killing me."

Andrill grinned and raised his eyebrows. "By mixing me a drink?"

"No, by mixing these two chemicals and creating a gas so toxic it will kill everyone in this room in seconds and most the people upstairs in a few minutes, at least those too slow or stupid to leave when they start to spasm."

"Now why would a young girl be carrying around something like that?"

"Just in case I run into an old man like you."

Andrill stared at the odd girl for several long moments and, much to Vera's surprise, began laughing. "Braxis! Did you hear that?"

Braxis sat unmoving, his chin tucked against his chest and his eyes closed. "Yep. Gonna kill us all."

"I'm not joking. If I pour these together, we're all dead." Vera looked over her shoulder. "Those by the door could get away, but you two won't, even if you hold your breath."

"You won't either," Andrill replied.

Vera shrugged. "Doesn't really matter does it, given the problem I've created for you?"

"You remind me of someone I once knew more and more. I struck a deal with him, much to my favor, and I am thinking perhaps I should do the same with you. Put away your poison and let's talk."

Vera moved the vial away from the flask but continued to hold them in her grasp. "What do you want to talk about?"

"Why were the soldiers chasing you? They don't seem to bother most folks as long as they take their silly oath and don't cause trouble. What did you do to rile them up?"

"I refused to take their stupid oath and caused trouble."

"I certainly see that. Why have you chosen to oppose our conquerors? You are clearly the academic type and don't look to be the typical rabble-rouser."

Vera tried to control her anger, but her posture and voice were tense. "They're holding my family in the Academy. At least my brother and sister, but possibly my father as well."

Andrill leaned forward. "Your family, they're wizards?"

"Yes, and my mother said they'll be shipped off to wherever they came from to indoctrinate them and make them fight their wars."

Andrill stared at Vera, his fingers tapping on his desk. "Vera...Vera Cossington?"

Vera turned her head and glared out of the corners of her eyes. "How do you know me?"

"Your father is Franklin Cossington, known as Rusty to his friends. He succeeded his father as the city's finance minister. I apologize for not recognizing the name. That's the problem with dossiers I suppose. Hard to put faces to names."

"Why do you have a file on my father?"

"I have reports on every citizen of note within the city and elsewhere. Information is a commodity, and often more valuable than gold. It is my stock in trade, along with a few other frowned upon activities, but information is my primary business. It's the one thing, other than prostitution, that is immune to market fluctuations."

"Since you know who my father is, then you know people will come looking for me if I disappear."

Andrill waved a hand in the air. "I wasn't going to kill you...probably not. I just wanted to gauge your reaction. As I said, I liked what I had heard of your run from the law and thought we might be able to help each other. As usual, I was right."

Vera gave him a petulant look. "How do you figure?"

"You'll need help to free your family from the Order's clutches, and I need help kicking their asses back into the sea. I think a few score of powerful wizards just aching for revenge might accomplish such a monumental task."

Vera curled her lip. "They weren't much help the first time. What makes you think they'll do any better the second go round, if they're even willing to try?"

"We were taken by surprise. They neutralized the militia, Watch, and Academy before the battle even began. And I wasn't helping them. This Order is the most professional military I have ever seen, and I wager that is because they have a great deal of experience fighting other armies. I would also wager they are not accustomed to dealing with people like me and my organization."

"You mean sneak attacks."

Andrill rolled his eyes. "In laymen's terms, yes."

Vera grinned. "I know a little about sneak attacks."

Andrill lifted his eyebrows and looked at the chemicals in her hands. "I thought you might."

Confident the thieves would not murder her just yet, Vera put away her concoctions. "What do we do first?"

"Information is the key to any battle. My people are out studying troop numbers, guard emplacements, and movements. I need to get eyes onto the Academy grounds to see what we're up against. It will take time to learn what we'll need to launch a successful jail break and secure a safe place for everyone, but time is not on our side. Your mother was correct, they are scheduled to be shipped off the moment reinforcements arrive."

"What do you want me to do?"

Andrill twirled a finger toward her pack. "You concoct whatever nasties will help us deal with the soldiers and anything else you think might advance our goals. Do we have a deal?"

Vera did not have to think long. As confident as she was in her abilities, she knew getting back into the Academy would be a lot more difficult than getting out had been. She needed the resources and skills Andrill brought to the equation.

"Deal."

Andrill clapped his hands together. "Wonderful! With the right information and a bit of divine intervention, we may well live to toast our success."

CHAPTER 17

Azerick stared at Southport's closed gates and the plumed helmets of the men guarding it from the parapet. "That bodes ill for the city."

Daebian nodded his head. "What little I'd seen of these soldiers, I expected the city would fall, but not this fast. What now?"

"We knock on the door," Azerick replied with a grin.

When they got within a hundred feet, a soldier atop the parapet shouted, "Stay where you are. This city is closed to all traffic."

"By whose order?" Azerick called back.

"By the divine command of the emperor and empress of Syrna."

"I do not recognize their authority in this land. On behalf of King Miles of Valeria, I demand your people leave this city, without plunder or prisoners."

Daebian glanced at his father. "That's a bit presumptuous of you, don't you think?"

Azerick shrugged. "I'm sure he would have said much the same thing if he were here."

The soldier shouted back, "There are no kings. There stands no man nor gods above the emperor and empress. Return whence you came and prepare to embrace the Order when we come for you. Your lives will be better for it."

"I'm really starting to dislike these people," Azerick said to Daebian.

Daebian nodded. "They have a way about them that truly gets under the skin. Now what, oh legendary sorcerer?"

Azerick raised several protective wards and drew in the Source. "I knock harder."

Daebian looked at his father and shook his head. "I don't recommend it."

His warning came too late, not that Azerick was of a mind to heed it. He thrust his staff forward and launched a silver ray of power at the gate with all the strength he could muster. The beam struck the barrier with little effect other than a loud clunk before the gates swung slowly outward.

Daebian frowned. "Well, that was spectacularly disappointing."

Horns blared as Order soldiers marched out through the gates, their ranks moving in perfect lockstep.

Azerick grimaced and raked lightning across their front ranks, the bolts so brilliant they dazzled the eyes and lit up the area like a second sun. The soldiers halted. A shimmering nimbus surrounded their shields. The lightning struck the wards with another brilliant display but did no damage to the troops on the other side.

"Buggering hell!" Azerick shouted as the soldiers advanced once more.

"Told you," Daebian quipped.

He clawed at the ground with arcane fingers and tore rocks and cobblestones from the earth and sent them sailing skyward. Seconds later, they returned as flaming meteors trailing smoke streamers. The soldiers tilted their shields upward as blazing rocks bombarded the squad and surrounding area with fiery, kinetic energy. The meteors cratered the ground around the men and shattered against their wards.

"I'm sure you don't want to hear this anymore than I wish to say it, but I suggest a hasty retreat," Daebian said.

Azerick glared his fury at the invaders before replying with a curt nod. He began casting one last spell hoping to slow down the enemy. Before he could complete it, javelins arced out and formed a rough ring around him and Daebian. Electricity struck him from every side the moment he tried to release his spell. Azerick's muscles locked up, and he cried out in pain.

Daebian grabbed him by the arm and urged him to run. "Sorry, I should have mentioned that!"

Azerick and Daebian raced toward the woods as the soldiers gave chase. Two of the Order's flying machines zipped over the wall and joined the pursuit. Azerick felt the Source return the instant they ran clear of the javelins. He tore open a gate and pulled Daebian in after him. They emerged deeper into the forest, leaving the soldiers far behind.

"Well that was a colossal bust," Azerick said as he caught his breath.

"I told you so."

"You said that already."

"Yeah, but I thought the scope of your failure warranted a second mention."

Azerick grudgingly nodded his agreement, but the droning sound of the gliders cut off his verbal response. "Damn it!"

He ripped open another portal and jumped through, closing it the instant Daebian followed. Within minutes, he heard the gliders' unmistakable sound once more.

"You have to be kidding me!" Azerick shouted and opened another gate. "They must be able to track the magical emanations of the spell. Stay on my heels. This will be…intense."

In a rare show of unquestioning obedience, Daebian followed his father through the rift. Even as he was stepping out, Azerick was opening another, and another, and another until Daebian found himself looking at the shimmering image of his own backside.

"Whoa, now that's just plain disturbing," Daebian said.

"It's going to get worse."

Thick plumes of fog rolled out of the end of Azerick's staff in a haze so thick Daebian could not see his hand in front of his face.

"Grab the end of my staff," Azerick ordered.

"Regardless of your opinion of my quasi-incestuous inclinations with Ellyssa, I am absolutely not grabbing your staff."

Azerick jabbed the butt of his staff into Daebian's stomach. "Grab hold, smart ass, and try to stay on your feet and hold your lunch."

Before Daebian could question him, Azerick pulled him through one gate and into the next. Azerick had conjured several portals in a massive circle, like points on a compass, covering several square miles. Daebian kept ahold of Azerick's staff with as much effort as he exerted to contain the contents of his stomach.

Azerick continued to race through the rifts, spewing dense fog until it blanketed a massive swath of the land in white mist. Daebian was stumbling drunkenly and ready to let go of the staff, and his lunch, when Azerick finally stopped. He was only slightly pleased to see that Azerick was almost as unsteady and sickly as he was.

"Let them find us now," Azerick snapped as he braced his hands on his knees and fought to catch his breath.

Daebian stared into the fog. "Don't be too pleased with yourself just yet, Father. We aren't alone."

Azerick's head snapped up and stared into the thick vapors. "Surely not the soldiers?"

"No, I'm afraid not. I think you might be a spawn magnet."

"There may be more truth to that than you know. If the Scions are able to sense my return, they will likely put a lot of effort into killing me."

"If this is to be our last battle, there is something I wish to tell you."

Azerick moved closer so he could see his son's face. "What is it?"

"I told you so."

"Now is not the time!"

Daebian shrugged. "I think it's important to make time for the things that matter most."

"You'll forgive me if I feel your priorities are a bit skewed."

"Hm, no, I don't think I will."

"Under the circumstance, I suggest you elevate our current predicament to your highest priority."

"And I suggest you duck."

Azerick furrowed his brow. "What?"

He barely registered the movement out of the corner of his eye before the ravager leapt out of the fog. Azerick reacted swiftly, but not fast enough to avoid being struck. His quick reaction caused the ravager to hit his ward at an angle, but it still sent Azerick lurching. Daebian's sword flashed, and the spawn's blood spattered Azerick's ward like rain on a window.

Disoriented by their recent, and excessive, gate travel, the hard nudge caused Azerick to stumble to his hands and knees. He raised himself up and circled his staff overhead with an angry snarl. Frost formed in a wide ring around them before ice spires erupted from the ground like massive crystal shards. Yelps and other cries of pain issuing from inside the billowing haze rewarded his efforts.

"I know fighting like a man is distasteful to you, but if the Order is able to detect magic being used, it may be best to keep it at a minimum," Daebian said.

"Kicked your ass," Azerick grumbled but deferred to his son's logic and set himself for melee combat.

The spawn leapt over or crashed through Azerick's ice field and attacked with a concerted effort. Father and son stood back-to-back; their weapons held in tight grips as they awaited the onslaught. While Daebian could see the attackers approach, there were too many of them to defend against, so Azerick extended his ward to envelope Daebian. While doing so weakened it, it still created a substantial, but far from impregnable, barrier.

Daebian's sword darted in and out, piercing the ward and creatures like a needle through fabric. Ravagers slammed into the arcane shield and clawed and stabbed at it with talons and knives, chipping away at its defenses. Whenever a blade or appendage broke through, Daebian's sword was there to meet it, forcing the attacker to draw back, often with one less hand than it had started with. While his defense was strong, it was not perfect, and more than once he was too slow to prevent suffering a wound but, so far, they were minor.

Azerick morphed a short but thick blade onto the end of his staff, hacking and stabbing at any ravager that came within range. A lucky break in the fog allowed him to catch sight of one of the blue-skinned monstrosities, the runes on its flesh glowing with cerulean light, leaping toward him. His spear launched from his hand under its own stored power like a ballista bolt and caught the creature in its chest in mid-flight, hurling it back into the miasma before exploding. The staff returned to its master's hand with a thought.

"I think we're seeing the last of them," Azerick said as he thrust his weapon into a ravager.

The attacks had decreased, the number of spawn rushing them dwindling to a trickle.

Daebian shook his head. "No. More are gathering just out of sight. Out of your sight anyway. I suggest we retreat again. Fighting these creatures gains us nothing."

"Each one we kill is one that cannot threaten someone else."

"Let that be their problem. You set us on this mission, so we should focus on that."

Azerick hated the thought of leaving these creatures to wreak havoc on the countryside, but from what he had heard, it was not a new phenomenon, even if he was a new focal point. But Daebian was right. He was already fatigued by having created so many gates, and every minute they spent fighting spawn increased the chance of the Order finding them once again.

"All right, but it's another round of gate travel," Azerick said.

"If you can manage it, so can I."

"I'll try to place our exit point inside the walls. Hopefully, the city hasn't changed so much that we emerge somewhere we don't want to be."

"Like inside the castle?" Daebian asked with a grin.

"I was thinking more like inside the castle wall," Azerick replied, wiping the smile off Daebian's face.

Azerick slashed at the air with his staff and opened another series of rifts. Daebian grabbed ahold of the butt of his staff when Azerick prodded him with it.

"Wait, won't—" Daebian began to say, but Azerick pulled him into the portal and cut him off mid question.

Azerick's mounting exhaustion showed as he could only create half a dozen gates. He stumbled to the ground when they passed through the last one and spat out a mouthful of bile. Daebian wavered on his feet but maintained his balance as he glared at his father.

"As I was saying, won't these people investigate any magical surge inside the city, and why in the abyss didn't we exit here first?" Daebian snapped.

"Because I had hoped to enter the city by more mundane means instead of risking the possibility of transiting somewhere undesirable, like in the middle of their barracks," Azerick replied just as sharply. He had not considered the likelihood of the Order checking out any use of powerful magic within the city, but he was not about to admit it to Daebian.

Daebian opened his mouth to reply, but shouts and blaring horns made him snap it shut. He grabbed Azerick by the arm, hoisted him to his feet, and pulled him toward the crude shacks. Azerick had brought them to the squatter's district, a place he knew well. While much of the old structures had been destroyed or salvaged, the new ones looked much the same. Only the faces peering out of the glassless windows had changed, and they bore the same haunted eyes, bereft of hope, that Azerick remembered.

"We need to get off the streets," Azerick said as he scanned his surroundings.

Daebian pulled him behind a crumbling wall. "I'm open to suggestions. Preferably one that does not involve fighting our way through those pricks."

Azerick looked around and tried to make sense of the wreckage surrounding them. "See that tumbled down building over there?"

Daebian followed Azerick's eyes. "Yeah."

"Can you take us through the shadow ways and put us about ten feet beneath that support beam?"

"Beneath it?"

Azerick nodded. "I assume they can't track your shadow-stepping."

"Not that I'm aware of, but you're asking me to perform a blind exit, and I can't guarantee we'll be alone in there."

"Would you rather deal with them?" Azerick asked, dipping his head toward the sound of clanking armor and the pounding of heavy boots.

"Yeah, I suppose you're right. All right, get ready."

Azerick stood up from behind the wall and raised a field of stone spires in the legionnaires' path. Their shields might make them invulnerable to his magic, but it didn't help them pass through obstacles.

He ducked back behind the wall. "Let's go."

Daebian grabbed Azerick by the arm once again and pulled them both into the wall's shadow. Blackness as deep as when he had been trapped inside his own mind by the psyling enveloped him, and it took considerable willpower not to panic. Azerick focused on keeping his breath steady and tried to slow his rapid heartbeat. He conjured a brilliant light at the end of his staff, but the darkness seemed to trap it like a bug in a jar, not letting it shine more than a few inches from its source.

"By the gods, can you see anything in here?" Azerick asked.

"Sort of." Daebian stopped so abruptly that Azerick bumped into him. "Crap. We're not alone. I was afraid of that."

"You can see them?"

"No, but I know they're there."

"Should I put out my light? It doesn't seem to be doing much."

"Does it make you feel better?"

"A little, yes."

"Then it's doing something," Daebian replied. "The shadow spawn can see us regardless of the light. They're coming."

"What do you want me to do?"

"Fight, but whatever you do, don't let go of me. If we get separated, you can travel a long way in a short time, and I might never be able to find you."

Azerick took a deep breath and let it out slowly. "Lovely place you have here. Give me a direction and distance if you can."

Daebian focused on his senses, particularly those not possessed by most mortals. "About twenty meters and drawing closer."

"Which direction?"

"All of them."

Azerick grimaced and swung his staff over his head and ringed them in a wall of fire. Like his light, he could see the flames, but they illuminated nothing more than a few inches away. He spied several glistening black forms caught within the inferno as they screeched in pain and leapt away to vanish back into the abyss.

"Did I do any good?" Azerick asked in an urgent voice.

"Not really."

Daebian knew the creatures could meld into the darkness and bypass the flames. He had no more finished the thought when the creatures sprang from the shadows. Most of the shadow spawns used their freakishly long, taloned fingers as weapons, but a few wielded obsidian blades, their glossy, onyx form so similar to the spawn themselves.

Daebian swung his sword in a swift arc that hissed like a willow switch. A pair of night stalkers cried out when his blade found their inky flesh. While his sword cut deep, it was Klaraxis snatching a piece of their life force away that caused the greatest pain. Daebian filled his other hand with a long dagger and parried a third clawing attack as he spun out of reach of two more.

Azerick tried to stick to his son's side as he stabbed out into the darkness with staff and magic, but a shadow spawn leapt out of nowhere and struck him head on at the same time Daebian spun away. He tumbled into the impenetrable darkness and grappled with the spawn as it tried to rake its claws across his face and throat. The sorcerer grabbed at the slashing hand, caught it in his grip, and sent a surge of arcane power coursing up the creature's arm until blue fire erupted from its mouth.

He shoved the charred corpse away and rolled to his feet, spinning around and swiping blindly with his staff. Azerick conjured as bright a light as he could make to hover just over his head. While almost blinding, it still left his knees and feet shrouded in darkness. He watched one creature step back with a hiss just before it slashed at him with its obsidian knife. He was elated to find that his light had some effect on the shadow spawn even if it were minimal.

While the brilliant orb had saved him from one attacker, his distraction allowed another to dart in from behind and inflict a cut across his back. Azerick struggled to reinforce his wards, but these were creatures born of magic, created by powerful gods, and his wards were far from invulnerable to their attacks. He was also tiring. His own stores of energy were all but depleted and he had been drawing power from his staff, but its reserves were not infinite by any means.

Azerick suffered another raking claw attack when he spun around to face the first one, but it had vanished back into the gloom before he could even catch sight of it. He lashed out behind him at the newest source of pain, but his staff met nothing but emptiness. Azerick knew he needed to do something to either make these creatures visible beyond an arm's length, or slow them enough to give him time to react.

A smile crept onto his face at the thought of a distant memory, a memory that brought with it a pang of remorse for the loss of Duchess Mellina's old guard captain, the first victim claimed by the spell he was about to inflict on these abominations. Since he could not see them to target them, he needed to fashion the spell so it affected everything within a large area. He suffered two more shallow wounds while he fit the pieces of this newest arcane puzzle together. There was no grand spectacle of light or fire, just a slight reverberation echoing out into the nothingness.

Azerick held his breath and listened. In the span of a few heartbeats, the sound of a jingling bell intruded upon the silence and was followed by several more all around him. The chimes sounded with every step and movement the shadow spawn made, giving Azerick a good idea as to their direction and distance, thus defeating their greatest asset.

He stabbed out at the nearest jingle and laughed aloud when his staff pierced the chest of a charging shadow stalker. Azerick cackled with glee as he whipped his blade-tipped staff in wide arcs, cutting and driving back the horde of spawn trying to take him down. His success flushed away fear and fatigue as the monstrosities fell around him or retreated deep into the shadows. Azerick stood still, listening for the sound of chimes over his heavy breathing, but no more attacks came.

"Daebian!" he shouted into the darkness.

His son's muffled shout came back to him. "Father? Where are you, and why in the hell am I jingling?"

Azerick grinned. "Over here!"

"Stay put. Don't move."

Azerick did as he was told, and within moments, he could hear bells approaching. He could tell by the tone and frequency it was likely his son, but he would not let his guard down in this hellish plane and held his staff at the ready. Daebian's face appeared out of the darkness when he came within an arm's length from Azerick.

"What did you do?" Daebian asked. "Not that I'm complaining. Being able to hear them made them much easier to fight."

"An old trick."

"I don't suppose it will last forever?"

"No, but it will linger for several days, at least on the ones I inflicted it upon."

"I assume you can remove it from me?"

Azerick bobbed his head from side to side. "Well, I could, but I think it suits you. Makes you more approachable, less dour and threatening."

"End this accursed jingling, or I'll show you threatening."

Azerick untied the threads of magic clinging to Daebian. "You need a sense of humor."

"I have a fantastic sense of humor—when it's at the expense of others." He took Azerick by the arm. "Let's get out of here before more come. Ones that don't sound like sleigh bells."

They walked for less than a minute before stepping out into a narrow, dank passageway. The interior was gloomy, but compared to the perfect darkness of the shadow ways, it appeared as brilliant as the streets above.

"Ha, nailed it!" Daebian crowed. "I am awesome!"

He took another step into the passage only to find that they had exited a shadow about a foot off the floor. The unexpected drop caused Daebian to stumble and fall onto his hands and knees.

Azerick hopped down and stood over his son. "You're right. That was great."

Daebian slapped at Azerick's proffered hand, stood on his own, and took a step forward.

Azerick tried to grab his shoulder. "Wait!"

The warning came too late, and Daebian stepped on one of the old floor plates in Azerick's lair. Azerick dove forward and tackled his son from behind, riding him to the ground. But instead of the crossbow bolt he expected to shoot out of the wall, sticky liquid poured from a pair of holes in the ceiling just above them. The two fluids exploded into foam the moment they came in contact with one another and hardened into a pumice-like stone an instant later.

"Oh yeah, great save, Father," Daebian snapped as he struggled to break free.

"So much for you seeing everything."

"Obviously I wasn't looking!"

"Obviously," Azerick replied. He looked up at as a bespectacled girl carrying a device with a flame licking out of its end appeared. "Who in the abyss are you?"

"I'm Vera. Who the hell are you?"

"I'm Azerick Giles," he replied with as much bravado and dignity as he could muster.

"I thought you were dead or something."

"Irrefutable proof that birthday wishes never come true," Daebian said with a sigh.

"Could you get us out of this please?" Azerick asked.

Vera pursed her lips. "If you're Azerick Giles you could get out on your own."

Azerick huffed. "Look, I'm tired, we've been chased and fighting…everything, and I would rather not expend the effort if I don't have to. So, could you get this stuff off of us?"

"I could. But you might make a better piece of art than a visitor. I think I'll name it *Two Curs Humping*."

Azerick glared at the back of Daebian's head when he chortled. "You think this is amusing?"

"I didn't until picturing it just now. You know, you need a sense of humor," Daebian replied.

"Vera, please. We're here to help," Azerick said.

"Fine," Vera replied and walked off. She returned a few moments later carrying a watering can. "If you try anything, I will torch you." She squeezed the trigger on her flamer and shot a gout of fire from its tip as a warning.

Azerick assured her once again of their good intentions and behavior. Vera set her flamer down to free her hands and poured the liquid from the watering can over the two trapped men. The concoction washed away the artificial stone like it was sand.

"Oh, gods!" Daebian cried. "Why does that stuff smell like fermented ogre piss?"

"Probably because it is," Vera replied. "Except it's mostly horse with a bit of human urine mixed in. Ogre urine would be much more effective, but it's difficult to procure. It might also cause chemical burns."

"Oh yeah, this is so much better," Daebian quipped.

"Yes, I should think so."

Enough of the hardened foam washed away that Azerick was able to climb off Daebian's back and stand, soon followed by Daebian. Vera set the watering can down and picked up her flamer, giving it a few more pumps for good measure.

Vera turned and beckoned to the men over her shoulder. "Come on. I have some fresh water you can use to wash off the smell."

Daebian rapped his knuckles against a hardened piece of his shirt. "I'm pretty sure our clothes are beyond salvaging."

"Probably, but I don't have anything here that would suit you in either size or fashion," Vera replied.

She led them into the central chamber that Azerick knew well. The alchemic apparatus resting on a table drew his attention, and he forgot about everything else.

"Hey, that's my alchemic set."

"No, it's *my* alchemic set. My father gave it to me for my seventh birthday."

"Your father? Wait, are you Rusty's youngest child?" Azerick asked.

"I am. I've read your notes on the formulas you had created. I found many of them mediocre at best and improved upon them."

Daebian looked at Azerick with a wide grin. "I think I'm beginning to like her."

"And who are you?" she asked.

Daebian drew himself up. "Daebian Giles. Azerick's son."

Vera traveled her eyes up and down Daebian's body. "Huh, I thought you would be bigger and more...demonic."

Daebian's shoulders slumped. "That would be my brother Raijaun."

"Oh, is he coming? We could really use his help."

"Hey, I killed a god!"

Vera recoiled from Daebian's outburst. "With what, your breath?"

Daebian opened his mouth and snapped it shut. "I don't think I like you anymore."

Vera clasped her hands under her chin, her eyes wide and her voice pleading. "Oh no, whatever shall I do? Where will I ever find another man in a sewer, reeking of horse piss?"

Azerick laughed. "Now *I'm* starting to like her!"

"Oh good, even if we all become enslaved by the Order, I will still be filled with joy knowing you view me with favor."

"And now it's gone."

"I'm coming back around," Daebian said.

Vera snapped her fingers. "Hey, how about we rise above the schoolhouse game of who likes who and focus on something important, like the fact an invading army has captured the city and is holding my family prisoner while they wait to ship them across the sea where I'll probably never see them again."

"You don't have many of friends do you?" Azerick asked.

"I don't need friends. Friends are just a distraction from things that are important and people who have haven't screwed you over yet."

"Amen to that, sister!" Daebian said.

Vera glared at him. "I am not your sister."

"Clearly. I would have drowned you at birth," Daebian grumbled.

Azerick steered the conversation to a more immediate topic. "Vera, how did the city succumb so easily? What happened to the mages at the Academy?"

"From what I've learned, the wizards were the first to fall. It was a smart strategic move as they presented the greatest challenge and support to the soldiers of the city. Although, given what I've seen, I'm not sure it would have mattered much. We might still be fighting, but it would be a losing battle."

"How did they neutralize them?"

"They created a magic dead zone. From what I understand, no one inside the Mage's Academy's main building can so much as light a candle using magic."

Azerick nodded. "I've recently experienced their ability to counter magic wielders firsthand. The fact they can block access to the Source over such a large area is troubling. Where do they plan on sending them and why?"

"These people make everyone swear an oath of allegiance. Breaking that oath, meaning acting or even speaking out against the Order, is a death sentence. The Order is on a crusade to eradicate the spawn."

"That's good," Daebian said.

"But their mantra is there is the Order and enemies of the Order."

"That's bad," Azerick replied.

Daebian added, "Yeah, I heard that one myself. They're pretty fond of it."

Vera continued. "Most of the common people conscripted into their army take additional oaths and are divided up amongst loyal units. They shackle anyone with magical aptitude to control their power and ship back to their homeland for indoctrination. After that they send them off to fight either spawn or nations not yet subjugated by the Order, and there are few of those remaining from what I've heard."

"And that's what's going to happen to every mage at the Academy?" Azerick asked.

"Yes, as well as the Martial Academy officers and children of influential or powerful people."

"And they have your family?"

Vera nodded. "My father, brother, and sister."

Azerick clenched his jaw. "We have to free them. Do you know when they're being moved?"

"Not until their main force arrives, and I don't think we have much time."

"What can you tell us about their forces, particularly around and within the Academy?"

"Follow me."

Vera led them to a side room. A large map of the city covered a section of one wall, and a map of the Academy adorned another.

"There are approximately a thousand enemy soldiers in the city," Vera said. "Of those, we've only seen a handful of wizards. A dozen, maybe as many as a score. We haven't had much time to get a good count, but their shackles make them easy to identify. I've marked most of the static guard stations and their numbers on the map and the timing and routes of patrols."

Azerick looked at the map and the information Vera had written in the legend. "You did this? It's very impressive."

Vera shook her head. "I didn't gather most of the information myself. I'm working with an old, creepy thief named Andrill. He has a good network of people doing most of the legwork. I mostly sit down here and make stuff like my foamstone trap and other concoctions that might come in useful."

Azerick's eyes widened. "Wait, you know Andrill?"

"Yeah. Why, do you know him?"

"Yes. We're acquainted."

"Good. He's a suspicious sort, and I wasn't sure how he'd react to me bringing in new people."

"I'm still not sure how he'll take it, but we'll cross that bridge when we come to it. What about the Academy? Do you know what we're dealing with there?"

Vera shook her head. "Not really. It's difficult to know since it's almost impossible to get inside. Our best guess is three shifts of twenty or thirty soldiers. That's what we've seen coming and going."

"That's it?" Daebian asked. "They don't seem very concerned about the wizards getting loose."

"I can see why," Azerick replied.

"To be fair, these are not regular line units. The emblems on their breastplates are different, and so are the plumes on their helmets. I'm getting the idea they specialize fighting mages."

Daebian looked at Azerick. "And sorcerer's too."

Azerick nodded. "I imagine so. Given how effective their standard patrols were at neutralizing my magic, I'm not eager to tangle with them."

Daebian flashed him a fake, sympathetic frown. "I know, it must be awful to actually face a challenge. It must really take you out of your comfort zone."

Azerick countered his son's condescension with a glare. "I've triumphed in the face of challenges you cannot even imagine, boy."

"You two want to stand around here waving your swords at each other to see whose is bigger, or are we going to go rescue my family?" Vera snapped.

Azerick tapped the butt of his staff against the floor. "I think it's obvious whose is bigger."

"Compensate much?" Daebian asked, twisting his mouth into a sneer.

Vera snatched her flamer from the table, sparked a striker at its nozzle, and shot a meter-long gout of flame at the two men.

Azerick raised his hands and took a step back. "All right, let's go see Andrill."

CHAPTER 18

Vera led them through the sewers, exiting at one of Andrill's secret locations located in a warehouse. The trap door opened inside a large shipping crate just tall enough to walk in if one hunched over. The back of the crate opened into a hidden room of a connecting building. Several men stood around or sat at a couple of small tables. Their postures stiffened when Vera entered the room and elevated to alert when Azerick and Daebian followed behind her.

Most of them relaxed a bit when Andrill stood. "Azerick my boy, is that you?" He nudged a slumbering Braxis sitting next to him. "Braxis, look, it's Azerick!"

Braxis snorted, his rheumy eyes flying open as he jerked awake. "Huh? Fire!"

Andrill patted him on the shoulder. "No, no, nothing like that."

Braxis relaxed, sank back into his chair, and closed his eyes.

"By the gods, you're so young! You look like the last I saw you. How is this possible?"

"Just as you said, by the gods," Azerick replied.

"And who is this with you?"

"This is my son, Daebian."

Andrill's face fell. "Ah. Too bad you didn't bring the girl with you. She was most impressive. I hope she is well and not too angry with me. I still feel awful for what I did to her."

Daebian's face colored. "Hey, I killed a—"

Azerick laid a hand on his shoulder and shook his head. "Nobody cares."

Daebian scowled and muttered, "I care."

Azerick ignored him and returned his attention to Andrill. "She is well and holds no grudge. We had to leave her in North Haven in case these invaders decided to expand."

Andrill looked grim. "I am sad to say that is precisely their goal. The good thing is that they do not appear to be planning any expansion until their fleet arrives."

"We need to get word to the king. If we can oust this advance contingent and display a large enough show of force, perhaps the Order will leave us be."

"It's certainly our best option, but from what little we have learned of these people, it is a thin hope at best."

Azerick frowned. "That's unfortunate, but let us focus on the matter at hand. If we're going to have any chance of driving these people away, we'll have to free the prisoners at the Academy."

Andrill nodded. "I assume our young friend here has filled you in on the details?"

"She has."

"Quite the mind on that one. I feel a great deal better about our chances of success with your help."

"And mine," Daebian said.

Andrill looked at the man, noting that he carried a sword, and looked unimpressed. "Yes, I'm sure."

Azerick broke in before Daebian could reply with either words or blade. "Daebian brings a lot to any fight, and given these people's ability to negate my magic, possibly more than I do."

"There's no maybe about it," Daebian said.

Andrill shrugged. "We can use all the help we can get."

"Your enthusiasm is staggering," Daebian replied.

"Andrill, I assume you have formulated a plan?" Azerick asked.

Andrill nodded and directed everyone's attention to a series of maps and sketches tacked onto the wall. "The central facility, where we believe the mages and students are being held, has been cordoned off by whatever devices they use to negate magic. There are about two score soldiers guarding the interior grounds with reserves just minutes away, so a frontal assault, even with your power, is likely a suicidal mission doomed to fail."

"I have to agree with you," Azerick said. "The soldiers' defenses are too strong. We need to get our people out without the Order knowing we were even there."

"Precisely what we had planned. Vera has an extraordinary knowledge of the campus and just about every building, street, and sewer built in this city. We'll go in much the same way she got out, by traveling beneath the streets and coming out inside the Academy grounds."

"Can we get to them from the tunnels?"

Vera shook her head and pointed at a large, circular room depicted on one map. "The only place with enough space to contain all the magic students and faculty while maintaining security is the auditorium, and there is no direct access to it by sewer or hidden passageways. It's also nearly in the exact center of the nullification field."

"So their location is more than just a hunch?" Azerick asked.

"It is," Andrill replied. "I have people on the inside that are able to get messages to me. It's how we know their strength and many of their guard points. They aren't allowed anywhere near the auditorium, so I cannot say for certain what you'll encounter once inside."

Azerick nodded. "All right, so how do we get in?"

Vera poked the map with her finger and traced their route. "We follow the sewer to one of the access points in the central building's sublevel rooms. There are only two, and I have to assume they found the one I used to escape, or at least know of its general existence and increased security around it. That leaves this one. It's an undercroft beneath the chapel. It's packed full of old furniture and temple stuff, so it probably hasn't been thoroughly investigated. We'll be in the open here, here, and here, but we can traverse the rest of the route using the secret passageways."

Azerick studied the diagram as she talked. "I assume we'll get our people out the same way?"

Vera nodded. "Optimally."

Azerick digested the information and sighed. "If we get caught, especially inside the null magic area, we're in a lot of trouble."

Andrill leveled his gaze on Azerick. "Don't get caught."

"Easier said than done," Azerick replied. "These people are clearly professionals, not some slack-jawed local watch or militia." He tapped a finger against his chin. "How do they create the magic dead zones?"

Andrill traced the auditorium's exterior with his finger. "They have placed several silver spear-like rods around the building. Most of them are on the outside grounds, I assume at the farthest point to cover as much area as possible while still being effective. My people have counted about a dozen in total."

"Could they get to them and remove them?"

Andrill took a deep breath and held it a moment. "They would almost certainly get caught, and that's a death sentence."

"I imagine the same is true for all of us."

"Not so. They consider us enemy combatants and afford us a certain amount of leniency. It is only after you have taken their oath that acting against them brands you as a criminal. The only way my people were able to remain inside the Academy was to take their oath. If they catch them acting against the Order in any way, their judgement and execution will be swift."

Azerick considered Andrill's words, something that would have required no thought not long ago. His answer was the same regardless of his rediscovered humanity.

"Andrill, your people have accepted the possibility of dying for this cause. If the Order catches us freeing the mages, we are almost certain to fail. What are our chances of driving them from the city if that happens?"

Andrill looked at the table and shook his head. "None."

"They're your people, and I'll leave their orders to you."

The old guild boss nodded. "I'll get a message to them before dark. If the guards raise an alarm before you've had time to get the wizards clear, they'll do their best to bring down the devices."

Azerick laid a hand on his shoulder. "Thank you, Andrill. I promise you; I will do everything I can to keep your people safe as well."

"I know you will." Andrill sighed. "I'm getting too sentimental in my old age."

"You and me both."

Azerick was only passingly familiar with the city's sewer system, and that bit of knowledge mostly extended to the area around the squatter's and common districts. He had no idea of where they were in relation to the streets above, but Vera appeared fully aware of their location as she unerringly led them beneath the Academy grounds.

When heavy iron grates barred their passage, Azerick knew they were nearing their destination. Not wanting to alert the Order's magus by using magic, Vera splashed her caustic acid on the bars, weakening them enough that Azerick's morphed arcanum blade hacked through them with relative ease.

Azerick knew they were close when he detected several wards protecting the passageway. With no other choice, he dismantled them, plucking apart the magical threads holding them together. He was not concerned with his actions alerting anyone to their presence. It was a passive act that required no real magic on his part, and anyone they might have notified was likely a prisoner inside the magical dead zone and would not feel obliged to inform their captors even if they knew of the wards' destruction.

Andrill had sent four of his best people to accompany Azerick, Daebian, and Vera. As master thieves, their dislike of not taking the lead was evident, but Vera's knowledge of the sewers and Academy grounds surpassed even theirs, and they were not much help with dismantling magical wards.

This being a mission of stealth, the four thieves were chosen for their skill over brawn. They were lean, fierce, and smart. Keaton and Baldur were indistinguishable in their dark clothes and face wraps. Devin stood out as the tallest of the group. Keanna, as the only woman, was thinner and shorter. A discerning eye would notice that she moved even more fluidly than her dexterous and graceful male counterparts.

Their subterranean excursion ended at the foot of a short set of stone steps leading to a door about half the height of an average person. The four thieves emerged from the darkness like shadows. Other than Daebian, no one would have known they were with them without having had prior knowledge of their existence.

Devan checked the door for mechanical traps after Azerick declared it free of magical wards. A few seconds of prodding unlocked it, but something on the other side kept it from opening. Devan pushed harder, wincing at the sound of the obstacle sliding across the floor. It was pitch-black inside, but Vera transferred a liquid from one glass vial into another, creating a greenish light that illuminated enough of the room for them to navigate past cloth-draped furniture and an assortment of objects crammed into the undercroft.

Their passage disturbed the dust covering everything, creating a haze that tickled uncovered noses and irritated lungs. Vera, Daebian, and Azerick envied the thieves' face wraps as they fought to keep from sneezing or coughing. The thieves crept up the stairs without a sound, but the steps creaked terribly under the weight of the others.

Devan held a finger to his covered lips before pulling the door open. He peered through the crack before opening it wider and stepping into the room. The others followed behind him and found themselves in a small aps chapel. Being late at night, the chapel was empty and dimly lit. As Devan led the way through the circular temple, keeping close to the wall, they noted that the massive, gold disc representing Solarian, the sun god, was gone, as were the relics and decorations depicting any of the gods.

They skirted the chamber until reaching a side door leading into a narrow hall containing the priests' rooms. There were only a few chambers set aside for the resident priests as the temples housed their own students. Vera pointed to a tapestry, behind which it hid a secret door. They hurried inside the narrow passageway as the sound of booted feet echoed down the hall.

"Did you see they struck the temple icons?" Devan asked. "I imagine they'll be putting up statues of their emperor and empress soon. Theirs is the only worship they allow."

"How do you know so much about them already?" Azerick asked.

"We've a keen intelligence service."

"And they give everyone a pamphlet," Vera added.

Devan grinned and shrugged. "That helped too."

Azerick arched his eyebrows. "They have pamphlets?"

Vera nodded. "They want everyone to know the law, their history, and their motivations."

Azerick grunted. "They're very progressive for conquerors."

Keanna scowled. "Bunch of gobshite propaganda, and the stupid ones fall for it hook, line, and sinker. They'll sing another tune when they start taking their family and half of everything they earn, grow, or make to fight their wars."

"We'll pack up their pamphlets and send them off with whatever remains of their army," Azerick vowed.

"Better to leave them in the privy where one could put them to proper use," Daebian chortled, earning him a few muffled chuckles.

The group shuffled through the narrow passage before Vera stopped them at another concealed door. "We'll have to traverse three halls to reach the next passageway, and there's bound to be soldiers in at least one of them."

Vera's assumption proved to be prophetic. Devan held his hand out behind him and extended three fingers as he peered around the corner at a small group of Order soldiers. Keanna, Keaton, and Baldur moved just behind him. The three men readied hand crossbows. Keanna pulled out a light repeating crossbow from under her dark cloak and readied a bolt by working the slide attached to the underside of the carriage. The weapon was not powerful enough to penetrate armor stronger than boiled leather, and its range was limited, but she could launch half a dozen quarrels in as many seconds.

Devan looked back at Azerick. "I would very much like to get closer. Their armor creates a lot of openings, but at this range we might not get the three of them before one sounds an alarm. Maybe you want to take them down with your magic?"

Azerick shook his head. "They might sense any use of magic. They're certainly looking for it this close to their wizard captives."

"I can help," Daebian said.

Daebian moved to the front, peeked around the corner, and sought out the magical lights affixed to the walls. He tapped into the power of Klaraxis' stone and used its dark energy to steal away the light. Shadows deepened, especially where the walls met the floor.

"Tell me when the shadows are sufficiently dark," Daebian whispered.

Devan looked past him. "That should suffice."

Daebian stepped back, and the thieves moved forward, diving into the shadows without a sound. The soldiers stopped talking and stared down the hall.

"Did it get darker?" one asked.

"It's night. Maybe the lights are supposed to dim," another answered.

"They didn't last night."

"What's the matter, you scared of the dark now?" the third needled.

The twang of the thieves' crossbows issued down the corridor. The first four shots sounded as one, followed by three more loosed quarrels from Keanna's repeating crossbow. The soldiers gave a sharp bark or grunt of surprise, but the thieves' virulent poison stole the air from their lungs and the life from their bodies before they could do little more.

Azerick saw the look of restrained horror on Vera's face as they stepped past the corpses. "Best get used to it. There will be a great deal of death before this is over."

Vera steeled herself. "I can handle it! I'm not a weak, silly girl."

"Perish the thought," Azerick replied with a wink and grinned.

Vera returned his look with a scowl, uncertain if the sorcerer was making fun of her. The thieves dragged the bodies into a nearby study room and hoped no one came upon them until they were far away with their freed captives. Vera guided them down two more halls, avoiding a roving squad, and entered another secret passageway.

Azerick stopped mid-step. "I've lost my connection to the Source."

"We're getting near the auditorium," Vera said. "This passage will take us to the connecting corridor."

Azerick nodded and pushed onward. He had expected this, but it was still a disconcerting feeling. He imagined it must be what a fish out of water feels like, or a bird with its wings clipped. Azerick refused to let it trouble him. He had experienced such a thing on more than one occasion in the past and triumphed. This would be no different.

The only bright side, ironically, was the increased darkness. When Vera led them into the next hall connecting to the corridor leading to the auditorium, they found the magical glow lights extinguished and oil lamps and candles in their stead. This created for gloomy, shadow-filled hallways, the natural environment for those whose profession relied upon remaining unseen.

Devan scouted the hall. "We have a problem. There are two groups guarding this entrance. A pair in front of the doors and a small squad near the end. There's no way my people can take out both groups fast enough to prevent them from sounding the alarm."

Daebian looked around the corner. "I can deal with the ones by the door if you can take out the four in the hall."

Devan nodded. "If you can get past the forward group and silence the door guards, we should be able to handle the others."

"It will happen fast, so be ready to strike when their backs are turned."

"Just tell us when."

Daebian looked to Azerick. "Father, you will have to go with me to keep the baddies off my back. We can't have them delaying us."

Azerick hesitated before answering. "I should be able to do it. I doubt their Source blockers reach into parallel planes of existence."

"We had best hope not. I trust you can you can work your magic one-handed?"

Azerick ducked his head. "With the other tied behind my back."

"No, with it tied behind *my* back. We'll be moving fast, so hold onto my belt." He looked to Devan. "Get ready."

Daebian dove into a nearby shadow, pulling Azerick in behind him. The instant darkness enveloped them, Azerick unleashed arcane fire in a wide swath. Hisses and unintelligible curses howled in the blackness. They had taken only a handful of steps before light exploded before their eyes. They returned to the prime material plane on the guards' left side. Daebian threw his arms wide without slowing his steps, shoved the nearest legionnaire into the other, and forced them both into the shadow on their right.

Only a brief exclamation of surprise and the sound of colliding bodies echoed down the hall before the four men disappeared into the shadow ways. Daebian leapt over the two soldiers as they fell to the ground and sprinted past them. The tinkling of bells sounded behind them for a moment before the screams began.

Azerick struck out blindly ahead of them with his magic before Daebian returned them to the Academy. There they found the other four Order soldiers lying motionless at the feet of their allies. They paused, ears cocked toward the doors, and listened for any sign that anyone had noted their presence. After a moment of not hearing any shouts of alarm, they made their way to the large double doors.

Devan pressed an ear against the wood. "I can hear people, but it's locked and barred from the inside. The lock isn't a problem, but the only way to remove the bar is for someone inside to lift it."

"I can use acid on the door and probably the bar as well," Vera volunteered.

Azerick scrunched up his face. "An interior lock means there's guards inside. Breaching the doors by any means will alert them."

"What do you suggest?" Devan asked.

"We have two options. Daebian and I can use the shadow ways to enter and try to take out the guards ourselves, or I can cleave through the door and bar from outside and we storm in."

Devan looked to Daebian. "What are the odds of neutralizing the soldiers quietly?"

"Not good," Daebian replied. "It's a blind jump into an unknown number of soldiers in a location I've never seen. Vera, how many entrances are there?"

"Two primaries besides this one and a small door behind the stage," she replied.

Devan grimaced. "Then we're likely looking at four groups of interior guards of at least two per post. Our odds are not great. If they were ordinary soldiers, I wouldn't be too concerned, but with their damnable shields…"

Azerick nodded. "Aside from separating me from my magic, that is what makes them truly formidable."

"If those are our only two options, then I suggest we charge through the door and hope we can neutralize them before they get organized," Devan said.

Azerick looked at Vera and thought. "I have another idea."

CHAPTER 19

Azerick shuffled down the hall toward the soldiers guarding one of the other doors. "Um, excuse me."

The legionnaires snapped to attention and leveled their spears. "What are you doing out here?" one demanded.

Azerick pointed over his shoulder. "Um, the, uh, other soldiers said I'm supposed to come here."

"You're a wizard?"

Azerick plucked at the student robe he had found and donned. "My instructors might argue the point, but yes."

"What are you doing out here? Why weren't you with the others?"

"I was off campus when you came. It was only afterward when soldiers came to my home and informed me that all mages are required to come here. So here I am."

One of the guards looked at the other. "We don't have any more shackles."

Azerick sneezed, sniffed, and pushed Vera's glasses farther up his nose. He hunched down and tried to look as innocuous as he could.

"They're shielded. Besides, he's as close to being an archmage as I am a dragon." He gestured toward Azerick. "Come on, boy."

The other soldier pounded on the door. "Open up. We got a straggler coming in."

Azerick heard the crossbar being lifted before the door swung open.

"In you go and don't cause any trouble."

Azerick ducked his head and tripped on the hem of his robe. "No sir! You won't have any trouble from—" Azerick sneezed so hard he nearly dislodged his glasses, "—me. Gods how I hate allergy season."

He stepped into the enormous chamber, slipped his borrowed spectacles into a pocket, and rubbed his aching eyes as the doors closed behind him. It did not take long for him to find the people he sought. Headmaster Maureen Florent stood as tall and stern as he remembered her. Not far away was the pudgy alchemy teacher, Magus Morgarum. He also recognized several of the council members and a few of the other instructors.

Azerick made his way to Headmaster Florent and cleared his throat. The archmage turned and looked as if she had seen a ghost. She composed herself, her look of shock replaced by one of suppressed disgust.

"I shouldn't be surprised to see you," the headmaster said. "Whenever the abyss shits on us, it always leaves two piles."

Azerick grinned despite the elder mage's venomous words. "Should you ever retire as headmaster, you will make a fine poet."

Headmaster Florent turned her hate-filled eyes toward the soldiers standing near the doors. "It appears my retirement is at hand, but I do not see poetry in my future." She looked back at Azerick. "Whatever future I imagined now seems uncertain."

"I do love to disrupt people's plans."

"Yes, you certainly do. Tell me, do your actions still haunt you?"

"Now that I am mortal once again, more than ever."

A smile crept onto the aged wizard's face. "Good. I said I would never forgive you for the death of my students, but if you have a plan to get us away from these people, I would be grateful. They mean to send us to war once they've properly broken us. I will not see more of my students die like that. Not again."

Azerick nodded. "Nor I. I have friends just outside the door."

"I hope you brought an army."

"Just my son, a few thieves, and a girl named Vera."

The headmaster's thin eyebrows rose. "The younger Cossington girl? She is a clever young lady. I'm not surprised these buffoons failed to nab her."

"You know her?"

"Magus Morgarum introduced us. She came to him for alchemy lessons years ago. Although not a Magus Academy student, she had shown such talent he tutored her in his spare time."

Azerick nodded. "We wouldn't be here without her."

"So what's your plan? You said you were mortal once more. Are you as cut off from the Source as we are?"

"I am, but I'm not defenseless."

"I wouldn't imagine so."

"I plan on taking down as many of the interior guards as I can and letting my friends in. Once we neutralize the soldiers, we'll lead you out of here through the secret passageways and into the sewers below the temple. I've prepared a place that should accommodate everyone and prevent us from being scryed out by their arcanus." Azerick looked around the room. "Although it will be crowded."

"You can stack us like firewood if it gets us away from here and out of these damnable shackles."

"All right. Once I lose the element of surprise, I'll need you to hinder any guards still standing."

The headmaster glared. "One of the paramount purposes of your so-called rescue is to avoid turning these children into soldiers."

Azerick shook his head. "No fighting. Just get in their way. I don't think these people will use lethal force against them as long as they aren't posing a threat. It should be over quickly. Where are the students from the other schools?"

"They kept the scholars confined to their dorms. The martial students who took part in defending the Academy were brought here, but they returned them to their dorms once the Order finished securing the city."

"As much as I wish I could free them tonight, I'm glad they aren't here. Just getting you out will be difficult enough. We'll have to help the martial students escape at another time."

Headmaster Florent pressed her thin lips together but gave him a grudging nod. "What do we do next?"

"Next, I need to use the privy."

The archmage gave Azerick a dubious look. "Behind the stage. They're nothing more than buckets with chairs lacking a seat placed over them."

"Ah, so that's what that smell is."

"It is indeed. These conditions have been quite intolerable."

Azerick grinned. "Look on the bright side, traveling through the sewer won't come as such a shock to the senses."

"Small favors I suppose."

Azerick navigated his way through the crowd and climbed the short set of stairs leading up to the elevated stage. Behind the back wall, he found the scene drop area and the small door Vera had mentioned guarded by a pair of soldiers. The smell of waste buckets wafted out of a corner curtained off for modesty. He made a show of entering each of the three makeshift privies before approaching the guards.

"Excuse me, sirs, but the buckets are full."

"I guess you're the lucky one who gets to empty them," one man replied.

"Where should I do that?"

He rolled his eyes. "Take the bucket to one of the proper privies outside and pour it out. Someone at the door will escort you."

"Thank you. That's all I needed to know."

Azerick's staff leapt to his hand, its arcanum sphere morphing into a halberd head in an instant. He swept the poleaxe across the necks of both soldiers, cleaving through them in a single swipe. As he had suspected, the anti-magic barrier did not block the power stored in his staff. It only prevented mages from reaching the Source, otherwise it was unlikely their shields would function inside the barrier.

The sorcerer left his staff on the floor next to the bodies, grabbed one of the waste buckets, and carried it into the auditorium. He approached Headmaster Florent, who was speaking to a small group of Academy instructors.

Azerick set the bucket near their feet. "Someone carry this to the door over there. When the soldiers open it, get out of the way."

"I'll do it," Magus Trent volunteered.

The magus was on the young side, and Azerick did not recognize him. He was likely in the advanced classes when he had been a student.

Azerick nodded. "Just get them to open the door and get out of the way. My people and I will handle the rest. Headmaster, are your people prepared to run interference?"

"Against my better judgment, yes."

"Okay. I'm going to the other guarded door. When I see the soldiers open the door for you that's when I'll strike. That will leave only the pair of soldiers guarding the third exit. With any luck, I or my people will take them out before they can shout an alarm."

Headmaster Florent glowered. "If you were anyone else, I would say you risk far too much on luck."

Azerick smiled back at her. "Good or bad, luck has always been something I've had a surplus of."

"Let us pray it is for the good this time."

Azerick made his way to the door he had used to enter the auditorium and watched Magus Trent haul his foul burden to the other exit where his compatriots waited. He saw the mage speaking to the soldiers before the two men lifted the cross bar. Azerick did not wait to see what happened next. Just as he had with the two soldiers behind the stage, he summoned his staff and swung with all his might as the doors at the far end crashed open.

The empowered weapon cut through the first man with little resistance, but the other reacted with surprising speed. The Order soldier brought his shield up and intercepted the blow. Azerick's weapon struck the arcane nimbus surrounding the buckler with a crack of thunder and a shower of cerulean sparks.

The guard thrust his short spear at Azerick's stomach, but he swept his staff down and knocked it away. The spear tore a bloody gash in his side but failed to inflict serious harm. Azerick reversed his swing and swept the blade at the soldier's lower legs. The guard tried to interpose his shield but was a fraction of a second too slow. Azerick's axe head skipped across the bottom of the arcane shield, cut through the metal greaves covering his right shin, and bit into the bone.

The soldier cried out and fell. Azerick raised his weapon high and brought it down where his shoulder met the neck, silencing him for good. He spun toward the remaining legionnaires and sought out both his allies and foes. The soldiers who had opened the door for Magus Trent were down with several poisoned quarrels sticking out of their exposed flesh, but the remaining two guards were trying to open the door while holding back the press of bodies shoving against them.

The shield of the soldier not wrestling with the crossbar flared, and bodies tumbled away. Those struck lay motionless or groaned and fought to get back to their feet. Daebian and the thieves struggled to reach them, their progress hampered just as much by the mob as the soldiers had been. More so now.

Azerick drew power from his staff and launched a stream of arcane bolts over the heads of the crowd, but they fizzled out before making it halfway across the room. There seemed to be a dampening effect inside the dead zone once the magic distanced itself from its source of power. He rushed toward the guards, desperate to keep them from opening the door and allowing reinforcements to join the fray. Azerick knew he would never make it in time.

He saw Daebian shadow-step and emerge between the two soldiers. His sword struck the one lifting the bar in the back. The beam dropped down into its cradle as the man fell. A second guard turned and stabbed at Daebian, but he avoided the thrust and countered with his sword. The soldier blocked the swing with his shield, but that left his back unguarded. A pair of crossbow bolts struck him in the neck and shoulder. He tried to skewer Daebian in a last act of defiance, but his thrust lacked strength as the poison stopped his heart.

"Everyone, out through the door!" Azerick shouted over the inevitable tumult. "Follow Vera!"

Vera stood in the doorway waving her arms. Shouts and horns rang through the halls as the outer guards bashed at the doors to get in. Devan, Keaton, and Keanna pushed to the head of the fleeing mob to act as the lead guard while Azerick, Daebian, and Baldur covered their rear. The halls were chaos with over a hundred people, many children, pressing toward what they prayed was salvation.

The guards had given up on the door and raced down the adjoining halls until finding the rear of the escaping prisoners. Baldur shot his hand crossbow, but the soldiers raised and joined their shields, and the bolt skipped off the shimmering barrier.

Azerick gave the thief a light shove toward the fleeing mages. "Stay with them. Daebian and I will deal with the soldiers."

Daebian and Azerick strode toward the advancing legionnaires. Azerick noted a fresh wound on Daebian's arm, likely received during his last shadow-step. They needed to figure out a way to rectify the problem with the shadow spawn. Daebian's ability to use the shadow ways was one of his best assets. Given their foes' capabilities, maybe the most important one of them all.

Azerick rushed forward and struck with his axe-headed staff. He drew energy from his weapon and used it to increase his power. It struck a shield with a brilliant flash of light, but the ward held. Spears darted out between shields, forcing him back. Unable to create wards of his own, even the weakest blow would do significant harm should one connect.

Daebian leapt into the shadows. Azerick's heart skipped a beat when he did not reappear. He lunged forward, shifting the halberd head into a long, narrow spear tip. More sparks flew amidst the flash of competing magics. There was no doubt in Azerick's mind which would ultimately prove triumphant—assuming he did not die first.

Swift, alternating thrusts forced him back once again. The soldiers sounded off with each step forward, their feet moving in unison. Daebian appeared behind the Order soldiers and struck at their backs. One of them spun around and blocked the surprise attack with his shield. Azerick reversed his retreat and poured power into his staff. The weapon glowed brighter than his enemies' shields and hummed and crackled with pent up energy.

Two spears leapt out to meet him. He avoided one and tried to bat the other away with his left hand. The soldier shifted his aim and stabbed his spear through Azerick's forearm. Azerick ignored the biting pain and thrust with all his might. The stiletto-like blade punched through the arcane shield with a thunderclap. The breastplate beyond may as well have been made of paper for what little good it did its wearer.

Azerick bent his wrist and grabbed hold of the spear shaft with the hand of his impaled arm and pulled. He swept the blade of his staff across and sheered through the wood and metal. The sorcerer plowed headlong into the disarmed soldier as he tried to draw the shortsword hanging at his side. The legionnaire collided with his fellow, throwing them both off balance. Daebian took advantage of the opening and ran him through the heart. Another thrust of Azerick's staff ended the life of the last soldier.

Azerick looked Daebian over. "More trouble in the shadow ways?"

Daebian gave him a grim nod. "We really need to do something about that."

"My thoughts exactly. No time for it now. We need to catch up with the others."

Azerick gulped down one of Vera's healing potions and dribbled a few drops into the open wound as they ran after the mages. He had to admit, her potions were better than his. They caught up to Baldur and the rear group moments later.

Azerick jumped up to look over their heads. "Why aren't they using the secret passageway?"

"It's too narrow. It'll take too long to get through. Half would be caught out in the open. Faster just to use the halls," Baldur said.

Coarse shouts and a blaring horn sounded ahead, followed by the clash of weapons.

"Come with me. Make a hole!" Azerick shouted as they rushed to the fore.

Azerick, Daebian, and Baldur got close enough to the front to see the other thieves engaging a squad of legionnaires. Rock-hard foam spattered the walls, floor, and the leading soldiers. It was probably the only thing that had prevented them from being overrun. Azerick could not see Vera, but the mages were streaming around the corner toward the temple, and he assumed she was at their head.

Azerick pointed at a door located down an adjoining hall. "There. Follow me!"

The trio ran into what appeared to be one of the temple priest's bedrooms. Azerick shaped the end of his staff into a mallet and struck the wall a mighty blow. Stone shattered and exploded into the squad's unprotected flanks. Azerick, Daebian, and Baldur charged through the hole in the wall and laid into the legionnaires.

Pressed on three sides, and half their number lost in the opening encounter, the squad had a hard time bringing their shields around to block every attack. Swords, staff, and poisoned bolts slipped past their defenses, and the Order soldiers began to fall. Baldur took the last man standing in the back when he tried to rush Daebian in a final desperate attack.

When Azerick had time to catch his breath and look around, he saw that they had not escaped the battle unscathed. Keaton was down and not moving. Devan had a belly wound that would have been fatal if he did not have one of Vera's potions. Blood soaked both of Keanna's sleeves and ran down her left leg and pooled on the floor. Azerick breathed a sigh of relief when both thieves thumbed the cork out of small metal vials and drank the contents. As good as the healing draughts were, it would take time before the two were back in top shape.

No matter how badly they needed rest, they would not get it. The sound of shouts and horns filled the hallways from two directions. Order soldiers appeared, raised their shields, and marched toward them.

Daebian looked down the hall at the fleeing mages and back to the advancing legionnaires. "They'll never make it if we don't stop them."

"You're willing to die to save them?" Azerick asked, surprised at his son's response.

Daebian grinned. "Not in the slightest, but I don't like these invaders, and I'll kill as many as I can before fleeing. I will then spend the rest of my life making them fear the darkness."

"I suppose that will have to do." Azerick flicked his eyes between the three remaining thieves. "What about you?"

Keanna shrugged. "I'm with Daebian. I've no desire to die here, but I'll take as many as I can with me. If I can escape, so much the better."

Her compatriots nodded their agreement. Azerick took a deep breath and set himself to sell his life dearly. His entire body stiffened as power flooded into him. His first thought was that it was an attack, but then came the familiar warmth and energy his connection with the Source gave him.

A smile spread across his face. "Our friends have taken down the nullification field. Go, all of you, get the others to safety. I'll handle the soldiers."

Daebian gave him a tight-lipped wag of his head. "You know their shields severely limit your magic."

"There was once a suit of armor that was supposed to make its wearer impervious to magic and most forms of harm. It didn't work out well for him, and it won't for these people. Hopefully our allies and innocents are clear so I can take off the kid gloves."

"Limiting yourself thusly has always been your weakness. Kid gloves indeed," Daebian scoffed before leading the thieves after the mages.

Azerick faced the oncoming soldiers and slammed the butt of his staff onto the floor. A semi-circle of force exploded outward, cracking stone and slamming into the legionnaires' flaring shields hard enough to stop them in their tracks.

"I will give you one chance to leave this city and my kingdom alive. To stay is to invite your own doom," Azerick called out, using his magic to amplify his voice.

The soldiers set their shields and resumed their steady march.

"So be it."

The sorcerer unleashed a torrent of power. Not at the soldiers, but at the walls and floor beneath their feet. The stone and timbers shattered, and the legionnaires fell into the Academy's sublevel. He turned his magic onto the ceiling and brought it, and several rooms above, down upon the soldiers' heads, entombing them. Even if their shields protected them from the falling stone, furniture, and debris, it would take hours to exhume them.

With a wave of his hand, cut stone lifted into the air and created a walkway over the destruction he had wrought. Azerick strode across his bridge and let it collapse after he passed. He could hear numerous soldiers forming up outside just beyond the doors as officers barked orders and signalmen blew horns.

Azure fire leapt from his staff and struck the door and much of the wall, reducing them into their basic components and sending them blasting into the Order formations within the courtyard. The brutality of the attack took many of them by surprise, striking down entire ranks before they raised their shields.

The legionnaires reformed their ranks with expert speed and precision. Many sets of eyes widened, and spears trembled in grips as a form grew out of the cloud of dust to tower fifty feet over their heads. Orange and black flames licked over Azerick's body as his image flickered between that of a giant man and a terrifying demon.

Azerick's voice sounded like thunder. "I am Azerick Giles. Lord of the Realm, Defender of the Crown, demon prince of the Fifth Circle of the Abyss, and the hand of the dark goddess Sharrellan. You trespass upon my land and murder and enslave my people. This will not stand!"

He slammed his tree-sized staff against the ground, causing the land to shake and shatter windows. More than one soldier tumbled to the ground and quaked in fear. But not all. Javelins arced out and encircled the colossal form. Azerick shrank, his illusion dispelled as he lost control of the Source once again.

"Aw, shit..." Azerick pointed a shaking finger at the sky over the soldiers' heads and screamed, "Dragons!"

Almost comically, the legionnaires raised their shields in a turtle formation and scanned the sky. Azerick sprinted into the darkness as the soldiers shouted their fury and took up pursuit. A flurry of magical attacks exploded around him as he ran. Free of the javelins' effect, Azerick erected as many wards as he could as fire, lighting, and searing arcane strikes slammed into him. His wards flared like those of the soldiers' shields. He felt the impacts, and he began to sweat profusely as heat bled through the arcane barriers and threatened to roast him alive.

Azerick slashed open a portal and dove through headlong. The gate snapped shut behind him, but he had only taken a few steps when a larger portal opened not far away. The Order soldiers marched through, their shields blazing and spears leveled, followed up by the three arcanus who had created the rift.

"Oh, come on!" Azerick shouted before tearing up a wide swath of the street and hurling the cobblestones at the soldiers with his magic.

The stones struck with significant force. Their impacts caused shimmering ripples across the translucent shields like hurling a handful of gravel into a luminous pond. The Order charged and tried to envelope him. Their arcanus raised walls of fire, ice, and stone to impede his flight. Azerick aimed his staff and shattered a wall of ice and ran.

Spells chased after him, splintering the sides of buildings, cracking and uprooting cobblestones, and filling the air with smoke, fire, and the smell of ozone. Azerick's mind and body worked as one, opening numerous portals throughout the district to fool the arcanus as to his location. He raced through one almost at random, depositing him near the market square in the business district.

Azerick sought the deep shadow of an overhanging awning attached to the front of an apothecary where he fought to catch his breath. He was still coming to terms with his reduced limits of both body and magic. He hoped his current level of fatigue was due to his newly resurrected status, and that it would improve with time. Given the strength and determination of his enemies, he needed all the power he could muster. Far more than he had now.

He pressed himself into the doorway when one of the Order's flying vehicles buzzed overhead. His relief after it passed by was as short-lived as was his respite. One of the hovering wagons, a skimmer Daebian had called it, set down near entrance to one of the market center's streets and disgorged a full score of soldiers. Several had bright stones set in the middle of their bucklers. The shield's polished surface reflected the light, enabling them to direct it into the shadows to reveal what lay within.

Azerick tried to sneak away before they chanced upon him, but a beam of light caught him as he darted between buildings. The legionnaires raised a hue and cry and gave chase. But Azerick was tired of running. He was tired in every meaning of the word, but more so of being chased like a rabbit by a group of hounds. Well, these dogs were going to learn he was no rabbit, but a badger.

The sorcerer whirled his staff, and a powerful cyclone sprang into being around the Order contingent. It pulled slate shingles from roofs and stones from the street, adding bludgeons and blades to the fierce wind. The soldiers responded swiftly, raising their shields and forming them into a protective dome. Sparks flew and light flared when the projectiles came in contact with the magical ward.

Azerick stabbed his staff at the black sky, and the cyclone flew upward, carrying its load of airborne flotsam. Able to see again, the soldiers leveled their spears and prepared to rush the sorcerer. Azerick swept his staff down and brought the tornado crashing onto their heads with extraordinary power. The kinetic energy coupled with his arcane power was more than the soldiers' battered wards could withstand. A weak point opened in the barrier, and like a breach in a dam, that was all it took.

Stone, slate, and wind poured through the small opening and exploded outward, scattering soldiers, and pieces of soldiers, throughout the plaza. Azerick wanted to drop to the ground and sleep, but fury overruled his exhaustion. Tonight was about showing the Order he and his people were not to be trifled with.

Azerick walked around the square and used his staff to carve runes into the ground. The Order was not the only ones familiar with such magic. He hastened back to a shadowy doorway when he heard marching feet and the droning of skimmers approaching. As he suspected, the battle had not gone unnoticed.

The levitating troop wagons arrived moments ahead of the foot soldiers. The first one glided over one of Azerick's runes and was engulfed in blue fire. Men cried out before their lungs were seared into useless, black husks. Anticipating another such trap, the second skimmer juked hard to the left, but not far enough to avoid triggering the rune.

Another blast of azure flame streaked into the sky. The legionnaires that had avoided immolation threw themselves from the contraption, rolled across the torn-up ground, and brandished their shields. The stricken soldiers were too disorganized to form a cohesive defense, and Azerick was not going to give them the chance to join ranks.

He dropped a barrage of flaming meteors upon their heads. The ground exploded around the legionnaires, sending shards of stone and fire through the gaps in the defenses of those unable to join their shields with others and striking them down. Azerick's hair stood on end a moment before the world exploded around him. He felt himself lifted into the air and hurled across the plaza. His wards shattered beneath the magical attack, but they held long enough to save him terrible injury, or worse.

He struggled to his feet and gazed through the dust at the Order soldiers streaming into the market square. They predictably formed into ranks, their shields glowing with energy. Azerick noted the handful of arcanus ensconced near the middle of the centuria-sized formation. His anger continued to swell, and he tapped into the powerful emotion to strengthen his hold on the Source.

Azerick jammed the arcanum tip of his staff into the ground and spent the last of his and the powerful weapon's energy reserves. The street split open, eldritch fire jetting out of the fissure that raced toward the legionnaires. The running crevice forked when it came into contact with the soldiers' crafted wards and tracked along the barrier's border until rejoining on the far side.

Cobblestones broke apart as the cleft widened into a crevasse until there was nothing to hold up the ground upon which the soldiers stood. The small, crowded island fell into the sewer tunnels below, taking its passengers with it. Another surge of power caused the fissure walls to collapse inward, but Azerick was not yet finished. A small, shimmering pinhole appeared over the crater and expanded like a soap bubble, growing until it was large enough to encase a grown man.

It appeared ready to burst, but it instead collapsed in on itself. A strong wind tore at Azerick's clothes as the deflating bubble tried to swallow everything in the plaza. Debris created by the titanic battle streaked toward the implosion, the powerful vacuum sucking in everything not rooted in place. The vortex pulled shingles from roofs and siding from nearby buildings. Loud cracks of shattering timber and the shrill squeal of nails being ripped from studs sounded above the roaring wind.

Azerick struggled to crawl beyond his spell's deadly influence and grasped a stout post holding up an awning. The gale-force winds lifted his feet into the air as he clung to the beam. He tucked his chin to his chest and looked back at the destruction he had wrought. A massive ball of wood, stone, and bodies hovered above the crater, growing every second as more flying objects added to its mass.

The spell ended with the abrupt finality of a snuffed out candle. The enormous sphere of debris crashed into the hole, plugging it like a cork in a bottle. Dust clogged the air and drifted across the destroyed market square now gripped in a deafening silence. Azerick stood upon shaking legs and summoned his staff to hand, momentarily lost to the spell, and shuffled toward a glowing orb emerging out of the haze.

The shimmering sphere popped and deposited a battered older man onto the ground near Azerick's feet. Azerick shaped the end of his staff into a slim spear point and leveled it at the arcanus' wrinkled throat.

Doncho's eyes traveled from the liquid silver blade, up the blood red shaft, to the pitiless, hazel eyes of its wielder. "Who...are you?" he asked, his voice weak and raw.

"I told you. I am Azerick Giles. Protector of Valeria, and the Hand of Sharrellan. What is your name, wizard?"

The old mage swallowed and struggled to find the breath to answer. "Doncho Filipov of Tish. Arcanus of the Order."

"This is the last act of mercy I will show you or your people, Doncho Filipov of Tish. Leave my land, and never return, or I will destroy you. Once I purge you from my kingdom, I will seek you out in yours and bring your Order to its knees so they might never threaten another peaceful people ever again. Look in my eyes and know I speak the truth. I have defeated far greater threats than you."

Doncho closed his eyes. "There is only the Order and enemies of the Order."

"Your Order chose to be my enemy. It was a poor decision."

Doncho opened his eyes and found himself alone, the only living thing in a field of utter destruction.

CHAPTER 20

Azerick's feet felt as though they were encased in lead as he plodded toward a sewer entrance. He could already hear the sound of soldiers converging on the plaza and needed to get out of sight. The last spell had drained him and his staff of every last vestige of power. He doubted he had the strength to create a light much less open a portal to spirit him away to safety.

Memories flooded back to him as he sidled through the narrow alley. This was where Hugo and his crew had chased him. Where he had found his secret lair. Where his life had changed forever. Azerick could not think of a single defining moment that guided him on the path he had chosen, but that had certainly been one of the more prominent events.

Azerick groaned under the strain of shifting the grate covering the access tunnel. It was even harder getting it moved back into place, but he could not leave it askew. To do so would be a sign even the most inattentive searcher not overlook. The water level was low, leaving the walkways elevated, as well as the stench.

He sought even the smallest tendril of power and found it. It was a wispy thing, little more than a single thread of fine spider silk, but he gently wove it into a pattern with his mind, fearful that if he lost it he might not be able to draw another. The arcanum orb perched atop his staff glowed with a feeble light, but it was enough by which to see. He could not recall ever having had such a simple spell challenge him, not even when he was a failing novice at the Academy.

Azerick found the secret door and located the hidden catch without pause. It seemed like a lifetime ago he had first discovered it. No, more like three lifetimes ago, he corrected himself. The fake wall swung inward. Someone had hung overlapping blankets up just a few feet in to block any light from spilling out into the tunnel. He could tell there were people beyond it. Too many to keep silent despite the hushed orders to do so. It brought him a great sense of relief. At least some of the prisoners had made it.

He used his staff to part the blankets and threaded his way between them. A sword tip hovered just before his face, and Headmaster Florent's hands arced with restrained power. She let the energy fade upon recognizing the sorcerer. A tall, middle-aged man with red hair rushed forward and wrapped Azerick in a tight embrace.

"It is you!" Rusty cried. "You came back."

"Like a bad rash," Daebian drolled.

Rusty ignored him. "I thought I recognized you during the escape, but I didn't believe my eyes. Why didn't you look for me in the auditorium?"

Azerick grinned at his old friend. "Because you're a terrible actor and I needed to remain anonymous. Then things got kind of crazy."

"Everything gets crazy when you're involved." Rusty held Azerick at Arm's length, looked him up and down, and clapped him on his shoulders. "I should have figured anyone who can defy the gods can defy the ravages of time as well. Colleen would love to know your secret."

Azerick shook his head. "The price is far too high to pay."

"I can believe that." Rusty shook his head. "Back again, and just in time for our newest travails."

"Yes, dark tidings often call for an even darker savior," Headmaster Florent said.

Rusty turned to the archmage. "In times like these, I welcome any help I can get. We all should." He turned back to Azerick. "You saved us. You saved me and my children."

"I'm not sure I've saved anyone yet, but we've at least hindered their plans. I didn't do it alone either. Daebian deserves as much credit as I, and Vera probably more than us both."

"Ah, yes, my little Vera is something, isn't she?"

"She is indeed."

"Father, I expect you fared well while we made our escape?" Daebian asked.

Azerick flicked his eyes between his son, the headmaster, and the mages standing nearby. "I did. Far better than they did, I assure you. The Order has several score fewer soldiers now than they did just this morning. They are a challenging foe, but they are not invincible. It will take power, and we must deploy it intelligently, but if we work together, fight together, we will drive them from our shores."

Several cheers answered his pronouncement.

Headmaster Florent's eyes bored into his. "These children are not soldiers or war wizards!"

"You are wrong, Headmaster. They will fight here, for their homes and family, or they will fight in some foreign land wearing shackles and Order livery. I will not have them charge into their spears, but everyone will have a role to play. It is the only path to freedom."

The archmage looked as if she wanted to argue, or even exchange magical blows, but she spun away and stormed down the passage.

Azerick turned back to Rusty. "Are we secure here?"

Rusty nodded. "As secure as we can be. We're packed like fish in a barrel ready for market, but we've improved upon the wards you put in place, particularly the ones against scrying. Their mages won't find us at the least, but we can't stay here forever."

"We won't, not most of us anyway. Andrill has safe houses and smuggler caches throughout the city. Those who can fight will go to those along with Andrill's people. Daebian and I will stay here, and I assume your family. At least the ones wanted by the Order"

"Can't we sneak the younger children home to their families?" Rusty asked.

Azerick shook his head. "The soldiers will search their homes first, and I expect they will be very thorough. They'll assume they will come home eventually and so will make repeated inspections until they find them. No, we need to get them out of the city. Despite what I told Headmaster Florent, many of her students are too young and too weak to be anything but a liability."

"How will we get them out of the city, and where will we take them? All the way to North Haven?"

"North Haven would be best, but we don't have the time or resources for such a journey. I have somewhere closer, I hope. As to how to get them there, I don't know yet."

Daebian said, "We also need to deal with the shadow spawn. I like a nice scar as much as the next man, but I'm getting tired of being carved up like a winter fest goose every time I shadow-step."

"I have an idea on that front," Azerick replied. "It's fairly simple, but I think it will work."

Rusty asked, "What do we do now?"

"For now, we wait and rest. We kicked the hornets' nest tonight. We don't dare move until they calm down," Azerick replied.

"More like set it on fire," Daebian said with a grin.

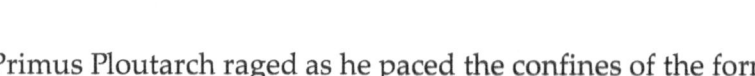

Primus Ploutarch raged as he paced the confines of the former duke of Southport's office. "Ten percent of my legion, two of my arcanus, destroyed in a single night, much of it by one man! I want those prisoners recovered tonight, Arcanus Filipov."

Doncho sat in a plush chair, wishing for nothing more than to sleep off his aches and exhaustion, but there would be no rest, for anyone, tonight. "We have roused the entire legion. They are scouring the city, particularly the homes of those who escaped. If they are in the city, we will find them."

"*If* they're in the city? Where else in the abyss could they be?"

Doncho shrugged his shoulders and winced at the pain the gesture brought. "They are wizards, Primus. They need not use conventional gates or scale walls to depart. We have not detected the conjuring of any portals within the city other than those opened by the sorcerer and do not believe they used any of them. The port is secured, our glider scouts are prepared to race to any use of magic in or near the city. Particularly transdimensional magic, which is very easy to spot."

"We must reclaim those wizards at any cost."

"Would you have me contact the primus arcanus and inform him of our setback?"

Primus Ploutarch's eyes opened wide. "Absolutely not! I will not have the empress thinking I cannot control a middling city with an entire prima cohort at my disposal. Besides, it would serve no purpose. The main host has already been dispatched, and their ships can only move so fast no matter our need. We will secure and pacify this city, in its entirety, before they arrive. Do I make myself clear?"

Doncho nodded. "Perfectly, Primus. My people are watching the city for any signs of magic. It is only a matter of time before the architect behind the escape reveals himself."

"Who is this man who so brazenly defies us?" the primus demanded.

"He declared himself to be Azerick Giles, a name I learned when we captured the wizardess and her warlock husband."

"They knew him?"

Doncho nodded. "She said he was her master, and her man's father. The survivors of the attack on their Academy described a man fitting Daebian Giles' description."

"What else do you know of them?"

Doncho took a deep breath as he recalled Ellyssa's words. "The mage, Ellyssa, warned that Daebian was not a man to be taken lightly, that he was dangerous beyond our estimation. It appears she was not overstating his abilities or tenacity. She also said Azerick was a demon lord and consort to the goddess Sharrellan, and that he had returned in the past when this land and its people were threatened."

Primus Ploutarch's face reddened, and his forehead creased into several deep furrows as he scowled. "There are no gods beyond the emperor and empress. Do not give me tales of folklore and superstition!"

"I merely repeat what the woman said. The figure outside the Academy declared much the same as did the man who issued his demand for us to depart this land."

"An illusion, conjured to frighten the weak-willed and feeble-minded! We are the Order. We do not run from phantasms and harsh words," the primus spat.

"The man was real enough, to which our depleted rosters can attest."

The primus spun on the other man in the room, who had so far remained silent in a desire to avoid the furious leader's wrath. "What do you know of this Azerick Giles?"

Terrance Beaumonte, former duke, now harmost pro tem of Southport, shifted in his seat. "I can tell you he is not myth or folklore.

He is real, or at least once was. He murdered my son when both were students at the Magus Academy some forty years ago. There are many credible claims of him having resided in the abyss and returned to lead the Gods War. His role in that I can personally attest to. While I was not present when the gods returned him to the abyss—" Terrance wilted under the Primus' glaring rebuke. "The false gods, I mean. I spoke to some who were there and witnessed his exile."

"Could he have come back?" Primus Ploutarch asked.

"I cannot know. He returned once, so I believe it is possible for him to do so again. If he has, you must not underestimate him. Few who do live to tell of their folly."

"Fated," Doncho grumbled.

"What was that, Arcanus?" the primus asked.

"He's fated," the old wizard repeated. "There are forces, while subtle, that are more powerful than gods. Even gods must bow to the fates and the ones chosen to do their will."

"You are dangerously close to speaking heresy, Arcanus," Primus Ploutarch warned in a low voice.

Doncho chuckled. "Heresy, gods, emperors, the desires and ambitions of man; the fates care not a whit for any of them."

CHAPTER 21

"It is as I feared," Andrill said as he raised a glass of brandy to his lips. "The blasted Order captured several of my people when they took down their anti-magic projectors."

"How many?" Azerick asked, sitting across the table from him.

"Five. Some managed to escape."

"And we freed the mages. Are they situated well?"

Andrill shrugged. "As well as can be. They've warded the safe houses and smuggler holes as best they can, but they're occupying every corner of my private little kingdom. It would be best to get the young ones gone sooner rather than later."

Azerick nodded. "I'm working on that, but they'll have to wait. What of your people, the ones taken prisoner during the escape? Have the Order marked them for execution?"

"Most likely, but I hear they're trying to get them to give us up before they do. They won't," the thief assured him.

"Then they will have to wait as well."

"Says the man hiding in a hole with me and not having his fingernails pulled out," Andrill scoffed.

"I will do everything I can to free them, but dealing with Daebian's problem first will yield us better results. I exhausted myself during the escape, and it will take a few days for me to recover the strength I'll need to carry out either of those two missions. Daebian's situation is the easier task."

"I'm glad you think so," Daebian said with a smirk.

"Were you able to get what I asked for?" Azerick asked Andrill.

"I did." Andrill retrieved a cut, polished piece of onyx the size of a quail egg set in the center of a gold disc from his pocket and slid it across the table. "It's the closest I could come given the short notice."

Azerick picked up the stone and examined it. "It's better than I had hoped for. Thank you." He stood and shook Andrill's hand. "I promise to try to get your people out."

"I know you will," Andrill replied.

Azerick and Daebian pulled the hoods of their cloaks up over their heads, exited the safe house, and walked openly on the streets. While taking the sewers almost anywhere in the city was possible, it was not always practical, and never pleasant. They figured the last place the Order would look for them was out in the open, and as long as they did not draw attention to themselves, they should be able to enjoy the relatively fresh air and easy walking.

"What are you going to do with the onyx?" Daebian asked.

"I'm going to make it into a soul stone."

"I already have a soul stone." Daebian patted the pommel of his sword hidden beneath his cloak. "And mine has a demon in it." He looked at Azerick and smiled. "We'll trap one of the shadow spawn in it! If you can project their essence, I might fool them into thinking I'm one of them. Very clever, Father."

Azerick gave him a sidelong nod. "Clever of you to figure it out so quickly."

"I always was the sharp one of the family."

Azerick knitted his brow. "And Raijaun and I are…"

"As thick as a tree… at times."

"I'll not argue your assessment of me, but Raijaun might have a different opinion of himself."

Daebian waved his hand as if swatting in insect. "He's ugly. Nobody cares what he thinks."

The pedestrian traffic increased as they walked. Azerick stood on his tiptoes and looked over the crowd. The people were bunching up near a squad of soldiers ahead.

"Looks like they're checking papers," Azerick said.

"Andrill needs to hasten his forgeries," Daebian replied.

Azerick checked the nearby side streets. "Let's go this way. We can skirt around them using the alleys."

The two exited the street and ducked into the narrow gap between buildings. They came upon an intersection when two soldiers stepped into view ahead of them. Azerick made to turn left, but two more legionnaires blocked the passage from that direction. He turned and found soldiers approaching from the right as well as behind.

"Where might you two be going?" one of the men asked. "It's against the law to avoid a checkpoint."

Daebian rolled his eyes. "What isn't these days?"

"I'll need to see your papers," the sergeant, what the Order called a decanus, said.

Azerick forced a smile and reached into a pocket. "Of course. I have them right here.

The decanus cradled his short spear in the crook of his arm, took the piece of paper, and unfolded it. The ensorcelled page exploded the moment he read the words. Azerick summoned his staff to hand, but Daebian's sword was already out and slashing through the stricken man's scorched neck as he reeled away.

Azerick thrust at the soldier standing behind the decanus, but he interposed his shield between him and the deadly weapon seeking his heart. Horns blared from behind them as the other legionnaires rushed through the narrow passageways toward them. Azerick raised a small field of crystal spikes behind the legionnaire. While the soldier's shield protected him from direct assault, it could do little against simple brute force. Azerick parried the thrusting spear, and he and Daebian lowered their shoulders and bull-rushed the man, knocking him down, and impaling him on the crystal spikes.

They used the dead soldier as a foot bridge across the piercing shards and ran. Azerick turned, cupped his hands with splayed fingers as if he were holding a large ball, and brought them together. Stone spikes grew from the walls, some finding their way past the legionnaires' shields to score their flesh. The soldiers angled their shields for better protection and charged ahead, the conjured spires shattering against their wards.

The sound of blowing horns joined the others as Order soldiers raced toward the calamity the two rebels caused. Charging legionnaires brought the pair up short as they approached an intersection. Azerick raised a series of stone pillars, creating a stairway to the rooftops. He and Daebian sprinted up the cylindrical steps. Azerick waved a hand behind him once they gained the roof, and the columns collapsed back into dust.

Daebian grabbed Azerick by the arm and pulled him down just as a glider dove at their heads like a hawk on a pair of rabbits. The glider wheeled around in a lazy arc, the rider's spear readied for a second strike. Azerick empowered his staff and hurled it like a javelin. It struck the glider just behind its beak-like nose. As Azerick had assumed, it was warded much like the soldiers' shields, although not as powerful.

While the projectile failed to damage the craft, it struck hard enough to foul the rider's attack and cause him to veer away. Azerick summoned his staff back to his hand and launched it at the glider's rear as it sped past. The weapon struck the ward with a brilliant flash and penetrated the back of the machine. The sorcerer made a bursting motion with his hand, and arcane energy exploded outward from around the staff. Pieces of metal broke away, and the glider disappeared behind a distant building, followed by a loud crash.

"Ha! How do you like that!" Azerick crowed.

Crossbow bolts rained down, glancing off his ward and sticking into the roof. Four more gliders appeared, their riders cocking their crossbows for another pass.

"We need to get out of here," Azerick said.

Daebian held up his arm to display the quarrel sticking out of it. "You think?"

Azerick summoned a thick fog to conceal them from the aerial scouts as he pulled Daebian across the roof.

Daebian drew up short a moment later. "We're out of rooftops, the alleys and streets are crawling with soldiers, and they have the building surrounded."

"Are you sure?" Azerick asked, squinting to see through the haze he had created.

Daebian scowled and pointed at his eyes.

"I guess you are. Take us into the shadow ways."

"Are you sure?"

Azerick ignored his son's mocking tone. "I don't want to expend energy opening multiple portals. Besides, we need to capture a shadow spawn."

"But you haven't prepared the stone yet."

Azerick shrugged. "We'll have to do it a little out of order."

Daebian spied a deep shadow where the building they were on met the ground. There were numerous soldiers milling about, looking for a way to reach them. He found a narrow opening in the pressing bodies, pulled Azerick close, and leapt off the roof.

The two dropped twenty feet to the street. The jump was like threading a needle, but Daebian's aim had been true. As luck would have it, none of the soldiers moved into their path while they were falling. One of the legionnaires was standing within arm's reach, so Daebian summoned a shadow blade to his free hand and stabbed him as they plummeted past.

They disappeared into the shadow before the man's dying scream cleared his throat. There was no true ground in the shadow ways, so there was no abrupt impact, although Azerick stumbled as his brain insisted there should be.

"Are they near?" Azerick whispered.

"Of course they are. They're always waiting for me. They seek me out here like the ones in our world search for you."

"You believe they're pursuing me?"

"I'm certain of it."

Azerick nodded. "I think you're right. Andrill said there have been more attacks around the city in the last few days than they have seen in the past several months. I had hoped it was not due to my presence, but it's too much to it discount as mere coincidence."

"It must come as something of a shock to you to find out you are not universally beloved."

The blackness hid Azerick's grin. "It's a good thing I have your reminders to help inure me against such emotional trauma."

"We all must play our allotted roles in life. I just perform mine with more enthusiasm than most."

"Your work ethic is commendable."

"Being exceptional at whatever I do is but one of my many talents." Daebian cocked an ear. "They're coming."

Azerick reinforced his ward just in time to deflect the attacks of a pair of shadow spawn. The spawn recoiled from the sparking impacts with hisses as they faded back into the darkness. Daebian hacked at one with his sword and stabbed another with his shadow blade.

"You do know we need them alive, right?" Azerick asked.

"I understand that, but I hope you agree that I also need to be alive for this little experiment of yours to be a hundred percent successful."

Daebian lunged forward, leading with both weapons. Azerick could not see either of them, but he heard the creature's shrieks and his son's curse.

Daebian's voice spoke out of the darkness. "I have one. I could use some help in securing it."

Azerick conjured a bright light and was just able to make out the shadow spawn Daebian had stabbed through its shoulder and thigh. The creature fought and hissed, flailing wildly. It's shrieks and thrashing increased when the light washed over it. Azerick wrapped the dark spawn in cords of arcane power, reducing its struggles to whipping its head about.

He extinguished his light, unsure if it was merely painful or potentially lethal to the creature. "Got it. Can you get us out of here?"

Daebian took Azerick by the arm, slashing at the shadow spawn that ventured close to them. The spawns' attacks increased as their captive continued spitting and hissing its wrath. Azerick lashed out with wide sweeps of magic, striking several creatures with every attack and driving back many more. Daebian tugged on Azerick's arm, and they found themselves standing in fetid water.

"I guess modesty and aim didn't make your list of exceptional talents," Azerick griped as he lifted one foot out of the sewer water.

"I'm sorry, maybe you want to lead a blind shadow-step next time?" Daebian snapped.

"You're right. I apologize. I'm tired, and standing knee-deep in other people's waste has soured my mood."

"Trust me, it isn't doing much for mine either. We're close to the entrance. I'll guide us so you don't have to make a light. Our friend does not seem to care much for it."

The shadow spawn writhed against its invisible bindings and resisted its captors. A small light conjured by Azerick got it moving quick enough. The creature did its best to avoid the light, which made it easy to direct. Daebian spoke true, reaching the hidden doorway into Azerick's old lair a minute after slogging to the sewer's walkway.

Daebian entered first and found Rusty and his family working on shoring up their defenses. "We need to douse the lights in the hall and one of the unused rooms."

Rusty finished putting the final touches on the ward he was creating. "What's going on?"

"Things happened that required us to move up the timetable on operation *take back the shadows*."

Rusty's eyes widened. "You nabbed one of those shadow spawn? You have it here?"

"Right outside the door, so we need to dim the lights and prep the room."

Rusty turned to his two magically-gifted children. "Elias, darken the passageways as much as you can without leaving us blind. Trisha and I will prepare the room. Daebian, give us five minutes before bringing it inside.

Daebian nodded and returned to Azerick. "How's our friend?"

"Unhappy but still here."

"He's going to become even unhappier. Rusty and his ilk are making ready the room. How long will it take you to prepare the stone?"

Azerick calculated the work involved in his head. "Three, maybe four hours."

Daebian studied the shadow spawn held in the grip of Azerick's spell. "He doesn't look too good. Hope he lasts that long."

"If not, there's plenty more where he came from."

Daebian gave his father an appraising eye. "Well, look at you, being all ruthlessly practical."

"I don't know why you act so surprised. I've plenty of examples of breaking from social convention to do what must be done."

"Yeah, but you agonized over it interminably."

"These creatures are a pestilence. They deserve no mercy or remorse."

Daebian flashed his father a smile. "If only you could apply such sentiment more universally, you might become tolerable company."

"I wouldn't hold my breath."

"I would. Have you smelled this place? I've broken wind twice during this conversation with no one the wiser." The creature struggled against Azerick's grasp. "No one asked you."

The door slid open, and Rusty poked his head out. "The room's ready."

"Wonderful," Daebian said. "Let's go make our guest uncomfortable."

The shadow stalker writhed the moment they entered the passageway despite the magical lamps putting out little more light than the blotches of phosphorescent lichen dotting the walls. Azerick goaded the creature with physical force and the occasional jolt of electricity when it refused to budge. He guided the shadow spawn into a small room and forced it to sit in a stout, wooden chair. Once seated, Daebian and Rusty secured it with thick leather straps and even a couple of chains.

"Will that hold it?" Rusty asked as he held a dim light near the creature, causing it to thrash against its restraints.

"It should," Azerick replied.

Daebian sat on a stool near the door. "I'll keep watch while you prepare the stone."

Azerick nodded and left the room with Rusty trailing close behind him. At a nod from Rusty, Trisha and Elias turned up the hallway lights, providing not just illumination, but another, less tangible, barrier to keep the shadow spawn contained. Azerick sat at a workbench covered in small tools and set the pendant with its onyx center stone in a jeweler's vice.

Rusty watched over Azerick's shoulder as he began the intricate task of carving runes into the gold disc. "So, we haven't had much time to talk. Is now OK, or is it too much of a distraction?"

"I can talk while I work," Azerick replied without taking his eyes off the pendant or lifting the tiny chisel from its surface.

"You seem well. Better than the last time you came back."

"I feel better. I feel...normal. For the first time in a very long while, I feel like a human being."

"What happened?"

"The demons revolted and imprisoned Sharrellan so they could destroy me. Raijaun and I freed her."

Rusty chuckled. "I can't imagine the punishment she levied on the ones that survived."

Azerick shook his head. "No, you cannot."

"So she sent you back here?"

"It was more complicated than that, but that was my demand for freeing her. I thought she had conceded and granted me my wish on my behalf, but now I think it was yet another ploy of the gods to use me to further their aims."

Rusty nodded his understanding. "Because of the Order."

"They have denounced our gods and seek to convert the entire world. I do not know what it takes to elevate a mortal to that of a proper deity, but with enough believers and power, I see how they could achieve it."

"So you don't think their emperor and empress are actual gods, as they claim?"

Azerick shook his head. "Not yet, but they may not be far off. I've taken time to study the shackles we removed from you and the others. They are not just devices used to limit a mage's access to the Source. They create a conduit to another source of power, one I believe their leaders control."

"So they're more like the Chosen priests, their power doled out by the gods for use in their name."

"Precisely."

"No wonder people think of them as gods," Rusty said in a heavy voice.

"If they have their way, we all will."

Rusty's face grew dark. "They imprisoned me and my children and would send us to fight wars they started. They will never be anything but my enemies."

Azerick grunted his reply.

"You think I'm wrong?"

"Friends and enemies are a fluid concept. Rigidly holding to one or the other is a good way to bring about failure."

"After what you've seen, the imprisonment, conscriptions, the executions, you can envision a circumstance where they are our friends?" Rusty asked, his voice rising with his mounting anger.

Azerick continued to carve the tiny runes into the gold disc, his voice as steady as his hand. "While their methods are flawed, their goal, at least on the surface of things, is noble enough. They seek to destroy the spawn the Scions have unleashed on the world."

"What about the death they have inflicted? They are evil!"

Azerick paused his tapping and drew a deep breath. "No, Rusty. I have seen evil, lived surrounded by evil incarnate, I have committed acts that many believe were evil, enough so to warrant my death. You need look no further than to our headmaster to bear witness against me. Evil as a concept is as fluid and malleable a notion as friend and enemy."

Rusty lost much of his bluster. "You had to do it or we would not have united against an enemy that would have destroyed us. You had no choice."

"I had a choice. I knew the spawn were coming. I could have led my people to the Academy and saved most of the people, the children, who died that night."

"And the mages would have thought they could defend against what was coming and not have joined together. You said so yourself!"

"Of course I did," Azerick replied with a mirthless chuckle. "How else could I deny the accusations of my complicity of such an evil act? I do not deny you your anger, Rusty. You are entitled to it, for today the Order is very much our enemy, and their actions foul. But tomorrow is another day, and we must accept and adjust to whatever it brings."

"You've become quite the philosopher."

"I've had many things to ponder, and much time to do so."

After a time, Azerick held up the pendant and studied his work. "I think this ought to do it."

He secured the talisman back in the vice and touched the tip of his staff to the gold disc. The arcanum orb sent out a silver tendril, tracing each rune and filling it with the precious metal. Power flowed from his staff into the pendant, causing the runes to glow like a piece of steel heated for shaping into a sword before "cooling" back to their normal, brilliant shine.

Rusty followed Azerick back to the room in which Daebian kept watch over their prisoner and soon to be sacrificial lamb.

Daebian stood and stretched when Azerick opened the door, ignoring the creature's wild thrashing and keening when light from the passageway washed over it. "About time you finished. I got so bored I named him and invented a back-story."

Azerick closed the door behind him and handed Daebian the pendant, now dangling from a gold chain Rusty had provided. "I told you it would take a couple of hours."

Daebian took the amulet. "Tolerating idleness is not one of my stronger attributes." He summoned a shadow blade in the hand holding the soul stone and turned to his prisoner. "Sorry, Fred, but you should have stayed on the farm and married Genevieve like your mother wanted. This is what ultimately comes of choosing a life of adventure."

He stabbed the conjured black blade into the shadow spawn's heart and tore its essence from its body, forcing it into the soul stone. Daebian slipped the necklace over his head and tucked it inside his shirt collar.

He opened the door to let in the light from the hall so it could create shadows within the room. "Time to see if it works."

Daebian stepped into a shrouded corner and disappeared. Azerick and Rusty stood by, growing nervous as several minutes passed. Both men jumped when Daebian leapt back out of the shadow, covered in black blood and looking as though he were a bad stage performer and the crowd had thrown inkwells at him instead of rotten produce.

"It works!" Daebian announced with a broad smile. "They completely ignored me. It was like stabbing fish in a barrel."

"I'm glad it was a success, but you should avoid going on killing sprees. The creatures could identify you as a threat by the aura you project."

"I thought of that. That's why I soul syphoned several of them. I can change my shadowy identity at will."

"Still, there's no need to draw unwanted attention to yourself."

Daebian rolled his eyes. "Yes, Father. Don't worry. I got it out of my system. For now. What's next on the agenda?"

Azerick yawned. "I get some much-needed sleep. We must meet with Andrill, Headmaster Florent, and probably a few members of the Academy council to plan our next move."

Rusty nodded. "Getting the noncombatants out of the city."

"And break Andrill's people out of jail, if it's not already too late," Azerick said.

CHAPTER 22

"We're out of time," Andrill declared the moment Azerick and Daebian arrived. "The Order has gotten everything they're going to get out of their captives. They're set for execution first thing in the morning."

"We need to get the children out of the city before we attempt another rescue," Headmaster Florent declared. "Whether you succeed or fail, the city will be abuzz with soldiers in the face of another assault."

Andrill glared at the archmage. "There was no such prevarication when my people rescued you lot. They risked their lives to get you free!"

Azerick interposed himself between the two leaders. "Headmaster Florent is right. Freeing your people is an escalation the Order will not ignore. These people dislike anyone challenging their authority. But we cannot delay the attack any longer. They have spent far too much time in those people's hands. We'll need to split our forces and execute both plans at once."

"Who leads which assault?" Andrill asked, his tone making his preference clear.

Azerick took a breath. "Since we're arriving unannounced, and Marley knows me, I should be the one to go with the students."

"I'd feel a lot better if you led the jailbreak," Andrill said. "No offense to Daebian or the wizards, but I know you. I think my people stand a far better chance with you being the tip of the spear."

Daebian said, "As much as I hate to admit it, Andrill's right, Father. This is a glorified babysitting task. I assume Magus Florent will insist on going with her students. That leaves the arcane role to you and the handful of mages left behind that know their asses from a hole in the ground."

"The only other person they might listen to is you," Azerick replied. "With you being able to travel the shadow ways, your help would be invaluable in freeing the prisoners."

Andrill slapped the tabletop. "It has to be both of you! Since they no longer need to guard the mages, they moved those magic barrier-making standards to the castle. Magic is useless inside the inner curtain wall. Daebian and my people will have to get them out. Azerick and the wizards remaining in the city will deal with the resulting uproar. There's no other way to get it done."

Azerick sighed. "He's right. Headmaster, you will lead the noncombatants out of the city yourself with a team of your choosing."

"And take them where?" the archmage asked, her voice rising.

"To the forest northwest of the city. You and your students will have to hide until Daebian or I can lead you to Marley's village."

"And how long will I have to camp in the woods with almost a hundred children while soldiers hunt us down, not to mention the abominations prowling forest?"

Azerick gave her a resigned wag of his head. "I don't know. Hopefully not more than a few hours. Take whoever you need to keep yourselves safe."

"I can send a score of my people with you," Andrill offered.

Azerick added, "You're mages. Even the youngest among you is not defenseless. That being said, you have to avoid using magic. The Order is looking for power surges near the city, and their scouts with their flying machines are not likely to give up the chase soon. Hiding is your best defense."

Headmaster Florent pressed her lips into a thin line. "I don't like it. Not one bit."

"The only other option is to stay here, but whether we succeed or fail, the Order will tear Southport apart looking for us, and since we have people crammed into every safe house in the city, they'll find some of them."

"And once they discover one, they won't stop until they find the rest of us," Andrill added. "They probably assume you've already left the city, given that they have scaled back their active searches of late."

Daebian said, "That and the need for more guards on the walls thanks to the increase in spawn attacks."

"Thank the gods for small favors," Azerick said.

Andrill arched his eyebrows. "Exactly which gods should we be thanking?"

"Let us hope the creatures continue to focus their attention on the city and not on a bunch of children and an old lady mucking about the forest at night," Headmaster Florent grumbled.

Andrill flashed the archmage a smile and winked. "Not so old to me."

The headmaster curled her lip in a sneer, but Azerick did not think she held as much contempt for the thief as she had hoped to convey with the look.

"We need to scout the city without fear of being arrested," Azerick said. "Andrill, have you managed to forge papers for us?"

"Yes and no." The master thief pulled out a folded sheet of paper from a vest pocket and laid it onto the table. "This is a valid license belonging to Lord Cossington's wife."

Azerick turned his head to look at Rusty. "She swore their oath?"

Rusty shrugged. "I insisted on it. She's not a combatant, so there was no reason for her not to. It was the easiest and safest way to get a valid certificate."

Azerick turned back to Andrill. "Can you duplicate it?"

"No. Examine the ink closely."

Azerick picked up the piece of paper and studied it with his mage sight. A thumb print adorned the lower left corner near Colleen's signature, and the ink had a glimmer of magic to it.

"When the soldiers check you for papers, you must place your thumb over the print created when you sign it," Andrill explained. "If the thumb matches the print, the words glow blue. If they are not the same, they glow red."

Azerick sighed and shook his head. "There arcanus draft the papers much in the same way a wizard pens a magical scroll. I was afraid of something like that."

"We can recreate the writing but not the magic," Andrill said. "I was hoping you could."

"It requires special paper, ink, and quill. I don't have the materials. I doubt any of my old supplies survived the destruction of my tower. Even if they did and Miranda hasn't thrown them out, I would have to go back to North Haven to retrieve them."

"I have plenty of materials in my office," Headmaster Florent said.

Azerick scratched his chin as he thought. "The guard is somewhat light now that there are fewer prisoners, particularly around the Magus Academy."

"You should let me go, Father," Daebian said. "I can get in and out far easier by myself."

"Can you be certain to get the proper materials?" Azerick asked.

Daebian frowned but nodded his head. "The magic in them is subtle, but I should be able to detect it."

"But can you retrieve them from the magical safe keeping them secure?" Headmaster Florent asked.

"No, I cannot."

"Then I have to go with you," Azerick said.

"But you aren't safe in the shadow ways," Daebian replied.

"We'll just have to make do."

"Always the hero," Daebian said with a shake of his head.

Azerick and Daebian traveled the sewers leading toward the Academy as far as they dared. It was unlikely the Order was ignorant of their previous secret egress, and the area was probably under heavy guard. Coupled with the enormous destruction Azerick had wrought during their last foray into the hostile territory, the route was a poor choice. It was only a matter of time before the soldiers figured out how they were traversing the city unseen.

Azerick led the way to one of the grates set in the floor of the Martial Academy's expansive stables. It was a chore, but they shifted the heavy iron barrier and climbed out of the shaft. While they had rebuilt the enormous structure after the war, it was still much as Azerick remembered it. Memories of Travis and his cronies crept into his mind, and he smiled at the childishness of it all compared to so many of the true hardships he had faced in his life. He longed for such simpler times.

Voices echoed down the long aisle flanked by stalls.

Azerick pointed toward the nearest empty stall. "In there!"

The two darted into the vacant stable. Azerick propped his staff in a corner and picked up a shovel as the sounds of approaching soldiers drew closer. Taking a cue from his father, Daebian grabbed an armload of hay from a wall-mounted manger and waited. Not wanting to surprise the men, Azerick scraped at the floor with his shovel. As he had hoped, their presence may have been unexpected, but it did not cause the legionnaires to become alarmed.

"What are you two doing in here?" a guard demanded.

Azerick put on his best idiot face and looked between his shovel and the soldiers. "Uh…shoveling shit, milord."

"No one is supposed to be out on the grounds without an escort."

Azerick shrugged. "We just did what the fellow with the sideways brush on his head told us to do. I guess he didn't want to stand around and watch us shovel ankle-deep horse crap all day."

The soldier looked at Daebian and noted the dark glasses hiding his eyes. "Why do you wear those spectacles?"

"Got in a fight with a wizard a while back. Bastard nearly blinded me. Now I gotta wear these things during the day," Daebian replied.

The man looked him up and down with a professional eye and noted the bulge of Daebian's sword hidden beneath his cloak. "What's under your cloak?"

Knowing their ruse had failed, Daebian glanced at Azerick before hurling the loose hay into the legionnaires' faces and drawing his sword. Azerick summoned his staff to him with one hand while he called and shaped magic with the other. Black tendrils sprang from the ceiling and struck like vipers, wrapped around the soldiers' necks, arms, and body, and lifted them off their feet.

Daebian's sword was free and seeking vital organs when Azerick lunged forward and stabbed out with his staff. Three of the men died in as many seconds. The farthest from the stall doorway had the presence of mind to activate his shield and used it to slice through the tendrils holding him aloft. His feet were churning before they touched the ground and propelled him through stables.

Daebian glanced down the long passageway before stepping into a shadow and leaping out ahead of the fleeing soldier an instant later. His sword cut low, just clipping the bottom of the legionnaire's shield, and bit through his greaves and the shins they failed to protect. The man went sprawling with a shout, but Daebian silenced him with a thrust through his back.

"So much for getting in unseen," Daebian said as he cleaned his blade with the soldier's short cape.

"Drag him into a stall and cover him with hay," Azerick ordered as he pulled the other three corpses out of sight.

Azerick hastened down the passageway to join Daebian after completing his quick cleanup. "With any luck, no one heard us."

Luck was with them but fleeting. While they heard no alarms and saw no soldiers, or anyone else, in the area, there was a large tract of open ground between the stables and the Martial Academy's central structure.

Daebian studied the ground between them and the distant building. "I think I can get us across."

"Can't you just shadow-step us into the Magus Academy?" Azerick asked.

"If I was alone, without a doubt, now that I can avoid the shadow spawn. But the last time we were there, the lights were out due to the anti-magic field. Now they're probably back on, thus changing the shadows I'm passingly familiar with. That means a blind step which takes time, and dragging you with me like a ripe piece of bait doesn't make for a swift, trouble-free journey."

"Baby steps it is then," Azerick said with a shrug.

Daebian looked as if he wanted to issue a retort, but he grabbed his father by the arm and led him into a nearby shadow. They emerged a moment later in a dark patch of ground between thick shrubs and the building wall. Daebian pulled Azerick into a crouch and deepened the shadows surrounding them when he heard approaching boot steps.

A squad passed by a moment later, oblivious to the lurkers just a stone's throw away. Daebian led the way along the side of the building as he maintained the cloak of shadows concealing them. They skirted the Academy building until they could see the magus quarters and central structure. There were more Order soldiers standing guard and patrolling here, but their numbers were still light.

They had to wait, squatting in the bushes, for almost half an hour before Daebian saw his chance and shadow-stepped across the courtyard. He and Azerick emerged next to the Magus Academy just as a squad of legionnaires marched through the doors. They ducked down, and Daebian enveloped them in another shroud of darkness. The squad halted behind their leader, who turned and stared at the dark patch of ground near the wall. He approached with caution, summoned his arcane shield, and made it glow like a tiny sun. The light washed away the shadows to reveal nothing but the base of the wall and the flagstones beneath it.

Daebian pulled Azerick through the shadow ways, doing his best to avoid the spawn he sensed lurking in the perpetual darkness. Perhaps his proximity to Azerick confused them enough to cause them to hesitate, but he knew that would not stay their attack for long. They exited an instant before the shadow spawn overcame their confusion and surged toward them.

Azerick looked around the dark chamber and figured they were in a cloakroom near the door the soldiers had exited. Daebian cracked open the door and peeked out into the hall. He motioned to Azerick, and the two darted into the passageway, ducking into rooms and alcoves whenever they sensed someone approach.

Daebian had to shadow-step them past two guard stations and a roving patrol before they reached Headmaster Florent's quarters. The door was open, and the room was in a state of disrepair. Given the room's disarray, it was clear the Order had searched her office, but the painting the headmaster had told them of still hung on the wall, although slightly askew.

Daebian entered and pulled the portrait away from the wall. "I don't see a safe."

Azerick strode up next to him and smiled as he studied the image of a former headmaster sitting at his desk and penning scrolls. "The painting is the safe."

Azerick focused on the invisible strands of energy until they became visible to his mage sight and manipulated them with his mind. The weave was complex. Nothing like the simple ward he had unraveled on Allister's door a lifetime ago. To compound the challenge, he was not trying to unravel it. To do so would render the safe useless and the painting inoperable. What he had to do was the magical equivalent of picking a very sophisticated lock.

Daebian's eyes darted toward the door that still lay open. "Hurry, someone's coming."

"I need another minute," Azerick whispered.

"You don't have a minute."

"Then buy me some time."

Daebian stole the light from the nearest magical globe and created a veil of shadows. Moments later, a troop of soldiers appeared in the hall just outside the door. Daebian recognized them as the same ones that had almost caught them outside. The decanus leading the squad glanced into the open room and looked as if he would march past, but he stopped at the last second and studied the interior with a look of suspicion across his face. He took a step into the room and stared at the shadow hiding the intruders from his sight.

Azerick finished picking the ward, reached into the painting, and began relieving the portrait of the paper, ink, and quill. The decanus' shield flared to life, and he increased its glow to banish the room's shadows, which it did. All but one. He reeled back his spear and hurled it in a single, fluid motion. His spear struck something in the shadows and stuck. The squad rushed in, brandishing weapons and blazing shields. Their shields banished the darkness and revealed the decanus' spear protruding from the portrait wizard's chest.

Darkness enveloped them as Daebian pulled Azerick into the shadow ways. He led them toward a familiar shadow within his father's old lair. It was a long step, and they had to navigate the shadow ways for a minute or two. Unfortunately, the shadow spawn did not give them anywhere near that much time.

The creatures leapt out of the darkness, their attack directed at Azerick. His wards flared beneath the assault, illuminating the spawn's ghastly visages. Their obsidian blades punched through the arcane shield in several places, but it stopped them well short of reaching the sorcerer's vulnerable flesh.

Azerick lashed out with magic, driving the creatures back. Daebian's sword flicked out, finding flesh with each strike as the spawn forced him to defend himself. The efficacy of his aural disguise failed under the monsters' scrutiny and his attacks. Azerick shuffled after his son as Daebian pushed through the impenetrable darkness. He beat back a second wave of attacks before they burst out of the shadows, causing Vera to let out a surprised shriek as she hunched over her alchemic set. Rusty stood nearby with a blazing ball of fire cupped in his hand, ready to hurl it at the intruders.

"Oh, it's you," Rusty said as he shook his hand, dismissing the fireball as if it were something foul sticking to his flesh.

Azerick clapped his old friend on the shoulder and grinned. "Good to see you on your toes."

"These bastards caught me flatfooted once. I won't let them do it again. Were you able to get what you needed?"

"We did. We're taking it to the headmaster and Andrill now."

They used the sewers and walked to Andrill's safe house instead of braving the shadow ways once more. Daebian's sharp vision had no problem finding the secret doorway leading to the hidden basement beneath one of several inns the guild master owned. Azerick was certain his son saw the thieves hidden from his own eyes just as he knew there were others neither of them could see, watching from behind secret passages, ready to slip a poisoned blade or quarrel between the ribs of any intruders.

A second hidden door opened into the room itself. The occupants were on guard but not startled by their arrival. The headmaster sat at a table with Andrill and a dozing Braxis. Half a dozen other men stood or sat in chairs near the walls with hands touching the hilts of blades or cradling crossbows.

"Did you get them?" Headmaster Florent asked the moment the two stepped through the door.

Azerick set the quill, ink, and paper on the desk. "We did."

"Have much trouble?" Andrill asked.

"No more or less than expected," Daebian replied.

Andrill elbowed Braxis. "You're up, old man."

Braxis snorted awake and blinked the sleep out of his eyes. "Who are you calling an old man, old man?"

The guild boss slid the writing materials over to him and he copied the writ. Braxis did not just reproduce the words. He mirrored the writing style and the arcanus' signature in every detail, at least to Azerick's untrained eye.

Braxis turned the page around and slid it across the table to Azerick. "Just sign it and make a thumb print on the bottom."

"Does it have to be my name?"

The corners of Braxis' mouth turned down. "That's a good question. I don't have the foggiest idea."

"As long as your thumb and the print are a match, it should be fine," Headmaster Florent said.

"I'm risking a lot on should be."

"We all are."

Azerick took the quill and signed a pseudonym. He then touched his thumb to the ink blotter before pressing it against the paper.

"Hold it there," Headmaster Florent said as she wove magic into the document.

The glittering ink glowed for a moment before going dark.

"That should do it," the archmage announced.

"You're sure it will work?" Azerick asked as he studied the page.

"It should fool any of the soldiers, but it won't hold up to more than passing scrutiny by one of their arcanus. Best to avoid them if possible."

Azerick nodded at the needless warning and studied the archmage's work as she enchanted Daebian's writ once Braxis finished forging it.

"Think you got it?" the headmaster asked Azerick.

"It's simple enough. I shouldn't have any trouble recreating it," Azerick replied.

"It's getting late," Andrill said. "Best we get to our positions."

Daebian and Azerick took the stairs and exited the inn with their new papers in hand as proper citizens of the Order instead of traveling the sewers like a pair of bipedal rats. Headmaster Florent and her teaching cadre took charge of several groups of students. Each wizard capable of the feat would cast multiple dimensional gates in and around the city to confuse the watchful eyes of the Order's arcanus just as Azerick had done.

It was a long walk for Azerick and Daebian to get where they were going, and they were stopped twice to present their papers. Both times they had to press their thumbs onto the print they had made at the bottom. The letters glowed with the appropriate green light, and they allowed the two men to go on their way without further disruption.

Father and son sat on the ledge of the fountain decorating the plaza outside the main gates blocking access to the castle grounds and waited. It would be another hour before the sun set and the mages fled the city with their younger students.

Daebian looked over his shoulder at the statue standing in the center of the fountain. "I can see why you chose to wait here."

Azerick followed his gaze and sighed. "I chose this spot because that is where I expect the bulk of the forces to come from."

Daebian looked from the statue to his father several times. "It's not a very good likeness."

"I've changed a lot, and I imagine people's memory of me is shaped by our interactions at the time."

Daebian looked up and nodded. "I can see that. That explains why this one makes you look like such a prick. The one in North Haven is less prickish…a little."

A boy of around five walked up to the fountain with his mother and pitched a copper penny into the water. His eyes bounced between Azerick's face, partially hidden beneath the hood of his cloak, and up at the statue. His eyes widened and his mouth gaped open. Azerick pressed a finger to his lips and winked at him. The boy clamped his mouth shut and looked back at him several times as his mother led him away by the hand.

"I guess there's still a resemblance," Azerick said.

The two passed the time watching the comings and goings of people through the square and the castle gates, paying particular attention to the soldiers' activities. Shadows stretched across the ground as the sun set, and the plaza slowly emptied of people.

"Best get to our positions," Azerick said. "We're starting to look conspicuous sitting here by ourselves."

Daebian nodded and crossed the square. Azerick walked off in another direction and took a seat inside a nice tavern from where he could watch the plaza through the window. There was little to do now but wait for the Academy mages to make their move. They did not have to wait long.

Azerick felt a surge in the Source, like a pebble tossed into a pond disturbing the placid water. It was subtle as he was not searching for it, but the gates the wizards tore open shone like beacons to the arcanus on guard for such magical use. Horns blared in less than a minute. Two minutes later, half a score of gliders hummed over the castle walls and streaked across the dark sky. Within five minutes, skimmers loaded with squads of legionnaires floated through the plaza and raced toward the outer gates and districts where the arcanus detected the portals.

Azerick looked around the room and recognized several of Andrill's men, and he knew there were many others nearby, including Rusty and several Academy wizards, ready to do battle should Daebian fail to escape with the prisoners without being detected. For now, all they could do was wait.

CHAPTER 23

Daebian watched the soldiers streaming out of the gates or flying over the walls. When it appeared the last of the legionnaires sent to investigate left the compound, he crossed into the shadow ways and appeared inside the castle courtyard an instant later. He skulked in the wall's darkened confines, noting the increased guards stationed within due to the alarms being raised. There would be no sleep for any of them this night.

He picked out a distant patch of darkness and shadow-stepped to the castle's exterior near a postern door. The shadow spawn ignored his intrusion into what they considered their realm for now, but Daebian knew they would eventually detect his false aura and attack. He needed to hunt and trap one of their souls before long to maintain the ruse.

Daebian elected to use the door to gain entrance instead of taking a blind step into the castle interior. The door opened to a narrow hall with a few small rooms off to each side, likely a servants' entrance with changing rooms and cleaning closets. He ignored these, wrapped himself in shadow, and slinked down the passage with his back pressed against the wall.

The hall opened into a larger area with many branching hallways leading to other parts of the castle. The castle had a few cells in the subterranean levels for special prisoners, and Daebian assumed that's where Andrill's people were being held since they were not in the city's jail run by the Watch. While the Order conquered the city with little resistance, they knew their hold was a tenuous one despite their confident bearing. All it would take was a spark of discontent to ignite a full-scale rebellion.

The Order's numbers were small compared to the populace at large, and with the freeing of the wizards, they had reinforced their position within the castle grounds as a defensible redoubt that could hold against an uprising until the rest of their forces arrived. It was why they held any dissidents they captured here instead of in the proper jail.

There was less light in the underground levels, making Daebian's infiltration that much easier. The moment he thought it, a nagging feeling crawled up his spine telling him that this was too easy. He shoved the thought aside. He was not worried about getting in regardless of how hard they might try to keep him out. The problem was getting Andrill's people out once he freed them. It was an easy matter for him to escape through the shadow ways should something go wrong, but he could only take two of the dissidents with him at most by literally holding their hands. Then the problem would be keeping them alive long enough to reach the outside, an unlikely prospect.

He stopped halfway down a set of stairs when a flickering torch revealed two legionnaires standing guard outside a sturdy door near the bottom of the steps. Daebian paused for just a moment to study them before plunging into a shadow and erupting within their midst. His sword slipped beneath the first soldier's breastplate, killing him in an instant. The second legionnaire's shield flared before Daebian could pull his blade from his fellow's corpse and brought it around to smash into the attacker's shoulder.

Daebian rebounded off the wall and slashed at the soldier with a series of strikes. The corridor's narrow confines made it easy for the legionnaire to block the flurry of blows and even riposte with his short spear. He dodged the spear thrusts and changed tactics. He stole the light from the burning torch, leaving only a weak stream of illumination coming through the small, barred window at the top of the door.

The guard's shield flared brighter to battle back the darkness. Its light revealed Daebian in mid-leap, his feet coiled to strike. The soldier raised his shield, and Daebian struck it like a battering ram. The legionnaire cried out in surprise when he continued to fall back instead of fetching up against the door, and his world plunged into total blackness as if his sight had been stolen.

The man rolled to his feet and willed his shield to banish the darkness, but it failed to cast a light farther away than his elbow. He spun toward the sound of jingling bells. Daebian returned to the dungeon before hearing the man's death cries.

The door was locked, and the soldier lying dead in a pool of his own blood did not have the keys. Daebian summoned Klaraxis' abyssal power and corroded the lock and bolt mechanism until he could shatter them with a swift kick. The door swung open, and he burst into the passageway. Barred cells lined the left-hand wall. There were five in total and were large enough to hold a dozen prisoners each. The Order must not have wanted to put all their prisoners together, because none of the cells held over three people. Three men stood huddled near the wall in the first cell, two in the second, two women in the third, and three more men in the farthest one.

Daebian thought it was unusual for there not to be any interior guards, but there was no other way in or out of the cell chamber except through the door he had entered. Lacking keys, Daebian had to destroy the locks on the cells as well.

"You must be Daebian," one thief said as Daebian freed him. "Is Azerick here as well?"

Daebian forced down the bile in his stomach, but it did not dull the sharp edge in his voice. "No, most of the castle and just beyond the wall is shielded from magic, rendering him next to useless. You'll just have to settle for me."

The man raised his hands in surrender. "Hey, I didn't mean nothin' by it. You got them wizards out. I'm sure you'll do the same for us."

Daebian ducked his head and handed out the few daggers and shortswords he had brought with him. "That's the plan. Most of the guards are chasing the mages, so with our skills, we should be able to get out little fuss."

"I thought there was two out here?" the thief asked as they stepped past the lone legionnaire's body.

"The other one is gone from this world in every sense of the word."

The man looked at Daebian with an appraising eye and reassessed his first opinion of him. Daebian stretched the shadows out enough to cover the entire group as they made their way up the stairs. The connecting hall appeared as empty as when Daebian had arrived. He crept out into the corridor to the end and studied the large open area with its network of hallways.

His eyes cut through the shadows like knives through gossamer, commanding them to reveal anyone trying to hide within their depths. He saw nothing but plastered stone and decorations. His ears probed for anything his eyes did not see, but he could hear nothing, not even the breathing or beating hearts of the thieves hidden in the shadows behind him.

After a long minute, Daebian motioned to the group, and they slunk up behind him without a sound. Daebian did not speak. He gestured with his hands in a silent language known only to people whose lives depended on stealth that they needed to traverse the hallway on their left to reach the exit.

Daebian led the way, clinging to the wall. He had almost reached the passageway to the exit when a blinding light erupted from every wall, floor, and ceiling and obliterated the shadows in which they hid. Dozens of Order soldiers double-timed into the open area, streaming in from every connecting hall. A man in resplendent armor walked to the middle of the room.

"Did you really expect me to fall for the same trick twice?" Primus Ploutarch asked.

Daebian glanced back at the thieves gripping their weapons behind him but did not respond.

The primus flicked a hand over his shoulder. "Take the warlock alive. Kill the others."

Daebian and the thieves exploded into motion and threw themselves at the soldiers. The legionnaires' shields flared with violet energy, and they marched forward to do battle. Daebian ran straight for the primus, his sword held low in front of him. Arcane energy flared from Primus Ploutarch's twin, silver bucklers. A shield surrounded the arcanum disc strapped to his left arm while a translucent blade four feet long and more than a hand span in width jutted out from the one on his right.

Their weapons clashed in a shower of purple sparks. There was nothing insubstantial about the primus' blade except for the impossible speed in which he wielded it. Had Daebian's sword not been enchanted, he was certain the arcane weapon would have sheared clean through it. Daebian heard cries of pain and death over the lightning-like cracking of their colliding blades, and a quick flick of his eyes showed that the battle was already lost.

The last two thieves standing tried to make a break for the hallway from which they came. It was the desperate act of men who had no other options. They knew there was no way out in that direction, but they grasped at the slightest chance of staying alive just a few seconds longer.

Daebian knew he had a chance to get them out through the shadow ways if they could break free of this damnable light. The corridor leading down the stairs might still have shadows he could use. Getting the two survivors through the shadow ways alive was slim, but it was far better odds than they faced out here.

The choice disappeared an instant after it floated through Daebian's mind. Short spears and crossbow bolts flew across the room and struck down the fleeing men. Daebian focused on keeping the primus' ethereal blade from his vulnerable flesh until he remembered that they wanted to take him alive. He lowered his sword, spun, and tried to race back toward the dungeon, but something akin to the fist of an invisible giant struck him in the back and sent him tumbling headlong.

Daebian tried to create a shadow in which to flee, but the brilliant light blazing from every surface tore it apart like smoke in a hurricane. He tried to climb back to his feet and make another dash toward freedom, but the unseen giant's foot crushed him to the floor. Primus Ploutarch stepped on Daebian's wrist and kick the sword from his outstretched hand.

Daebian glared up and saw Doncho hovering over his shoulder just behind him, and he understood the true source of the invisible beating. Primus Ploutarch vanquished his sword and shield and bashed Daebian in the back of the head with the arcanum buckler, sending Daebian to the darkness he had fought so hard to reach.

CHAPTER 24

Headmaster Florent waited in the large warehouse, surrounded by scores of students and several Academy instructors and members of the council. As the daylight faded, her anxiety increased and, by the look on her fellow mages' faces, she was not alone in that regard. The minutes ticked past, and time seemed to slow until she was certain it would soon come to a stop altogether. The sun finally dipped over the sea's horizon.

"It's time," the headmaster announced, her voice carrying across the expansive warehouse due to the preternatural quiet.

She and several full wizards tore open numerous portals. Other mages stepped through them and ripped open several more gates, their destinations scattered throughout the city and beyond the walls. Spellcasters leap-frogged through the rifts, opening more portals to random locations to confuse any arcanus tracking such blatant use of magic.

Headmaster Florent and the mages tasked as team leaders rushed their students through the portals without pause. By the third transit, even the strongest wizards wavered on their feet. Several students were vomiting and near to falling down, but those with steadier balance grabbed them up and forced them through the next gate until all were standing in the forest as far from Southport as they could reach.

"We'll pause here. I want every team leader to get an accurate headcount," Headmaster Florent ordered.

The instructors counted their charges while everyone else fought to regain their composure. Several gliders flew overhead, but the dark clothing they wore hid them from prying eyes beneath the heavy canopy.

"All accounted for," Magus Trent informed the headmaster a minute later.

Headmaster Florent nodded. "We need to get away from the portal exit. It's only a matter of time before the soldiers come looking for us."

With a spattering of mumbled complaints, the large group made their way north toward the hidden town Azerick had described. It would take about two days to walk the entire distance, but they were prepared to make such a trek, however exhausting it might be.

It was impossible to move quietly, and the headmaster thought people back in Southport could hear their passage. People stumbled and cursed when they tripped over rocks and sticks, but they dared not risk creating a light with the gliders still buzzing overhead every few minutes. Those who were able cast spells that allowed them to see in the dark, and they guided the others past obstacles as best they could. They were minor spells and shouldn't be detectable unless the arcanus appeared in the middle of them.

Traveling was still slow-going. Because they needed the treetops to conceal them, they had to travel over rough ground and avoid open areas. They pushed through their pain and exhaustion until the youngest could go no farther.

"We'll rest here," Headmaster Florent announced.

Magus Pugh sat next to the headmaster and looked up at the treetops. "Haven't seen any of those flying machines in a while. Think they've given up?"

The headmaster's eyes flicked skyward. "I wouldn't count on it. We'll need to maintain light discipline at least for tonight."

"How much farther do you expect us to travel tonight?" Magus Trent asked.

"We need to get at least another five miles before we stop. That should give us four hours or more of sleep before starting out again in the morning."

Magus Trent wagged his head. "The children will still be exhausted."

"They'll manage. We've seen the alternative."

Magus Douglas bustled toward the group, panting with labored breaths. "Headmaster, I think there's something out in the woods watching us."

"Soldiers?" she asked.

The councilman shook his head, dislodging beads of nervous sweat. "I don't think so."

"What do you think it is?"

Magus Douglas leaned in and spoke in a whisper. "Spawn."

"Gods preserve us," Magus Pugh whispered in a hoarse voice.

Headmaster Florent stood. "Gather everyone together. Put the youngest in the middle. I want everyone capable of creating a ward on the outside. If we begin hurling fireballs and lightning, we'll bring the Order down on our heads as well. Have you informed Andrill's people?"

Magus Douglas nodded once. "They're aware of the threat and are standing ready."

The mages gathered their students and huddled together. Those who were able, raised overlapping wards not unlike those created by the legionnaires' shields just as glowing eyes appeared in the distance. Headmaster Florent conjured an invisible wizard's eye and sent it flying out into the darkness. She gasped and almost lost control of the spell at the sight of scores of spawn approaching them and trying to surround their position.

"We have to fight, but don't use spells that can be seen or heard from a distance. No fire or lightning or such," Headmaster Florent ordered. "We're still too close to the city and those scouts."

They had planned their tactics for such a possibility before leaving the city, and most mages had selected their spells accordingly. The mages stood with their backs pressed together while the thieves Andrill had sent with them pointed their crossbows outward or held knives to fling at anything that moved. Only the suppressed sobs of the younger students broke the forest's eerie silence.

More than a dozen spawn slammed into the barrier the wizards had raised. Their snapping jaws flung ropy spittle, and their blades hammered against the invisible surface. Magus Trent created a wall of ice twenty feet long and caught several of the creatures inside it. They thrashed at their icy prison and hacked at it with blades and claws.

Several mages used staves, sticks, and rocks pried out of the ground to bash the trapped spawn until they ceased their struggles. Magus King's spell caused dozens of fist-sized stones to raise out of the ground and sent them flying out into the mass of ravagers and other spawn. Sharp barks of pain accompanied the sound of stone striking flesh.

One of the small, blue-skinned spawn came hurtling out of the darkness and penetrated the wizard's wards like a needle through cloth. Headmaster Florent's eye's widened in terror, and she struck the creature with an invisible battering ram of force. She had seen the destruction these mage-killers could wreak during the war.

The ripper's trajectory reversed course, but it exploded an instant after the archmage struck it. Several mages and thieves went down, and not all got back up right away. The spawn sensed the weakness in the ward and converged upon it.

"Seal that breach!" Headmaster Florent cried.

Mages fought to reinforce the barrier while battling back the thronging creatures clawing to get through. The archmage gritted her teeth as she assessed their situation. There was enough arcane power between them to obliterate the foul creatures with ease, but doing so would almost certainly give away their position. As magus Sorenson struck down a ravager that had penetrated their wards, she knew they had little other recourse.

Headmaster Florent began shaping the Source into a powerful spell that would incinerate the bulk of the spawn piled against one section of the barrier. She paused her casting when several creatures howled in pain and began writhing on the ground. She saw crossbow bolts and javelins jutting out of the monsters' backs, their wounds smoking as if struck by red-hot brands or acid. The spawn turned almost en masse and directed their fury at the newest threat.

Ropy tendrils launched out of the darkness, wrapping around the creatures' bodies and sticking to their flesh. More projectiles flew out of the trees ahead of a line of men wielding shields and barbed pikes. The pikemen jammed their shields into the ground and leveled their long spears to hold back the spawn that fought their way free of the constricting tendrils while archers and javelin throwers unleashed volley after volley of death.

The Academy mages struck at the creatures' rear with shards of ice and stone, and the remaining thieves loosed their quarrels and throwing knives with deadly effect. Caught between two sides, the spawn began falling until the few that remained fled into the night. The wizards held their wards in place, not knowing who had saved them or why. As the new group approached, it was obvious they were not part of the Order.

They looked rough, with piecemeal armor and a wide assortment of weapons. Headmaster Florent was shocked to recognize some of the faces of the men and women approaching them as former Academy students.

"Headmaster Florent, is that you?" a young woman asked.

The archmage squinted and tried to put a name with the face. "Sibyl Arbeit? What are you doing out here with these people?"

Sibyl smiled. "I would ask you the same question."

Headmaster Florent motioned her people to relax, and several of her people dropped their guard and tended to the wounded. Once they lowered the barrier, a few of the newcomers strode forward without asking with bandages and poultices in hand.

"Foreigners have invaded Southport. They captured us before we could raise a defense." The headmaster took a deep breath. "Azerick Giles has returned. He and some others freed us. We thought it best to get the younger students out of the city to avoid the fighting and being recaptured and sent off across the sea should things go badly. He told us to head north and find a group of people he met before arriving in the city."

Joah cleared his throat as he stepped forward. "We know about Azerick, and you've found the people he mentioned."

"I was my understanding you are based at least two days north of here."

"We are, but we've been tracking this group for a while," Joah explained. "That's what we do, among other things."

Headmaster Florent stared at Joah and his group for a moment. "You're the people who have been robbing travelers."

Joah smiled. "Among other things. But Azerick put a stop to that. The question now is what do you want with us?"

"Azerick thought you would welcome some Academy students and keep them safe."

Joah dug the toe of his boot in the dirt. "Welcome is a strong word. Marley isn't the welcoming type."

"These are magus students. Even the most inexperienced would be a benefit," the headmaster insisted.

"There's also a lot of them, each having a mouth to feed and needing a bed," Joah countered.

"You can't just abandon children to their fate!"

"You'd be surprised at what we can do," Joah replied, a subtle warning to the wizards not to press him and his people.

The archmage swallowed her simmering frustration. "Azerick said they could find safety with your people."

"Azerick, regardless of his opinion on the matter, is not in charge. That would be Marley. Where is Azerick now?"

"He's in Southport trying to drive out the invaders, but he said he would meet us once they freed some prisoners marked for execution."

Joah looked around. "Looks to me like he missed his appointment."

Headmaster Florent let out a slow breath. "Yes, it does."

CHAPTER 25

Azerick kept his eyes locked on the gates, his concern for Daebian so consuming he almost jumped out of his chair when Rusty sat across from him.

"He should be been back by now," Rusty said.

Azerick let out a sigh and nodded. "I know."

"It's getting late. Most of the mages and Andrill's people have gone back to ground. We should too if we want to get back before curfew."

Azerick gave a slow shake of his head. "Daebian is hard to pin down. Even if he wasn't able to free Andrill's people, he should have been able to get out."

"These people aren't stupid, and they aren't weak. Something went wrong, but there's not much we can do about it tonight. You're supposed to be making introductions between Headmaster Florent and Marley. You need to focus on the mission you can affect."

"He's my son," Azerick said as he watched soldiers marching back through the gates far sooner than they should have been.

"And if he's still alive, we'll figure out a way to get him back, but there's dozens of sons and daughters out in the woods in the middle of the night filled with all manner of danger."

Azerick sighed again. "You're right. I abandoned them once. I cannot do it again. Let's get out of here."

Azerick and Rusty left the tavern, sticking to alleys and dark streets to avoid the soldiers marching toward the castle. Azerick was certain they were expecting an assault, and the idea concerned him a great deal. He found the Order's entire response to Daebian's infiltration disturbing. They should have been out investigating the numerous portals they had opened and hunting for them, but the squads had returned far too soon. That meant either they had expected a jail break and planned for it, or they caught someone more important than the wayward mages. Azerick was thinking it was both.

"Can you open several gates at once, a few near the outer walls?" Azerick asked when they were several blocks from the tavern and hiding at the end of a pitch-black, dead-end alley.

"I can open a few. Gating isn't one of my better skills, even when I was in practice," Rusty replied.

"That's fine. I want to get as close to the outer wall and then as far from the city as I can before opening another portal. I think the arcanus are focusing their attention near the castle, so they shouldn't detect me once I'm in the countryside."

"Let's hope not. I'll get with Andrill and the rest of the wizards and work on a plan to get into the castle. If they caught Daebian, we'll get him back."

"Like we did Andrill's people?" Azerick replied with venom in his voice.

Rusty laid a hand on his shoulder and looked him in the eye. "We'll get him back."

Azerick nodded. "Yes, we will. If we have to tear down the castle around them, we will."

Azerick and Rusty opened several portals and stepped through the ones that saw them safely away. Azerick opened another rift the moment he appeared near Southport's northeastern curtain wall and gated as far out into the forest as he could reach. Another dimensional step took him almost five miles from the city and he began walking. He hoped it was enough to avoid the Order's watchful eyes.

Two of the flying machines buzzed overhead in last hour, but they did not see him. They appeared to be flying patrols. Whether they were routine movements, or they were searching for him or Headmaster Florent and the runaways he could not say. Azerick plodded through the dark forest, heading north in the direction he had sent the Academy mages. He slowed and went on alert when he came upon the scene of a large battle. Dead spawn and blood littered the area, many of the bodies bent and broken like the surrounding trees. He knelt and looked at the quarrels sticking out of several bodies.

"Azerick, is that you?" a woman's voice called out of the darkness.

Azerick turned toward the voice, still in a crouch and prepared to defend himself. "It's me. Who's there?"

Several people in woodland garb approached. Azerick recognized Sibyl when the group drew closer.

"What happened here?" Azerick asked and felt foolish the instant he said it. "Were the mages here?"

"They were. We came upon them mid-battle."

"Is everyone OK?"

"A few suffered injuries. Some of them serious. A few may not recover," Sybil replied.

"Where are they now?"

"A couple miles north. We didn't want to stick around in case the fight drew unwanted attention."

Azerick nodded. "Did you get the wounded to your camp? You have healers there don't you?"

Sybil shifted her posture and looked at her feet. "Joah refused to take them to Freehold."

Azerick bolted upright. "You said some of them were badly hurt! Why haven't you seen to them?"

"I thought you understood our need for secrecy."

"Didn't Head Master Florent tell you what was happening, why I sent them to you?"

"Yes, but that doesn't change anything."

"It changes everything!" Azerick tore open a portal. "You said they were a couple of miles north? Let's go."

Sybil and her group followed Azerick through the gate. She looked around to get her bearings and led the way. They marched through the woods with Azerick spurring them on the entire way. They reached the camp after about half an hour of walking. Azerick saw several people being tended to, but his blood still boiled at the sight. He felt responsible for them. He had been the one to send them out on their own, and it ended up proving to be a bad decision that may well cost lives.

"Joah, why didn't you at least take the wounded to Freehold?" Azerick demanded.

Joah stiffened his spine at the sight of the angry sorcerer. "Because Freehold ain't a tourist town. It's my job to keep people out, not bring them in in droves."

"These people are hurt!"

"We're well-versed in tending to wounded, especially when it comes to spawn attacks."

"They need a real healer. If Freehold has one, then we need to take them there. Then we can talk about the rest of them."

"It ain't your call," Joah said in a firm voice.

Azerick glared at the recalcitrant man. "Are we really going to do this again?"

Joah crossed his arms and returned the sorcerer's stern look. "No, we're not."

Azerick turned to Sybil. "Do you have a way to contact Marley?"

The wizard's eyes darted between the two men before she nodded. "There's an arch not far from here. I can take you to see him."

"Sybil!" Joah snapped, "It's not your place to reveal the arches!"

"It's also not my place to leave a bunch of kids in the middle of spawn-infested woods! We'll go talk with Marley. It's his place to say, not yours."

Joah spared a glance at Azerick and replied, "You sure about that?"

Sybil motioned to the sorcerer. "Come on. It isn't far."

Azerick followed the mage and had to jog a moment to catch up with her long, agitated strides. "I don't think Joah likes me much."

The corner of Sybil's mouth turned up. "You think?"

"There was a time I would have painted the forest with his blood over something like this."

"It's a good thing you're not that person anymore, or you would have had to fight me and the rest of us as well. He's not a bad sort, nor particularly good. Joah likes to follow the rules, and you forced him to break them once already."

"You don't mind breaking the rules?"

"I've never shied away from sharing my disagreements regarding some of our less than noble pursuits."

"Like highway robbery?"

Sybil frowned and looked uncomfortable. "That's one of the big ones."

"Then why stay with them?"

"Spawn killed my family and many of my friends. Marley's people kill spawn."

Azerick nodded, understanding far too well the desire for vengeance and the satisfying feeling of enacting it. "He's not the only one surely? I imagine King Miles would welcome all talented mages in his ranks."

"Miles can barely protect his crown. He doesn't care about us out here. If he does, he's impotent to do anything about it. This is my home, and I won't abandon it."

"Believe me, I understand."

Sybil sighed. "I know you do, that's why I'm taking you to Marley."

They walked in silence for several minutes before the wizard spoke again. "I was there that night, when the spawn attacked the Academy. I was just a novice when I saw a lot of my friends die."

"I'm very sorry," Azerick choked out.

"I was eight. No eight-year-old should see death like that."

Azerick shook his head. "No, they shouldn't."

"Headmaster Florent blamed you for it, for a lot of the deaths. I always thought she was wrong."

"I wish she was, but she's not. I chose not to intervene."

Sybil looked back at him over her shoulder. "That's probably not the best answer to give someone who's trying to help you."

"No, but it's an honest one."

"I suppose there's some value in that."

"You're not going to ask me why?" Azerick asked when she said nothing further.

"I think I know why, and so does Headmaster Florent no matter how hard she clings to her anger. A better question is where is your son?"

Azerick held his breath and looked at his feet. "I fear they captured him…or worse."

"And yet you're here and not there."

"I promised the headmaster I would see her students to safety."

"You seem to make a habit of choosing the greater good. It is unfortunate that the greater good often requires a greater sacrifice."

Azerick gave her a grim nod. "You are wise for your age."

"I've seen much in my years. This world is much less forgiving of fools than it once was." She stopped at a stone archway hidden by tall shrubs and crafted camouflage. "This is it."

Azerick studied the permanent portal. "Your people made this?"

Sybil nodded. "We made a few. Some of our people helped make the larger ones used in the Gods War to evacuate the cities. It wasn't much of a leap to recreate smaller ones, even without access to the Source pool. They don't reach as far, but they can cut several days off our travel."

Sybil wove her magic into the arch. Within a few seconds, the inner archway shimmered. The scene beyond looked much the same as the surrounding forest, and only someone with an astute eye would notice that what lay beyond the arch was miles away. They walked through, the mild disorientation leaving no doubt they had traveled much farther than the few steps they had taken.

"It's Sybil and Azerick," the mage said the moment they crossed through the portal.

Just like his last trip through the arch, several people hid in the trees and brush, guarding the portal with weapons and magic. No one spoke or challenged them as Sybil led the way toward Freehold. There was little activity this late at night, but the village was not entirely asleep. A few people lurked in doorways, alert for any dangers that might get past the exterior guards.

Azerick followed Sybil up the short steps and into the lodge. Marley sat on a throne of hewn timbers atop a raised section against the far wall. He did not appear to have been roused from his bed.

"The hero returns," Marley said. "Have you once again saved us from evil?"

Azerick ignored his mocking tone. "Not yet. You're up late."

"As are you. I wonder what else we have in common? If you did not come to inform us of your triumph, what brings you here?"

Azerick gave Marley the abridged version of events over the last few days. "I evacuated the student mages along with a handful of instructors and wanted to bring them here."

Sybil added, "The large group of spawn we were hunting attacked them. Several of them suffered serious injuries."

"So there is some urgency to my request," Azerick said.

Marley's eyes widened and he showed his teeth as he smiled. "So it's a request this time? Was there a declaration of friendship I missed?"

Azerick let out a long breath. "I handled our last meeting poorly. Things have been chaotic since I returned, and I have not had time to adjust to the many changes in my life. I was surrounded by creatures every bit as foul as the ones plaguing this land but far more cunning. My concept of diplomacy has been somewhat singular for a long time."

"I admit, it strokes my ego and warms my cockles to get what I can only presume to be an apology from a notorious hero."

"It serves both our interests to bring them here."

"How many are we talking about?"

Azerick winced inwardly, knowing this was not an argument in his favor. "About a hundred."

Marley's eyebrows crawled up his forehead. "A hundred mouths to feed and bodies to shelter? How could this possibly be to my benefit?"

"You count only a handful of mages with power and talent beyond that of a journeyman wizard. I'm bringing you the headmaster herself and no less than two archmages and several full wizards, some of whom, including the headmaster, will stay with their students. Even the youngest can provide a measure of security and help continue to keep Freehold hidden."

Marley rubbed his chin as he thought. "Headmaster Florent is a shrewish old hag, and her presence could be as disrupting as yours has been. I can't have wizards constantly usurping my authority."

"She and her people are guests, and I will press that point upon them." Azerick leaned forward and leveled a steady gaze on Marley. "Think about the long term. I told you I would convince Southport and North Haven to leave you be and even provide material support as long as you ceased waylaying travelers. This act would almost certainly secure their goodwill. With any luck, they won't even be here that long."

Marley pursed his lips and nodded. "Speaking of your campaign, I can't help but notice your god-slaying son is not here. Is he attending to other, more important business?"

Azerick took a deep breath and looked at the floor. "He was… detained."

Marley smiled, seeing through Azerick's prevarication. "It sounds to me like the war is not going well, and that my guests might be staying longer than you claim."

Azerick laid a baleful glare on the man. "I have been trying to convince the Order that coming here is not in their best interest. I'm done with forceful diplomacy. Now I'm just going to kill them."

The power of Azerick's words pressed Marley back in his chair. "All right. If the headmaster and her wizards promise to follow my rules and understand that I am in charge here, then I will tend to their needs."

"Thank you, Marley."

Marley chuckled. "Don't thank me just yet. Save it for when you take them back."

Azerick ducked his head and turned to leave. He let Sybil take the lead as they stalked toward the arch. Neither of them spoke until they crossed through the portal and hiked back to their people.

"You did well with Marley," Sybil said. "Better than last time."

"Yes, I'm becoming quite the diplomat."

"Did you mean what you said about the invaders?"

Azerick nodded. "I did."

"You have a plan then?"

Despite the dark night, a shadow washed over Azerick's face. "I most definitely do."

CHAPTER 26

"Tell us where the rebels are hiding, and this will go away."

Daebian was strapped to a stout chair set in the middle of a room that seemed comprised of nothing but brilliant white light. While the speaker was nothing but a silhouette to his abused eyes, he knew it was Arcanus Joakim Karpos. The man had been interrogating him for hours, possibly days. Daebian had little concept of time.

The Order appeared to avoid the more standard forms of torture. At least so far. They refused to let him sleep, deprived him of food and water, and bathed him in bright light, which was the worst of it so far. Daebian was a creature of darkness, and his tolerance was rather low, even with his eyes closed.

"We'll find them soon without you," Primus Ploutarch said, his coarse voice the opposite of Arcanus Karpos' soft, hypnotic tone. "There's only so many places they can hide in a city this size. Someone will give them up. All we have to do is drop enough coin in the right hand."

"We want to avoid as much bloodshed as possible," the arcanus said, his dulcet voice laced with magic. "The Order is here on a mission of mercy, to save the lives of those tormented by the spawn, and to raise your people's culture and standard of living. If they but yield—" The arcanus cut his words short, and he cast a furtive look around the room.

"What is it?" Primus Ploutarch asked.

"The nullification field is going down."

A dark line severed the air not far from where Daebian sat tied to his chair. It widened in an instant to reveal what appeared to be a narrow egress somewhere in the city. A searing red ray lanced out of the portal and struck Arcanus Karpos in the chest. Unprepared for the assault, the beam cut through him and melted a hole in the stone wall behind him several inches deep.

Azerick flew through the gate behind his arcane lance and hurled his spear-tipped staff like a javelin. Primus Ploutarch summoned his shield and brought it around just in time to block it. The powerful weapon stuck in the magical shield, creating a series of sparks and loud crackling as the two magics fought to destroy one another.

The force of the blow caused the primus to stagger back. He conjured a sword in his other hand while he backpedaled away from the onrushing sorcerer to bide enough time to set himself for battle. Azerick was not going to let him. Stone hands extended from the wall behind the primus and latched onto his arms.

Azerick recalled his staff and drove it into the Primus' chest while the stone hands pinned back his arms. The leather straps securing Daebian parted with a wave of Azerick's hand.

"We need to get out of here," Azerick said as he tugged on Daebian's arm.

Daebian pulled away. "We need to get my sword and the stone."

"There's no time! They'll get their damned emitters back up soon. We'll figure out a plan to get the stone back after we meet up with the others and end these bastards once and for all."

Daebian paused for just a moment before jumping through the portal ahead of his father. The gate snapped shut the instant Azerick crossed through. Azerick cocked an ear toward the sounds of shouting, horns, and clashing weapons.

"Come on!" he shouted at Daebian and ran out of the alley.

Daebian saw they were close to the castle gates. A squad of legionnaires streamed out in pursuit of several men racing across the plaza. Azerick struck out at the soldiers, smashing the lead element with a powerful blast of energy from his staff. The energy wave halted them in their steps and blasted the front rank back into those behind them. Shields flared from within the Order ranks, and they turned their attention to the newest threat.

Azerick pushed Daebian ahead as gliders streaked out over the wall. "Go, I'll defend our backs! We need to get to the others."

Daebian took off at a sprint with Azerick following close on his heels. The sorcerer lashed out at the flying machines. It became clear that mages manned some of the gliders when magical strikes accompanied loosed crossbow bolts. Azerick's ward shrugged off both types of attacks, but they would not hold forever.

Azerick stopped, turned around, and swept his arms up into the air. A large section of the street cracked and buckled before the cobblestones shot into the sky. Glider riders tried to swerve away, but the attack was too swift and expansive to avoid. Wards flared around the machines and their riders, but not all were able to withstand the onslaught.

Machine and man spiraled to the ground with a loud crash of metal. Azerick swept his arms down and pummeled the foot soldiers in a hailstorm of stones. Their shields sparked and crackled like lightning under the barrage, some failing to hold and allowing a few stones to break through and bludgeon those sheltering beneath it.

Azerick turned and ran once again and shouted to Daebian. "We need to get off the streets as quickly as we can!"

Daebian nodded and ran. The remaining glider pilots changed tactics and hurled javelins. Azerick cursed as the javelins rained down and tried to flee their area of influence. They had almost escaped the ring when a fireball erupted behind them. Both men felt their feet leave the ground and went tumbling headlong.

Daebian snatched up a javelin as he stood. Azerick raised a ward to protect them in time to block another magical attack. He swirled his staff over his head and conjured a vortex that grew into a lightning-spewing tornado. It divided in two, then split again. Eight miniature electric cyclones harried the glider riders, who had to focus their attention on their piloting skills to avoid destruction.

"That won't keep them busy forever," Azerick said. "We have got to get to ground. The others are waiting for us."

Daebian nodded. "We can escape this way. It's not much farther."

Daebian led them to a narrow, dead-end alley just a block away. "It's here, but there's one thing I have to do first."

Azerick furrowed his brow. "What's that?"

"This."

Daebian plunged his lance into Azerick's chest. Azerick looked dumbfounded for a moment before falling to his knees. The alley disappeared as a bright light flooded in. Daebian could just make out Arcanus Karpos stumble before catching his balance.

"Clever. How did you figure it out?" the arcanus asked when he caught his breath.

"Little things," Daebian replied. "That you never mentioned anyone by name, as well as your insistence I lead us to the others. Azerick could have gated us out of harm's way. I'm also rather astute and not easily fooled."

Primus Ploutarch's deep voice came from just over his shoulder. "Your cleverness may well come at the expense of a great deal of unpleasantness. My patience has its limits, and I will do whatever it takes to pacify this city before the others arrive."

Daebian smiled at the threat. "I can appreciate a man who's willing to set aside the notion of a code of conduct to achieve his goals. I hope my father has not changed so much that he has forgotten that. I've seen what remained in his wake when he set aside his code in order to do what must be done, and the destruction was glorious."

As Azerick had expected, Headmaster Florent stayed with her students, but a handful of wizards and a few of the older journeyman mages returned to Southport with him hoping to liberate the city. It took time to convince Joah to heed Marley's accord with the mages and getting Headmaster Florent to concede that she and her people were guests and that Marley's word was law within Freehold. Should she find the conditions intolerable, she was free to lead her people to North Haven.

Getting back into the city had been more difficult than leaving. Order patrols were out in force and were diligent in checking papers. The arcanus were also prevalent. While their numbers were few, there always seemed at least one was nearby no matter where Azerick and the mages appeared.

Despite traveling through numerous portals and opening several decoy gates, they barely escaped into the sewers without getting caught. They had to flee ahead of patrols on three of their five transits before eluding their pursuers. Azerick could not risk attracting attention to any of his lair's entrances, so he and his small group had to walk through the rank tunnels for several minutes before reaching it.

Azerick opened the hidden door to his old lair and found Trisha and Elias playing cards, using a barrel for a table. "Where's your father?"

Trisha looked up and turned her head toward him. "He went topside to check on mother and our grandparents."

"Any word from Daebian?"

Both mages shook their heads.

"I assume Vera is in her lab?"

"Of course," Elias said.

Azerick left the twins to their card game and sought Vera in the room she had commandeered for her laboratory. The mousy girl was busy as usual making minute adjustments to the alchemic set to ensure her current brew was at the optimal temperature and mix.

"I'm back," Azerick announced as he entered the room. "Have you had any success with your latest project?"

Vera pointed at a stack of well-padded crates containing a dozen bottles each. They looked like nothing more than a shipment of wine, but what was in the bottles was no simple beverage. It was a concoction based on dragon spit, or demon fire, as it was commonly known to those who handled the destructive incendiary. He had made some long ago and destroyed the chapter house of the thieves responsible for murdering his extended family, but that was tame compared to what Vera had produced.

Azerick's eyes widened in surprise. "You made that many already?"

Vera explained in her typical deadpan tone. "Yes. Andrill managed to procure enough dragon spit, which cut production time in half. I also figured out a way to use a simple catalyst to achieve the desired effect without excessive distilling. I'll double the number of bottles by morning."

Azerick smiled and softly wagged his head. "You're brilliant, you know that?"

"Of course I do. It's only now that other people are realizing it. Have you figured out how you wish to deploy it?"

The sorcerer's genial grin turned sinister. "I have. It's time to go rescue my son."

Azerick unleashed another powerful fireball against the castle walls. It exploded like a small sun going super nova, but the anti-magic emitters kept it from harming the soldiers manning the wall.

"Primus, you have my son!" Azerick's magically amplified voice rang out. "Release him, or I will tear down the walls around you and raze the castle in which you cower!"

Scores of cobblestones tore free from the street at a gesture and hovered several feet in the air. Azerick whipped his arm forward and sent them streaking out like a flight of arrows. While the emitters blocked magic, they did nothing to stop the hurtling stones once in motion. Legionnaires raised their shields, overlapping the shimmering wards as the stones struck.

"Come out and face me, Primus!"

Primus Ploutarch's plumed helmet appeared over the parapets, protected by his soldiers' wards. "While I appreciate your courage in defending your land, you must know that your efforts are futile. Your city has been defeated, and soon your kingdom will follow. Surrender yourself, and I promise to treat you fairly, and you will come to realize that the Order is the only path to salvation."

"You know nothing of defeat, Primus, but I will gladly show you."

Azerick raised his arm and dropped it. At his signal, dozens of people ran out of nearby buildings and alleys and raced toward the walls with no visible weapons other than the wine bottles they gripped by the neck. They hurled the bottles in a high arc to shatter against the wall. Mages within the small assault force raised wards just in time to shield themselves from the fiery explosions created when the small glass vials inside the bottles broke and mixed with the dragon spit.

While not powerful enough to destroy the wall outright, the damage was far from inconsequential. The blast shook the stone beneath the legionnaires and created a blistering sheet of fire that continued to burn.

Primus Ploutarch cursed and leapt back. "Enough of this! Bring them to heel!"

Gliders raced over the wall and hurled javelins and magic at the insurgents. The gates opened, and two full centuria double-timed out into the plaza. Boxed in by the javelins, Azerick was forced to retreat with his compatriots.

"Get to ground!" he ordered. "I'll try to draw them away."

Once free of the javelin's punishing effect, he launched a stream of arcane bolts at two of the flying machines, followed up by a raking blast of lightning into the nearest rank of soldiers bearing down upon him. He raised a field of stone spires between the legionnaires and his people, forcing them to turn their full attention his direction.

Azerick ran as more javelins arced overhead and tried to deny him his use of magic. He raced through the streets, leading his pursuers away from his people. Seeing the sorcerer as the far greater threat and prize, the legionnaires were more than willing to give chase. They dogged his heels and buzzed overhead through the city streets.

After the second ambush comprising hurled explosive bottles, heavy stones, and crossbow bolts, the soldiers wizened up and avoided the narrower alleys, choosing to keep to the primary streets while the glider riders kept them informed of their quarry's location. The destruction wrought by the ambushes was unfortunate but unavoidable. They had warned the citizens away from the areas, and the only loss of life was their enemies' when a shield failed to protect them and let fire and projectiles pour into their ranks.

After more than half an hour of running, Azerick decided it was time to give his pursuers the slip. He opened half a dozen portals and leapt through a short series of gates, eventually returning to the safety of his underground warren.

Primus Ploutarch bottled his mounting fury and did his best to project calm. "What is the tally of this recent assault?"

"Twenty-eight legionnaires killed, most of them by fire in the ambushes during the chase, and another two-score with moderate-to-severe burns," Optio Timaeus reported.

"Do we know to where the insurgents fled?"

The scout officer pointed to several shapes on a map of the city. "Our aerial scouts saw many of them run into these buildings, but by the time we got a contingent of soldiers to search them, they were gone. We arrested several of the proprietors for giving aid to the enemy, the ones we could find."

The Primus' face grew darker. "What of the sorcerer? He is the key to this insurgency."

Doncho cleared his throat before speaking. "He obviously knows we are able to track any strong use of magic and used a series of portals to make his escape, any of which could be his final destination."

"Show me where each of the gates went."

Doncho referred to his notes and pointed to several spots on the map, none of which were closer than half a mile from another.

Primus Ploutarch tapped a finger against the large map as he thought. "Is there any point that stands out from the others?"

"One exited below ground. That is the only anomaly."

The primus turned to Optio Timaeus. "Do we have a diagram of this city's sewer system?"

"I believe so. I'll send someone to fetch it."

The scout rushed from the room and did not reappear for nearly an hour. He unrolled the schematic and held it against the much larger map hanging on the wall.

"See if you can correlate where the insurgents went to ground with where the tunnels run," the primus said.

Optio Timaeus' eyes flicked between the city map and the schematic several times, pointing out each location he could find.

Primus Ploutarch smiled as he saw that every bolt hole was atop one of the sewer tunnels, including the one portal the sorcerer had conjured. "I should have known the rats were hiding in the sewers. I want Every exit we can find sealed off. We will send a centuria in at each of the primary tunnels to herd them to this central location and crush them once and for all. Each centuria, along with the squads you delegate to watch the entrances, will carry nullifiers with them so their wizards cannot gate away."

Optio Timaeus shifted his feet, but kept any hint of objection from his voice. "Primus, that will require the bulk of our forces."

"And strip several of the nullifiers in use around the castle if we are to create a null magic area large enough to ensure none of their wizards can escape," Doncho added.

"Leave enough nullifiers in place to secure the castle proper. Take the ones in use around their Academy officer trainees," Primus Ploutarch ordered. "They aren't serving much use there. That should allow us to create a large enough noose to encircle all their necks at once before pulling it tight."

CHAPTER 27

Optio Timaeus heard the shouts of men and women and saw the flickers of movement as the insurgents fled the light of his men's torches. He did not order his centuria to run them down. This was not an apprehension mission. It was a routing maneuver preceding a culling. His and the other six centuria sent into the sewers were to herd the insurgents into the large central intersection of mainline tunnels. It was then they would slaughter the city's resistance. It was a distasteful mission, one lacking honor expected of the Order, but these people had brought it upon themselves.

A soft, blue light cast a glow up ahead. The scout leader could hear heavy boots marching in unison not far away and knew they must near the intersection. The legionnaires' movement precision allowed them to arrive within seconds of each other despite their lack of communication.

Optio Timaeus called a halt the moment his centuria rounded a slight bend in the tunnel. He had expected the enemy forces to have prepared a hasty defense to mount their final stand. But he saw only a lone figure standing near several glass orbs emitting the strange blue light to one side of the open intersection.

He looked into the conjoining tunnels and saw the orange light of the other centurias' torches a moment before the units arrived at the mouths of their respective tunnels. Somehow, the dissidents had escaped. They had most of the known exits leading to the surface guarded by a handful of soldiers, so they could not have fled that way. It did not matter. With them being denied the sewers, they would ferret the insurgents out from whatever bolt hole in which they had crawled.

It took a moment in the strange light, but Timaeus recognized the man standing alone against seven hundred of the best soldiers to ever walk the world. Perhaps this venture would yield acceptable results after all.

"Sorcerer, you are surrounded. There is nowhere to go, and I assume you realize you cannot wield your magic. Surrender, and you might still be given the opportunity to take the oath of allegiance."

Azerick shook his head and let out a long breath. "You are correct on two counts. I am surrounded and cannot use my magic thanks to your devices, but it is you who have nowhere to go. I asked you to leave my city and kingdom in peace. You refused. You came to this land seeking to conquer it. You delved into these tunnels seeking to put an end to those who refused to yield to your tyranny. But you found neither. Here, you will reap only your demise. Farewell, Optio. You may tell Sharrellan yourself that you no longer believe in her, and give her my regards."

Azerick turned, opened a hidden door behind him, and disappeared through it. He pulled it shut, blocking the legionnaires' angry shouts as they rushed forward. Vera touched the tip of a device looking similar to her flamer and ran a thick bead of what appeared to be mud around the door seam. Azerick shouted down the passageway, his command repeated by dozens of voices until it reached one of the Academy mages on the surface.

Outside the nullifiers' sphere of influence, the wizard launched a bright red ball of light into the sky. Outside the walls, Rusty and Magus Trent opened a pair of dimensional gates in the middle of the river, their exits just inside the primary sewer entrance, bypassing the floodgates used to flush the tunnels.

Optio Timaeus ordered a halt to his men's attempts to pry open the secret door the sorcerer had used to escape and called for silence. The sound of a heavy cavalry charge roared down the tunnels until it became deafening. The optio experienced just a few seconds of horror when he understood the trap into which he had led his men before walls of water erupted from several of the tunnels and crushed their bodies against the stone walls before eventually flushing them out to sea. Geysers shot out of the grates and covers all across the city, flooding low-lying areas and drenching the streets and passersby.

Doncho hurried through the castle halls and burst into the room Primus Ploutarch had commandeered for his headquarters. The old arcanus' face was ashen, and his voice trembled as much as his hands did.

The primus looked up from the map he was studying at the arcanus' abrupt entrance. "What is it? Is there word of the mission?"

Doncho swallowed and worked his jaw to get his words out. "Yes, Primus."

"Well, did we get the bastards? Speak, man!"

"No, Primus. The insurgents, they flooded the tunnels."

The officer's jaw fell slack and his eyes went wide. "My soldiers?"

Doncho shook his head. "There has been no word of survivors."

Primus Ploutarch could only stand in mute disbelief. He had sent seven hundred men, nearly his entire remaining force, into those sewers only for them to be wiped out to a man. His invasion had failed. He had failed. Even if he could escape this accursed city, his career was over. His name would carry shame for all of history.

His door crashed open once again and broke him out of his stupor. A young Optio, probably the last officer in his cohort besides himself, burst in.

"Primus, the insurgents attacked the Academy! Given what I know of their numbers and incendiary devices, they likely overwhelmed the guard and freed the prisoners."

Primus Ploutarch bunched his fists until his knuckles were near to bursting through the taut skin. "Order everyone left to the ships. We need to inform the approaching host of our...my failure. I may have lost this battle, but these people are fools if they think they have won the war."

The optio saluted and raced from the room to order their withdrawal. Muffled explosions echoed down the corridors. It appeared as though the populace would not allow them an easy retreat. Primus Ploutarch hurried through the hall. He had a prisoner that could provide valuable intelligence and a possible bargaining chip. He would not leave this land empty-handed.

A figure stepped into the light at the end of the hallway. The primus stopped, his heart hammering in his chest in a mix of fury and exultation. His name and honor was in tatters, and his career as dead as the legionnaires he had sent into the sewers, but at least he would get his revenge.

"Where is my son?" Azerick asked, his voice low and menacing.

A smile played across Primus Ploutarch's face. "Tucked away, ready for transport back to Syrna, as you shall soon be."

"Once again, you claim victory before the battle has ended."

"The nullifiers are still active in this area of the castle. There is no magic to protect you."

"Unlike your arcanus, I can be just as dangerous without it."

A shimmering sword almost as long as Azerick's spear projected from the arcanum disc strapped to the primus' forearm, and a shield from the one on his left. "We shall see."

Azerick strode forward, twirling his staff in his hands as he met the Primus near the middle of the hallway. He wasted no time and took the offensive from the start. His staff stabbed and slashed in a series of crackling sparks as the primus deflected the blows with sword and shield. While the nullifiers prevented Azerick's weapon from extending power beyond the point of origin, they did not render it totally inert. A good thing seeing as how the primus' arcane blade sheared through the stone wall as if it were soft leather.

Primus Ploutarch waded in, taking the initiative with a flurry of swings with his ethereal blade, driving Azerick back through the hall and into a foyer of intersecting hallways. Azerick's decades of experience was almost a match for the primus. Almost. Azerick was a sorcerer with combative skills that bordered on exceptional. Primus Ploutarch was a soldier whose sword skill met and likely exceeded his own. Without his magic, Azerick was fighting a losing battle, and both men knew it.

With every parry and dodge, the Primus' sword came closer to reaching flesh. Even if Azerick could conjure a ward, he doubted it would do more than mitigate the damage inflicted by the blade of pure magic. Without such protection, it would cleave him in two with the ease of cutting a loaf of bread. As if to expound the point, he felt a burning pain and the hot trickle of blood running down his side from a grazing thrust.

Primus Ploutarch's eyes narrowed in excitement, then widened in surprise in the next instant as both men felt the nullifiers' anti-magic effects vanish. Azerick threw himself back, spun, and ripped open a portal. He dove through it, his free hand weaving a spell even as he gated across the room. He made a clawing and tugging motion to complete the spell at the same time he stabbed at the primus with his staff, screaming with the effort of simultaneously weaving a spell and unleashing his staff's awesome power.

Primus Ploutarch brought his shield around to block the spell, but he was unprepared for the strength of the staff's kinetic force. He flew backward at the same time stone spikes erupted from the wall behind him and pinned him in place like a bug on a board. His concentration lost to pain and impending death, Primus Ploutarch's sword and shield vanished. Azerick stalked toward him as he tried to speak past the rasping expulsion of blood from his mouth.

"You think you've won?" the primus sputtered. "You only delayed the inevitable."

"Every second not shackled by tyranny is a victory."

"The Order brings hope and peace, not tyranny."

"Peace through force of arms and servitude through indoctrination is the very definition of tyranny."

The primus' body shuddered and released a racking cough. Azerick thought he had expired until the man opened his eyes again and spoke. "You ruined my name, and now you have taken my life. I ask that you allow my men who still live to leave in peace. Grant me this one dying wish."

Azerick ducked his head. "I am not your precious Order. I do not hold people against their will or compel them to serve me. As long as they swear to never return, I have no objection to allowing them to leave. It's all I wanted from the start. You brought about your own ruin."

Primus Ploutarch nodded weakly before letting out a final breath. Azerick spun toward the sound of feet running his direction from one hallway. Rusty, two of Andrill's people, and a handful of Martial Academy students and officers burst into the foyer a moment later.

"What's the status outside?" Azerick asked.

Rusty took a few breaths to control his breathing. "There's a few score of soldiers left, but they've barricaded themselves in a small courtyard on the southern side of the castle grounds. They've got a few of those nullifiers, and we're having a hard time ousting them."

"Go back to whoever is in charge out there. Tell him to parlay with the survivors and give them the chance to get on their ship and leave as long as they swear never to return to Valeria's shores. I need to go find Daebian."

The men rushed off in the direction from which they had come. Azerick searched the rooms on this floor, assuming Daebian was likely held nearby. He found his son several minutes later, strapped to a chair in a room filled with light. The illumination was magical, so he had to assume either the room was shielded from the nullifiers' effect, or the spell was attuned to them much like the soldiers' shields and the primus' sword.

Daebian looked up at his entrance and rolled his eyes. "Great. Rescued like a damsel in distress by my father. Talk about adding insult to injury."

"I could leave you here if you prefer."

Daebian appeared to ponder the option a moment. "Cut me free. It's been hours since they let me relieve myself. You rescuing me is ever so slightly less embarrassing than pissing myself. If you could avoid telling Ellyssa, I would consider it a personal favor."

Azerick's eyebrows rose. "A favor? Well, that is quite the reward."

"It is, and not one I give lightly. Did you find my sword and my demon? There are people in desperate need of killing," Daebian said as he stood, rubbing at the chafing on his wrists.

"I promised to let any survivors leave as long as they swore never to return."

"The operative word being you. I never made such a promise."

Azerick glared at his son. "Let them go."

"Do you really want to call in your favor so soon, and for such a pitiful cause?"

"I do not consider my word a pitiful cause."

Daebian sighed and shrugged his shoulders. "Fine. How you have lived this long crippled by such morality and sentimentalism is beyond me."

EPILOGUE

Azerick, Daebian, Andrill, and Rusty and his family stood on the dock, watching the solitary Order vessel sail over the horizon. The other ships they had arrived on Azerick kept as spoils of war. Their city had been conquered, many of its citizens killed or held against their will, but they had come away victorious.

Daebian's keen eyesight picked out red dots against the grey backdrop of the sky. "I see sails."

Rusty squinted his eyes. "Are they coming back?"

More sails appeared. First a pair then scores. Within minutes, the sea looked like the mouth of a shark with its mouth agape and pointing its bloody teeth toward the sky.

Azerick sank into his power and sent his consciousness streaking out over the sea. It was a form of scrying, something he was not skilled in, but he could manage the relatively simple feat. The swells raced beneath his incorporeal form as he sped toward the ships, and his heart raced. His rough count tallied around a hundred vessels, each bristling with weapons and legionnaires.

His consciousness detected a powerful figure standing near the prow of the lead ship. He guided his ghostly form toward it and alighted on the deck. A woman of extraordinary beauty stood with regal bearing just behind the bowsprit. Despite the ship's rolling deck, she stood as steady as if she were on solid ground. She turned her large eyes toward him, and her glossy red lips, standing out in contrast to her dark skin, turned up into a smile.

"You must be Azerick," she said in a soft but commanding voice.

Azerick stood mute. She should not have been able to see him without casting a spell to detect divination. It was then he realized she was not physically here. She was a projection, same as him. Azerick prayed she was on one of the ships. The power it would take to appear before him were she not was staggering.

"I understand you defeated Primus Ploutarch and his cohort. I must commend you on your fleeting victory. You intrigue me. Kneel and swear fealty now, and you and your people will avoid needless suffering."

Azerick found his voice and glared at the woman. "I have faced archmages, armies, demons, and gods. I did not yield to them, and I will never yield to you. What gives you the right to invade my homeland? Who are you to demand my subservience?"

The young woman's teeth flashed; their pearly surface even whiter than the snowy, pristine field of her eyes' sclera. "I am Princess Sylvianne Attar, first daughter of the emperor and empress of Syrna and most of the known world. We are the Order. Goodbye, Azerick. We shall meet again soon."

Sylvianne touched the tip of her middle finger to her thumb and made a flicking motion at Azerick as if he were an insect. Azerick's spiritual form flew in an uncontrolled flight back toward the shore. Spirit and body collided, and he felt himself launched into the air once more until he crashed into the side of a fishing shack.

Rusty and the others ran toward him as he struggled to get to his feet. Azerick had not been struck like that since the last time he had angered the dark goddess Sharrellan.

"Azerick, what happened?" Rusty asked.

"Their...their army is coming," he gasped as he levered himself to a standing position by bracing his hands on his knees.

"What do we do?"

Azerick turned his eyes toward the approaching ships. "We run."

To be concluded in:

DESCENT INTO CHAOS

Book Ten of The Sorcerer's Path

FROM THE AUTHOR

I hope you enjoyed this tale and will try my other works. Feel free to look me up on Facebook! You can also check me out on my website **http://brockdeskins.com/** where I write serial fiction, free for your enjoyment, and answer questions!

Author page:
https://www.amazon.com/Brock-Deskins/e/B005M6VQ1O

Facebook:
https://www.facebook.com/brocksbooks/

Twitter:
@brockdeskins

PLEASE **REVIEW** **MY BOOKS** (Especially if you liked it). Customer reviews are the primary means of enticing others to purchase them. I am dependent upon the sales of my books to earn a living that will allow me to continue writing stories that I hope bring you some measure of entertainment. Thank you for your support.

OTHER BOOKS BY BROCK E. DESKINS

The Sorcerer's Path is an epic fantasy series.

The Sorcerer's Ascension: Torn from a life of comfort and luxury, his family destroyed by political intrigues and aspirations, a young boy must quickly grow into a man before the deadly streets of Southport devour him. Follow Azerick through a page-turning adventure that pits him against thieves, thugs, murderers, and men of power that will stop at nothing to achieve their goals.

Azerick must fight just to survive, but for him survival is not enough. A hunger to avenge the wrongs committed against him burns deep within. But that is not all that lies within the young man. There is a power waiting to be unleashed that may be the key to achieving the justice and security he seeks--if it does not destroy him first.

The Sorcerer's Torment: Azerick flees The Academy but quickly falls prey to powerful beings that use his skills and power for their own amusement. What these creatures do not understand is the power of the young sorcerer's will and the lengths he will go to for vengeance. Despite becoming a prisoner, Azerick finds his first true love, but can he keep it?

The Sorcerer's Legacy: Azerick has found himself a home and tries to settle down. He takes on an apprentice and tries to put all the death and desire for vengeance behind him. But when the Rook finds him, Azerick is once again pulled back into Ulric's schemes. Knowing that all he has worked toward and everyone close to him is in danger as long as these schemes are ongoing; Azerick decides to put an end to it, once and for all.

The Sorcerer's Vengeance: After narrowly avoiding being killed in his own bed by the land's most feared assassin, Azerick leaves his school behind to find out who sent him and to put an end to the threat once and for all. Azerick's search will take him to the very pits of the abyss and back to unleash hellish fury upon those that threaten him.

The Sorcerer's Scourge: With the siege broken and Ulric dead, Azerick can finally relax, study his magic, and run his school in peace. Unfortunately, Jarvin's reign is far from uncontested and the true usurper decides to make his move. Jarvin escapes with help from an unlikely source—a vampire named Landrin who still clings tenaciously to his own humanity. While Azerick and a large force from North Haven race to save the king in exile, evil forces are preparing to unleash a nightmare upon the kingdom that may well destroy them all.

The Sorcerer's Abyss: Now the master of the Fifth Circle of the abyss, Azerick is challenged by another demon lord for supremacy. Azerick must face this threat as well as his innermost demons, all the while searching for a way to escape his hellish prison.

Ellyssa fears she is going insane as she plagued by nightmares of her capture and enslavement. Deciding the key to saving herself lies in the total destruction of the object of her fears, she embarks on a crusade to find and kill the slaver, Captain Jake, and eradicate the slave trade.

Ellyssa's nightmares and battles spill out onto the streets of North Haven and gains the attention of The Academy. Fearing Azerick's school is turning out rogue wizards, The Academy decides to hunt down and destroy the rogue and place the school within their control.

The Sorcerer's Return: Azerick has come back from the abyss in order to try to unite all the races against the return of the old gods who seek to destroy them and subjugate the few they allow to survive a brutal purging. However, fighting ancient gods may be the least of his troubles as he battles to save a fractured kingdom, a brilliant son traveling a dark path, and the splintered soul of his own humanity.

The Sorcerer's Destiny: Brutally purged of his demonic influence, Azerick continues the struggle of uniting the kingdom to face the coming of the Scions, ancient gods banished by the mortal races during the Great Revolution two thousand years ago. The fallen gods' prison is crumbling, and Azerick is powerless to stop them from breaking free and enacting their cataclysmic vengeance upon the world.

The humans must ally with the other races in a final battle against impossible odds while their entire world crumbles to the ground and is trod beneath the feet of an unstoppable foe. How can they set aside their distrust of each other when they fear the very person trying to save them?

Rise of the Order: Banished to the abyss after helping defeat the Scions and saving the world from eternal darkness, Azerick languishes in perpetual misery as Lord of the Fifth Circle. The denizens of his hellish realm view him as a usurper and outsider. The chaotic creatures form an alliance with one goal in mind: destroy Azerick Giles, but Sharrellan stands in their way.

A powerful spell tears through the demonic planes, and when the dust settles, the dark goddess is nowhere to be found. It is up to Azerick to return her to her seat of power, but he has a price: return him to his mortal form and send him home.

Back home, a vast empire is on a crusade to conquer the world, and it has set its sights on Valeria. Their goal is to unite the world under a single banner, eradicate the spawn infestation unleashed by the Scions, and replace the gods who they feel have forsaken them with their mystical rulers.

Can Azerick save the dark goddess from the clutches of her demonic subjects and become mortal once again? Will he have the power to protect his people from The Order if he does?

Descent Into Chaos: The Order has arrived in force, and the fate of Valeria, and perhaps all the world, is poised to come under their iron-fisted control. Azerick and Daebian are forced to flee Southport and make a contentious alliance when King Miles capitulates to the invaders. Reduced to insurgent warfare, Azerick and his allies attempt to battle The Order's vastly superior forces in a series of hit and run strikes, but the enemy legions may not be his biggest threat.

Princess Sylvian Attar, daughter to The Order's godlike emperor and empress, has taken a personal interest in Azerick. Herself a powerful sorceress, Sylvian hunts Azerick in hopes of removing Valeria's legendary hero from the battlefield thus sapping her enemies' will to fight. Azerick decides there is but one course of action he can take against this unstoppable foe. It was time to inject a little chaos into The Order.

Brooklyn Shadows is a modern-day vampire tale. Full of action and snarky dialogue, Brooklyn Shadows is an enjoyable read for anyone who enjoys the supernatural underworld and butt-kicking vampires.

<u>**Shrouds of Darkness**</u> (Brooklyn Shadows Book 1) Leo Malone has been a vampire for the better part of the twentieth century. Once a prominent Sherriff (vampire cop), he now earns his living as a private eye and occasional bodyguard for anyone that requires some serious protection. Leo is hired by the daughter of a mob accountant who has gone missing.

The fact that her father is also a werewolf has Leo following a trail of grisly murders that will lead him through a web of intrigue and conspiracy involving his fellow vampires and the local werewolves that make New York their home, all the while trying to keep one particularly determined cop off his back and himself out of jail. Leo is not some pretty-boy vampire that all the girls ogle over, but a hard-eyed, remorseless killing machine who does not take crap from anyone.

<u>**Blood Conspiracy**</u> (Brooklyn Shadows Book 2): While dealing with the aftermath of the failed vampire council coup, Leo discovers that the modified Cure has fallen into the hands of a black ops government project designed to create vampiric super soldiers. When the inevitable happens, the off-book Homeland Security operation forcefully enlists Leo to help them resolve the situation. Worse yet, he has to work not only with an antagonistic werewolf named Meat, he is reunited with his hated creator, Lesile.

<u>**Primacy of Darkness**</u> (Brooklyn Shadows Book 3): Jack the Ripper, sadistic madman of old London, once thought long dead, has returned

to New York in an effort to quench his thirst for blood and mayhem. When the city's vampire enclave finds itself insufficient to deal with a madman of Jack's caliber, Vincent, the enclave head, enlists Leo Malone to put the maniac down before he reveals the existence of vampires as he throws the city into the throes of chaos and terror. Leo soon finds that Jack is not the only monster with which he must contend. A ghost from his past has also seemingly crawled from its grave and seeks to put an end to him and the rest of his kind.

The Transcended Chronicles is the story of an outlandish young man as he goes from being a troublesome youth to one of the kingdom's greatest secret agents. Blessed (or cursed) with an amazing ability to both fight and abuse his body with every conceivable vice known to man, Garran Holt is either the kingdom's greatest hero or its biggest embarrassment.

The Miscreant (The Transcended Chronicles Book 1): Garran Holt is a troubled young man. Unable to tolerate his self-destructive ways, his mother sells him into indentured servitude as part of a work crew building King Remiel's new trade road. When mercenaries sent to disrupt the road's construction attack his work camp, Garran discovers an inner power capable of turning him into a warrior of unparalleled ability. When the leader of his work crew recognizes Garran as being one of the transcended (a fighter able to slip into the swifter currents of time), he is trained as an agent, one of the kingdom's elite spies. Crude, abrasive, and deeply committed to destroying himself with drugs, alcohol, and debauchery, Garran might be the kingdom's only hope against falling to The Guild, the powerful trade cartel bent on becoming the true and undisputed power in the land.

The Agent (The Transcended Chronicles Book 2): The Guild rules the kingdom through their puppet monarch, and Garran must race to save the last living heir to the throne before the powerful syndicate's assassins complete their extermination of anyone who could oppose them. Garran and Prince Adam Altena struggle to find allies in hopes of rescuing Adam's sister, who was forced to marry the usurper in order to prevent even the thought of rebellion, and raise an army capable of defeating The Guild. With The Guild now in control of Anatolia's powerful army as well as their legion of mercenaries, their future is grim. How can a disreputable agent and a deposed prince convince their neighboring rulers to oppose The Guild, an organization that has had them cowed for decades?

Empire of Masks is an exciting and explosive new series that takes place in the world of Hedon and takes you across the land of Eidolan where ships sail through the skies and men and women wage war with magic, swords, muskets, and cannons.

Highlords of Phaer (**Book one of Empire of Masks**): Born a slave, descended of kings, Jareen Velarius just wants to provide the best life he can for his family, but Eidolan is a realm that challenges even the most stalwart of souls. Caught between his masters and those brave or foolish enough to strike against them, Jareen struggles to reconcile his role as a dutiful slave with that of a man who desires to be free. His goal: to return his people to a life stolen by the highlords more than a millennium ago.

Auberon Victore, sorcerer, alchemist, son of a powerful overlord, and Jareen's master, creates an alchemic compound he is certain will change the world; he just does not know how. Jareen sees it for the weapon that could break the sorcerers' iron grasp wrapped around the necks of every lowborn in the empire. It will change the world, but not in the way his master desires.

Across the Tempest Sea, a mighty storm has raged for a thousand years, keeping a terrible, long-forgotten enemy at bay, an enemy whose cruelty knows no bounds. Only the perpetual storm and their fear of the sorcerer highlords keep the Necrophages from returning to Eidolan and cloaking the empire in death and darkness. But the tempest is waning, and the dissidents' freedom may well come at the cost of their total destruction.

Nightbird: The Great Revolution ended the highlords' tyranny two hundred years ago, but the legacy of that epic war, and that of the principal architects' descendants, lives on. With the highlords' death and their taking magic, as it was once known, to their graves, Eidolan fell into a time of darkness and its cities lived in isolation. However, some people, dubbed arcanists, discovered a new form of magic and the airships returned to the skies, rejoining the cities in trade as well as conspiracy, but a new darkness, more dreadful and deadly than any they faced before, is coming.

Kiera is a fifteen-year-old nightbird, one of many who flit about after dark, stealing whatever they can find in order to survive. She lives on a derelict airship in the poorest part of the city with Wesley, a young man who plies his trade as an escort to wealthy older women, and his little brother Russel, an autistic savant who communicates only through sign but who could secretly be the most powerful techno-arcanist the empire has ever known. Deep in debt to the underlord Nimat, Kiera dives into evermore dangerous schemes that put her at the heart of a secret war that could spell the destruction of not just the city, but the very empire.

Kiera is caught in the center of several factions on the brink of war. When she can no longer tell friend from enemy, there is only one side she can trust—her own.

Mourningbird: A creature of darkness lurks in the shadows of Velaroth, wearing the skin of its victims, and grips the city in terror. Dorian, a Necrophage bent on sowing chaos and paving the way for his people's invasion, has declared war on the humans of Eidolan, and there appears to be no one capable of stopping him.

Kiera's world is shattered by those who hold power, and she is forced to seek an ally. The nightbird is coming into power of her own, but can she stay alive long enough to seize it? Russel's behavior has taken a turn for the worse, and his actions have drawn the attention of those who would use his amazing talents for their own gain...and everyone else's loss.

The battle for Velaroth, and perhaps the world, has begun. Who will win? Who will live to mourn the dead? Will there be anything left for the victor to claim as their prize?

Standalone books

The Portal is a fun and exciting story of some less than popular teenagers that accidentally open a portal to a mystical land during one of their role-playing games. Drew, a dour and anti-establishment teenager, is pulled through and captured by evil creatures lying in wait on the other side. Now it is up to his friends and older brother to rescue him, but who will rescue Drew's captors from him?

Amelia (Battle for Ardentia): Amelia is a precocious, ten-year-old girl with a powerful imagination. In her alter-ego guise of a demi-goddess warrior princess, Amelia fights against a powerful demonic sorcerer named Romut and his horde of monsters in a never ending series of battles to protect the people of her imaginary world. However, the true battle strikes home when Amelia is diagnosed with a brain tumor. Now Amelia must fight not just the evil living in her imagination, but for her very life.

ABOUT THE AUTHOR

Brock Deskins was born in a small town located in rural Oregon. At age twenty, he joined the army and served as an M1A1 tank crewman, dental specialist, and computer analyst. While in the military, he became an accomplished traveler, husband, and father of three wonderful children. His military career completed, attended college to brush up on his skills as a computer analyst and gain new skills as a writer. Brock received his degree in computer networking and is now devoting his full time and limited attention span to writing.

BIBLIOGRAPHY

THE SORCERER'S PATH
The Sorcerer's Ascension
The Sorcerer's Torment
The Sorcerer's Legacy
The Sorcerer's Vengeance
The Sorcerer's Scourge
The Sorcerer's Abyss
The Sorcerer's Return

The Sorcerer's Destiny
Rise of the Order
Descent Into Chaos

BROOKLYN SHADOWS
Shrouds of Darkness
Blood Conspiracy

THE TRANSCENDED CHRONICLES
The Miscreant
The Agent

EMPIRE OF MASKS
Highlords of Phaer
Nightbird
Mourningbird

OTHER BOOKS BY BROCK E. DESKINS
The Portal
Amelia: Battle for Ardentia

Curious about other Crossroad Press books? Stop by our website:
http://crossroadpress.com
We offer quality writing
in digital, audio, and print formats.

Subscribe to our newsletter on the website homepage and receive a
free eBook.